JOURNEY TO COLONUS

JOURNEY TO COLONUS

A NOVEL OF RACE, ESPIONAGE AND REDEMPTION

FRANKLIN DEBROT

SilverWood

Published in 2016 by SilverWood Books

SilverWood Books Ltd
14 Small Street, Bristol, BS1 1DE, United Kingdom
www.silverwoodbooks.co.uk

This book is a work of historical fiction. It contains the names, as well as the words, of some real people; and some historical events are described. It also describes events and characters that are the products of the author's imagination. Any resemblance of such non-historical persons or events to actual ones is purely coincidental.

ISBN 978-1-78132-503-2 (paperback)
ISBN 978-1-78132-504-9 (hardback)
ISBN 978-1-78132-505-6 (ebook)

British Library Cataloguing in Publication Data
A CIP catalogue record for this book is available from the British Library

Page design and typesetting by SilverWood Books
Printed on responsibly sourced paper

Journey to Colonus was long in gestation. Some persons have been especially important in making it possible. Starting with two wonderful women: my wife, Jean, without whose patience over the years as my best editor with numerous altered and re-altered versions, and her invaluable secretarial duties, constancy and moral support, *Journey* would never have been born; my mother, Marie-Louise Alice, who bequeathed a love of books, and whose heroic fidelity was an inspiration. There were others, too, who played a critical role early on: Jeanne Renner who, in spite of everything, did what is so very rare – when it mattered, she didn't pass by unseeing and indifferent; Elaine Renner, my cousin but more like a sister, who at twenty-two when other women are starting out in life, passed from this life; and David Henrickson, who one day was a stranger and then the next was a brother, who encouraged and promoted me, and pointed me in a new direction.

Author's Note

Journey to Colonus is an historical novel but written not in the mode of a tourist visiting that most remote world, the Past. Its cast of characters are still very much with us – in fact, they are essentially us; and its account of recent history will show effects still shaping our lives. The reader may feel that he is visiting a familiar place but seen in a different light. It is only fair to warn, then, that for some, reading it will pose a measure of risk.

PART 1

1

Superman

It was America's sixth year in Vietnam and late in the summer that man first walked on the moon. From inside his eighth floor hotel room, Vincent Brown listened to loud, intrusive voices in the hallway, white male voices with heavy Southern drawls. Lighting a cigarette that trembled between his fingers, he stepped over to the window and parted a thick curtain, smelling of years of accumulated smoke, to watch the Greyhound buses below inch their way in and out of the city station. Sprouting from the upper story of a small brick building across the street from the Hotel Carolina was an electric sign, a flashing, curved arrow pointing to a red, white and blue display: *EAT... EAT... EAT.*

"We deal in basics in America," he mused, mumbling to himself. Yes! Fill up, refuel! EAT! The sound of the buses at this height, with the windows sealed and the air-conditioner humming, made just a low, distant growl.

"We're going to make it work here, Mr. Brown," Ronald Montbanc, that little banty rooster, said when they'd first met. "The people's movement is going to have a new birth, beyond New York and Chicago and the West Coast. We're going to weld together all of those disparate eruptions of the spirit – of the black soul of the people..." That's the way he spoke: lots of welding, he liked that word, "weld". Yeah! "Because we're pure..."

Pure? The Alliance, yes, was to be wholly black. An umbrella organization, loosely confederated, but spread over the entire country, bringing together people previously uncoordinated, often bickering, sometimes warring, that on broad issues would speak with one voice. President Montbanc had made it his signature goal ever since his hotshot days as professor and then an administrator at California State University in Sacramento. And now the most significant movement of people in the country, centered here in the South, with the potential of being everything that Paul Robeson, Vincent's hero, had envisioned...

Years before, he'd met the famous actor, singer, and world figure at the AME Zion Church in the heart of Harlem. His parents, his younger brother Basil, and he went to hear the great baritone who mesmerized the world. Vincent was in the most impressionable of years, budding adolescence, and he would never forget the man and those incomparably moving, melancholy songs: *Swing Low, Sweet*

Chariot; *No More Auction Block*; *Water Boy*; *We Are Climbing Jacob's Ladder*. Afterwards, encouraged by the friend who'd brought them to the church, he shook the great man's hand, so large that it fully enveloped his. He remembered Robeson didn't just nod to everyone he met; when he shook Vincent's hand, he said in that tremendous, resonant voice, "Your mother says you are a very good student – keep studying hard! Our people need outstanding students – future leaders!" Since then he'd read everything Paul Robeson said and wrote, moved by his stirring message in words and in life that people of color should join together as one in a movement of liberation. The message became Vincent's own.

He'd tried to explain this to his skeptical younger brother, who'd barely a month before joined the brotherhood of the Black Panthers. "It's not just economics or politics, Baze. It's something else. It's something beautiful. Like this neighborhood of ours, this block we live on."

Basil had been studiously gazing at his feet; he'd heard as many of these heaven-inspired, uplifting talks as he ever wanted to hear.

"Remember how when we were growing up all the older folks pulled together? Folks different as can be. Take Pop! A lot of folks thought him arrogant with his West Indian, Trinidadian airs. But you know still, quietly, he pitched in too. There were people who didn't have money and still he took care of their teeth. Remember he spoke to that Martin kid for his mother?"

"And then there was that businessman: Elsie White's father. Remember Elsie?" Basil started laughing as he began to recite a lecherous, very personal, reminiscence of the buxom Elsie.

"That's right, White." Vincent nodded vigorously. "Yeah, he was the one businessman in the neighborhood. Remember how he threw in to support our anti-lynching campaign?"

"That was kids' stuff."

"But that's not the point. People joined together. We began losing that, I don't know when. But that's what I'm talking about. See?"

So when he heard Ronald Montbanc speak in New York about the need for community action across America, that they'd been too long like a Third World nation depending on others to market the raw commodity of their energies, and the Alliance was to change all this, he was 'welded'.

But that night at The President's Welcome he'd met them all: the Peters. The Albrechts. Sister Mary O'Keefe. Bob Keech. Loewenstein. Others. And the thought struck him a hammer blow: *these* people really own this place. Not Montbanc. Not *us*.

"Mr. Brown, I'm so glad to finally meet you. I heard so much about you and what you did at Columbia, and now you're joining us here at Baxter University."

Join 'us'? Who did she think he was joining? Montbanc supposedly settled all this. And here was this fool of a woman, Albrecht. Did she know what they'd done at Columbia? Join *her?* For one thing, they'd broken with the white organizations. The point wasn't how radical they were, but that they had their agenda "and we have ours".

"This is white America," Raskin Perrin, Vincent's newfound Alliance friend, would say. "They expect to be the proprietors, and we the property."

Raskin understood.

Back at Morningside Heights, everyone understood. There were the white boys from Scarsdale and Riverdale and all the other dales wanting to join their cause. But they didn't let them take it over like they'd done in Atlanta and Birmingham. The Alliance was to be the center of a bright new community of the future. But here they were, pushing their way back into bed with them.

"Don't laugh now, Professor Brown," the gray-haired Sister Mary was saying, "but I'll be teaching black literature." Anomalous in this Baptist-affiliated black college, this Protestant, white-establishment Colonus, she was wearing an outfit that made her look like she belonged to the Salvation Army. "Until I began as visiting professor a year ago, I didn't know *anything* about black literature," she said, nodding, speaking in a soft welcoming voice. "I think of myself more as a student, my students as my teachers. But I think that's not such an unhealthy situation, don't you?"

He smiled obligingly, but visualized Montbanc, actually seeing that little dancing midget in his mind's eye more vividly than this holy woman standing there in front of him. Well, he'd never contradicted the good sisters at St. Bridget's parochial school on the edge of Bedford-Stuyvesant; he wasn't starting now. Is this, he thought, what Montbanc has in mind as the "spirit of the black soul" emerging in the new South? Damn Montbanc!

On to credentials-swapping. Continuing to summon his good manners, Vincent shared a dirty little secret.

"Oh, a Filmore Scholar!" Mrs. Albrecht cried. Astonishment all around, as if he'd won the Nobel Prize.

"That explains why you're such a perspicacious young man," Sister Mary said. Mrs. Albrecht, gently touching his shoulder, glowed.

They were in a large room – actually more a ballroom. Comfortably air-conditioned in that otherwise sultry night, the room had high ceilings and elaborately decorated floral and grape-garlanded plasterwork; and in the center hung a chandelier, the crystals blinking and twinkling in a thousand diamond-like reflections.

Perspicacious. What would the sisters at St. Bridget's have thought if they'd heard him called that? These people, they all talked like this. So full of. . .he laughed.

As he made nice and they all chatted, pretty coeds with come-hither smiles made the rounds offering sweet tea, soft drinks, and cookies.

Vincent would surely have left by then, but his friend Raskin had, minutes before, buttonholed him with bad news. He pointed to the other side of the room to a young, beet-red white guy and said that this was "the new man". The fool was being dragged across the room by Mrs. Albrecht, a silly grin plastered across his face!

Oh, this *was* bad news! When Vincent first got President Montbanc's invitation earlier in the spring to join them at Baxter, he'd been nothing but frank. He said he wouldn't fit in. Besides, he had other fish to fry. He said there was the work he'd begun as an undergraduate in upper Manhattan. They were agitating for improved representation in the higher councils of the city government. But Montbanc said he could do all of that, and a whole lot more, as part of the Alliance. He told him if he'd thought he was a faculty type he wouldn't have been interested in hiring him. No, his intention was to have him "*weld* the spirit of the people in the fiery idealism of our youth" – nationwide.

He *was* flattered. But then what he said was soon amended when Dean Middleweek notified him that working exclusively with the Alliance wouldn't pass muster with the trustees. Vincent would have academic duties. It was stressed they'd be minimal. "A few lectures" in something he'd be "interested in". His real work would be with all phases of the Alliance's development, especially its upcoming convention. This "itty bitty teaching" was merely a cover to satisfy Baxter's "hopelessly antiquated trustees".

Then odd bits of news started drifting through the summer air like thistle-winged seeds on the Carolina breeze. For starters, it looked like he'd be 'helping' with Great Books – Great Books being headed up by Thomas Doswell, a man mockingly characterized as "a champion among Uncle Toms". Raskin's quip: "An Olympic contender."

OK. This wasn't so good; still, mostly it wasn't so good for Doswell. But then the story started shaping into something else that included *team teaching*, which meant regularly *coordinating* with the old guy. The notion that Vincent would be free and easy with his own Alliance affairs went out the window. And that wasn't all. He'd begun learning about a vaguely-referred-to third person, necessary, he was assured, "to keep his load light", but in reality one more individual to complicate matters. All this was shaping up into precisely what Montbanc said he would *not* be doing. The most infuriating part of it was the way the revelations came to light in carefully doled-out portions. But then as he began to threaten rebellion, another, pleasanter message came down the pike via Baxter's usually cheerless Dean Middleweek: it was that this third person was to be Raskin.

Raskin was one of the few people who was not an unknown, having been delivered into his care by the President himself his first day in the city. The day he arrived his debonair new acquaintance drove him back to the hotel and all over Colonus, introducing him to friends as though he'd known him all his life.

In contrast to Montbanc's imperial aloofness, Raskin's warm enthusiasm was the proverbial breath of fresh air. So on hearing that Raskin, his ally and daily confidant in the Alliance preparations, was to be the third person in the Great Books Triumvirate, he was greatly relieved. Just as long as it wasn't some Chuck, he'd jokingly bantered with Raskin back then.

Now he was looking across that brilliantly lit room, having earlier spoken to Raskin and learning that it wasn't to be him after all, but a new guy. There he was, in the flesh. It may have been unthinkable, but it was a fact that he was no brother. And whatever the story they'd come up with, bottom line, he'd been suckered, monkeyed with – screwed! The boyish, grinning, red-faced Mr. James Allan, the latest in the President's package of surprises!

"My undergraduate training was at a little Catholic girls' college you never heard of." Vincent was hearing the tinkle of Sister Mary's soft but chirpy Midwestern speech."I was very fortunate, you know, because at the time you were considered a candidate for apostasy if you went to a secular institution."

Wide-eyed expressions of dismay all around.

"If you didn't go on to a Catholic graduate school – Notre Dame or Catholic U or Fordham in New York, or some other such place – you were suspect."

Great gales of laughter.

"Really?" Vincent had reached his limit – his internally regulated chatter-tolerance alarm system was ringing away!

When Sister Mary O'Keefe, chubby Joseph Keech, the Peters, Chuck and Rosie (Chuck being another visiting professor from Wisconsin), and the giant Rev. Baker took up with a cookie platter making the rounds, he bolted.

Outside there was a breeze and a full moon. One of those luminous nights that people sing odes to. But he wasn't. As he walked past storefronts with closed roll-down gates, graffiti scrawled, some offering invitations for Sunday and weekday church services – lots of Jesus, Glory and Hallelujah business in this part of town – past a huge mural of a 'fro-bedecked Jesus and the Lincoln Theatre, his thoughts ran over and over in his mind. He'd learned that this 'Tom', Tom Doswell, from the beginning wanted no more to teach with him than – they all laughed – the Grand Wizard of the Ku Klux Klan. Raskin framed it all as a great comedy, drawing a picture of Tom Doswell woefully shifting his massive bulk within the President's corset-like constraints. But now Vincent was wondering about the obsessive nature of this quarrel. And the picture was growing clearer every day: all these empty promises and this accumulating web of old scores to be settled, every bit of it wasted energy. Indeed, in dealings outside the university – within the Alliance itself – he'd already begun to see a similar pattern. And he wondered not only if all of this quarreling would stop with Doswell, but if it would stop with anyone.

Had Montbanc, this arrogant little Sammy Davis lookalike, been at his own party he'd have made for him then and there, throwing the fact of this Allan boy straight into his face. But of course he'd quite presidentially danced his way out after a half-hour's appearance.

After wandering for hours through the East End, he walked back to the hotel and took the elevator to his room. It was still early to his adrenalin-pumped body. Sitting in this smoke-suffused space brooding, slumped in the couch with the monotonous sound of the tube washing over his mind, a sudden racket burst outside in the corridor: loud, boisterous voices and slamming doors. It was some kind of event-filled weekend at the state university and they were arriving in droves, aging college jocks and their wives or faded dates whooping it up, singing corny college songs.

There was no way he could sleep anyway. In New York, on upper Broadway, there'd be places you could spend the night on a bar stool with some soul, some blues; where there was someone with whom you could split your sides laughing, or at least find fraternal solace. So he took his keys and some change, crushed out the stub of his cigarette, and made again for the door.

Colonus in North Carolina, Corinth in Mississippi, Athens and Sparta in Georgia, Memphis in Tennessee – so many Southern towns with classical Greek names. Modern American Colonus was larger than the village of Greek antiquity where Oedipus went into exile after his unspeakable crimes; yet then it was still a relatively small city, and it didn't yet sprawl with rows of prefab housing and checkerboard malls, though it was beginning to. A man could still walk from one end to the other in a few hours. Vincent had been all over the East End that night and on previous days – the scorching days when the sun cooked you inside out – amidst barefoot, shirtless kids running in and out of cinder-block bungalows on little plats with plastic-molded ducks, deer, and Jesuses; but something in him revolted at the requirement that he confine his wanderings, that he must continue as he'd begun the evening, by *their* rules.

So he took a turn down Gadsden Avenue in the opposite direction, a shopping area by day: hardware and sports stores, dress shops, a luncheonette, and brides' boutique; all rolled up for the night, except for a movie house which had a late-night showing of some gung-ho John Wayne war movie set in Vietnam, and a drinking establishment where earlier he'd seen from Raskin's car some soul folk loitering outside.

But as he stepped inside the place and approached the bar to order, a couple of white guys standing nearby reacted like something slimy with pointed ears had just appeared. A dozen or so other patrons scattered about were listening raptly to the whiny country/western sound coming from the jukebox. Prudence might have prevailed, but he'd already ordered. Leaving now would be running with tail between his legs.

No way. All I want is a lousy beer, he said to himself.

He sat at a small table at the far wall opposite the bar, then crushed out the stub of his cigarette. After a moment he lit a second. The place was dimly lit, and there were colored Christmas lights hanging along the ceiling, and small, brightly lit-up animated signs advertising beer brands. But he was feeling defiant.

"This is supposed to be the new South, Dean Hyzak's wonderfully progressive Colonus," he muttered. That was when several heads turned, one man leaning against the counter at the other end of the bar, glaring.

A waitress came around who seemed perfectly normal. Her blond-dyed hair was in a beehive, brown at the nape of the neck, the color of her skin pasty, washed out. He took a long, meditative last drag on his cigarette; then stubbed it out, adding carefully to the mound of butts in the black plastic ashtray.

"Sir! Would ya like a sandwich or some peanuts?"

He was grateful. She wasn't unfriendly. She was doing her job, every bit professional.

He was thinking – thinking simultaneously of looking casual – how strange being in the old Carolinas, not far from where his mother's people came, and near where she herself had been born but would never return. He spotted several patrons that were speaking in lowered voices, their eyes, hawk-like, glued on him.

He'd already ordered and finished a few beers (one in the hotel), and was feeling that looseness you feel when you've downed a few.

"Stay away from white bars!" a woman friend told him just days before his departure for Colonus.

"Are you kidding?" he'd laughed at her then.

But he laughed now at the absurdity of his having stumbled into this place anyway.

"Colonus is no berg." Wasn't that what Mr. Sunshine, Ozzie Hyzak, said? Yeah, and North Carolina is so *progressive* nowadays, he silently mocked the invisible Dean Hyzak.

He swaggered over to the juke, feeling eyes boring into him, and was surprised to actually find a couple of Aretha Franklin records. Cheerily drawing some coins from his pocket, he thought, how did the Queen get in here? How did *we* get in here? Laughing to himself – gotta pee bad; gotta pee bad, hold it, bladder! – and feeling a little woozy, holding himself steady, he crossed over to the men's room.

A few minutes later, he was repeating the words in a mumble as he zipped back up. "The pause that refreshes," he chuckled as he emerged from the stench of that foul, closet-like enclosure. And in the background, his Aretha having played out, the country music was whining away about the truck driver's long-lost loves in Dallas and Baton Rouge, and there was a guy standing near his table with a pot belly that hung absurdly over his belt like a water-inflated balloon.

"How a' you? How do you do?" He nodded in a languidly menacing way. Slowly turning his head round to look at the two men who'd materialized behind him, then turning back again to Vincent, he said with a sneer, "Where you from? Where you come from?"

The red and green, yellow and blue Christmas lights and dancing signs advertising popular beer and cigarette brands were luridly hypnotic in their effect. Tammy Wynette was belting out *Stand By Your Man*, and he was saying to himself, I'm alone here – I'm dead if I don't get outta here; yet he was also glued to the spot by a strange fascination, almost as if he was looking in from outside on an American scene played out on a stage under klieg lights, a scene reenacted numberless times and wondering in some kind of stupefied fascination if it would begin to whir away again with him in it.

"*Stand By Your Man!*"

There was a sea of angry white faces.

"You know you're pushing it, bo-yy," another man now pushed his way to his table, not speaking so much as growling like a vicious yard-dog, "when you don't even know better than to use a white man's washroom."

"OK, Wayne. OK, Wayne," someone was suddenly shouting, "that's enough! That's enough."

"He don't remember what happened to that nigger Martin Luther King who went around causin' trouble!"

"No trouble! No trouble!" a shrill voice was yelling from somewhere in the back.

He was pushed, but a curiously gentle push, as someone somewhere cried, "You figger you another Martin Luther King?"

All the while there was that insistent, whiny, dreamlike wailing – *STAND BY YOUR MAN!*

He was pushed again.

He shoved back.

In the same instant someone struck him a glancing blow from the side. Adrenalin-charged, he exploded, kicking and swinging wildly, at the same time trying to break for the door. And then terrifying moments as he felt an iron grip around his neck, several men pushing him back in the same direction, and a wave of pushing in the opposite direction and someone screaming, "Get that boy outta here! Get that boy outta here!"

A woman was screaming hysterically, then a man yelled, "I'm gonna kill that nigger! I'm gonna kill that nigger!"

Within seconds Vincent was flying headlong. Just barely catching himself before striking the sidewalk, shaking trembly-boozy and with the sound of shouting-cursing following and a violent scuffle from inside, he righted himself, making tracks. After no more than a minute, he fell on his hands and started retching. For a minute he remained in that dog-like posture, throwing up. Then lifting himself painfully, aware suddenly of how vulnerable he appeared, he tottered to his feet.

The street was thankfully deserted.

For critical moments, first leaning against a lamppost to keep his balance, he stood, relieved; then something more: a surge of good feeling rising; drinking in the victory, the cool, breezy night air!

"You dummy, Vincent!" the lovely and combustible Gwen Randolph blasted him months later when he told her of his misadventures. "Didn't you know that when you were all by your *lonely* – you *fool!* – that's when you *really* were in danger?!" She really burned him. "That kind of trashy behavior only makes trouble for all the folks. I thought better of you."

Gwen had a point. But the fact was that he was lucky. No one followed him.

As he made the rest of the way to the hotel, feeling like Superman changed back to Clark Kent, he began to hear sirens; and he thought, too, convinced that if he could face down a mob of racists, he could face down anything Montbanc would throw at him. Wasn't it, after all, ultimately about the business of ridding the world of just such as Wayne? Dwayne and all the rest? He'd be the good soldier, suppressing his own preferences; the more intolerable the demands, the greater the merit in the sacred effort!

Now he had the greatest opportunity ever in his life to achieve momentous ends.

2

Good Intentions

Jim Allan woke late Friday morning on the anniversary of his third week in the city in a supremely unsettled state. Unable to connect with Thomas Doswell after more than a week in Colonus, he'd learned since then that the man had inexplicably done everything he could to keep from ever meeting him – or, that is, teaching with him. Dean Ozias 'Ozzie' Hyzak, Dean of Students, first dropped the news.

Hyzak, smoothing his pencil-sharp moustache with a long, finely manicured finger, while bemoaning the fact it was so late, that he was "busy as a bee", and wouldn't have the time to take Jim on a tour of Baxter's tree-lined walks and "fine old buildings", or even for lunch in the dining room of the Grand Hotel, fixed the long-haired, bearded young man with a benevolent smile, and finally blurted it out.

"Doswell was against hiring you."

"What?!" Jim murmured, feeling like the man had punched him in the solar plexus.

"Dean Middleweek thought he'd change his mind, but he persists on being against your working with him in Great Books."

The contract he'd signed was to teach Great Books with Doswell and another man named Brown, another New Yorker, he'd been told; something he'd planned on and was well prepared for. Young men Jim's age were being drafted for the war in Vietnam, and without this position the reason for the deferment he hoped to get would be removed.

The Assistant Dean was immensely busy. He glanced awkwardly at his office door; the noise of a crowd of rowdy students anxious to see him for some urgent practical living problem boiled up from outside. Realizing the time that he was wasting, and wearied by the Dean's cheerful recitals of Baxter's – and the city's, and the state's – many amenities, Jim suddenly rose from his chair, ready to leave, but then paused, and suddenly facing the Dean, asked desperately, "What does he have against me?"

"That is a good question." Hyzak nodded and then chuckled. "I don't pretend to know the ins and outs of things – you know I'm only the Assistant

Dean." Leaning towards Jim, the oil he put on his hair (smooth, brilliantined like Nat King Cole's) giving off a sweet, unpleasant coconut smell, he added in confidence, "Let me tell you, I have *so much* on my plate!" He sat up, turning his arm to the door, his voice rising. "The Food Manager just now frantically called. He tells me —"

Jim jerked away. "I'm taking your valuable time." And as he said this, he thought bitterly, Why was I told to talk to *you* and not to Dean Middleweek?

As he opened the door, about to step outside, Hyzak called, reminding him of something he'd told him earlier. "Everyone who's anyone will be at the President's Welcome," to which he'd begun incongruously laughing like he'd made an uproarious joke. "The home economics department puts on a grand show! The hors d'oeuvres are *deeee*...lish! Make sure you come."

Jim often did his best thinking while he drove. So that day, as he cruised in his muffler-blasted Volkswagen Bug to calm his mind and collect his thoughts, he thought seriously of quitting. He certainly had reason to. But squinting through the heat waves to the billboards and a glossy magenta, yellow and green motel at a crossroad, mired in a slough of despondency which the energy-sapping heat of the day did not improve, he felt little inclination to do or even to think anything decisive.

Late in the afternoon, after driving back to the Hotel Carolina where he was staying temporarily at reduced rates, he picked up a *New York* magazine and a copy of the *Colonus News-Herald*, and decided on taking an early supper at the Belk cafeteria. Lingering at his table in the cafeteria's refrigerated coolness, he scanned the headlines: daily tallies like sports reports of dead Americans and Vietnamese; cheery pictures of local beauty contest winners; NASA's plans for a second moon walk; an understanding by Colonus' City Council to upgrade the city's parks. Shirking the *for rent* section of the classifieds, he glanced through an interview with an "urban guerilla" in California who explained why they'd bombed the Bank of America.

No, Jim thought, his draft status would be in great jeopardy if he resigned.

Later that week, he took Hyzak's advice, planning to speak with the ever-busy Dean Clarence Middleweek, and hoping on an offchance to catch the elusive Doswell in the President's palatial home. But as it turned out as he arrived in the hall where the gathering was taking place, he found neither Middleweek nor Doswell nor Brown, his fellow New Yorker – and it was as Hyzak said. Shortly after arriving he was taken in hand by Raissa Albrecht, a fifty-ish dowdy white lady, to acquaint him with his "*new* chief", Doswell's replacement, a tall, café au lait African-American of middle years by the name of Raskin Perrin.

"Jim, Professor Perrin here is going to head up the new Humanities Core," she said by way of introducing them, her smiling eyes falling dotingly on the frowning Perrin.

Once again someone took the wind out of Jim, for other than throwing them an irritable glance, Perrin sidled away, barely acknowledging her.

Then, seeing across the room an affable-seeming group of men, and desperate to get away from the gabby Mrs. Albrecht, he managed to detach himself, and approached them with the trepidation of the new kid on the block. Hearing energetic Spanish accents going on about a play which had just opened in the city's Johnston Arts Centre, a Broadway play called the *Latin Stripper*, with an over-compensating exuberance brought on by shyness, he asked with roguish humor about the expected length of the *Latin Stripper*'s stay in Colonus. With this there was a sudden hush.

After eternal seconds and long, pointed looks, one of the men broke into a loud laugh and sang out, "Ah, no! It would be truly wonderful. But you mean the *Satin Slipper!*"

As Jim made off that night, feeling like a human billiard ball bounced from one corner of the room to the other, from one day to the next, an older black gentleman of immense height introduced himself. "I'm Cleon Baker! Some people call me 'the Rev'. You must be the new man in Books. Now you just come on by my office whenever you like and we'll talk."

Rude, brusque, with hardly a reply, he flew, mumbling to himself over and over what a fool he'd been not to come down first and check everything out before putting his name on the dotted line.

That was how the night ended, driving back alone to his room at the Hotel Carolina, shouting profanities through cranked-down windows into the sleeping Colonus night.

Since then, resigned to making the best of the situation, knowing it was too late to turn back with thought of the great national meat grinder at work, he'd begun routinely visiting his office and looking for an apartment. Then out of the blue later that Friday, astonished, he found a memo from Thomas Doswell in his mailbox. With covering copies for Deans Middleweek and Hyzak, it said nothing of Perrin, of any changes, any mix-ups or delays, and it offered no apologies; but it gave a time (that very day) and place to meet and discuss plans for the coming year. And it was dated a day or two before his conference with Dean Hyzak. Why was it so late in coming? Could the Dean have been aware of Professor Doswell's calling this meeting when they'd first spoken? But why? Regardless, Jim had little time to think, for it was necessary to meet him in a couple of hours.

Frantically, he rushed back to the Hotel Carolina to grab a shirt, a tie and suit jacket, completing the makeover he'd begun that morning when he'd had his scraggly beard and long brown hair shorn in the downstairs barbershop.

As he approached the man's previously hidden office, not far from his own, in a row of three identically drab frame cottages, something struck him as odd: all the time he'd been searching, no one had so much as hinted that his office was under his nose. What'll he be like? he mused. Ever since Hyzak had said he was "not a man who'll give an inch" – oh yes, "a charming man, a man of great learning and culture", but not one to give an inch – he had imagined him as pedantic and grim-visaged, sporting a fake Anglicized accent, like a prof he'd once known in the city. As the avalanche of contradictory messages came pouring in, it became clearer to him: unreasonable, vaingloriously professorial, and surely the unctuous Hyzak with his Voodoo contributed much to the picture.

But the individual he met was startlingly different. He was none of that. He was fat and carelessly, even slovenly dressed, hardly looking the part of a professor. As Jim faced the solitary, Angus-like bulk, in a half-finished office off a dingy plaster-begrimed upper floor hallway, the contrast would have set him to laughing but for the sad inauspiciousness of the man. He could have been one of Baxter's over-the-hill janitors, bulky in his ill-fitting, crumpled, tieless suit with faded fedora, now perched carelessly atop some books. But amidst the harsh smell of some industrial-strength disinfectant that filled the building, in that solemn, careworn, sweat-glistened face, there brimmed an inner light.

As often happens when people have a thousand important matters to talk about, Jim Allan awkwardly launched into talk about the weather. He didn't know what else to talk about, and he was beginning to catch on: there was academic foul play operating at the highest levels. Earlier he'd met his office mate, Dr. Emil Szereszewski, long-haired like Einstein, middle-aged and grumbly, who'd said this much: that President Montbanc and Doswell had been in a quarrel since Montbanc's arrival from California a few years before.

"If the President has his way, they will be studying Buddhism and Confucianism alongside Shakespeare and Aristotle," he said in a tone which made no secret of whose side he was on. And then, glancing sharply at Jim for a second, he seemed to reconsider: "I imagine it is well the young people know about the great literature of other people around the world."

No. He wouldn't step into this domestic squabble, he thought now while gazing about this drab, disheveled room, scattered books and student papers piled high against the walls.

Doswell busied himself with filing, and over the next several minutes Jim felt from the older man the discomfort of his ruminative silence. Carelessly the younger man launched again into a round of hackneyed conversation about unfamiliar Southern weather in the mode of the newly arrived Northerner.

"You were in Birmingham in the summer of '63 weren't you?" Doswell said.

He felt himself turn red. But of course, how ridiculous – he'd put that in his resume.

"You must have been pretty young," the old man said after a moment, breaking off his awkward ramblings. "Still in high school? You were in Birmingham to join in the marches?"

"I didn't actually go to Birmingham for that," Jim said, this time careful to be absolutely candid. He was running from home, he said, and he hadn't intended to go to Birmingham, but to New Orleans. "I got waylaid. I didn't have a very good car."

"Running from home..." The words trailed off in the other man's mouth.

Jim wondered then when Brown would be appearing. There was no air-conditioner, but it was unseasonably cool. As a strong breeze blew in through opened windows, the silence between them was broken only by the insistent beat of soul music and the chatter and loud laughter of youthful voices passing below.

It was shortly afterwards that they heard the downstairs door in the front open and then shut. Footsteps bounded two steps at a stride; after a few seconds there was a hard, insistent knock.

Doswell answered the knock and a 'fro-bedecked, muscularly tall and slim, light-skinned young black man entered the room.

Jim stood as the other settled himself; as he reached across to shake his hand, Vincent seemed not to notice as he simultaneously spoke a few words to Doswell.

"I went to your old office first, that's why I'm late." He had a slight accent that was hard to place.

Doswell said nothing.

Jim, gazing long and hard at Vincent, wondered at his rudeness.

As Doswell outlined routine items of business: attendance policies, mechanics of grades, Vincent kept his gaze centered on the old man. He did so even as Jim registered a long complaint about the university's mail service.

But for now most of Vincent's thoughts were on seeing this through as quickly as possible. Vincent had another meeting and wondered if it would be OK to leave early.

Doswell agreed, and so after a few minutes, Vincent said a hearty goodbye to Doswell, and nodded just barely in Jim's direction.

Jim was not disappointed to see him go.

It was then that Doswell rose from behind his desk, snap-brimmed fedora in hand, and announced, like it was a matter of no small importance, that he liked orange juice.

"The Student Union in Ford Hall squeezes its own, want to join me?"

It was cheering, this invitation, so together they strolled over, and as they went the older man began telling Jim a little about Baxter's history.

"Butler Hall is the original Baxter Freedman's Academy," Doswell said, facing a large, red brick building, with a cupola and a great bell set in the center of its roof. Idle and disheveled, it had been standing for years amidst other, more recently constructed buildings. Doswell gazed long and hard at the old place.

"The Academy, as they called it then – the whole of it was right here," he explained with some warmth. As he waved his thick arm, he spoke of it as being constructed by "freedmen" with bricks fired on the site and timber cut from the land. He paused as students walked past and waved. Others stopped and wanted to talk, share something about their summer. Jim watched and nodded and waited, and then they resumed their walk, Doswell continuing in the same affably personal vein; Jim listening, caught up in increasingly thick traffic jams of laughing young people, drawing some of them along, Pied Piper-like, on the way to the Union.

As they approached the building, Jim recognized two persons he'd seen the night of the welcoming party: Sister Mary O'Keefe and Blissie Carter, the latter a very pretty young woman who'd earlier attracted his attention. He'd caught sight of her at the center of a group arguing noisily about the nation's space program; someone saying it was an unnecessary drain on the economy, and that the money spent on it might be better spent on the problem of hunger. And Blissie, her sweetly tremulous voice weighing in with all the force of youth, announced that this was one of those things about "the white American power structure" which made her "blood boil".

He gazed over at her wistfully. As he watched her, gay and animated at Sister Mary's side, taking in the full vision of her loveliness, he felt a tingle in his chest, and the blood rushing to his scalp. Why didn't he strike up a tango with Blissie right then and there? He could have, he might have, but he simply didn't.

It was mid-afternoon and the dining hall was almost empty, but they could see steam rising from the stainless-steel serving tables and hear the clanging and shouting of student workers from the kitchen. They took in the pleasant smell of fried chicken and potatoes being prepared for the upcoming dinner as they ordered their orange juice.

Amidst their talk over the next several minutes, sitting at a table surrounded by empty tables, Doswell said that he'd moved into his new office the week before, which may have explained why no one said where he could be found. As they gazed about themselves, the talk returned to Jim's earlier stay in the South, in the summer of '63.

"Yes, Birmingham, yet you ended up in Kelly Ingram Park just when Bull Connor was turning on the water hoses?"

Jim smiled. He was fishing. So he told a more expanded, lighthearted version of his story: how he'd left New York the winter before, and had come to Birmingham after an uneventful stay in Castle, a small city in Mississippi. "I'd like to say I was run out of town by the town fathers because of my shameful conduct with their lovely daughters, but that would be a lie – but then," he grinned puckishly, correcting himself, "I guess I did get benefit from my New York accent with one of them."

Doswell smiled. "So you spent your time there mostly thinking about the girls."

"I worked as a clerk in a farm store selling the local farmers on the most effective pesticides available for the cotton weevil..." Jim's chuckle as he said this turned to ready laughter as he noted the incredulity forming on the other man's face.

"You advised them with that New York accent?"

"I didn't say they took my advice."

"Yes, yes. I hope not."

"Anyway, I didn't stay in Castle long, only long enough to buy a used car with the money I'd saved, and long enough to get bored with the place. So I drove to Birmingham, which wasn't too far away."

"So there you were. It's a big city. What got you involved with King?"

"Some of his activities, by accident – not with him."

A smile played on the older man's face.

"I was working in a Sears store and met this guy who'd lived in New York a few years before, a real friendly guy. We struck up a friendship. He hated New York – he loved fishing, and gaffing frogs and turtles too. I'd never done that, I mean, the frogs and turtles bit. So he invited me to come with him to where his grandfather lived in the country an hour away. He and the rest of his family lived in downtown Birmingham – I should say his extended family, cousins and aunts and stragglers here and there. They lived in this crowded apartment near the park.

"We went there whenever we caught something to eat, and sometimes when we had a really good catch we'd call ahead, and we'd have a feast, everyone invited. Mrs. Bland's cooking was memorable – the fried catfish and frogs' legs, they were very good, but the brandied peaches, they were especially good." Jim grinned.

"You put on some pounds, I suppose?"

Doswell's orange juice glass was reduced to miniature by his large, beefy hands. And he had the odd habit of filling his cheeks so they bulged squirrel-like as he swallowed.

Jim volunteered stories about the Blands – about his friend Marston, and Marston's cousin 'the Indian', who never spoke a word to him, but spoke about him to the others in his presence. Those were the days when pictures of police dogs tearing at demonstrators' pants legs, and children being hosed down by power fire hoses near the park, had been flashed around the world.

"He'd say, 'Marston, if some redneck don't get him, some damn fool could.' He'd glare at me." Jim mimicked the frown. "I think he thought mostly about the troubles I posed to them."

"You *could* have been a whole lot of trouble to them if you'd been harmed."

"Yeah. And *I* could have been in a whole lot of trouble if *I'd* been harmed."

Doswell laughed. "No doubt."

Jim told in a lighthearted way the mock-heroic tale of his political actions later after he'd returned to New York, blocking traffic to and from the World's Fair.

"That was something Jim Farmer was behind, wasn't it?"

Jim looked puzzled.

"CORE?"

He smiled. "I don't remember. It was mostly the adventure. It had little to do with ideas."

But Jim did have a zest for ideas – that is, with books and great authors. And he had more than an inventory, Doswell noticed.

Their talk drifted from the great authors on Doswell's course list and then to philosophy: to American philosophy first, William James and his novelist brother Henry, then to French philosophy and novelists – and to one Doswell particularly disliked: Jean-Paul Sartre and *Nausea*. "The man is nauseating," he stressed, to Jim's discomfort. But the younger man's mind was instantly put at ease again with Doswell's critique of Auguste Comte. The old man was easily at home in this world of French literature.

He talked of his appreciation for Flaubert's perfection of craft, and his love of Hugo's *Les Misérables* – only he'd retained his love for this last while Jim had since moved on. Jim was especially struck by the fact that he'd committed to memory the Bishop's words to Jean Valjean in the novel's early pages, reciting them with flair and dramatic resonance: "*Jean Valjean, my brother, you belong no longer to evil, but to good. It is your soul that I am buying for you. I withdraw it from dark thoughts and from the spirit of perdition, and I give it to God.*"

As they talked of Victor Hugo's strengths and weaknesses as an author, a lone student approached their table. He was tall and thin, butterscotch in color, atop his head a topiary-like 'fro, adding half a foot to his height – the grandest 'fro Jim had ever seen. And he was giggling strangely.

He opened by saying something teasing about the orange juice.

Jim noticed Doswell gave him little margin. The lamp of benevolence that had been growing brighter over their table in the last hour dimmed as the boy continued, "There was a rumor round you wouldn't be back, that you was quittin', Mr. Doswell."

After some moments, Doswell said quietly, "No, Alvin, I'm a fixture around here. The students will have to bear with me a *long* time."

Alvin was laughing. "Hey! When you plan on havin' that party o' yours? You had it this time last year. You said as soon as everyone comes back. Ya not gonna have it this year?"

The old man was bristling. He said nothing, and only relented when the boy turned towards Jim and said that Doswell gave "the wildest parties" he'd ever seen, that "they were better" than even he knew they were.

In the months ahead Jim would learn that while the old man welcomed a surprising degree of casual give and take with the young people, for some reason on this occasion he didn't.

"Listen, Alvin," he broke in, "we're having a professional conference here, so why not go and find yourself a fine woman to take to that great party you're going to next?"

The boy, who was the very essence of awkward, still responded to this better than Jim might have. In fact, he didn't miss a beat. "I know when I'm not wanted. I know when I'm getting the royal brush-off too." He play-acted sudden indignation. Then turning as if to leave, he wheeled around, facing Jim. "Hey! What's yo name, Professor?"

"James Allan. Alvin – Alvin who?"

"Alvin Foote, like what you got at the end o' both your legs." He giggled. Then strolled off, moving like a palm stalk carried in the wind.

Alvin Foote, this impertinent boy, let the cat out of the bag. Or more: dropped the cat in Jim's lap. Jim had earlier resolved not to venture anything in this matter of Doswell's leaving, or his previous confusion; but now, led by the boy's opening the subject, he let slip a remark on the great strangeness of the last few weeks. The older man only nodded, saying little, but he did something unexpected: he said that they should take supper together.

So after a few finishing swigs, squirrel-jowled, from his juice glass, and a hiatus just long enough to note the relative lateness of the hour and the fact that students were noisily filing in for the evening meal, Doswell excused himself to make a quick telephone call.

As they drove off in Doswell's boat-like, late-model Olds, the old man returned to what Alvin Foote had brought up: the rumors and the gossip about his imminent departure. Jim, encouraged by this, mentioned the irksome Mrs. Albrecht at the President's social, and her assurance that he and Great Books were no more.

Doswell listened attentively, carefully negotiating the heavy traffic. After a minute or so he said softly, "She's usually got her rumors and her humors all mixed up."

Their destination was a soul establishment called the Jolly Roger, just outside the East End in Colonus' downtown.

Now, as they spotted a parking space the second time around the block, Doswell said, "It's true. I didn't want you. And I didn't want Vincent. I preferred to go it alone. I tried it with help before and I had nothing but trouble."

In silence, he parallel parked the big car with ease.

Jim sat alert and on edge, noting that there wasn't a trace of defensiveness in his words. At the same time, he was hardly surprised or offended by this explanation.

Jerking the emergency, the old man continued, "People who don't believe in what you're doing, no matter how able they may be in their own right, are obstacles."

Jim nodded and said he'd begun to suspect as much.

One thing noticed back then by anyone who'd lived any time in the American Southland was the profound social conservatism of the black middle class. Jim had noticed this on his previous trip south. It had contributed to his early picture of the old man. He was reminded of it again in Colonus. It was also an awareness of this which, days earlier, had led to his spending more time in the Hotel Carolina's barbershop than he'd spent with all the barbers he'd seen in the previous several years put together. Respectable men bedecked in fashionably tailored charcoal gray, earth-brown, and dark blue suits, with pinstriped shirts and button-down collars; their opposites dressed in elaborate, flower-adorned, wide-brimmed hats, flouncy dresses or figure-hugging suits, were apt to frown on excesses in drink, slovenly dress, and personal appearance. And in all these particulars Doswell clearly failed.

In New York Jim had known of quarrels fought among those who wanted to conserve a traditional curriculum and others who sought revisions to bring about an "expanded political consciousness". But never had one of the defenders of tradition appeared so out of character. With Doswell's sweat-stained fedora by his side, facing Jim in a booth of his favorite eating place (a seedy joint that was near the city bus station), he observed that the older man liked his beer as much as he did fresh-squeezed orange juice.

Perched on a shelf behind the side counter of this grayish-yellow, fluorescent-lit diner, there was a radio tuned to Baxter's radio station and an interview with one of Central University's professors. It was strange, amidst the clatter of dishes and the barking orders of the waitresses, hearing a Baxter student interviewer ask and receive answers to his questions on 'dissent'.

"It's an increasingly costly commodity in America today," they heard, Jim straining to hear better, Doswell sucking industriously at a pig's knuckle, taking occasional swigs from his beer. "The system forces people into being cogs in the machinery of the system, lopping off and discarding what it can't use – *automatons*, that's what they want us to become...and remember, there's a growing brutalization—"

The radio cut off as some patrons with coins in hand triggered the howl and throb of the jukebox.

Doswell, studying his plate of pig's knuckles and finishing his second beer with a working man's gusto as Jim still nursed his first, cracked in a loud but casual tone of contempt, "Here, a tragic song to be sure – it should be set to music and the Baxter Chorale given a shot at it."

This remark gave Jim a moment's surprise, but the younger man was already explaining, in the spirit of their newfound camaraderie, his enthusiasm about teaching "the Canon"; underlining his warrior-like stance, criticizing the wrongheadedness and sheer folly of the partisans of curricular change. No, he added needlessly, he certainly couldn't see any betrayal in anyone's "advocating great books". But then Doswell said something that once again began to send Jim back to the drawing board.

He didn't agree that the partisans of curricular change were simply wrong-headed, and it wasn't illogical what they were doing.

What did he mean, Jim asked, puzzled, upending the last of his beer.

Its very incoherency followed a certain logic, Doswell stressed over the noise of the juke. "Great literature has everywhere to do with asking what is good, and these people not only fail to ask this, but have made it a creed to exclude the asking of it."

"A creed?" Jim drew a blank.

Then Doswell added, "A tyranny." For in them – he paused, taking nail and finger to mouth, dislodging something between his teeth, and then speaking even louder to be heard over the din – a "good will" was supplanted by a "naked will".

The meaning of the words broke like a wave over Jim, and as they settled uncomfortably, the old man continued in a similar vein.

"They view their task as creative wreckers – by destroying they think of themselves as clearing away the wreckage of the past and bringing on the new millennium."

"But isn't it also about what's good? I couldn't teach great books from other cultures, but surely someone else's teaching them can't do any harm? They—"

"As an addition," Doswell spoke without reservation, without sign of self doubt, "once a person knows the best of his own. But what they're about has less to do with enlarging the vision than blurring it. And that's only its face. A benign front. The object is to trash great work by mixing it with trash, mixing Ginsberg and Hopalong Cassidy with Shakespeare. Relativize everything. And then once you've destroyed the foundations, you lay down new ones."

Jim returned the bottle he'd been playing with to the table. The old man returned his attention to a side dish. Jim grew more thoughtful as he watched him forking fries and the last of his green beans. In fact, inside those seconds, had Doswell been white and stated this theme of his, Jim would have begun to disengage himself, for the older man's remarks he instantly took as not only wrong but oddly indecent. Bitter-sounding and irresponsible. Over by the juke he noticed a few patrons swaying to the velvety pulse of a soul version of 'When You Look Upon a Star'.

The old man felt the young man's resistance. His eyes on Jim, estimating, he said, "If values come down to mere cries in the primeval night," he interrupted his chewing, speaking barely loud enough to be understood, "why shouldn't the enlightened consider it reasonable to reshape them into something hopeful for the future? What should stop them from doing so? When all our 'shoulds' and 'should nots' are mere material, artifacts of our animal origins? Wasn't this what our friend Comte had in mind?" His voice had grown increasingly harsh as he finished this food-in-the-mouth speech.

Jim murmured, following indecisive seconds, "But I don't think this is what *these* people have in mind."

Doswell tilted his face as the juke blasted away, nodding a glazed acknowledgement as he took jowl-filling swigs of his beer.

Jim knew he hadn't heard, but he let it go. As it was, he saw no signs of conspiracy. His old comrades were very open. As for the archetypal positivist in the flesh, he saw his father, whose book jobbing firm had sewn up the New York textbook market. He couldn't imagine the people Doswell had in mind associated with his thoroughly business-minded father – his father, who vigorously believed in nothing beyond dollars and cents and testable achievement. What he and his Movement allies had set themselves against was precisely the overbearing class elitism and materialism embodied in so many just like him.

And yet, in the midst of the Jolly Roger's clatter and the scream of the juke breaking into the clamor, watching him draining his beer, Jim thought he knew well the people Doswell had under *his* broad net. He knew they could be extreme, could be willful in their destructiveness. He knew the peculiar combination of verbal felicity, brutality and high morality of his Movement comrades. Following his return from Birmingham, Jim's doubts growing about certain directions the Movement had taken, like the toy soldier in the Diehard battery commercial, he had gradually ground to a stop. That's why he'd come south – to be recharged!

Stealing appraising side-glances at Doswell, who ordered another beer and was casually gazing at some patrons as they entered the diner, Jim might have thought of him as an articulate fool who confused passion and immaturity with treachery, but he didn't because he was feeling no small affection for this stubborn old bull of a man.

"Give my friend another, Jenique." Doswell, drawing the attention of the waitress, pointed to the empty bottle in front of Jim.

Watching Doswell now, Jim *couldn't* disengage himself. He couldn't, not only because of his affection and respect for the old man, but because he was *not* distinguished, he was *not* polished, he was *not* white. No, nor was he even a properly bourgeois Negro. The aloof black middle-class professional, as he initially imagined him – and Hyzak guided him by the hand in visualizing, Oreo indeed! – yes, that might have allowed an easy write-off, with that dank-cellar odor of a foolish and bitter kind of middle-class resentment. But Jim knew there was too much that he didn't understand. Were Hyzak, Middleweek – who else? The President – were they right about him? None of this meshed. All of it was too complicated and constrained by the authority of his dismal appearance, his generation-old fedora, his horny, beefy hands; his simply being – what? Jim didn't know, but not the cliché he'd expected.

"Heyyy! Dr. Doswell!" A man with a pronounced case of scoliosis, a powerful black Quasimodo with a prominent scar that reached from just under his right eye down his cheek to his chin, materialized from behind the counter. Broadly grinning as he approached Doswell's side of the booth, he spoke familiarly and loudly, in a heavily laden New York or northeastern-inner-city accent. Doswell responded in kind, replying warmly. The man glanced over at Jim and continued grinning, glancing back and forth from Jim to Doswell, repeating, "My man, my man! Dr. Doswell."

Doswell tilted his head Jim's direction and said, "He always calls me Doctor. I long ago stopped trying to break him of the habit."

The man seemed to have a proprietary air about the place. Was he the Jolly Roger who owned the diner? He engaged Doswell in a back-and-forth that had to do with regulations governing public eating places. Yes…Jim's mind drifted further into something of a trance. Why does he say such things? Am I getting it right? Am I missing something? Is he testing me?

As they chatted his thoughts were a jumble. For the first time he really noticed the less prominent puckered, pinkish-white scar tissue over Doswell's left eye, and he thought, what does he have to do with this man? What does he really know about any of this? Who is this unsavory friend of his? And what is this business of the *shoulds* and the *should nots* which in the end have no justifications over one another but the naked will? Yes, *Do It!* they say… True. But isn't all this bitter? – the thought entered deeper into the tunnel of his mind – even childish? Someone who still admires the monumental sentimentality of a Victor Hugo?

"So you'll call him? Explain?"

Doswell nodded.

"Hey! Jenique, gimme the check!" the man bellowed as he approached the waitress, who towered over him like a Tutsi beside a Bushman.

"Mo! Don't you go taking my check like that!" Doswell gestured, discernibly annoyed.

Mo, check in hand, turned and flashed a triumphant grin.

Jim smiled, thinking, I'm going to annoy him some more now.

Doswell was more than annoyed. "Damn it, I tell him not to do that. It makes me want to stop coming here!"

Jim grinned. Not to be distracted, he remarked with softening words on what he thought was the old man's earlier failure to appreciate good intentions.

For a second Doswell gave him an uncertain look. But then, as he gained his bearings, his reply was hardly conciliatory. "Useful idiots there are many," he said sternly.

But Jim, blushing, uncharacteristically pressed on, stressing what had been cooking in his mind for a good part of the night. "Battles don't have to be blood feuds," he heard himself saying. "People start by thinking each other idiots and then they grow deaf to each other." But as the thought came from his mouth he grew embarrassed at his own effrontery, ending inconclusively with a self-effacing laugh.

He would say years later that he remembered a weary smile come over the old man's face. Doswell had been drinking all night. Jim hadn't finished his third, nursed so long it had gotten too flat to drink. But Doswell was steady and clear, while he was lightheaded. Now there was an edge to what he began saying.

"Jim, you mean we need to listen to each other here and—" With that the words were swallowed up by the piercing screech coming from the juke. He was saying something about intentions, but just exactly what? His eyes had nothing of the softness of the ox he bodily resembled; they gripped Jim's forcefully. Jim, still feeling himself blush, heard, if not much by way of the words, the severity in the tone of the words.

But after a minute or so, the blast of impenetrable sound subsiding, Doswell said something over the remaining din that took him by surprise once again: "This fellow Brown, I would try not to let it bother me."

"Brown?" Jim returned the gaze, his manner giving the appearance of a bafflement that he didn't feel. He was unwilling to concede even by a look that there was anything about Vincent he'd noticed, much less been bothered by.

Doswell lifted his glass in the gesture of a toast. "To good intentions."

3

An Ivory Angel

Institutions like Baxter University couldn't long survive without substantial infusions of private funds. Ask where did Baxter get the bulk of its support, and the answer would come back that since the end of the nineteenth century it had enjoyed the largesse of the Burwell family, local gentry that originally made their fortune in millinery manufacturing and had since branched out into half a dozen other money-making ventures.

Wallace Burwell, a member of the latest generation of these displaced New Englanders, also happened to be the most generous member of the family in all its three generations of prosperity. Nor did his generosity end with funding for Baxter. It went as well to Central State University, and the local art museum, and to many other causes, artistic, educational and political. It even included sharing his house for semi-philanthropic purposes.

Raskin Perrin, who seemed to know more of the intricacies of the Burwell family than anyone else, philanthropic or otherwise, went over there regularly. It was a huge Georgian affair, one of the state's grandest mansions, in an exclusive residential district that took its name from the estate, Laurel Hill, and which Burwell, a bachelor, a man of Raskin's generation, often shared with a gaggle of vagabonds, with whom it was said he had business and personal relationships mixed in ways that were "very untidy". Raskin was on the edge of this little troop, an intimate of at least one or two who seemed to permanently reside there, Burwell himself being absent much of the time. With a home in New York and in the south of France and where else no one knew, even when he was in residence he had his private sanctuaries on the estate. But whether absent or present, Laurel Hill served as a kind of Colonus analogue to the Parisian salons where the smart set gathered. Occasionally prominent individuals visiting the state university, or on occasion famous friends of Burwell, would stop by. Gore Vidal and Lillian Hellman came later that year; and on the evening of one Friday late in September, following a distinguished author's address at CSU, James Baldwin was due to appear.

Until the news of Baldwin's imminent appearance Vincent hadn't visited the place, and was sure he never would. Someone had accused him of avoiding visits because Raskin and most of his friends were gay. But it was a different kind of wooing which till then had dissuaded him from going. It was that competitive intimacy among whites, each of them vying one with the other to be first in the special affections of the bad jungle boogies, that sealed it for him. But in the end, Vincent went because Raskin assured him he would be certain of getting to talk to the famous author in the informal setting of the big house. Baldwin, after all, was a favorite. Colonus was bleak; Vincent needed a break amidst the gray monotony. And no doubt he would have talked with James Baldwin had he shown up as planned, but the man didn't show. The evening turned out like many others except for certain natural and synthetic mind-altering agents being in extra-sumptuous supply – and for the fact that it was the night he got to know Blissie Carter.

He remembered he was standing in the interior courtyard and garden of this grand American manor house, leaning against a column, gazing at a gushing, sculpted granite water fountain, taking in the general richness of his surroundings…and then he heard from off the courtyard, out of sight, the chime of girlish merriment.

Minutes later someone quietly approached from behind, wakening him from his reverie.

"I hope you won't bite my head off," came the softly melodious Southern belle drawl.

Turning uncertainly towards the voice, he began clearing his throat.

"I don't blame you for what you said about all of us wallowing in 'romantic utopianism'. I really thought you were impressive."

It was clear she was talking to him. She was very attractive. Vincent had noticed her earlier on campus. How could he not have? She had butter-colored hair, cut about shoulder-length, that hung loose and came straight down and moved freely when she swung her head (which she did often). She wore a tight-fitting pink sweater, and she had a bright, animated face that seemed to be constantly taking in a little joke all her own.

He knew she was referring to some things he'd said at the 'sensitivity training' session Gerald Loewenstein and his friend Colin Murphy from Central had organized earlier that month. He'd said to Raskin then, tongue in cheek, that he doubted anybody's consciousness had been raised, and here she was saying things which suggested *hers* had been.

Vincent was a bit uncomfortable with his own reaction, though. Blissie looked the part of the giant 'Goodrich girl' in boots, cowgirl hat and figure-hugging mini-skirt, reclining provocatively along the length of America's highways. Yes, that same billboard perfection of Madison Avenue, but with a bright Ivy League smirk.

"You know what makes me want to *screeeeam?*"

Vincent smiled. He was certainly not about to bite her head off.

"It's people who take things for granted… By the way, do you believe that because a woman bears a child she is primarily responsible for raising it?"

He hesitated. "I haven't given it much thought."

She put on a sour expression. "Ahaaaaa!"

"I was raised by two parents. I've always thought of child-rearing as the business of both parents."

He'd forgotten his racial grudge for the moment. Her bright, laughing, blue eyes and amiable defiance made him reflexively seize the initiative, responding to her both playfully and aggressively. He told her the sexes were made for each other, that they complemented each other.

"You mean you get to give the speeches, and we get to run the mimeograph machines and make the coffee?"

He laughed heartily.

They bantered back and forth for a while, and it turned out that in a couple of weeks she and a contingent of students would be driving up to Washington to participate in the first Peace Moratorium that fall. Was he going? As a matter of fact he wasn't. No, he was going to a very important pre-summit of the Alliance. And it was being held in Washington at Howard University where he was to see to some urgent business (rumblings in the ranks). She was impressed with this mysterious business of his. (His telling her so little made it even more mysterious and fascinating.) One thing led to the next, and there she was suggesting he help to make a full car for the drive up.

"We're looking for one more person. I think I've found him." She grinned radiantly.

But afterwards, he regretted the hastiness of his decision. When he'd first come to Baxter there was his earlier determination to stay clear of these people – and that included white women. Over the next several days he reminded himself to call and say he couldn't make it; yet in the end, that's all he did, remind himself. They left on a late Friday morning in Blissie's shiny blue and white '68 Buick Le Sabre, four students, Blissie and Vincent. The trip was quite pleasant, there was a lot of exuberant horsing around which was contagious, and he enjoyed himself more than he had in a long time. Blissie was in fact very nice. She was witty and gay but left the limelight to a few girls and a boy who were full of raucous tales and outlandish jingles and songs, all the while stealing glances Vincent's way with knowing eyes and a wise grin.

As for Washington, it was draped in gray the evening they arrived. It had always seemed to him more a Southern city, a city of sun and light (at least as he imagined Southern cities before). Now it could just as easily have been New York or dreary Philadelphia in early fall. The students went home to stay with their families, with much fanfare and hoopla over time and place to meet the following day, leaving Blissie and him to fend for themselves.

They were parked along Constitution Avenue, the car facing the Washington Monument, her mini-skirted thighs splayed at the steering column, making it hard to gaze serenely out at the city, but he tried (at least he thought he did) to appear undistracted. He'd always tried not to be an obvious person, but he was challenged by this nonchalance. How many colored boys in earlier generations had gotten into serious trouble this way? But such thoughts made it no less tantalizing – more so.

And then she came across in a refreshingly direct manner. For as long as he would know her, there would always be something piquantly unselfconscious about her, something very clear and direct and confidently certain.

His original plan had been to stay with a friend with whom he'd stayed before when the Alliance meetings were being held. But then she got the words out before he did.

"I've got friends in Georgetown where I'm going to crash. You can stay over there. They've got plenty of room."

The picture flashed through his mind of God knows how many strewn about on the floor in their scrungy sleeping bags, and the usual pot-laced adolescent hijinks – with him in the midst of it all. He made a face, and she read his thoughts.

"You'll like them. And there won't be a crowd. There won't be anyone else."

"I hate dropping in on people unannounced," he said coldly, belying the instant excitement in his blood. "And they don't know me. Better skip it. I appreciate the offer though."

It was funny; she was very spontaneous, not at all inhibited, altogether vital and vigorous. "Vincent! Don't be ridiculous! You're a stick-in-the-mud. What do you want, a silver-plated invitation? I'm telling you they won't mind!" Then as an afterthought she added, "I'll call them first if you want me to."

"The question is, will *I* mind?" he said softly after a moment, all the more thrilled at how strong she was coming onto him.

She shrieked, "You're impossible!" and punched him in the arm hard, like a man would, straight, with closed fist and knuckles, none of that cat's paw business.

He yelled, in not altogether mock-pain, "Ow! If I don't go are you going to beat me up?" He was thinking all the while, I can't believe this!

"Damn right I will, you stick-in-the-mud!"

The blood coursing, tingling through his veins, his whole body fully alerted, he ended up staying at her friends' apartment.

He had a vision at the time. He imagined her with her father at their home in suburban Charlotte, the old man deeply distressed; after all his darling daughter, his very own dear little Blissie of the golden curls and alabaster skin, was hobnobbing with a…a…well…

"Blissie," – deep basso profundo, grave – "you're not really thinking of getting serious with this Nig-ro?"

Blissie: "Oh, Daddy! Don't jump to such conclusions!" Cooing. "No. I just like sleeping with Vincent."

Which is the way he too felt about Blissie – he just liked sleeping with her. But then there were her friends.

John and Susan were career government people, John with the State Department, and Susan who was maybe ten years younger than John and with another department or branch of government. And maybe it was the fact that they were with the government, especially John, that made them so anxious to please.

Susan said, "I've been saying for a long time now that if we can spend billions to kill people, why can't we spend billions to save people?"

China was in the news at the time and John was supposed to be some kind of expert. He and Blissie obviously had an ongoing conversation on this subject.

"You remember, Blissie? I said we'll soon recognize that China is a major country with solutions to problems we'll all be soon facing: well, now it's official, if you look..."

The strangest thing about John and Susan was that Vincent couldn't remember afterwards what they looked like. Usually he remembered people's faces, their mannerisms, their posture, their general physical appearance – at least, if not their names. But this would never happen with these two.

Blissie was very attentive to her hosts, nodding vigorously, adding a thought here and there.

"They've made tremendous strides, think of the starvation that existed..."

"They've learned to avoid waste in ways we certainly..."

"And all you hear about them from our press is the regimentation and the hatred for America. Well, as for hating us – can you blame them? I would hate us too!"

"They have always had a regimented society," John said. "That's nothing new. And that's changing, certainly. Did you know, Vincent, that in their armed forces everyone wears the same uniform? There are no rank insignias?"

Vincent, who'd been growing increasingly impatient, and aggravated by Blissie's seeming indifference to him, listened, but didn't half-care one way or the other what these right-thinking white folks had to offer. This is what he'd sought to avoid at Laurel Hill. There was something about being around people like this, something that reminded him of an insinuating suitor trying to win over the coy, seductively reluctant belle – people just like him – which he found revolting, most so when he sensed he was intentionally being drawn into these little courtship dances himself.

"...and everybody shares in the labor – bringing in the harvest, in the mines, in the work of the basic industries—"

"Would you like to work in a mine? Or maybe harvest cotton out of a cotton field?" Vincent broke in. He was being his difficult self, and he was curious just what kind of answer they or Blissie, wrapped up in her increasingly irritating female obliviousness, would give to that.

There was a second of silence. "You've got me there, Vincent. I wouldn't want to work in a mine and I doubt I'd last long in a cotton field," John said.

"But that's now," Blissie piped up. "Where everyone shares equally, where there's a community feeling, you'd probably want to participate in that way. Don't you think?"

"Well..." He hesitated, taking his time to reply.

Blissie was suddenly laughing, a note of apology in the laughter. Then hastening on, glancing from John then back to Vincent, she said, "If you're brought up to believe in the individual first, in your own selfish interests first – and I admit that's the way I am – then it's hard to contribute to the community without feeling a great personal sacrifice." She looked around. "But doesn't everyone feel frustration at not being able to contribute? That's because it's only human to want to work with others – it's the system that frustrates."

"Well, I don't think mining would ever be my thing. I'd probably be one of those who'd have to be sacrificed for the future... Vincent may be right."

"Good riddance too!" Susan was giggling as she stepped sideways into the kitchenette. "He can't even do his part to wash the dishes."

John laughed. But Blissie only smiled feebly. And Vincent, yearning only to jump into the sack with Blissie, gave them not even the feeblest smile – which made for a tense silence.

After a moment, Vincent glanced at his watch, stubbed out his cigarette and said to no one in particular, "I'm going to pack it in for the night. I got a big day ahead of me. Hope you don't mind."

Don't mind? What relief showed on their faces as they pleaded with him to stay up and talk a bit longer.

At that moment he wished he'd never have to see John and Susan again. And the incredible fact was, that's exactly what happened. By the following night they'd quit the place. He never knew why; Blissie never told him, and he never asked.

When Vincent said that he had a big day ahead of him, he wasn't just making excuses. He did. Alliance business had been growing increasingly burdensome since the start of classes the month before. He alone had been hired to oversee on a day-to-day basis preparations for the upcoming convention: he was responsible for lining up speakers, sorting through proposals for topics, exercising the delicate diplomacy required for dealing directly with the many VIPs invited to appear. And then his work doubled with Great Books.

It's been said that no servant can serve two masters, but Vincent was trying anyway. He knew that the President never supposed that he would try, but a sense of pride would not allow him to do less – after all, there were the students that he had to face every day in class! But now he was really being put to the test. It wasn't just that Alliance-related labor grew as the convention weekend approached, or that some of the proposals for topics were outlandish, demanding a delicate diplomacy; but that dealing with first class prima donnas – and no one was more deserving of the laurel than Ronald Montbanc – was more aggravating than anything he'd ever previously experienced. His behind-the-scenes maneuverings, his sudden sulks and his unexplained decisions without consultation made Vincent's job far more difficult than it needed to be. He'd been cleaning up after Montbanc's trails of destruction since the beginning, and now at the first session on Saturday morning, he learned about more than the usual rumblings and complaints and threats. He learned about the defection of the most important leader of the largest patch in the wide mosaic that was to make the Alliance the inclusive voice it was intended to be. This spelled looming catastrophe for the new movement.

Malcomn Tupper was the distinguished leader of Southside Chicago's largest church. Most importantly, he was the informal leader of a larger segment of people, not just from Chicago but from around the country, who were a patchwork held together by their emphasis on community, educational excellence and personal responsibility. Still, if someone asked where Tupper stood on precisely this or that issue, the clearest thing they'd hear was that he wasn't to be locked into one political philosophy or party. So he was difficult to place. And this was true of his many admirers. Yet the tone he set, certainly for his critics, was disconcertingly moderate, at least Vincent felt as much; and it was not only his overall message but his style: epigrammatic, McLuhanesque – sometimes impenetrably so. Vincent often thought his dialectical thinking not just plain wrongheaded but nonsensical. Still, sometimes the man did have original insights. And like Vincent, and his hero Paul Robeson, community was critical to him. So though Vincent was clearly *not* a disciple, he respected the man; more importantly, he'd long been cognizant of the fact that while his presence gave no guarantee of his admirers being winnable to the cause, without him it was unlikely they could ever be won over.

Vincent's longtime concern, given not only the President's leanings, but the leanings of virtually everyone else actively involved in the formation of the new movement, was that this segment's interest in the Alliance, already weak, would die on the vine; that the Alliance would slip into becoming simply one more organization in the shopping mall of competing organizations pushing another line of political nostrums – precisely what it was intended as an alternative to, and why he'd promoted Tupper in the first place.

Maxine Scales, a member in good standing and Vincent's most dependable contact with Tupper in Chicago, now gave him the bad news. "I think, Vincent, that your President Montbanc never really wanted Dr. Tupper to come. He was jerked around so much over that matter of scheduling we talked about, I was surprised he stuck it out as long as he did."

If Maxine, or Tupper, had known something of the intractable scheduling problem he and the other Baxter planners had had at that time they might have been more understanding. It was unfair to put the entire blame for this on Montbanc. The convention had been set to meet in November many months earlier; there was a lot going on that fall; it was to be held on the same weekend that the second National Peace Mobilization had been called, and so Tupper wasn't the only person put out by the scheduling. Indeed, Vincent argued vigorously that everything was set, that they were too far into the final weeks to be backing out at this late a date.

However, to take such a position was one thing, and to believe that anyone who failed to fall instantly into line was a fool or a cur, or both, was another. And that's the place from which Montbanc habitually came. Thus it was his manner and his tone that set people off. And Vincent couldn't always shield him or them from the unpleasant exchanges that Montbanc brought on.

Vincent learned that Saturday morning that the straw that broke this camel's back was more than a problem with scheduling. It was Montbanc's sudden turnaround on a decision to invite Jon Molumba to give an address side-by-side with Tupper.

At that time Jon Molumba was the nationally known leader of a small and militant black nationalist group centered in Oakland, California, which had achieved notoriety (or prominence, depending on your point of view) for the most anti-white rhetoric heard anywhere in America. He'd also been an acquaintance of Montbanc's for years. Maxine told Vincent the full story.

"When he learned that Molumba was coming, and was to appear on the same program Friday afternoon, he said, 'enough is enough. That fool with his get-me-a-white man get-me-a-gun talk – I'd have to be dead', he said, 'and they'd have to roll me up on that stage in my coffin, for me to be up there with him.' I said, 'Dr. Tupper, isn't there any way we can change your mind? I know that Vincent and Dr. Montbanc, they really want you to be there. What if that crazy man is taken off the program with you? What if he's set for a different day?' He stopped me dead right there. He said, 'Maxine, I've made my final decision. I'm satisfied with it. My mistake was to say yes in the first instance. I'm not going to repeat it.'"

So what finally ended it all with Tupper turned out to be a matter Vincent had settled – or thought he'd settled – weeks before. The Rev. Tupper had expressed himself in no uncertain terms: he would never share a stage with Jon Molumba.

And the ironic part of it was that President Montbanc, who'd invited him after agreeing not to, routinely criticized the kind of violent, "foolish" rhetoric that the knob-headed Molumba made his trademark.

In fact, this matter of inviting Molumba had in the beginning been a regular seesaw for Vincent. But after giving it much thought, when he decided against him, his final argument to Montbanc was that the Alliance was already widely represented by militant wings of the Movement; not only that Molumba's presence would antagonize conservative elements, but given the Mora's long-standing rivalry with the Panthers, possibly lead to open war. It was a tactical stance, hardly personal or ideological, and Montbanc seemed to understand this, and so Vincent thought it was settled.

As Vincent later wandered downtown by the Lincoln Memorial, the mall teeming with Peace Marchers (Blissie had pestered him to accompany her, but he wasn't about to join this latest march of the innocents), looking to the Washington Monument and thinking about the first time he'd been here in the summer of '63, he gazed through the prism of these latest troubles out over the tumult of the Reflecting Pool and remembered that first time. Not just him alone, but the whole family – everyone, that is, but Pop; Mom, who rarely did anything alone, made an exception on that one occasion, for she'd *believed* in this – the Movement! So without Pop she'd boarded a bus with a group from church; and Vincent's brother Basil, two years younger and seventeen at the time, going on another bus with friends from high school – and then there was Vincent, too, but in an overcrowded car with some SNCC people.

Afterwards, when they got home, they argued for days about what had occurred. He told them, then, what they didn't know: that John Lewis was going to give a speech that threatened Sherman's March all over again, and came close to giving it; that he was going to tell the Kennedy Administration where to go with their too-little-too-late, and did, *almost*, but for some last-minute arm-twisting by John Phillip Randolph. And on hearing this, Mom was glad he hadn't; Vincent stayed mad that he hadn't; and Basil, full at that time of the deep insights garnered over seventeen years of rich experience on this earth, which in a few years would lead to his joining the Black Panthers, sided with the ultra-conservative Mom. And Pop? With his West Indian all-knowingness, he remained fully aloof.

Now, in the fall of '69, it was Vincent's turn to stay aloof. There they were by the Reflecting Pool, just as many innocents as six years before, some still kicking up the water like children. With dusk coming on the air was growing crisp, and there was a slight breeze. Thousands were there, nearly all white, in loose-fitting farmer overalls and jeans and shorts, watching the candlelight procession that wound its way to the White House as they chanted the names of dead veterans. Watching: wholesome, handsome Wonder Boys and freckled buttercup girls in blue-striped overalls embroidered with the words *Make Love Not War* and a strawberry decal pasted on their fannies, signaling peace signs and waving flags, wearing jackets reading *DAVENPORT HIGH Champs '68*... Yes, again, the march of the innocents! They were holding hands, faces so clear and open and sweet, all gentleness! Wait till you get bumped around some; wait till the hard knocks come; yes, these thoughts kept pulsing through his brain. And as he drifted, making his way, he listened to the names, many colored boys' names, no doubt – Martin N. Colley, Leroy G. Croft, H. Bobby Crofton – words, names, lost in the open air, as the lights of the procession moved steadily forward.

Days later he met with President Montbanc, along with the officious, efficient, and almost white Middleweek and the rest: Hyzak and Baker and Perrin, approaching Montbanc's inner sanctum, a procession of supplicants. When Vincent had first gone to these meetings he was very much like those innocents in the candlelight processions on the mall: the flush of a naive revolutionary fervor infusing his imagination, blinding him to all else. Now he was no longer prepared to sit idly, answering when called upon, as the little tyrant dictated from his swivel throne.

"I saw Maxine Scales in Washington and she told me Malcomn Tupper has changed his mind about coming. He won't be here next month."

Tupper? It was as if the President was uncertain to whom he was referring. Then he turned to Dr. Middleweek with a puzzled expression, and suddenly, as if it had all come back to him, asked, "How often has the Rev. Tupper changed his mind, Clarence?" But he didn't wait for an answer from the man who was always ready with an answer. "He really is like an old lady, isn't he?"

Dapper Baker was laughing so hard he looked like he was about to bust an artery.

Vincent waited for the laughter to die down. "I don't know how often he's changed his mind in the past, but he's not about to change it now."

The President gave him a quick, sharp look.

"I'm sure we can prevail on him to change his mind, Vincent." Middleweek, who'd been largely silent until now, took up where the President left off, marshaling his words with the supportive competence of the perfect number two man.

"Dr. Middleweek is right, Vincent," Raskin added. "Rev. Tupper is angry about that business with the scheduling. But the peace issue, as we've all agreed," he nodded in the President's direction, "has become essentially a white issue. We're not just another ad hoc group jumping to the tune of a bunch of white boys. What we're about is long-term power: who has it, who disposes of it, how to get it, how to shape it for the future. Just as soon as everyone understands this, we'll be on track."

Vincent looked intently at Raskin, searching his face for some sign, a sign of something other than this sycophant's game he played. On previous occasions he'd urged Vincent to be patient, appeasing him with easy references to Montbanc's "imperial presence"; his not appreciating his status as "vassal to the king of Baxterland", but now in President Montbanc's presence the satire was nowhere to be seen or heard.

"The issue isn't scheduling," he replied sharply. "The issue is sticking to what we agreed to. Rev. Tupper refuses to appear on the same stage with Molumba..."

"Well, we can't let him dictate—"

"Excuse me. He's not dictating. There are a whole lot of people who represent views like Molumba's at the convention. And Molumba is the head of only a very small organization – Tupper, and people like Tupper, they represent a broad spectrum that we've got to bring on board. We agreed to accommodate these people. Then we went back on our word."

The 'we' Vincent had in mind was President Montbanc, and everyone knew this.

"Vincent, we never promised anyone who we were or weren't going to invite to the convention," the sinuous Middleweek stressed. "If I understand rightly, in fact, I think that was one of our early decisions: having all doors open to everyone, to keep our options open."

Middleweek was speaking the official line. But as a practical matter, decisions were being made and had been made about who could and could not be represented. This was unavoidable. It was Montbanc who made all final decisions. But he himself had established early on that he would do so with Vincent's recommendations. He at least owed him the courtesy of letting him know when he changed his plans. And Middleweek certainly knew this.

Baker and Hyzak rarely spoke at these meetings except to address nuts-and-bolts issues. Dr. Baker now departed from his usual course.

"I met Mr. Molumba not long ago, Vincent, when I was on the West Coast, and he is a thoroughly charming gentleman. I think that if the Rev. Tupper were to talk to him as I have, I'm sure he would be very impressed – as would you."

Vincent said nothing to this. It was totally irrelevant. He once again gave Raskin a grim look. Was there even a glint of irony in his face? When they were alone he could be uproariously funny, mimicking the President's pomposities at these meetings where everyone did Montbanc's bidding on reflex. Now he was part of the solemn phalanx which stood against him.

Within that same week they met twice, and the following week at least twice again. Nothing was said about Tupper. Other matters were on the agenda. Vincent shared a proposal from a contingent of the recently formed Republic of New Africa to make the case for a late-twentieth-century Southern secession. The idea was to liberate subjugated areas in Mississippi, Alabama, Louisiana, Georgia and the Carolinas; a plebiscite being administered by the Republic of New Africa and the United Nations, and reparations of two hundred billion dollars for sufferings endured during and since slavery to be demanded. Montbanc thought much of this unrealistic, but was not against letting them make the case; after all, he lectured, obliquely referencing the situation with Molumba and Tupper, the Alliance was intended as a big tent, accommodating all viewpoints, no matter how extreme – and "even if personally repugnant". There were other issues that came up at those same meetings, and through all of them Vincent waited expectantly for a discussion of the gaping hole in the speakers' schedule.

Then one day Montbanc brought it up at the tail end of a discussion Dean Hyzak introduced about food service problems that in the end he was confident could be resolved.

"The miracle of the loaves and the fishes," Vincent muttered to himself as Montbanc announced, without preliminaries, that he'd decided to draw on the "Baxter family, the abundant talent of the old U" to fill in the Tupper vacancy. All this was said without a snicker. "But who?" he asked, gazing about and grinning, as though searching for ideas from his battery of yes-men. He himself was already giving the welcoming address. Dean Middleweek had ruled himself out earlier; he would be too involved in day-to-day activities to take on this additional burden. Raskin and Vincent were too junior, and – here Montbanc winked – too notorious for their militancy.

But there was one among them, aside from Hyzak, whom he hadn't mentioned. Following a dramatic pause, and facing Cleon meaningfully, Montbanc said, "A man with gravitas," breaking into an indulgent smile that fell on the giant who until that moment seemed to have his thoughts focused elsewhere. "This is what we need."

Raskin started everyone laughing when he added, as he arched his eyebrows theatrically, "And mellowness."

Alarm registered on Baker's face. "Oh, I don't think I could do that, Dr. Montbanc," he gasped. "You need someone who can give a stirring address. That's not my forte."

"Nonsense, Cleon. You're too modest. You underestimate yourself. Anyway, the point is, we need an intelligent address, one that appeals to people of a less militant bent than some of these, these *firebrands* can give." He winked again. He was in a rare good mood.

Baker had once before recommended Mildred Braithwaite, a sociologist who'd taught at Baxter many years, for a more active role in the weekend's activities. She was, he now said frantically, an absolutely charming lady, "professionally quite able" and "fully willing to participate in any way she can". But everyone knew she was death as a speaker. And so now as Cleon enthused over her as a perfect candidate, Vincent groaned, not only over her, but for the alternative – Baker. He'd feared all along it would come to this: that for the large and influential constituency of a Tupper there would be a blank.

The talk went back and forth and while the President still talked up Baker – it was clear all this didn't really matter to him, otherwise he would have dictated his choice long before. Montbanc ended by asking Baker to further consider the matter, and for someone to sound out Mildred Braithwaite.

These days were a foreglimpse into the most challenging times Vincent would be seeing in his tenure at Baxter. Getting arrested on Morningside Heights, in Chicago and in Washington, was a lot easier than dealing with Montbanc and Company. The former was part of a holy war, and could be exhilarating; the latter were deadeningly tedious sessions dealing with a crisis no one but he discerned. Still, it was only a foreglimpse, and he was now intimate with Blissie Carter, who took his mind off these migraine-inducing convention details.

And then there was this: a curious matter; a wholly unexpected turn. Just before departing from Washington, a couple of delegates who'd accompanied Maxine from Chicago buttonholed Vincent and asked if Tom Doswell was still teaching at Baxter. Yes, he said, surprised they should ask; and yes, he added, puzzled on seeing their eager faces, Doswell was his "chief". With that there was an explosion of high-spirited laughter as they relayed, to his amazement, fond stories they'd heard from friends on the Southside about a couple of summers some fourteen and fifteen years earlier. The warmth of their comments carried over to the entire delegation, as suddenly everyone, even Maxine, said something they'd heard about him: his many contacts in their city, his work in establishing a permanent channel for several inner city high schools to the University of Chicago. The university was in the neighborhood, but as remote until then as the pinnacle of a Swiss alp. There were other things as well which Vincent didn't quite catch, but it didn't matter – the fact was, he was a regular celebrity among these folks. And they'd never even met him personally.

It was this, and other discoveries made closer to home about the old man in previous weeks, that led Vincent, as he gathered his thoughts over the next several days, to an otherwise unthinkable idea.

4

Vincent's Unthinkable Idea

Even before his Washington surprise, Vincent's picture of Thomas Doswell had begun to evolve. Raskin had portrayed him earlier as an Uncle Tom, a holdover from earlier times that one and all were anxious to see on the way out. And indeed, everyone he knew, with one or two exceptions, shared Raskin's sentiments. But Vincent had his own eyes, and the picture he'd been given didn't match what he saw. Not that he'd changed his mind about Doswell being some kind of reactionary old bird. But slowly something else became obvious to him: he didn't fit the mold. There was something more, a force of character that contradicted previous expectations. And the fact that he was disliked by the Montbanc admirers, of whom Vincent had been growing more and more critical every day, only reinforced this opinion. All he had to do was visit the President's office, as if attending King Minos in the Throne Room at the Palace of Knossos, to be reminded of how hopeless they were. At first he'd held out hope for Raskin, but his readiness to go along to get along when the occasion called for resistance shrank his respect for the man.

When they were alone, Raskin tried to explain.

"Vincent, our dear Dr. Montbanc is a politician – he has to be in his job, but taking the long view, he's going where we all want to go—"

"I don't see it," Vincent interrupted. "He's a pretty lousy politician if he is one. One thing's certain, though: he wasn't elected emperor."

"Ah, Vincent," Raskin said then, his ugly mug grinning from ear to ear (actually, he wasn't so ugly that in his youth an orthodontist mightn't have put all right), "maybe you have a little more of the emperor in you than you care to acknowledge."

"Why? Because I don't want to be jerked around? I have to be happy about constantly picking up after his personal messes?"

"So you want a full-time secretary to be picking up after you instead?" Raskin's eyes grew large with merriment in these exchanges. He was in the habit of ribbing Vincent about the work-study kids he'd complained of being given instead of the secretary he'd been promised.

Now something else happened. Doswell had invited Vincent to his home.

And Vincent wanted to find out more about this business in Chicago, but the idea of broaching Doswell's past with the Lemon Face listening in was repellent. Why did he have to invite both of them at the same time? He recoiled at the thought of spending the evening with Allan. He recalled Thoreau remarking somewhere, *If I knew for certain that a man was coming to my house with the conscious design of doing me good, I would run for my life.* Here was this white guy come on his mission of saving the benighted ex-slaves, and he would have to exchange smiles with the humanitarian and not head for the hills. Still, he wanted to get to know the old man, and this was a perfect occasion. Even without the news from Chicago, he was an intriguing character.

The Bakers, for instance, told an interesting story. Cleon had been hired by the university the same year (1945, the end of World War II) as "a three-fer: religion and philosophy and basketball coach". But Doswell came with a past that contained, according to Mrs. Baker, nothing of comparable merit. He had no teaching experience, no experience with the military, no background in sports (always a valuable asset) – no experience at all, apparently. He'd never even gotten beyond a bachelor's degree; yet he was hired by the then-President of Baxter, Carey Robinson, a man known, even in those days, for upholding the importance of a doctorate. What was significant for the Bakers was that Doswell and Carey Robinson were childhood friends, a fact which Mrs. Baker relayed to Vincent with a sly, knowing smile, and a well-timed harrumph which spoke volumes.

But there was this, too: Doswell, at the end of his first student year at Baxter, back in the second decade of the century, had won a rare scholarship to Harvard. As someone said whose relatives had known the Doswell family (he was born in Colonus, grew up in Colonus, and his father had been a professor in the then-flourishing seminary), he'd left Colonus with "the prayers and well-wishes of many behind him, and never returned". That is, until some twenty-five years later.

When Vincent pointed out his Harvard connection to the ample Mrs. Baker, she had a ready reply. "Alright, he went to college in Harvard. But he never spent one single solitary day in graduate school. Cleon worked his way through graduate school, and believe me, it wasn't easy. And he'd already been teaching a few years. Well, *he* hadn't taught a single solitary day in his life! Oh – I forgot! But he *was* Carey Robinson's old buddy!"

"You think that's why he was hired?" Vincent asked.

"What else?" Eunice Baker's hands were planted firmly on her broad hips as she flashed him a sharp look.

But there was something he'd learned from Baxter's head librarian, Mrs. Majora Moxley, a rare Doswell supporter: there was a period sometime in the mid-to late '50s that he'd begun publishing on literature and the arts in major periodicals, in *Harper's* and several important scholarly journals. Neither Baker nor anyone else did anything similar. But then, rather strangely, after no more than five or six years, just as quickly as he'd begun, he'd stopped.

Aside from Mrs. Moxley, all the people Vincent had come to know had some complaint to register. But none of them were damning; on the contrary, in many instances they led to a better opinion of the old man. There was, for instance, the tale of President Robinson's falling into decline during his last days, suffering the effects of a malignant brain tumor, and Doswell's increasingly being seen when presidential decisions were made. Cleon declared him Robinson's "gray eminence", much pleased with himself over the historic reference. And when Robinson died he was convinced Doswell intended to "grab power", taking over the college's presidency. Doswell's putsch never came off, but within the year following Montbanc's accession to the throne, Doswell challenged the power of the emperor himself and refused to join their team effort.

It was this episode which impressed Vincent most about the old man, enabling him to see better why Montbanc viewed him as a standing threat. Listening to Baker and the rest of them, who'd joined in Montbanc's well-touted Baxter Plan to make the college over into a "model of educational excellence", one would have thought that Doswell was an out-and-out traitor because he wasn't willing to give in at every turn. The President, Vincent learned, had come three years earlier with an ambitious Millennial building program. What's more, he'd promised infusions of big foundation money (over and above Burwell's regular gift), and a variety of committee-recommended curricula changes, one of which included scrapping Great Books.

It was a measure of their tunnel vision that in presenting Vincent with evidence of Doswell's mule-like intransigence on this matter, they should think he would instantly adopt the official point of view. True, he had come to Baxter highly recommended as a man with a passion for scrapping obsolescent structures, but it was this same presumption, their lack of a moral imagination, which led him to focus instead on Doswell's incredible spunk, his cool competence and their general incompetence.

The details on that score were these: shortly after Montbanc arrived, based on his presidentially appointed Humanities Curricular Committee's recommendation, without consulting Doswell, he altered Great Books' independent status, making it essentially a satellite of the Humanities Division. In doing so, this gave the committee not only all of the usual prerogatives belonging to departments, such as recommendations for hiring and tenure, promotions, salary increases, and so on, but curricula planning as well. It was the classic political/bureaucratic maneuver: clothe everything in the impersonal garb of disinterested change made in the name of everyone's desire to achieve some abstract goal no one can argue with, and then with the hands of all (and therefore none) on the knife, slowly twist it hard into some very real individual's back.

What none of them counted on, least of all Montbanc, was their sacrificial lamb's response. No doubt they expected that, being near retirement, he would quietly fade away. Instead, he fought them with an obstinacy that resurrected, for a few old-timers, a memory from their early years of Doswell's father, a gritty bull of a man who breathed fire from the pulpit and was a presence everywhere else in life.

With three influential former students on the Board of Trustees insisting on the beneficial influence of Great Books in their lives, and bringing to bear a personal persuasiveness that outmatched his opponents' strenuously maintained equivocalness, in a situation where the presumptive power and decision-making authority lay with the President, Doswell retained control over Great Books. And this was unprecedented. Anyone else would simply have been ignored if he'd taken the trouble to protest. But it was the President, not Doswell, who was humiliated, for Montbanc was now faced with a man who, at least as it affected Great Books, could veto the substance of his decisions. No wonder he hated him! This little cock of a dictator who brooked no interference, even in matters dealing with conference schedules!

Vincent had long revolved all these thoughts in his mind. What they revealed were his abilities and his formidable virtues – but virtues which were damning vices as seen by his enemies. Was it a pipe dream, then, to contemplate Doswell's filling Tupper's slot? Was it impossible not only from Montbanc's perspective, but from Doswell's as well? But if it were possible, would it not be perfect, since the very people who best represented the Tupper constituency remembered him so favorably?

5

Forty Acres and No Mule

Devon, the small, rural community near where Doswell lived, was a singular place because it was a place where the bulldozers had yet to make their assault; where the gouging, the filling, the flattening, the blending, melding, coalescing *everywhereness-in-nowhereness* had not yet encroached from the nearby growing suburbs of Colonus.

James Allan pulled to the end of the lane, stepped out of his VW and greeted Doswell, who was dressed neatly enough in cotton slacks and a plaid shirt. He was accompanied by a middle-aged couple in a well-worn yard where grass grew in patches, and half a dozen pre-adolescent children were squabbling and running about like a litter of newly weaned pups. It was a day resplendent in the glow of an Indian summer, a crisp breeze touching Jim's face, rustling his auburn hair that was growing out once again and touching his collar. And then there was a sweetish, not unpleasant smell of farm animals in the air. Jim guessed at Doswell's grandson because when the woman chided one of the children for some bit of mischief he redoubled it with a warning of his own directed at "Billy".

As Jim gazed about this scene he grew thoughtful: here was Doswell's hidden and unfrenzied little farmstead, a kind of picture seen from afar on his earlier stay in the deep South. Was this the forty acres with a mule, the serene, rustic setting of a thousand Southern fables? In truth Doswell's place was forty acres, but if he'd once manned a plow he certainly did no longer. And while Doswell's neighbors, Mr. and Mrs. Lewis, were hardly affluent black people on the make in the newly developing suburbanite South, the wiry, light-complexioned Jim Lewis was no Old South sharecropper either. James Horace, the scion of the Lewis family, was an independent black farmer. He and his younger brother Harold, and his eldest son Luther, cultivated and pastured a thousand acres of mostly rented red-clay Carolina earth. Thus it was the case that he was a sharecropper and tenant quite literally, but not of the old mold, given the scope of his enterprise. They were entrepreneurs, with their many projects and cash crops and large expenditures in equipment. But Jim Lewis was a shy man, or at least not talkative, and so now it was Euretha, his wife, who quickly filled the breach of silence between them following Doswell's introduction.

"Thomas told me," she said as the broad-beamed old man looked on smiling, "that you are the best, the hardest working person he's ever had working with him."

Doswell first stifled a chuckle, then broke into hearty laughter when she noted his amusement. "I don't know about being the best, but I guess I've been working pretty hard."

"Ah, well, don't be too modest," she said, grinning. She turned to Doswell. "We'll keep Billy with us, then? Till just before supper?" She turned again to Jim. "It's been very nice making your acquaintance, Mr. Allan."

Then she glanced at her husband, and he spoke a few words to the children who were obviously anxious to leave, because in no more than seconds they came flying from all directions like iron filings to a magnet, and tumbled, squeezing, pushing, shoving, protesting, giggling and laughing into the back of his pickup, amidst a pile of chain and scattered farm tools.

As Doswell and Jim, smiling and waving, stepped back from the cloud of dust Lewis' truck was kicking up, backing and turning and starting on its way, Doswell announced that Vincent wouldn't arrive until late in the afternoon. This was good news to Jim that he covered with a studied indifference. Since their first meeting in Doswell's office a month earlier, Jim's grudge against Vincent had grown. It wasn't just the rudeness directed at himself that never let up from that day, but he'd noticed too, in the lecture hall at the weekly assemblies when Doswell addressed all their students, protracted, sullen stares, impatient glaring, little naysaying nods when the old man mentioned something that had an unfavorable reference to what was no doubt dear to Vincent's fervid heart. Nor could Jim resist comparing his own strenuous efforts with Vincent's feeble ones. He scheduled regular meetings with small groups of needy students outside of classes, early mornings, late afternoons, and even on a Saturday or two. While his colleague, the luminary that pulled the tides, was off to Washington, to the Midwest, to California, to Atlanta, a star at the center of the universe – and canceling classes in the process. Jim's only regret was that he'd be showing up at all. He'd be ready with an excuse for leaving shortly after dinner.

In the meantime, the old man offered to take him on a tour of his place, observing his gawking, wide-eyed wonderment, and thinking as he did what an odd fellow this Allan was.

They strode side by side in silence through the pasture, and then, as they came to a stream amidst a scattering of mature hardwoods, stately oak, ash and walnut, they began some idle talk. It was at first about Lewis, and the man's rare success as a farmer. Then Doswell told him about Mrs. Lewis: how she cared for Billy with the same devotion she did her own children; that he and Billy often took their meals over at the Lewises', and that they were "like family".

By now, two or three moon landings had taken place since the first in July, and the talk drifted to matters of technology: its mental and spiritual impact on people, people's tenuous connection to the physical world – topics that had come up occasionally in the weekly assemblies with students.

"I knew a man once," Jim said, "who when he looked at trees saw only board feet, how much lumber could be extracted from any given specimen." He raised his head, abstracted, gazing long and hard at one of the taller trees. "Someone said the step that took mankind out of the sea and down from the trees is now taking us to the stars," he said grandiloquently.

They came to a clearing, a place Allan would return to more than once later, a place beside the burbling stream where there grew a certain flame-colored wild flower which bloomed in springtime in such profusion that on a bright day it gave the stream the appearance of being on fire. Doswell squatted, his hand splashing at the cold, silvery-flecked water. He listened as Jim plunged on, saying that perhaps they were just like the grass, that it was only a kind of "cosmic joke" that humankind alone in creation thought otherwise. "Full of conviction and self-illusion, and that maybe we do effect a purpose, but in a bubble, and then we're gone without a trace, like everything else."

Jim could be extremely odd. Just minutes before this he'd said in passing, in a dreamlike reverie, that before coming south the previous summer, he'd been in the White Mountains in northern New Hampshire, and while there it occurred to him that if he'd died then, his death would be beautiful, it would have meaning – and so he'd thought of simply stepping off one of the mountain lookouts.

With virtually any other person this would have ended it. Doswell did not like melodrama, least of all melodrama such as this. Suicide being a subject he was better acquainted with than most, he wasn't one to brook idle talk of this kind.

"Yes," the younger man said thoughtfully in a near-whisper in response to Doswell's stern reproof, "I suppose there would be no beauty in that. I don't know why I said it. You're right. That would be a *very* grave sin. I'm sorry."

Jim Allan had never before uttered such a thought to anyone. On the contrary, it was a thought he studiously avoided expressing, even obliquely, though it would come to him at odd moments.

The shadows were growing longer, the day's light dimming; Vincent was soon due to arrive and Doswell was preparing chili for supper, along with a store-bought frozen fruit pie for dessert. They made their way back to the house, mostly silent, Jim only stopping to inquire about three or four leafless trees downed and lying at the edge of the wood. Doswell said he'd cut them down the winter before, and he was sawing and splitting them for the coming winter's heat.

"The wilting leaves of a wild cherry can be fatal to livestock," the old man said in passing.

"You mean at this time, when they begin to fall?"

"No, no. When they're cut green, in leaf, or a branch splits from the tree, and they wilt."

Jim marveled at this and everything else around him: the whispery sound of the wind and occasional distant, lowing cattle, the sweet fragrance of the long grass that had recently been mowed around the trees. He said he'd like to help with the firewood.

"You'll be sorry if I take you at your word and put you to work."

"No, I won't. I'm serious. I'd like to come back out. I love it out here."

6

The Little Maggots Burrow Deeper

Jim was going on with great earnestness about the virtues of various authors, making proposals for additions to the reading list; and as Vincent listened he thought of his recent student days at Columbia, where those just like Allan waxed eloquent over their love affairs with Sartre, Heidegger and Kafka.

"You know, back when I was at the student end of things," he addressed his fellow New Yorker for the first time in Doswell's kitchen, which also doubled as his dining room, heaping bowls of chili set before them, "there was a certain type I observed. My friends and I called them the existentialists because they'd take a course in Modern European Lit 211, or something of the sort, and the transformations among them were just short of miraculous. They'd read about dread and madness and angst and all that, and presto, they come out a couple of months later with these pained faces touched with melancholia, resignation and absurdity. Amazing: the Izod polo shirts peel off, they start shopping in Salvation Army outlets, and before you know it you see these Left Bank lookalikes spouting deep, dark profundities."

There followed a thick silence, except for seven-year-old Billy, who loudly announced his pleasure with the chili and called for a second bowl.

"Yes, Billy – here." Doswell filled a second and passed it to his grandson, the extra softness in his voice contrasting dramatically with the fire in his eyes.

His face flushing, Jim said he too had noticed something similar, only it was "the Politics 211 crowd", and added, "the posturing, the play of the campus revolutionaries: clenched fists, faces frozen in scowls like pretend cowboys and Indians and pirates – and Bolsheviki!"

Vincent's eyes narrowed and there was a second of silence; Doswell offered him a bottled beer, wryly saying, as he passed it to him, something about using too much chili in the meal. "Here is something to cool your mouth."

Vincent smiled and nodded. "Yes. There are phonies and frauds everywhere, no doubt about that." He spoke just above a whisper.

Doswell lifted a ladleful of chili con carne in the gesture of a toast, and offered more to Jim and then to Vincent.

But there was little else they agreed on that night.

Tension-filled dinners go better with a voluble child at table. Doswell's grandson, Billy, at first hung his head and spoke only in monosyllables, but after a short while warmed up to Vincent's attentions. In no time at all he became the fount of animated talk about critters he'd recently captured, games he and the Lewis 'cousins' played, and other detailed accounts of his Devon life. Though Doswell was a man of the old school, he listened patiently as Billy prattled on.

But Vincent had work to do, which meant he wanted an opening to talk about the upcoming convention with Doswell. Finding an opportune moment in Billy's sudden need to run to the bathroom, he warily broached the issue of the Alliance. Jim, who took no interest in the subject and had no desire to intrude on a matter which little concerned him, drifted to the sink to help Billy with the dishes.

The news of the upcoming convention had not been in circulation long, but the old man listened patiently while he watched Jim with a gimlet-eyed curiosity.

"Stop messing with those dishes," he said, following a few minutes of this. "Vincent here says that the Alliance is about democracy." He'd turned back to Vincent, shifting his bulk to face him squarely. "But I'm hearing a lot of folks talk about 'delivering the message' and 'getting people to see', and wondering, Vincent, about the message – and how much unity is going to be found without breaking peoples' arms."

Jim, standing by the sink, remarked that it was getting late, that he'd need to be leaving soon; there was work that needed finishing in his still-unfurnished apartment.

"Unfurnished? You mean you're buying chairs, table, refrigerator, the works?"

Vincent shuffled painfully.

"It was all I could find. It came with kitchen appliances. And I bought furniture cheap from the previous occupants."

"I wanted to talk some more about adding new texts, and perhaps dropping some, in an updated syllabus." Doswell nodded Vincent's way. "You have some ideas as well?"

Vincent offered none and ignored the question.

The old man turned to Jim. "Here's the deal: you'll get another bottle of Heineken's – you know it's my finest – if you agree to stay longer and give us some ideas." He said this with absolute earnestness.

Jim grinned.

Vincent shuffled in his chair and sat upright, sighing delicately.

The conversation at first went well, Jim warming to the subject as Doswell inquired speculatively, citing desirable qualities in a choice, while Billy wandered to the living room to catch a television favorite.

"You know," Jim said, "I was thinking about George Orwell's *Nineteen Eighty-Four*, or at least part of it: O'Brien's telling Winston under torture that reality is only in the human mind, and that 'truth' is whatever you wish it."

"Yes, and it's not a difficult text. It's something that could be readily excerpted."

"I thought of using it when I had a student say matter-of-factly the other day that the truth is only what the powerful say it is."

Doswell's head jerked back as if struck. "What did you say?"

"I'm sorry to say I was defensive. I said something in a vague way about wallowing in 'their subjective desires and impulses', something like that."

Doswell nodded.

"I finally did get around to saying, 'What you just told me, are you saying it is true?'"

"That was good."

"Yeah, but I took so long to say it I don't think he got it."

"I don't think he knew himself what he'd said." Doswell turned to Vincent, then to Jim. "What do you think of Dostoyevsky's *Underground Man?*"

"The students, with a little help," Jim said, "can understand it."

Vincent's voice had an edge. "Dostoyevsky won't be readily excerpted – at least it wouldn't be fair to the students' comprehension. And it's a difficult text already. Ellison's *Invisible Man* might be more accessible, something they could relate to."

"Hmmm, that's not a bad idea." Jim nodded Doswell's way.

"The work has merit, but it's somewhat derivative."

"From what?" Vincent made a low chuffing sound.

"*Underground Man.*"

Vincent didn't reply.

The conversation went on in mostly this way between Jim and Doswell, Vincent growing more impatient until the talk turned to a faculty orientation session about 'tolerance' just before the opening of classes, which Doswell, not having attended, asked about.

"I just loved Bob Keech saying that we are all like missionaries to move out into the big city of Colonus, and maybe, like right here in Devon" – Vincent was suddenly chuckling and talking as much to Jim as Doswell – "straighten out the folks, teach the Ku Kluxers, and the Roy Maddox and George Wallace admirers, the ways of...of..." – he spoke this last in a Raskin-like smarmy tone – "liberal-minded white folk."

Jim caught a sinuous invitation in this: Vincent's idea of an olive branch; invited to be the exception by way of acknowledging that there are no exceptions to the racial prepossessions of white people. But the still-chafing details of that gathering were uppermost in his mind: the Encounter session, which Colin Murphy from CSU and Gerry Loewenstein from Baxter's psychology department led as part of the university's 'greater sensitivity' goal, had begun with Bob Keech, following testimonials from others of racism and prejudice in and around Colonus, saying that there should be an effort at fighting prejudice in the community at large.

In the absurd seconds following, the talk bogged down with academic-style definitions and distinctions around the word 'prejudice'; and urged on by Murphy's and Loewenstein's oft-repeated "express yourself, speak from the gut, say what's *really* on your mind", Raskin, clearly happy to take their advice, announced that Keech was off to a wrong start, "like the fat kid in the touch football game that's running in the wrong direction". It didn't help that Keech was overweight by a good fifty pounds.

"You're confused, Mr. Keech. I'm not sure you know where you are, but I do. Isn't this the same place where just last year when I put on Hansberry's *Raisin in the Sun* and was assaulted by the *News-Herald*'s team of KKK assassins some of you joined in?"

Once he started, Jim remembered he wouldn't let go. "You and some other folks had some mighty cozy relations with Colonus' old-time KKK newspaper of record."

Keech, in those mesmerizing moments, grew flushed, he twisted; he was mumbling.

It was then that Vincent rose up and took command.

Up towards the center of the assembly, with a hundred participants sitting in concentric circles, Vincent, standing, with his back to Jim, was saying, in that slightly West Indian lilt of his, that there was a need to get Baxter finally on track as a black university after a hundred years of toadying to whites; that this was all typical of what Marx had in mind when he talked of a rotting bourgeois culture, its wallowing in idealism and romantic utopianism. He grew more heated as he spoke.

"If people seek a common goal with the black community they will have to submit to the agenda of black people."

Then Vincent stalked out, Jim noticing several individuals gazing at him like he was a screen star. One man stood and patted him approvingly on the back as he passed. And it was then that Jim leapt from his seat, stumbling over the startled Mr. and Mrs. Peter from Wisconsin, and made for the nearest exit.

The worst was yet to come. Furious, as he paused in the lobby of the building, standing beside a massive planting of palms and ferns and philodendra, the lovely Blissie Carter and Sister Mary came strolling by and, within hearing distance on the other side of the foliage, he heard:

"Whew! Wasn't he marvelous, Mary?"

"I certainly think he is a dynamic young man. Very impressive!"

"He is *so* real too. I think he probably put off a lot of people, though, but they needed to hear it."

"They certainly did. He has a lot to teach all of us," Sr. Mary said.

Now in Doswell's farmhouse kitchen, Jim's eyes fell on the teacher-of-all sitting across from him, his face the picture of smug self-complacency.

But Jim said absolutely nothing.

Doswell, obviously not unfamiliar with the previous year's "tempest over the *Raisin* in a teapot", spoke of Raskin's "tendency to go over the top".

"I wasn't here at the time," Vincent, his voice rising, said, throwing caution to the wind, "but I think if Raskin says that there were folks who were playing fast and loose behind the scenes to undermine him because they didn't like his militancy – well, I've already seen signs of that myself – I don't see any reason not to believe him."

Doswell sighed. "You don't see reasons *not* to believe him? Don't you think you need reasons to believe him?"

Jim joined in. "I think this idea that you can just throw your net wide and suppose you'll catch a whole bunch of people. . .well, that is a pretty good example of prejudice itself – which is what that meeting was all about stamping out, wasn't it?"

"You know, I'm getting a little tired of your sweeping moralisms. You don't know a damn thing. . ."

"Now, now. . ."

"*Not a thing* about what you're talking about."

"Not only his assault on Bob Keech, but yours on everyone else was. . . pathetic! Bigoted, prejudiced!"

There was a sudden silence that followed this last javelin-throw. In the quiet at the kitchen table there was only the sound from the TV, and Vincent and Jim were so situated that they could see the action on the small, nearly oval black-and-white screen. In the time it took Doswell to tell Billy to lower the sound and for Billy to respond, Walt Disney's Fess Parker as Davy Crockett had hurled Big Mike Fink, the river man, crashing against the cabin on the deck of his river boat, and the river man was battering Crockett over the head with an oar and then a chair. All of which registered with special irony on the younger men as they sorted out the awkward emotions of the moment.

Jim was embarrassed; still, he also felt exhilarated as if a burden had been lifted.

Much was at stake for Vincent. He had come to Doswell's home with a purpose, and his purpose was being sidetracked. The impulse to strike back felt like a throb in the side of his head, and yet it had to be suppressed. He'd come this far. And if he was to do anything with Doswell he'd have to make his pitch sooner rather than later. What had transpired in these last moments had come dangerously close to ending it.

As he looked at this old man, a cross-current of thoughts and impressions flashed through his mind. Seeing the massive, bull-like bulk, the broad, sweat-glistened, dark brown face, alone in this gray and faded kitchen, everything bespoke defeat. Here he was, solitary but for his grandson, self-exiled for some reason known only to himself in an isolated community of illiterate Negro farmhands, wood-cutters and share-croppers. Why would *anyone* want to listen to someone over whom history had passed like a steamroller? Yet he was a 'celebrity' – this was a fact – to some folks in Chicago who hadn't seen him in more than a dozen years.

So on that Sunday evening, remembering what he'd heard at a party in Maxine's big Chicago townhouse about an "experiment in reading" which had turned into lasting "mentoring" arrangements between half a dozen local universities and failing South Side schools, Vincent asked Doswell about those celebrated days. And Doswell, momentarily lost in a lapse of memory, then pretty much shrugged it off, mentioning Great Books and people he knew in Chicago who'd found him "a summer job".

Dinner was over. Jim was gone, and Doswell had seen to his parental obligations with Billy upstairs. It was late, but he'd asked Vincent to stay, a consolation since Allan's presence had made any progress in popping his long-gestating question about replacing Tupper on the speakers' schedule impossible. He'd been determined earlier not to allow himself to be drawn into a vortex of silliness with Allan, but still, when Doswell mentioned that Jim wasn't one of those who suffered from a "moral superiority complex", he forgot himself. He told the old man that he'd been annoyed at having to discuss Alliance affairs with Allan listening in.

Doswell laughed, and said Jim was no more interested in "listening in" than the man in the moon.

Vincent let this pass, but then when the old man added that he should "let up"; that "the man has given you no reason to act so damned offended all the time", he couldn't contain himself.

"These white leeches," he replied in a sizzling whisper, "trying to fill their void, they offend me."

It was late. They sat in his half-lit study. With a certain irresolute hesitancy, reaching awkwardly for a lamp, Doswell switched on an additional light and said, as he settled himself back down again, "You're a collector of offenses, you collect them like some people collect coins."

"It's a necessary part of being black in America," he muttered, conscious of holding himself in check, "something we didn't choose. I would have thought—"

"I mean you seem to take some perverse pleasure in it, like the more insults you can discover where nobody else thought to look, you announce as some kind of achievement, a distinction you expect everyone to applaud. I am not applauding."

Vincent felt the sudden throb and numbing bewilderment he once felt when his father had struck him hard in response to some disrespectful words he'd uttered. All of Raskin's insinuating talk about Doswell came rushing back at him. For a moment he thought to say that he hoped he wouldn't ever be so dead to the world that he'd fail to know when he was being condescended to – acting like an *old Tom*. He felt in that instant a powerful urge to walk out. But he didn't, and he just barely held his tongue.

Doswell poured and then shoved a shot glass with whiskey his way and said, "Here, have some of this." He grinned. "It tastes good."

The tingly taste of the whiskey lingered in Vincent's mouth. He waited several seconds as he tightened his fingers around the glass. He still felt like walking out, but there was also a reassuringly appealing expression in that imperturbable, scarred face.

Once again Vincent broached the matter of the Alliance convention, and once again the old man ventured his opinion that the convention was all thought up to advance "a few persons' ambitions".

"What if Montbanc is out for himself – or, for that matter, all of us are? The question is not one of morality, the question is whether change is being served."

"*Is* change being served?" the old man asked instantly.

Vincent's laugh was slightly forced. He fenced around with the old man at first. Then he plunged in. He told him something about Tupper. He told him that Tupper was out of the picture, and someone like him was needed. He told him about the ongoing plan to have either Baker or Braithwaite fill in. Weaving carefully, he said he'd settled on him as a far more appropriate alternative because "they'd be boring".

Doswell studied his guest. After a minute, and with the faintest smile, he said, "*You* settled on *me?*" As Vincent reached for a cigarette, and the old man reached over, pushing an ashtray in his direction, he added, "You assume a great deal, Vincent. Your naiveté encourages me."

The windows were cracked open. There was a breeze playing through the faded curtains and outside, beyond the shabbiness, one could hear the cacophonous cricket-sound of that mid-October night. Vincent sipped his whiskey as he studied the old man in the dim light.

"But aside from your incredible naiveté, the question, in fact, is one entirely of morality. If the Alliance is premised on some Marxist-Socialist agenda, I could never share in it."

"I'm a pan-Africanist," Vincent said quickly, "and as for Marxism, Lenin himself taught that Marxism is not a dogma."

He'd obviously said the wrong thing. For the old man shot back angrily, "Lenin taught Stalin!"

For the second time that night, and in quick succession, Doswell had taken Vincent by surprise. Like Allan at the Jolly Roger, he was struck by the reactionary character of this remark, only the word 'reactionary' hardly contained the dismay he felt.

Vincent said something which, though softened, still registered his dismay.

But Doswell didn't soften. Putting aside his whiskey glass, his head rising, the muscles in his broad neck tensing, he quoted Lenin word for word: "*The dictatorship of the proletariat is a scientific term stating the class in question and the particular form of state authority, called dictatorship, namely...*" Here he paused for emphasis and enunciated each word precisely, from what he took care to describe as "a 1917 directive" – "*namely, authority based not on law, not on elections, but directly on the armed force of some portion of the population.*" Then, gazing steadily at Vincent, he asked if he understood that.

Vincent didn't reply, but he wondered uncomfortably, what is this obsession?

Doswell took a quick swig from his whiskey glass, and pushed the bottle towards Vincent again. "Here. Help yourself."

Was he drunk? Not really. He was fully in possession of his senses.

Vincent, feeling a little less clear himself, said that there were no Marxists around. "I'm no Leninist or Communist, and neither is the President or Raskin or anyone else." He laughed dismissively. "I can tell you that for certain. For me? I'm a nationalist...a supporter of the dispossessed. Surely you, a Great Books reader and promoter, you know Marx's insights are helpful..."

"What do you do with the refuse?" The old man, neglecting his disavowals, charged ahead, his words full of accusation. "What do you do with the refuse, the heaps of human material that are part of the price of progress? The waste, the human shit that has to be flushed out of the system? *That* is the morality not talked about in polite company – the plumbing – an altogether necessary task for the making of the glorious revolution!"

The ground had been moving at Vincent's feet like an oncoming earthquake for some time. Now it was the sense of everything turning upside down and spinning out of control – the earthquake arriving. He would have violently and finally washed his hands of him then and there if the old man hadn't begun taunting him: "Vincent, you can't imagine: *they* are right and *you* are wrong – if there was ever a counter-revolutionary element, I *am* that!"

With this remark, Vincent watched the old man closely. His face was serene but there was a glint of humor in his eyes; an element of satire in the remark, directed as much at himself as at Vincent. Probably it *was* the booze, he thought. He felt less staunchly determined – strangely, all of a sudden even amused. If he felt anything besides this, as the night wore on, it was a certain tranquility amidst a puzzled affection, not unlike what he'd occasionally felt for his father! The old man had also begun asking judicious questions: about Tupper's reasons for pulling out, about this idea of an 'open convention' with all opinions welcomed, about the people in Chicago: the Rev. Tupper, Maxine, and others Vincent didn't know.

He was new to all of this realpolitik, this behind-the-scenes business of garnering enough delegates to draft him as a stand-in for the missing Tupper. Vincent didn't have any sure answers, and Montbanc was surely an unpredictable quantity; but still, as if in slow motion, he perceived his object coming into reach.

He was answering the old man's questions as thoroughly as he could. As it was, before the night was out, he'd managed to get him to cheerfully assent to his grand proposal.

"If you can get clearance from higher up – which you won't get," he added with a disconcerting confidence.

Still, the terms were sufficient. He already knew the rest was a higher climb, but appealing to "the entire neighborhood" was Vincent's plan if he was to fulfill both his and Robeson's long-ago dream.

By the time he was stumbling out his front door, dawn breaking, more certain than ever of him as this Paleolithic creature, this black mastodon out of the Ice Age, unearthed and defrosted, they'd become old friends and drinking buddies.

7

Brooklyn Summons

It all began with a telephone call from Vincent's Aunt Molina. A hundred pounds overweight, asthmatic, pushing seventy years, she was summoning him home to Brooklyn, no excuses tolerated.

Two years before, in the late summer of 1967, Vincent's parents, returning from a dental convention in Boston, drove into a bridge abutment and were killed on rain-slicked Merritt Parkway in Connecticut. His brother and he found themselves suddenly orphans, and the sole owners of the old brownstone house in Crown Heights. They'd grown up in it and shared it, along with their parents and Aunt Molina, their mother's oldest sister. Vincent's father, a dentist with a thriving neighborhood practice, had left a will with instructions that should his wife not survive him, his estate should be divided equally between his two sons. It stipulated, however, that as long as their Aunt Molina lived, Vincent and Basil should not sell the house, and that she be given the right to stay in it as long as she wished. In actual fact Vincent and Basil were happy to abide by these instructions. Aunt Molina, having lived with them for years, was a second mother, and the one close relative they had. Their other relatives from both sides of the family, in the West Indies on their father's side, and from the American South on their mother's, were hardly ever around long enough or often enough to register as more than intrusive strangers with odd names; staying over a few days, taking them to their bosoms, smooching them, or bullying them, bidding them goodbye, and then rarely if ever seeing them again.

Indeed, since coming to Colonus it had been Molina's pet project to get Vincent into contact with some of these long-lost relatives in the South, mostly living in the Carolinas. Her letters, all during the summer and early fall, full of gossip from the neighborhood, implored him to renew family ties. But by late fall the central topic of her concerns had shifted to his brother Basil: she feared for his life. Basil had received serious threats, anonymous telephone calls, and on this last occasion, a note left on his door, warning of violence and mayhem.

Vincent's brother at that time shared the house on Park Place with Aunt Molina. It was a big house, like so many houses in that part of the city, a rich man's place years before, with a walnut-paneled library, sumptuous living rooms and dining room, large bedrooms and a fully-finished basement that at the turn of the century had been servants' quarters. Basil occupied the basement apartment, his father's old dental office space with its separate entrance, and Aunt Molina and a couple of old lady boarders and friends the three upper floors. But though on the inside it was only slightly less grand than the setting for the WNET British-made television series *Upstairs, Downstairs,* of recent years, the sidewalks and streets of Crown Heights were hardly genteel Edwardian London. There were the not-altogether-rare rapes and muggings and murders that inner city New Yorkers know only too well. Aunt Molina had good reason to fear for Basil's life.

It began with the police coming over to the house on a few occasions, and Basil having been arrested once. They'd searched the basement for guns, and had come very close to moving up the stairs and ransacking the whole place, which nearly caused Molina to have a heart attack. At that time, there were internecine conflicts within not only widely various elements and militant wings of the radical black power movement, but within the Black Panther Party itself. And Basil was obviously in the thick of something. In the last letter Vincent got from his aunt, received within a day or two of his visit to Doswell's, and then followed up by a telephone call (a clear sign of her desperation, for his aunt *never* made long-distance calls), Aunt Molina demanded that he come to Brooklyn on the first plane out, and speak to Basil "face to face to talk some sense into him".

So it was that with his bags all but packed to go to Chicago, he canceled his classes and took a flight to LaGuardia for his home in Brooklyn.

It was certainly unlucky that he should have so much to contend with all at once, but his brother's welfare transcended all concerns. What to do? It was too late to talk sense to Basil. Getting him out of the city was the only sensible course. But how to make that happen?

"So, Vincent, do you think your church of the Holy Alliance will be born, I mean a live birth, November 25th?" Basil began the instant they met, in his typically good-natured, ribbing way. He was predictably ignoring Molina's concerns and the real reason Vincent was back in town.

"Good question," he said. "I'm doing everything I can to keep it alive."

"You mean his Royal Highest, the majestic and pompous Montbanc, is still giving you migraines?"

"I need help, Basil. They promised me a secretary, and I never got one. I have to do everything alone. And you're right, he doesn't make it any easier."

The one sure way of dooming whatever influence he had over Basil was to straight out tell him what to do. He'd learned long before that frontal assaults were the least likely to succeed. So he decided to go along with Basil's infuriatingly casual way of talking exclusively about Alliance business, suppressing all signs of his actual alarm. Basil was genuinely interested in the movement, and proud of Vincent's prominence in it. His Black Panther militancy was hardly at odds with Alliance politics.

Basil responded to his mention of Molumba as he knew he would. "It was good to learn Molumba and his band of traitors and cutthroats aren't coming to the conference. The brothers going down there were saying that if it came to that they'd be ready to defend themselves. You know what that would have meant?"

He did. And that was one of the reasons he hadn't wanted Molumba coming. Vincent informed Basil now that that decision had been reversed. Molumba was appearing after all.

"Huh? He's coming after all?" Basil muttered, his eyes grown large with astonishment.

So in New York, not wanting to do anything that would reveal his burning concern for Basil's welfare, Vincent tried to convince him to return with him to Colonus, quite honestly talking up his urgent need of help with the Alliance. Previously he'd told him about Montbanc with comic overtones, intending as much to entertain as to inform, and holding back his growing doubts about the man's suitability as Alliance leader. Now he told his brother the entire story: Montbanc's real character, the way he routinely alienated people, how the Rev. Malcomn Tupper in Chicago was the last and most important of those he'd infuriated, and how this was threatening their long-held plans for a movement that would bring together all segments of the community.

"You know, Vincent, you do need a warrior in your corner. Someone like Pop, I suppose. You were, what? The dreamer? This old dream of yours, this downright *spiritual* dream of a community that's above everybody's everyday concerns…?"

"No, no, that's not—"

"I mean, if you could pull this off it would be tremendous. In fact, it will be a miracle. I don't know about Tupper or this man…Boswell—"

"Doswell."

"Yeah, but I know about Molumba. He's bad news. You've always trusted too much…"

"It's not about my trusting—"

"You know how Pop always thought Mom was too hopeful about people? She trusted people too much? You—"

"Listen! God damn it, Basil! I've just finished telling you. I've gotten so I don't trust anyone anymore – certainly not Montbanc or Molumba."

"No. No. You don't trust *anyone* anymore. But you trust human nature – or nigger nature."

"Don't use that word, Basil! Mom and Pop, they'd knock you upside the head if they heard you!"

"Ooooooh! Ohhhhh! God damn!" Suddenly Basil was holding his head, and groaning like he'd just been struck hard by invisible hands.

After some of Basil's typical fooling around, Vincent told him about his late-night talk with Doswell in Devon. He told him about Chicago and its disgruntled delegates. He painted a grim picture that went beyond the Molumba affair. There'd been many delegates, not just from Chicago, he said, who'd been undergoing a slow burn over Montbanc's highhanded ways. This is why he'd originally been hired, in fact, to deal with these rancorous people in small but vocal pockets out in California and Atlanta – and elsewhere.

Now he told him about his discovery that Doswell was actually remembered in Chicago from a period of summer visits years before, and that he would make an ideal stand-in for Tupper. That he was looking to get delegates to support him.

"But those ideas? You told me once he was an old Tom. Why do you want to get him up there?"

"I wanted Tupper originally, not because I shared his views but because we needed people that wouldn't otherwise be interested in the movement."

"Yeah, but you have this idea of going *backwards?*"

"Can't you understand that the Alliance is supposed to be a tent big enough for everyone? That's what Robeson had in mind?"

"I hear you. But it's still going to be a bitch, I mean to convince people outside that Chicago bunch you mentioned."

"That's why I'm here in Brooklyn, Basil. I'm gonna go fishing."

Basil's eyes went large again. "Fishing?" Then he started laughing from his belly up. He made a face, the way he and Vincent used to when they were conspiring against Pop with a plan to get around some decree the old man set down. "Sounds like you planning on having some fun." He was intrigued, but he still shook his head, smiling. "I don't know if you'll catch any fish though."

But Vincent had already caught his first fish – or at least he'd hooked him! This fact regardless, he knew Basil was right to be skeptical. He knew how radical his New York Alliance friends' politics were. They were as radical as his own, but without his long-held dream.

"Whatever you do, don't go talking about Robeson and about all the folks working together, a big, happy COM-muuun-ity, that stuff. That puts people to sleep."

Vincent was pleased with his brother's interest, and if he was less than overjoyed with the critique of his persuasive powers, he wasn't surprised.

One of the first people he spoke to was a woman he and Basil had known since they were kids. Basil remembered that not so long before, she'd been unhappy with Montbanc's style of leadership. She'd mentioned this in passing when they talked about Vincent's role in the upcoming convention. Belinda Malcomn had a resemblance to Angela Davis, and she had a similar – though in her case not personal – admiration for Angela's mentor, Herbert Marcuse.

"Why do you want to go out of your way for people with bourgeois inclinations?" was what she said when he explained about Tupper and Doswell.

When he stressed what the Alliance was all about, she was unconvinced. She asked, "Should tolerance become a mask for faintheartedness? For cowardliness?" echoing Marcuse's latest ideas.

Among those he'd initially approached, Belinda's reaction was the most moderate. (She'd always had a soft spot in her heart for the Brown brothers.) Sullen indifference and even expressions of bristling antagonism were more the order of the day until Basil helped him with a little miracle.

At the start Vincent stuck like glue to his brother, watching like a hawk for assailants on every street corner; but when nothing out of place gave concern, Vincent became less vigilant, more so as he noticed Basil's interest in Alliance affairs begin to rival his own. Of course the teasing never stopped. He bragged about knowing more about Alliance people in Brooklyn than Vincent did, and added that he should go to folks in his own circle if he "wanted business taken care of".

One day he told Vincent about an elderly relative of one of his friends. The man, he said, was a delegate, "an old guy" who'd "seen it all", and was sure to be helpful in influencing others "like him" – if Vincent could just reach him.

So with Basil he watchfully made his way to a dark walk-up over a hardware store near a tree-shaded side street off Nostrand Avenue as he grumbled to himself about "wild goose chases", and that this just might be one of Basil's wildest. But as it turned out, his brother's intuitions were on the mark.

Vincent, Basil and Moses Walker talked in the kitchen, a menagerie of birds, yellow canaries, blue and green parakeets, singing and chirping from cages which hung precipitously over their heads. Basil earlier told Vincent that Walker was an old union man who had strong opinions and colorful stories. In fact he talked and talked, as old men love to do with younger men, the birds all the while raining down seeds and an occasional fleck of bird shit. But Vincent didn't really mind. Settling in, he was willing in those days to endure anything for The Cause. He listened attentively, reading this old guy who was well into his seventies, maybe eighty or more, for the possibility that he would be a likely candidate to take into his confidence – and if he was, how best to approach this delicate mission.

Actually, it wasn't hard to listen. He was long-winded but on the whole he had something to say, and he was clear-minded and vigorous, his stories going back as early as World War I. So he told, for instance, of intensely active union years following the war, then through the '20s, inevitable love affairs, heroic sexual triumphs, miscellaneous tales from long years before. As he spun his tales, Vincent still feared one thing, and it was that given his sweepingly revolutionary views, Moses would not be receptive to his message. So slowly he introduced his own more practical thoughts about Doswell, feeling his way as cautiously as he could into the live current of the old guy's present opinions.

They went that way for several minutes without any sign, and then Vincent began to notice a light in the older man's expression, a sudden merriment, inexplicable as it appeared in his dark, white-haired, stubbly-bearded face. He asked Vincent for a specific description of Doswell, and then, more animated, he asked for information about his age, and where he'd gone to school. Then he told Vincent he remembered a man from many years before who'd been a labor organizer, one who'd participated in and led several strikes, especially the big textile strike in Passaic, New Jersey "in '25 and '26, that rocked the whole country". He said he remembered for sure that this man had graduated from Harvard, and he wasn't sure but he thought he might have come from Colonus originally. As for the name, he was pretty sure it was different, but "in those days old organizers didn't use their real names".

For several seconds no one spoke as it dawned on them; Vincent thinking, at the same time, this is too much, but *wishing* it could be so.

Basil spoke up. "Is there anything else, Mo? Any way you can know for sure?" He was looking at Vincent and then at the old man as he said this.

The old guy looked ceiling-ways; he was murmuring to himself. "Uh, uhuh." After several long moments, like he was answering someone from afar, they heard him barely whispering and nodding to himself. "Yeah, yeah, that's right."

To them he said nothing. It was all slow motion, molasses-slow inside his head, and they dared not interrupt; they knew something was there and they didn't want to make it vanish with a distracting thought.

"There was a big battle – no, a riot: the police and company goons, the whole damned lot, they had us hemmed in. He was up front, he kept saying, 'We're just walking through here, we're not here to do anything else, just walking through', and they were shouting some shit, they weren't going to let us 'get away with that crap again'."

"What crap?"

"Oh, maybe we were five hundred, maybe more. He kept saying it – no, they said, that crap wasn't going to work again. And then they started swinging. He was the first to get it. Mounted police, billy sticks, fire hoses – we didn't have nothing. It was *their* riot. A couple of strikers were killed." The old man instantly pulled up his pant leg and excitedly pointed to a long scar. Then, without pulling his pant leg back down, excited for the opportunity, he gleefully pointed to his hairless scalp.

One of his grandsons, a skinny teenage boy who'd wandered towards the kitchen, started whooping it up. "Pop! Pop! We seen that old drawing before!"

"He has a scar," Vincent spoke as if awakened suddenly, "over his," he paused, "his left eye."

"Yeah, yeah! That's what I mean – he looked bad after that..." Moses grew silent again, and thoughtful. There was a murmur of voices outside the kitchen; inside there was only silence but for the birds. "He was the best-educated colored man I'd ever met, yet there he was, living down and dirty, and taking his lumps like the rest of us."

Vincent remembered his mother once telling him about visiting a strange city, and meeting a woman who, it turned out, had a mutual friend from years before in some third city. Such chance meetings were not uncommon in the African-American community that for years constituted, after all, a small nation largely turned in on itself. This was especially true in earlier decades, when people lived almost exclusively in ghettoized parts of cities and towns, and when traveling overnight, even in the North, they arranged accommodations beforehand with folks recommended from home, rather than risk insults at white-owned public accommodations.

So the fact that Doswell had once taught summer classes in Chicago, and then earlier worked as a union organizer in the New York area, and then had lived in such a way that there should be people who remembered him, was not so surprising. Yet when the connection was made, especially in the latter case, more than forty years later, coming from what seemed like another age, the effect was entirely startling!

Vincent laughed most of the way back to Colonus – perhaps he should make stopovers in all of America's major cities and steel himself for the old man's moon-faced mug appearing at the turn of every street corner! And then when he wasn't laughing, he was thinking: so this is why his past is a blank and he wouldn't talk to people about what he'd done before coming to Colonus. And he laughed again. Imagine putting *that* down on his resume! This put an entirely new light on everything.

It would take him a while to sort it all through, and perhaps at the right time he'd talk to the old man more carefully about his past. In the meantime, returning south couldn't be put off any longer. Vincent finally approached Basil with the idea, not unexpected by his brother, that he make the return trip with him, stressing of course the Alliance's urgent needs. Basil's declaration that he had a "hot lady friend" that he wasn't about to desert "just now" left him disgruntled but unsurprised. Predictably, he reverted to an older style of relating to his brother – he blew up. He repeated how badly the Alliance needed him; that Basil knew he was leaving him in the lurch when he needed him most, and finally that New York was dangerous, and Aunt Molina was rightly worried that he'd be murdered. Basil wouldn't budge, and he couldn't stay indefinitely.

So he finally made his flight out to the Midwest. And when he got out to Chicago again, he saw that he never had any reason to worry about how long it would take to sell his idea about Doswell. He met with about a dozen people, Maxine and even the Rev. Tupper; individuals he knew could be trusted. And sure enough, their response was electric. The one difficulty at the meeting was holding down the enthusiasm to keep it orderly enough to proceed!

And so obviously there was no selling his idea. That evening they gave Vincent assurances he'd be "talked up". There were dozens of other delegates elsewhere, both in and out of state, with whom they had excellent connections, and with whom they'd be in contact. Yes, they were certain they could begin a boomlet, a mini-movement; that they'd steamroll the President and he'd have no choice – this last Vincent wasn't so sure of, but he was certainly encouraged by their thinking so. In turn they promised to withhold all credit to Vincent for coming up with the idea – a helpful detail in his imminent dealings with an ordinarily intractable and shrewd President Montbanc.

Vincent left Chicago cutting his visit short, buoyed by their unbounded support.

8

Vincent and the Emperor

When he was preparing to leave Chicago, standing on the tarmac at O'Hare, surrounded by half a dozen of his Chicago friends and the scream of the jet engines, the muscular Maxine Scales cried into his ear, "Vincent! Damn! Don't you worry! We'll take the ball and run with it!"

Within days of his return to Colonus, as he caught up with his long-neglected teaching duties and his long-neglected Blissie, the letters started arriving. There were messages of commendation for Baxter University and the President, expressing surprise that Doswell hadn't been proposed for a major presentation earlier. Others advanced the idea that if he was *disinclined* to speak, the university might use *every bit of its persuasive powers, monetary or otherwise* to win him to the idea! The majority of them were from Chicago and the Midwest, but there were a few from Atlanta and from New York.

Most memorable was the one from Moses Walker. Scrawled in longhand, the misspelling and the crude grammar marked the bare literacy of the man. But like a yellowed scroll dug up out of the desert sands of some ancient, primogenitive land, it testified to an earlier generation's raw courage and faith. It recalled that more than forty years earlier a young Negro recently graduated from college became *the stike ogonizer wich parlize entir United States estern seabord*. But the *colord peoples*, it said, weren't the only people who saw this *colord man* as a leader; he was the leader of all *the peoples, black, brown, white too* – no doubt this last *slightly* exaggerated. Surely though, Vincent thought, this simple message should win him a place – this alone, he thought.

As he read the letters, mulling over how to put that bountiful harvest to best use, a departure from his original plan in approaching President Montbanc occurred to him. He decided that he would go and see Raskin and try to convince him first. Raskin knew the importance of history. And he had a reverence for those in the generations that came before who had fought the same battles as he, only isolated by the long and lonely years in the trenches. He remembered him telling about heroic folks he'd known as a boy in the '50s in Michigan where he'd grown up. There were veins of idealism that could be found glittering under the cynical, even elaborately cruel put-ons that were a part of his habitual trickster's personality. If Vincent could get him to see that there was more to Doswell – and the testimony of Moses Walker should if anything make that happen – who knows, he might win him to a different view of things, and have an ally that would help in persuading the President.

"I think, Vincent, those cookies of hers, that's all she could *put out* that anyone would be interested in."

Raskin was talking about Mildred Braithwaite, middle-aged, unmarried, and still attractive but in a prim, wooden kind of way; Cleon's candidate to fill Tupper's spot, and the person Vincent preferred if there was no other option. Mildred had taken to hailing Vincent in the walkways, stopping at his table in the cafeteria, and once even coming to his office. He knew she'd been lobbying him because Raskin had originally encouraged her to, a little joke to set the woman on his tail when he thought he was already in her corner.

Raskin was giggling, very pleased with his little joke about Mildred's cookies.

A flood of real annoyance came over Vincent. It was vintage Raskin. But he wasn't put off. Instead Vincent began to sing Mildred's praises: she regularly attended the annual convention of the American Sociological Society; she'd often read papers and commented on those of others; and occasionally she published her research findings in scholarly journals. In short, she was an active, up-to-date sociologist with standing in her profession.

In fact, to the sound of Raskin's chuckles, he said he'd recently read part of a monograph of hers about the problems of crime among teenagers, about black teenage pregnancy and single-parent homes. "Cleon was right, what he said about her."

"You mean our lady Demosthenes!" Raskin burst into a fit of hilarity.

Raskin's office was off the stage in the Morris Building (a gift from Philip Morris); it was shared with no one, unlike Vincent's, which he shared with Duro Ogunda, a Nigerian who taught Swahili and International Studies. Vincent's distracted gaze took in some of the book titles along its high walls: a large selection of dramatic works; Shakespeare, of course; a history of the theatre; a book on theatrical sword-fighting; a leather-bound set of the complete works of the Marquis de Sade; Casanova's *History of My Life*; a book on American Negro folk tales; the *Confessions of Jean-Jacques Rousseau*; and *The Immoralist* by André Gide was sitting atop Raskin's desk.

He glanced at Raskin, taking in the strong ambrosia fragrance of toilet water that he was in the habit of liberally splashing on himself. He said that he had some "serious thoughts" about the Saturday speakers' lineup.

Raskin smiled tolerantly. He crossed his hands behind his head, leaning back leisurely in his chair. It was late afternoon. Raskin was wearing his smart-ass grin, but Vincent ignored it and charged ahead. He began by reminding him about the President's grand style, his inflated ego, and the great harm he'd done in the Tupper affair. Now he reminded him once again of the Alliance's original purpose, its name emphasizing the object of bringing *all* people together, and how all of them had time and again testified to that conviction. Then he told him additional facts about the Alliance contingent in Chicago: about those that said they weren't coming, and the general apathy among the reduced numbers who'd said they *might*. The Alliance was coming apart, he said, and not just in Chicago.

"Whoa! Vincent!" Raskin broke in. "I don't know what you're building up to – it sounds good, but why are you telling me all this stuff? I think you're talking to the wrong man!"

"I know who I'm talking to," he said, "and I know I've got to talk to the President. But for once, Raskin, I'm asking you to stand up and stand by me. You know everything I've been telling you is so."

"Stand up? Stand up about what?" He looked at Vincent, a grin flashing across his face. "Did Mildred get to you with those chocolate chip cookies of hers?"

"Shit, Raskin! Get off that!" he yelled.

"Well, what the hell are you talking about then?"

"I'm talking about forty letters I've gotten this last week." He pulled them roughly out of his briefcase, rubber-banded into two packs. He pointed to the larger pack, saying it would take a while to read them all, but then he took two of the best among them, two that he'd put on the outside of the pack, and opening them, dropped them in front of Raskin. "Read a couple," he said.

Raskin relented, though he looked pained. Unlocking his clasped hands from behind his head he pulled himself up, lifting one of the letters to the light on his desk. He read soundlessly, but after a while a frown began stealing over his face. Then picking up the second letter, but holding it like it carried the germs of some contagious disease within its folds, Raskin started to read again. After a minute he threw it down.

"What is this? They're all like this!"

Vincent nodded significantly. "They all want him."

"How did this get started?" He said this in a tone more annoyed than surprised.

Dusk was falling; the overhead lights being off, the room was darkening. Raskin shifted heavily, restless in his desk chair as Vincent told him that they had underestimated Doswell – that they'd *grossly* underestimated him – for they'd been unaware of the fact that he had a reputation elsewhere, "a regular fan club, and in, of all places, Chicago".

Vincent could see Raskin's patience was being tried, and yet he sensed that he was still uncertain, that he was waiting to be sure where this was leading. He went on about his Chicago experience, and his discovery. He told Raskin about the ardor of the people who'd known Doswell, and Doswell's work especially with the University of Chicago in the early '50s. He told him how even Tupper had remembered him. Through it all Raskin sat there like a yogi contemplating. Then Vincent built up to Moses Walker. He said that Doswell's academic status was probably less interesting from Raskin's, and certainly his, standpoint than something else he'd recently discovered.

Still Raskin sat, his head and his chin resting on his clasped hands in the posture of a man in contemplation, unmoving.

Vincent removed Walker's letter from its envelope and placed it on Raskin's desk with the other two letters.

For a long several seconds Raskin said nothing, his face a blank. Then, his voice rising and quickening to a pitch of anger, he said, "Tell me what's in it! I'm not going to read all these damned letters tonight!"

"You don't have to read them all. Just read that one." Vincent pointed to it as if with the long hand of fate. "That's all."

Raskin looked in its direction, but made no motion to pick it up.

"Read it!" Vincent ordered. He had seen the shock and distrust in Raskin's face, and knew in his blood now the hopelessness of the situation, but this exercise had acquired a momentum of its own.

Raskin gingerly took the letter in his hands and put it to the light. Then Vincent, turning away in hopes of lowering the tension and to avoid hurrying him, heard first disconcerting giggles, then a high-pitched, gleeful, hyena-like laughing jeer.

"This is *bullshit*, Vincent! That old man has really put one over on you! I never thought you could be such a fool!"

"It's not bullshit," he shot back, more a reflex of the mind, the sudden, heavy creaking sound in the hot water pipes and the futility in his voice simultaneous. "I met that old man, he told it as he saw it, and Doswell didn't even know he existed."

"Doswell didn't know?" Raskin laughed louder and harder. "How do you know?"

"I know!"

"He was put up to it!" He yelled this absurd and yet, in a way, true accusation.

Raskin always said that the President was a survivor, someone who'd clawed his way up from the bottom. The son of a Louisiana sharecropper who, as a boy with his mother and half a dozen brothers and sisters, had trekked across the continent to California; there, despite numerous handicaps, he'd risen steadily in the sunny but highly competitive California environment.

Still relatively young (in his mid-thirties) he'd returned east, having advanced himself first as an academic, then an administrator in the University of California statewide system. He'd come with the purpose of transforming Baxter, as he'd first told Vincent in New York, "into the first genuine black university in the heart of the Old South". He was on his third year at the task.

Vincent, deliberating on all of this, the President's long-cultivated grudge against Doswell, and then his failed mission to Raskin, knew he was facing a near-impossible task. Why should he, after all, offer the old man a place in a movement he considered his baby? Answering his own question, Vincent reasoned, because the President had himself said very recently that all viewpoints, even if "personally repugnant", should be welcomed at the convention. But he was aware of a bout of unsettling cynicism taking hold in his brain as he put this thought into words.

The President was sitting bolt upright, blank-faced, motionless behind his great oak-varnished desk, obliquely facing the tinted plate-glass window that gave onto a broad view of the campus courtyard below. They were to be alone, of course. And in fact this was to be the first time Vincent had been alone with him in Colonus for more than a few seconds. Mrs. Schooley, the President's secretary, had motioned him to sit down, then stepped out.

Vincent gazed about the sumptuous office in this newest of two new campus buildings, part of the New Millennium Project Montbanc had announced when he'd first arrived at Baxter. Everything gleaming, expensive, efficient-looking, as one might expect of the office of a CEO in a Fortune 500 company. There was no telephone-fondling, no dictating machine he was talking into now. It couldn't have been more than half a minute that Vincent waited, shorter than on previous occasions, but it was long enough to underline that he, Ronald Montbanc, was President of the university, and he, Vincent Brown, hardly counted in the scheme of things.

Still facing the window, the President said suddenly, "What do you have to say for yourself?"

If anything Vincent had come prepared, or thought he had. Suppressing all signs of belligerence, he simply plunged in with what he'd prepared himself to say. "It surprised me as much as it probably did you that Doswell was so well-known out in Chicago and in New York. As you can see, people noticed him over the years." He laughed as he said, "You can blame President Robinson for sending him out to Chicago. He's the one who first encouraged him to go so often, and then sent him to do double-duty as an emissary from the admissions office. But as for New York, that letter from that old union man—"

"What do you have to say for yourself, Brown?" Montbanc broke in, repeating his bullying question, spoken as if to an erring, recalcitrant child. Vincent remembered some of Raskin's words about Doswell and the President the few nights before. "If Uncle Thomas was certified and stamped God Almighty Incarnate Himself there's no way Ronald would let him get up there and preach to those people. Don't you know that, Vincent?"

"You know, when you first talked about the Alliance," Vincent said now, as patiently as he could, trying his most reasonable voice, "and before that when I read about it, and about you, the one idea that appealed to me was that it was to bring *all* people of color, all people of African descent together. A united front..." His voice drifted into its lecturing mode. "It wasn't supposed to be easy, we certainly didn't have to agree with everything we heard, we weren't being asked to like all of our brothers, but we were supposed to *listen*, not just shout folks down or call them names when we heard things we didn't like. The idea was 'to bring in to the open the true spirit of the people,' you said, that's what you said. You reminded me of Paul Robeson – his ideas, I mean. I was impressed by that, greatly impressed. You won me over—"

"I'm asking you, Brown, what's your game?" the President pressed, impatient, obviously unpersuaded and unmoved.

"My game," Vincent said, his words quickening, "you ought to know. You hired me to play it. Remember? My job was to keep this thing together, to make it work, and it is falling apart. I'm giving you my best advice, which is what you hired me to do. You let that old man speak like they're asking and *you'll* come out smelling like a rose no matter what he says and no matter how upset anybody might be."

Montbanc tried interrupting again, but this time Vincent didn't let him, noticing for an instant the surprise in his face.

"Let me tell you. A lot of these folks in Chicago – and in Atlanta, yeah, in Brooklyn, in other places as well – I've met them, and I've done my best with them, but if you don't cut them some slack, you don't give them something, they're just gonna get ugly. I mean, we could have a whole lot of people just getting up and walking out, *if* they show."

Montbanc fidgeted.

"On the other hand, why should anyone be really upset by Doswell if he isn't to their liking? More likely, those who want to hear him will hear him, those who don't won't. This is a convention, isn't it? They'll be thankful to you that you let him. And they'll be *completely* right. Because you'll have kept your word. You'll have shown the Alliance is open to everyone, just like you said. Is he going to say something *against* you? You, who's hosting this gathering, you, who would be giving him this forum to speak? How could he? Why would he? And *if* there are some people who'll be unhappy with what he says, well, you can always play politics. You can always hedge on who exactly was responsible for getting him up there. You can play it from any angle, give it any spin. You can take credit where credit is due, reminding them that the Alliance is all about being a great big tent, or you can put blame elsewhere if and when that's convenient, yeah, and that's obviously with me because you'll have a story to tell, backed up by a whole lot of people."

Montbanc had swiveled his chair around after a minute or so, got up, stepped over to the window and placed his palms against the blue-tinted plate glass as he gazed out on the courtyard below. He seemed to be weighing what he'd heard, and Vincent was feeling the exhilaration of the power in his words.

Inside that room and between them there was not a sound; even outside the suite there was no sound to be heard. Cleon Baker had said that this building had been so designed that regardless of the noise vexing the outside world, from within its walls – within the Presidential Suite – there was only an enveloping, monastic quiet.

Montbanc finally stirred himself. "That old fool, he doesn't represent anything or anyone but himself. Who is he? Just a nobody who thinks he's somebody."

"I suppose Braithwaite and Baker are world-historical individuals," Vincent replied instantly.

There was a sudden hush as Vincent saw Montbanc's face turn rigid. He gazed past him through the same wide, blue-tinted windows, past some of Baxter's older buildings and some stately trees, to the gleaming Islamic Study Center, another recently finished building in the Millennial Building Project, and just beyond it, a part of the new library, still under construction.

After a moment Montbanc turned sharply and faced Vincent; he spat out his opening words. "Brown! You know Perrin thinks that you're just a fool, that that old Tom has put one over on you? But I say a fool is a fool no matter how he becomes one! And you're just as much a fool as he is if you think you're gonna *shine me up* and get me to start eating outta your hand. You think you and that old fool are gonna start running this show? You think you're gonna take this movement over and become chief nigger? Yeah. Maybe you're as big a fool as he is!"

He moved from the window towards the door. At the same time he nodded dismissively in its direction. "By the way, your career with the Alliance is over. Don't go flying around on our credit cards anymore. And don't go bothering to make any more calls on our behalf because you don't represent anybody but yourself."

"You don't *own* the Alliance." Vincent turned on him. "I'm just as much a part of it now as I've ever been!"

"Be careful I don't throw you out on your ear! I mean out of this university too!" Montbanc's voice rose several decibels. "You'll be looking for a job tomorrow."

"I've got a contract!" Vincent started yelling himself. "You can't fire me. I'll be here to the end of this year. And don't think I'll be silent!"

That's when the President lost it. "God damn you, nigger! You've got what I say you've got. You go when I tell you to go. You come when I tell you to come! If it weren't for me you'd still be picking lice out of your burr head!"

And that is, thankfully, when Mrs. Schooley (the much-admired soundproofing clearly inadequate to this occasion) slipped open the door, stepped in, and followed within seconds by a mute and wild-eyed Dean Middleweek, stammered, "What's... What's... Do you want me?" as she looked around anxiously. And then, seeing Vincent approaching the little runt with what she rightly thought was the intent to kill, she came between them. "Mr. Brown." She touched his arm gently. "Mr. Brown, I think you should leave now!"

Outside into the suddenly bright, sunlit courtyard, striding two steps in one, already fifty or a hundred yards away, in the shadow of a high-rise men's dorm, coming full-blast from a radio in a student's room with windows open to the great outdoors, Movement bard Gil Scott-Heron beat out a staccato rhythm with words anticipating the sound of rap.

The revolution will not be televised!
The revolution will not show you pictures of Nixon
And will not star Natalie Wood and Steve McQueen or Bullwinkle and Julio...

Vincent stopped suddenly in his tracks and listened, transfixed. "Yeah!" he sighed, taking in the utopian ludicrousness of it all.

Will not be televised...

And after the first shudder of surprise, he began chuckling, then laughing near-hysterically.

Green Acres, Beverley Hillbillies
Women will not care if Dick finally got down with Jane
On Search for Tomorrow
The revolution will not be televised!
Will not be televised!
Will Not Be Televised!
WILL NOT BE TELEVISED!

He made his way across the nearest faculty parking lot back in the direction of his office, repeating the staccato, rap-like sound and words. "*Because black people will be on the street, looking for a brighter day! A brighter day!*"

Earlier it had been gray and overcast, raining off and on, but it was now fully cleared. The day wasn't cold; the air had that fresh, utterly clean smell coming after the rains. There was the sound of cars and trucks on the avenue adjacent to the campus, roaring past.

The revolution will put you in the driver's seat!

And as he mimicked the rhythm and the words and the gaiety of that song, he thought the revolution will go on; that there would be no Ronald Montbanc leading the charge or in the Alliance's driver's seat…but the revolutionary and transforming idea of unity would continue on a brighter day, and he would never stop working towards that end.

In the days immediately afterwards, he acted more like a man celebrating victory than suffering defeat. He was exultant – exultant and exhilarated at finally and decisively breaking with the little dictator. In fact, if he'd felt anything like dejection, any disappointment at all over his failure at persuading him to bring the old man on board, it so paled in comparison that the memory of it was a complete blank.

It was now late autumn but Blissie and he were in the spring flush of their newly budded affair. Maybe all this nonsense he'd recently talked himself into, and talked to Basil about – what he called these "wearying rounds of encounters", and the need for someone "to rest oneself in" – could be bypassed and he could move on with life. Yes! The black knight and the white damsel. It wasn't his first love affair, but it was a first of its kind and mighty pleasant! As back in the days when he was manning the barricades on Morningside Heights, he felt the urge to make love long and hard. Triumphant in his ostensible defeat, he made love to Blissie and mixed it with living dangerously. Or then again, not so *very* dangerously, for it was the end of the decade, not the beginning, Colonus was no berg, and virtually all of their public appearances were at Laurel Hill.

PART 2

9

Jim's Two Love Affairs

It was the same weekend the second (November) Moratorium to Stop the War was gathering in Washington, and all over the nation, in towns and cities and hamlets across the land, activities in conjunction with the Washington gathering had been planned. TV news prime time, newsmagazine stories, newspaper headlines and radio airwaves crackled with reports of events: ecumenical services in churches around the nation; assemblies and rallies on campuses and courthouse squares, in the grand expanse of city parking lots and suburban malls, fanning out over the manicured lawns of veterans' cemeteries; marchers marching across the George Washington Bridge spanning the Hudson River, the Golden Gate in the Bay Area of California, bridges and walkways and thoroughfares everywhere between, banners waving, demanding, BRING THE TROOPS HOME NOW.

And indeed Blissie and Sister Mary, Loewenstein, the Peters, Raissa Albrecht and her engineer husband and teenage daughters, Keech and a number of others were going on trips up to Washington or to the state capitol. And in Colonus itself there was to be a candlelit procession joined by contingents from virtually all of the city's churches, complete with public readings from Scripture and the solemn recitations of names of fallen soldiers.

At Baxter in the noontime hour, and then sometimes well into late afternoon or evenings in the Union dining hall, there they'd be, not just Baxter people but townies and CSU people planning strategies: talks at the local high schools, telephone calls to key people around town and in the capital, to national organizers in New York and Washington. But neither Vincent nor Jim was engaged in any of these activities. Vincent was busy with the convention, though no longer in an official capacity; and Jim was concentrated on reading and thinking into the wee hours, his thoughts and reading kindled by the wind-borne upheaval. As a for-instance, he was reading a great book which would never be on the list: Hegel's *Phenomenology of Mind*, whose near-impossible German syntax and prolix abstractness eventually yielded up the Idealist's claim that the Incarnation had brought to the growth of human consciousness a recognition of selfhood both to oneself and others – others, that is, not opposed to oneself, but as bound together in the one God who was both God and Man. So in the ideal of practical action, the cultural life of the people, and the exercise of Christian life and belief, the God within and in others had begun the transformation of the stranger into one's brother. Of course he knew this didn't mean the age-old impulse to murder, to torture, to enslave had been banished from the face of the earth; but that a new stage in human life had supposedly begun, and, like the sprout from out of the living seed, it had sprung up, giving hope in this thousand-year spring. But what had happened to the promised equality, the fraternity that had come with the face of Christ on every man? Was this the meaning of the people's marches, the banners and prayers in the public squares, and the speeches amidst the throngs? *All we are saying...* Hands joined; songs in choruses a million strong?

Yes, he was preoccupied and thoughtful, living within the chrysalis of his apartment. Such thoughts were mostly night thoughts though; during the day they lingered on the frayed edge of consciousness. Then Jim got a telephone call from Enrico Carbonari. Rico was a childhood friend. He recalled during his first turbulent weeks in Colonus what Rico had said when he learned that he had a job team teaching with two others at a black university in the South. He'd noisily insisted that he'd been had.

"It's like three to a marriage," he cried, as they stood beside traffic-clogged Bruckner Boulevard.

It was the first he'd heard from his prophetic friend since leaving the city (he'd yet to answer Jim's letters). So, full of news from home, the two talked for easily half an hour, probably more. (Rico was footing the bill; he'd gotten his first professional engineering job, so he was rich.) He told Jim the neighborhood gossip, and local news about the Moratorium to Stop the War. This last had been washing over Jim's melancholic, Hegel-filled mind, registering as a background din of impressions which poured over the newswires, the television screen, the car radio, from virtually everywhere. He'd been attending to tasks, and when not clinching furniture bargains for his unfurnished apartment with his office mate Szereszewski, or sitting at his antique oak desk studying and reading, there was only one other thing he'd begun doing, and that was obsessing over his loneliness and racking his brain trying to figure a way out of his solitary state.

"I have blood in my veins," he murmured, feeling sorry for himself, as he looked into his solemn-sour, stubbly face mornings in the bathroom mirror. He quoted Emerson to the same mopey face gazing back at him. "Books aren't a substitute for friends." Of course, he'd ruminate, there were his strategy-planning luncheon companions at the Union that he was learning to avoid – and, he'd recently learned, had tagged him the Lemon Face. And there was his companionable antique stalker, Szereszewski, twice his age and friendly to be sure, but hardly a nighttime social companion.

There was one individual, however, who was – Ramatha Radhakathri, a youthful, binge-drinking East Indian of Brahmin caste origins with a passing resemblance in short form to the Egyptian actor Omar Sharif. Radhakathri was from Baxter's Political Science Department, and invited Jim out often. Jim had taken to having dinner with him, or joining him for late-night drinks. One great negative to his companionship, though: Radhakathri was an incessant whiner and complainer.

"You know, Mr. Allan, I am not a happy man," he'd confessed on one of their first outings around Colonus.

"Why is that, Radhakathri?" Jim asked, refusing to give in to his own dejection in the other man's company.

"This country, this country, I tell you, it is so cold. The people are so unfriendly. They have no grace. Oh! And…and look what they've done to their poor Negroes! Such violence! And such animosity towards strangers."

There was an element of pathos (he too was a solitary) and comedy, as well, in Radhakathri's complaint. He told Jim many times that there was nothing he would like better than to take leave of America's unfriendly shores, while on other occasions sharing the fact that he'd arranged with the Immigration and Naturalization Service to stay in America indefinitely. Jim couldn't help feeling a bit fond of him, as one often does with someone so transparently childish. But he also took to gently teasing him about the manifold contradictions in his complaints. At all events, even if Jim felt less ambivalent about his companion, his desire for companionship went to more than someone of his own sex. So when Rico, having finished his report, announced that an old flame of his was in the neighborhood, Jim pounced on the news.

Responding to Jim's enthusiasm, like Rico thought he needed to overcome the distance with his lungs, he shouted, "Yeah! Lee is real near you! She's over there with some do-good government outfit, VISTA."

Lee Bagby and Jim went back to the times of his politically active days shortly after returning from Birmingham to New York half a decade earlier. He'd met the slim, demure Lee outside the New York World's Fair, literally flopped prone on a road out there in the wilds of Flushing Meadows. Even then being politically active was a great way to meet girls. And they eventually became intimate in the carefree, careless way typical of those days and those circles, becoming as much buddies and comrades as lovers.

But where was Rico's "over there" where Lee could be found once again? All that he could learn was that it was somewhere in the Carolinas (North? South?) near the coast. So over a good part of the following day Jim called around among a maze of social agencies to pin down Lee's VISTA group. Eventually he learned they'd been operating out of a little crossroads town not far from Wilmington. It was then he decided that during the convention weekend he'd drive out to the coast to see Lee.

In those days Jim wore his hopes like an ever-eager night watchman, skeleton keys that had yet to open one locked door. Yet what did he hope for now – what had fizzled out two years earlier from lack of combustible energy? Could it be reignited? What did he have to go on? A change in setting? The fact that they were both do-gooders? That it was all fated? What he had most to go on was the little gasp in her breath, a little bird-like chirp in her voice when he telephoned. But had he really heard that?

In truth, against his own vocal self in his worst of moments, he was convinced Lee desired a reconnection as much as he, but in her own quiet and hidden way.

As they strolled along the beach near Wilmington that weekend (he'd wanted to see the ocean for months), the moist-chill, breezy salt air in their faces, the rhythmic surge and boom of the breakers pounding the shoreline, she began to tell him of her plans for the future, and eagerly asked him his. In his secret self, he thought, Can I hold you again, and will you hold me? Can I love you and be loved by you? Kiss your eyes? Your lips? Hold you and then lie with you in the lee of a knoll, with the sound of the ocean breakers pounding the shore?

These were his thoughts, thoughts which pushed, pressed and jostled into the present like an unruly mob, as she, quite sensibly and obliviously, spoke of her well-charted future, her earnest plans to continue in her present mode, working among poor people, community organizing, helping to familiarize them with complex regulations and programs – then on to law school to serve people as a public interest lawyer. All of this represented nothing but doing good. And it's this that originally attracted him to Lee, that had made her different – that and the ineffable sense in him of wanting to save her, and that in saving her he would save himself. Yes, and not least of all, the fact that Lee was pretty, that she was always the poised, intelligent WASP. Rico, who'd met her only a few times, had the impression that if Lee had been born a Catholic, she would have been a nun. One of his neat summations. And Jim knew exactly what he'd meant, even though he was regularly sleeping with her back then. Lee fit the description of those women Rollo May, the popularly read psychologist, described who, though capable of sexual intimacy, were otherwise coolly distant, businesslike, even with lovers. And yet, still, there was that delicate, glass-like vulnerability to which he was drawn.

So they had dinner together, at the women's house, about a dozen people, men and women, talking of the day's headlines, most prominently a local story favorable to the Alliance gathering in Colonus. Then Lee and he went to the movies to see *Easy Rider*, which was enthusiastically recommended by all. And afterwards, when they returned to the men's house, outside in the shimmery light and shadows of a yard fire, they talked well into the night about the movie and the stifling conformity of America. Those were days when drugs were still widely viewed as emblematic of a defiantly revolutionary ethos. The celebrated counter-culture gloried in the individual's self-definition, and mind-expanding substances were viewed as part of its expression. As they passed around a couple of joints, everyone leisurely identified their own experiences with the movie's theme of the Establishment's repression of the individual.

An earnest VISTA volunteer, an affable guy Jim's age, was speaking enthusiastically, approvingly nodding Jim's way, citing the reports that at Baxter they were joining "old-fashioned American patriotism with revolutionary change on race".

One of Lee's housemates was saying, "Wow! Wow! That's great! Cool!"

Lee was smiling; a dreamy smile playing in her eyes and across her slightly parted lips, her sweetly pretty, pale face radiant in the firelight.

"You must be proud, being part of that," the guy was saying.

Another guy who'd read about Baxter and the Alliance gathering in a national magazine added, "I don't suppose the publicity is hurting either."

Jim nodded, said nothing.

And as they went on about what they speculated the Alliance meant about bringing black people together, Jim felt increasingly irritable. Yet as the night passed amidst the pot-laced comradely talk, which drifted to more general talk of racism and reactions to racism, personal foibles and gossip, he joined in. Though he'd felt some initial reservation, it ended with his experiencing the easy, comradely sensation of being among kindred spirits.

But the following day when Lee and her friends were preparing to go down to the city to picket some federal installations, and they'd assumed that he was going, when they learned he wasn't, or that he was irresolute, there was once again some awkwardness felt all around.

"Well, you want to, or don't you?" Lee said in a prickly but childlike voice, the others looking on, baffled.

For an instant he thought he would go, the pressure of the moment being intense, but he knew he'd already cast his lot. "Well, no, I think I'll go to the beach," he said, as they looked at him with a mixture of distrust and disbelief on their faces.

That day, feeling he was in the furthest cold, outer reaches of space, spinning heedlessly, he left alone to visit Hooke's Point, a little town on the coast. When he returned that evening, he was shut out: the talk was all on the activities of the day, hopes for "a rebirth of democracy", the "end of the war" and Lee's plans for joining the American Friends Service Committee going to Cuba soon. To be sure they didn't quarrel, it was impossible to quarrel with Lee, but there was a clearly felt mutual alienation, and Jim's disjointed efforts to explain and to identify what he thought fell on deaf ears.

That night he didn't sleep in the men's house; he stayed in a motel by the ocean's edge, and he had a strange and vivid dream that he was a fish swimming along with all the other fish in the sea, but he was a very foolish fish because he was looking for the water. Just kept squinting away in search of the water under the strain of this impossible effort to see it. Making no headway, naturally, in seeing it, for he was *in it.* He woke in a panic, halfway still in his dream, with fish-eyes staring, bumping his head in half-sleep over and over against the headboard as a goldfish bumps its nose incessantly against its reflection in a glass bowl.

So it was that weekend, that same weekend in mid-November that the Alliance convention was taking place back in Colonus, and the week's major feature, the second Moratorium, was running all over America, that he spent kicking at sand dunes, finally deciding to leave the coast and Lee earlier than planned. What could be the depth of his feeling for Lee if he could leave her so easily? But it *wasn't* easy. And if it was true that a good part of what Jim felt was a desire for love rather than love itself, it is also true that with Lee he had come closer to something like love than he ever had with any woman. It is also true that his short stay with Lee and her friends had triggered in him a state as ominous as any he'd lived under his final months in New York the previous summer. He left without any thought of his break with Lee being permanent or otherwise.

As he drove back to Colonus, blasting the country roads in his muffler-damaged Volkswagen, fleeing the flat, red-sandy tidewater, the drab, semi-tropical palmetto and scrub, he kept bumping his nose up against that same blurred reflection – one reflection, that this whole life of his he'd been running just like this, running, fleeing from place to place, craving the between-places. As cow meadows and a measure of greenness began to appear in intermittent blurred and longer stretches, he thought of that first week in his hotel room in Colonus, gazing down from the tenth floor to the Greyhound bus station, watching-listening to the growling buses below as they inched their way in and out of the station, reflecting on the urgency to take one going anywhere, to join those people on the bus platform he imagined on their way to nowhere!

It was late afternoon Sunday, dusk approaching, as he approached Colonus, and he remembered the day, weeks before, when he'd gone to visit Doswell; that day out in Doswell's rickety jeep with the chainsaw, hacking away at wild cherry trees he'd been battling since he'd bought his place. There was a nip of fall in the air and it was breezy but sunny, and the two of them had worked up a sweat in minutes. Falling into a rhythm and a pleasure in the physical exertion and camaraderie, Jim was amused watching Doswell's surprisingly nimble, bulky figure like an adept fat man on a dance floor.

"You look like you're angry at those trees. I feel sorry for them."

"Yeah, you would – just watch what an old man can do!"

"Hey, don't over-exert yourself," Jim yelled back, laughing.

"Hey *you!* Get to work...boyyy!"

When it was over, and the trees reduced to chunks of firewood, the two of them, soaked in sweat, surveyed their work. The wind played through the rustling branches of the trees at the edge of the wood, and as he reached for a handkerchief to wipe his face, the cooling breezes sent a shiver over Jim. Presently they loaded the jeep with the tools and chainsaw, and part of the firewood, and drove back in silence over the bumpy pasture to the house.

It occurred to Jim, driving back now from the coast, how nice it would be to just suddenly turn off in the direction of Doswell's place. He was sure that he wouldn't be over in Colonus; at least he was sure that he wouldn't be at the convention. In that dusk-settling gloom of late autumn, he didn't want to return to his apartment where the four walls would echo no sounds but his own! But just dropping in on Doswell didn't seem appropriate. And maybe even more so, as a great author said somewhere, we don't care to confide in those who are better than we are. Still, he just had to confide, or at least be with someone following that bitter weekend.

He thought then of his habitually complaining friend, Ramatha Radhakathri; he would almost certainly be at the King's Table, the lounge and restaurant of the local Holiday Inn. The thought of Radhakathri's company in the foul mood he was in appealed more than Doswell's – indeed, was perfect for an evening of misery and complaint!

But then fate has a way of throwing a curve ball occasionally, and through little effort it sometimes happens that we hit a home run. He stopped at the Holiday Inn, and as it turned out on that evening Jim found an uncomplaining Radhakathri who little resembled his typically discontented friend.

"My dear Mr. Allan!"

He heard the cheery greeting and saw the new Radhakathri rising from his usual dimly lit corner of the restaurant, motioning him to his table, and in that combined English public school/East Indian accent of his, announcing with all the enthusiasm of a schoolboy that just two days before he'd met "a very fine lady!" And yes, he was seeing her again that very night.

And that was how it came about that Jim got to know Susan Weston and Chris Khalaf, the latter Radhakathri's brand new "very fine lady companion", the former, her friend, soon to be Jim's. Chris Khalaf, an old-fashioned Lebanese-American girl Radhakathri had met at his lawyer's office, had brought Susan Weston, a warm-hearted, athletic, not-so-old-fashioned North Carolina girl, along for the ride.

"You teach with Ramatha?" Susan said in a cute Southern belle drawl, which when she pronounced Dr. Radhakathri's already odd-sounding given name was particularly appealing.

"We teach at the same college in different areas."

"What do you teach?" Her eyes were bright, laughing emeralds.

Radhakathri broke in. "He teaches Great Books."

"Great Books? What is that, the best books? What kind of books?" She looked puzzled, but her eyes were still gaily lit.

The attraction was mutual. She was no intellectual. No, but she had other attractions. She had the athletic and vivacious prettiness of a cheerleader. Jim wasn't bad-looking himself. And he wasn't acting like any kind of Lemon Face. Slim but no longer a beanpole as in his early school years, he had an athletic build from years at track and field and as a wrestling standout in high school. His face, though serious, even etched permanently in melancholy, was at the same time quickly responsive. And he was responding. They hit if off instantly. Opposites attract. If Chris Khalaf hadn't been so backwards, had she been only half as socially and culturally advanced, as liberated as the rest of her generation, she'd never have asked Susan to accompany her on a first date. But she had!

Susan, on the rebound, would be his first sweetheart since he last set eyes on Lee twenty-four hours earlier.

"Well, who decides the best books? Are they the ones that are most boring?" Susan asked teasingly.

"Ah, dear lady, dear lady!" Radhakathri was shaking his head, laughing, thoroughly charmed.

"Susan! Don't be so silly!" Chris admonished her friend.

"That's what a lot of students first think. That's our first hurdle," Jim said, "getting over the expectation that they will be boring."

"It must be very hard to teach if you have many students like Susan here," Chris said, pointing her finger teasingly at her friend.

"Chris! You nasty thang."

Susan was smart-talking, affectionate, fun-loving, with no use for books and not a word to say on politics. Just what the doctor ordered!

During the next several weeks on Saturday afternoons, Radhakathri, Chris, Susan and Jim gathered together to play touch football in the often-nippy autumn air. Even Radhakathri played vigorously, protesting as usual (he was unfamiliar with American football) – but good-naturedly. After all, how could he do otherwise under both Chris and Susan's charming tutelage? Following these weekend sojourns, if they didn't go out, or if they did, they'd come back to Jim's now properly employed apartment on Hargett Street, with its romantic views from the back porch. Jim and Ramatha entertained the women with droll stories about Baxter personalities, or occasional political or worldly talk about New York, Washington and Tokyo (Radhakathri had spent some time in all three), accompanied by card-playing and games like Scrabble and Monopoly, sometimes dancing and talking and spooning into the evenings. But then as the Christmas holidays approached, their first semester at the college drawing to a close, life growing, for the first time in a while, very sweet, like a bolt of lightning from out of nowhere came an eviction notice. Out! Jim read with hot flashes, unbelieving. All of his furnishings, his many books, out with his papers piled high – out by the end of the month! Or else!

10

A Life-changing Offer

News photos taken in the Balkans, Southeast Asia, Latin America and elsewhere, showing the dispossessed carrying all that they can as they flee a catastrophe, are the stuff of everyday. And while Jim's situation, as he clutched his landlord's notice, was hardly so dire, it wasn't a mere inconvenience either. His apartment had been acquired with some difficulty and was now impossible to quickly replace. As Dr. Middleweek warned in one of his earliest letters, all of the decent places in Colonus would be taken if he was late in looking – which he was, with the confusion of those first weeks. So he'd ended up settling for unfurnished, not his original plan since he had no furniture, and hardly ideal since it wouldn't be ready for two weeks. But it was also an attractive place, and while there'd been a delay as the young couple occupying it, in the throes of a divorce, found other quarters, it went for a near-steal. Thus it was that this misfortune-gained place and the promptings of his office mate,Szereszewski, had led him to buy all the necessary secondhand furnishings that heaped up complications for his now-sudden eviction.

As he grimly gazed out onto a scene as Christmassy as the southern climes of Colonus would ever offer (dusted by the only snow of that season), Jim experienced a kind of Kafkaesque meltdown, and cudgeled his brain for some clue as to what might have been the cause of this inexplicable trouble he was in. And yet, as he did, no amount of self-scrutiny uncovered anything on his part that was amiss. He certainly wasn't being ejected as the result of torrid or overly merry parties; for the simple, boring truth was that there was nothing in those evenings that any landlord with the mindset of the '50s would have objected to, much less the late '60s. What he came to realize was that this was one of those darkly ridiculous incidents in his life that demonstrated a destiny to become the victim whenever some screwball combination of misunderstandings should by chance fall together. For what he eventually learned was that in the scarce several weeks he'd occupied the place on Hargett Street while seeing Susan Weston, he'd been scrutinized by a neighbor who'd been observing his comings and goings with Chris and Susan and Radhakathri, the neighbor no doubt concluding that Radhakathri, not being of the right hue, had African origins.

He remembered once talking to the man by the curb outside his apartment when he'd first moved into the neighborhood. Mr. Yancey was one of those cigar-chomping, pot-bellied older men that appear perpetually lost following retirement. Jim pegged him as strange; a measure of his strangeness: Yancey had told him, chewing as much as puffing on the stub of a cigar, that he and his wife had gone off to Canada "with the kids" one summer years before to see the Dionne quintuplets, reporting it as one might a visit to Disneyland.

Jim's downstairs neighbor, Bill McNally, a red-haired graduate student at Central, who fully looked the part of the jock engineer that he was, later reported a conversation he'd had with Mr. Yancey shortly before their landlord had sent him the notice. McNally was a bit apologetic when he told him how Yancey had cornered him and said there were wild interracial parties going on in their house: that he'd seen "a nigger, at least one, maybe two" coming in with Jim on several occasions, and wondered about other goings-on as well. So it had been this "outrage" which Jim's landlord mysteriously referred to, but did not name, when he was evicted.

Such were the absurd twists that made up the course of Jim's life that year. And then another twist: that he should be evicted for the crime of social concourse in his apartment with Negroes, a crime of which he was innocent, but which would now throw him headlong into the actual crime, and for this there would be no similar penalties.

It is a commonplace to observe that the Christmas season, with its frantically cheerful emphasis on celebrating family ties, can be the occasion for the most depressing of times for those from troubled families. Before his eviction notice Jim intended to make the obligatory return to New York for a few days around the holiday. Then with his apartment at Hargett Street waiting, he planned to head back to Colonus to spend the rest of the vacation with Susan. It was, after all, enough time to see his brother and for the requisite heart-to-heart with his mother, who was alone at the house. But now he'd come into a sea of uncertainty with this urgent need to find a place to live. And then it happened that he bumped into Doswell near the Student Union on a weekday soon afterwards.

"Jim," Doswell said on that leaden-gray, overcast December afternoon, "you look like you've just had something that's given you a stomach ache. What you been eating?"

He'd parried the old man's remark with a wisecrack of his own. But in fact, beside his concerns over finding a new place to live, another problem had arisen. He was upset over a clash with a student who'd accused him of not reading a paper that was turned in and graded, the paper so patently poor that after he read the first paragraphs he'd stopped marking corrections. The boy charged him with reading only to where the markings ended.

"He's threatening to take this up with the Dean."

"What do you think you'll do?"

Jim smiled. "I was planning to tell you."

"Well. That's done. Don't worry about it though, the kid doesn't have a leg to stand on."

They talked for a while of this and that. Then Doswell asked about his plans for the coming holiday, and that was when Jim mentioned his recent eviction notice. When Doswell expressed amazement at this new situation, Jim shared his own initial puzzlement and what he'd since learned. Then he told him how Susan and Chris had invited him to stay with them, but that their other roommate had vetoed the plan. He also told about Radhakathri's promising to put him up while he was looking for another place, a promise made amidst the camaraderie of their common victimhood, but later denying he'd ever made such promises.

"What about the hotel? You stayed there on a weekly basis before, didn't you?"

"It's the holiday season. They're only taking reservations for rooms on a daily basis, and they're at peak season rates. Every other place in town has the same story."

"When did you say you have to be out?" Doswell finally asked after listening to this protracted tale of woe.

"My final day is New Year's Eve."

"The man sounds like he's full of the Christmas spirit. When were you planning to go back to New York?"

"I'm not sure I can now – or, if I do, when."

"But when were you planning to go originally?"

One thing led to another in their talk, and then Doswell was offering Jim the spare room next to Billy's, and thinking aloud about his neighbor, Jim Lewis, and his son Luther, and if they could help move his furnishings into one of the outbuildings.

"You can stay with us as long as it takes to find a new place," he announced matter-of-factly.

It was a quick and easy solution, offering, of course, a lot of additional time. It was also an amazingly generous offer. So only on learning that all other reasonable options were closed with the busy Christmas season did Jim relent to what seemed foreordained, causing him, with foreboding, to change his plans. Rather than visit New York a few days, he'd stay with his mother in the Bronx the entire break to avoid imposing on the old man any longer than necessary.

11

Times Square, New York

Despite the life-line that now stretched from Colonus and Devon, this entrance into the city remained deranging – crazy making. Crossing Seventh Avenue and Broadway amidst flashing neon marquees and the infernal racket of the city, overhead dizzying rising construction, the drill blast of jackhammers, under diverted makeshift post-and-plywood walkways, boring through streaming crowds, Jim hurried as through a gauntlet for the subway station below ground on 42nd Street.

Past the prostrate, the drugged, the defeated…

> No Trespassing. Post No Bills.
> Fuck you. Phone 416-8701 Josie For…
> COME TO MARLBORO COUNTRY… AMERICA'S SEXUAL REVOLUTION
> HAIR
> SEX IN USA FOR CONSENTING ADULTS ONLY. LAST 2 TWO DAYS!
> IN BLUSHNG COLOR!… IN SIZZLING COLOR!!
> THE MUSICAL REVELATION…
> RATED XX! RATED XXX!!

Self-revulsively yet powerfully drawn to one or another item in this glossy heap/treasure trove of porn…

> LOVE THY NEIGHBOR RATED XXXX!!!
> PATTON – One Last Chance and Week … M*A*S*H Only!…
> GRAND FUNK RAILROAD
> THREE FACES… AMONG THE COUNTLESS… TO BRING US ALL… CLOSER…

"Heyyyy mannnn…" Jim turned, "how 'bout…" then descended along with the rush of hundreds streaming below ground for the hub shuttling trains blasting east to the Grand Central, south to lower Manhattan and Brooklyn, north for upper Manhattan and the Bronx...

STAR SPANGLED GIRL a patriotic, chaotic comedy!
REMAIN PERSPIRATION-FREE—NO ODOR, NO SMELL, NO STICKY FEELING solves ALL your wetness...

At his home hours later Jim's mother, napping in the room down the hall, called to him. The soul-stirring sound of Beethoven's Ninth Symphony, in its fourth movement, the Ode to Joy, flooding the room in high decibels, had, in the instant before, come to an end.

"Why didn't you drive up in the car then?"

Jim took half a minute to answer.

"I'm afraid it's going to break down on me on a long trip. I'm trying to use it as little as I can. Didn't you tell me Chuck would be here for dinner?"

"He said he would but I forgot to tell you he telephoned while you were out and said he can't come after all. He said Clare was worried about Kevin..."

Jim turned momentarily to the sound of voices coming from outside his window, hearing, as his mother spoke, a raucous exchange among passers-by below.

"Get outta here!"

Laughter.

"Yeah."

"Nah!"

"Get outta here!"

More laughter.

"Yeah! Yeah!"

She called out once again asking that he play something "sweet and soothing".

Lying back on his bed, shoeless, hands clasped in a cradle behind his head, he thought of Chuck. Two days after Christmas and he'd yet to appear. He thought of Greta and Elise in California, too far to come for a few days. With the sound of a Strauss waltz played at lower volume, he closed his eyes, and inside of a few minutes, in that murky zone between wakefulness and sleep, he heard chairs crashing, glass breaking, cries, sudden pained sobbing...

As a first-grader he stood guard at his mother's bedside, her still-youthful lips knitted as she frenziedly kneaded her face – her cheek – kneaded first slow and gently, then frantically, like a soft bread dough, flinching and jerking reflexively.

In the intervals between the shocks, when 'it' was away for hours, sometimes even weeks, she said it was like a hot iron thrust to the side of her face; it was "excruciating," she said. He didn't need to be told this; he *saw* it!

Yes, there were those longer stretches of time when she was free of her pain, but never of the impending threat. It was always ready to reappear at times of greatest tension. And Christmases were among those times, his mother making additional money requests over the usual household allowance – and with the additional burdens of the season, tensions grew. As Elise and he whispered among themselves, 'it', this most unwelcome of intruders, refilled her and reoccupied the house as well.

He always felt Chuck bore the heaviest burden; to him was owed the greatest debt. He remembered his brother with his stocky and pear-shaped father standing over him as Chuck flinched and dragged himself on his stomach, crawling as he tried rising to his feet from the force of a blow. His mother coming between them, wringing her hands, crying that once again "neighbors everywhere", "strangers outside!", "people upstairs!", on all sides and inside, could "hear everything!"

They lived in a three-family frame house, one of an identical half-dozen built within talking distance of one another, theirs standing at the corner of the block. On one side, the long, west side of the house, beneath Jim's first floor window, the sidewalk; the north window, on the narrow, back side of the house, the rust-brown brick rear of the older six-story apartment house which shared laundry lines with theirs and defined a part of the little box-shaped, weed-choked yard.

His sisters often remarked bitterly on how easily their family could have afforded a house to themselves with a broad enough lawn and garden to act as a shield against the outside world. Someone told him the entire city's higher education textbook market was sewed up by his father's book jobbing business, but they lived packed tight in this three-bedroom apartment, sharing the house with the second and third floor tenants.

As Chuck grew into his teen years, he'd stay out all day with friends, only slipping into their room late at night to sleep. Jim, on the other hand, found another direction. While still very young, he and Elise pursued something like his mother's rigorous devotion to early morning Masses, evening novenas, rosaries, fasts and abstinences. When he was even younger, he tried religious mortification. At ten he had no way of acquiring a hair shirt, they were nowhere to be found at the usual retail outlets, but as an alternative he occasionally slept without a mattress on the cross-wire frame of his bed, rising in the night with supplicating prayers in hopes of bending the Divine Will.

Three years younger than Chuck, like his sisters he attracted less attention from his father. But while later he found books and his pet dog and the world of his imagination an escape, it placed him, more than his brother at the same age, within the orbit of the house.

He remembered one late afternoon before he'd gone south the first time; an unusual day, for his father was at home, and Jim was stirring hot dogs and beans over the stove in the kitchen for supper, while his father sat at the table sipping coffee. Not having seen Buster, his large, black and brown hairy mutt, he asked with some anxiety about its whereabouts; and his father, who'd threatened on several occasions to dispose of the animal because the apartment was too small, and it was gotten without his permission, confirmed his fear with a taunting remark about his "enjoying hot dogs".

On that day, erupting into a fury like never before, they'd come to blows. Unlike his brother, Jim had no compunction about fighting back; in fact when he soon became physically stronger than his father, he'd throw his arms around him, half-carrying, half-dragging him to his room, ordering him like an unruly child to remain behind his closed bedroom door, waiting with a kind of predatory yearning, should he emerge, to repeat the humiliation. But then in the lingering quiet following, a disgust and sense of utter waste and shame, a numbness and craziness and feeling of being hopelessly defiled descended on him that he simply could not shake.

It was this last, the assaults on his father, that he would never tell anyone – absolutely no one. Only his mother knew.

And, yes, he fully understood why Chuck didn't want to come home. No one did.

His brother no longer believed in his mother's mysterious pain; his father never had. He had himself gone through successive waves of doubt which, especially in the last year following his father's death from cancer, led him to speculate widely on the why of it, and the why of his father. There was a time he wanted more than anything to understand him and his strangely cramped life. Now he wasn't sure what he believed, or if any of this mattered anymore. What mattered was the present – and that Chuck, his well-loved and sorely missed brother, knowing that he was here, still hadn't come. His mother said that the last time Chuck was at the house with Clare and the children, Clare had sulked through their entire stay. It seemed that she and Chuck were always angry about something: on one occasion it was photographs that they said disproportionately featured some of the other grandchildren over their own; on another…

History doesn't stop, any more than the seasons stop their relentless return; noxious weeds sown heedlessly in previous generations appear just as certainly in the far as near years. Such unspoken thoughts gathered in his mind like weighty pebbles in a glass jar as he gazed, grimly abstracted, across the yard at the wall outside his window.

Now alone with his mother, she was asking his advice on the wisdom of going on a pilgrimage to St. Anne de Beaupre outside of Quebec City, a Canadian holy site like Fatima or Lourdes where devout Catholics went seeking miracle cures. He was thus engaged in the delicate balancing act of giving advice on the wisdom of seeking a miracle cure to his mother's pain when he'd long since stopped believing in miracles; and then giving it for an ailment he wasn't sure existed in the first place.

Suddenly these rounds of insane thoughts triggered in him an instant decision – get away! Impossible to stay in this madhouse! Speaking these words out loud to himself, as quickly as he'd thought them, as though to a stubbornly quarrelsome and uncomprehending stranger. Thankfully he knew just where to go. He'd spoken to Susan by telephone several times since he'd been away, and she whispered that Chris and Sharon would soon be gone for the holiday.

He left New York as quick as he could, and for a week he and Susan were like a honeymoon couple with the house in Colonus to themselves; there were mornings breakfasting alone, evenings snuggled together, days seeing Susan in very fetching figure-hugging blue jeans or short, short skirts which revealed tanned cheerleader legs. When in the darkness of those nights she wrapped herself about him, his body in hers, her body engulfing his, her vital animal strength became one in him, it was a gift offering such sweet solace!

She would have let him stay the entire break but then Sharon returned, and unlike Chris, who was willing to let him remain for the time being on a sofa in the living room, Sharon wasn't about to have him "ogling" her early mornings and late evenings as she traipsed about in a bathrobe or less. A point he had to concede, since he would have had from that sofa of theirs a convenient spot from which to ogle. So he was ejected, not without a quarrel on an oblique other point. Susan needed suddenly to get back to her family in Berkely, a couple of hours' drive away. Jim now had, at the very least, to sleep in Devon until she returned.

In the angry exchange that followed, no doubt up to here with Jim's insufferable neediness so fully on display, she cried, "I have a life, Jim, you know? I have things I have to do that don't always involve *you!*"

This was a knife thrust to the heart! Choked up and alarmed, had he demanded too much? In fact when Susan finally did return, she assured him that her visit home was not her own choice, she was just as eager to have him with her as before; only now overnights were out, and protracted bedroom visits were increasingly awkward. And then, with Radhakathri's recent return from the West Coast for the break, and Chris' successful project of corralling Susan and Jim into foursomes which featured Radhakathri and his increasingly boring habit of running Colonus and America down, Jim began to question his previous half-thought-out rule to stay as much as possible away from the house in Devon.

Winter descended more fully with the coming of classes. Not just a chilly couple of days with a light snowfall that would disappear even quicker, but a Canadian front which led Lewis and the neighbors to talk about the threat these sub-freezing temperatures posed to the local fruit orchards. Driving out early for Baxter, Jim noticed in the morning light small clusters of cattle, the steam slowly rising from their huddled, sluggish bodies.

It was at this time that he began seeing a lot more of Doswell and Billy;

Billy, who had endless admiration for his grandfather whom he called "Popeye" – Popeye this and Popeye that; and then overhearing Billy in the room next to his over the well-heated kitchen admonishing the Lewis children with sage advice from the old man; or then again, tales of prodigious physical feats his grandfather had accomplished, and could on a bet accomplish again. When he wasn't driving back to Colonus in the early evening to see his honey-haired Susan, he began spending more time with the Lewises too. And what struck him most about them was the bond that existed between these uncomplicated people and Doswell. Seeing Susan was mostly a weekend affair now, both their early morning schedules making more frequent visits too high in price and too low in reward.

After Doswell's remark that Euretha Lewis more than anybody was burdened with tasks, and remembering how Jim Lewis and his eldest son, Luther, had so generously moved his things to Devon, in the afternoons he went over to the Lewises' to help where he could. And given his city-boy's love for the country, this wasn't a burden. On the contrary, there was the novelty of helping with the farm chores, occasionally helping to bottle-feed a dozen or more dairy calves Mrs. Lewis raised on a consignment basis for the local dairies. He began to gravitate, those weekday late afternoons, to the plump and warm-hearted Euretha, and as he came to see her and the old man together in Devon, he mused more and more about the secret connection between this uneducated farm woman and this Harvard-educated college professor. It wasn't anything that Jim Lewis should have felt threatened by, nor was he; for Jim immediately recognized their intimacy as something that exists between a devoted daughter and her father. And as he came to see more and more, he saw that it was as uncomplicated as this: that sometime in the past the old man needed just such a daughter, and that she needed a father, and that without either of them speaking it or thinking it, they adopted each other.

"I don't know why they do him like they do over there at the university," she said once to Jim at her house, in the large, professionally outfitted kitchen where she cooked up the gargantuan meals she prepared everyday for her husband, her brother-in-law, her children, and occasionally other hungry people – including Doswell and Billy, Jim, and even Susan on a couple of occasions.

On some of those afternoons, since Jim nearly always got away from the campus much earlier than the old man with his many administrative duties, he'd return to Devon, and go over to the Lewises', which was half a mile up the road from Doswell's, to help with the chores. Visiting with Euretha and the younger portion of her little tribe playing out on the expansive, worn-out yard, he'd drift to the house, sometimes carrying in a load of firewood for their woodstove (one of two cook stoves in the kitchen, the other a modern electric range), or occasionally, Solomon-like, resolve a clash between squabbling children.

One afternoon, as Euretha busied herself between chores, she told Jim some things that were on her mind and that he wondered about. "It used to be that Thomas would every year have a big gathering of all his students right here. I would put together a whole lot of food and Thomas would get a couple of the school buses when they weren't using them for something else, and between that and James and Thomas and a few boys' cars we'd have more than a hundred young people here for the day."

Exhibiting his sometimes sober-minded side, Jim asked about the cost of these day-long forays.

"Thomas always came up with the money and there'd be young men that drove up in the morning and helped with the preparations. Some of them even offered to help James out in the fields."

"What happened?" Jim asked, thinking of that impudent, audacious boy, Alvin Foote, months earlier in the Union.

"Dr. Montbanc. The school administration. There was talk about drugs. I don't know what they thought. That we were some kind of fools? Like we was having some kind of drug parties here? Then they said that the buses couldn't be used for anything but official school business. That was all just made up. He did it to ruin it – not why he said. But what I don't understand is why. Why would a man want to ruin such a good thing?"

Of course at this stage in Jim's career at Baxter, what Euretha was saying about the President and the school did not surprise him. He'd since come to see the picture pretty clearly. But Jim wondered at this and much else, taking in the delicious cinnamon and apple and ginger fragrances of Euretha's magical baking, gazing dreamily through one of the kitchen windows into the yard. It was still cold under these gray, leaden, overcast January days, but her youngest would be playing outside the kitchen window, a hundred or more feet back off the same gravel lane that ended at Doswell's place.

There may have been something, he thought, to the charge of drugs being used at these parties of theirs. Perhaps that's what irritated the old man about Alvin Foote. Some of those students, maybe Alvin, had been doing drugs out beyond Euretha's kitchen window, up in the woods, around the barn, out in the fields, with a thousand opportunities in a hundred hidden places.

But Jim knew something else as well: that if the college closed down every event where drugs appeared, no event – dances, athletic contests, maybe some classes – would have been open. Drugs were everywhere. In New York, of course, it was worse. In Gramercy Park, and in the streets around the Village, there was a regular bazaar going on day and night. The question was not whether drugs were brought to Doswell's fall gatherings, but whether their presence there would have represented a significant *increase* in their use. And that was highly unlikely for all kinds of obvious reasons; if anything more likely there would have been a significant decrease.

Sometimes in the evenings Jim talked to Susan by phone. Radhakathri's annoying habit of whining about Colonus and America and Baxter was getting to Chris, and Susan was finding him absurd. There were at least a few days of ice storms that January which kept him, like all sensible people, inside. So it happened that he sometimes spent long evenings in the house with Doswell and Billy. And there in the living room/study with the faint, musty smell of dust-laden books mixed with the fragrance of firewood smoke, and in the light of a single lamp, Jim and the old man would talk of far-ranging matters often spanning centuries, and as current as the day's news. They talked about the civil rights struggles early in the decade. They talked about direct action protests in Greensboro and Birmingham and elsewhere. They talked about revolution: Marx and Lincoln as revolutionaries – or Robert E. Lee, a man, Doswell observed, who'd said slavery was a blight, a monstrous evil, and that secession was a false doctrine; "yet when the shooting starts he takes the side of the secessionists and the slave traders".

They talked about great authors: Kierkegaard and Plato and Hegel (the last two in comparison), Cervantes, and Shakespeare and his *King Lear* (the tyrant within every man). They talked about authors on their Great Books list – and sometimes there was an element in these talks of something Jim feared. What had attracted him to the old man in the first place? His portentous, moral personality? His do-or-die convictions? Could his passion, say, just as easily be described as mania when under pressure? His defiant character as embittered? Relentless? Obsessive? Might he now painfully discover some such complex of truths in close quarters? Some taffy-like, smooth blend of passion/mania, valor/defiance/obsessiveness, and get caught in it?

One night, beer-swishing and squirrel-jowled, the old man spoke with demonic urgency of Descartes, the seventeenth century philosopher whose rationalism, he said, "crash-landed in the twentieth century. No one escapes," he thundered, "the shadow of the evil genius. Do you see? He's not certain that he feels heat, he's not certain that he hears noises! He's only certain that it *seems* that he sees light, that it *seems* he feels heat. *Seems...*" His bull-like shoulders hunched. "And he never shows us the way out...only that I become the creator of truth, creator of all that is – Creator! The truth to be destroyed and reshaped at will...everything! Spun out of the mind – lie at will!" The passion in his voice sounded like that of a man suffering the discovery of a wife's infidelity or a child's death – hysteria; mania-driven.

Jim thought, is this the madness they talk of? That Radhakathri mentioned and reported from Ekanem (Radhakathri's office mate, and once Doswell's)?

But Jim saw more and more that Doswell was a man conversant with texts – or texts less as texts than as voices still living, still speaking, faithful or faithless, quarreled with, combated, ridiculed, praised – texts which became a battleground over which arguments and counter-arguments were hurled amidst ghosts under the dim light of his study lamp. And true, too, there was sometimes a whiskey smell in the room, and it often gave the words an edge. Yet there was never on any of these evenings an absence of reason either; yes, perhaps séances of a sort, conjuring ghosts, but rational ghosts, living-idea ghosts – only one ghost, one subject, one topic which…he never…visited.

On occasions when Jim returned early from classes, and was at the Lewises' watching all those children noisily pouring out of their school bus, he would wonder at the circumstances which had brought Billy to live so fully in two houses – two houses with one orbit. In the early evenings when Doswell would put down his reading glasses and close a book, and then with a lumbering solicitude and sigh begin the nightly rituals for Billy's bedtime, Billy cajoling and negotiating for additional time before lights out, Jim would think about the mother and daughter – an absent wife or just plain woman – and this elderly man who was here alone, father, mother and grandfather rolled into one. Often, at such times, these were little more than passing thoughts taken up by the press of whatever it was Jim might more urgently be attending to. Yet, in the review of the day before drifting off to sleep, such questions – was she alive or dead? When had there last been any woman other than this filial Euretha? Why was he in this unlikely place, this city man who'd graduated from America's premier university, but living in this rural farming community so inconsequential that it went unmarked on every map?

It always came back to this: the absence of the woman so evident in the light of this little boy's large presence, and the void in anyone's inclination to talk of her. And this creating in itself a kind of spectral presence.

It would be that way – this compound of mysteries and this most pressing central mystery, Carole's existence – until one frigid day when Jim had gone to give Euretha emergency help; it was then that the forbidden subject was first broached.

He remembered it as a break following the storm, her sitting at the kitchen table, her hands in her lap, looking thoughtful, something plainly ripening in her mind. As he finished disinfecting one of the calf bottles, which he set top side down on its drying stand, he matter-of-factly asked, "What are you thinking?"

She glanced at him, distracted, as if pained. Then she gazed for a long several moments at the ceiling where overhead on the second floor Billy was getting over a bad case of the flu. "That child up there…" She hesitated, collecting her thoughts. "I was a little girl, maybe eleven, twelve, back when I first laid eyes on his grandfather and his mother, and she was a little girl herself, not much older than he is now…"

There was a long silence then. It was Friday, and Jim's weekend had just begun; he would be seeing Susan later that evening. He could smell the spicy fragrance of Euretha's apple pies baking in one of the ovens. There was no sound other than the crackle of the fire and the hiss of water, near boiling, standing in two pots on top of the wood-burning stove. She'd stopped what she was doing and was looking absently out of the kitchen window to a fence row of leafless trees. Then she turned in his direction, but seemed to be addressing the space between him and the stove as she told of that first day, shortly after the end of the Second World War, and some of the days that followed:

"What a frightened little bird she was – his mother." Her eyes flitted to the ceiling again. "Clutching his big hand that morning! But you know, I don't know who was really holding who, who was leading who that first day. The two of them so pitiful, so lost, both of them, when they came out of nowhere."

She told then about how he'd come to rent part of a "big old house" that "an old colored lady", who lived with her brother, owned at the time. "The house looked a lot better then. Her name was Mrs. Fleet, and they were the half-brother and sister of the president of the college, Dr. Robinson."

Jim leaned forward.

"I remember it so well because it was all so strange. One day they just appeared, the two of them, as if out of nowhere, that little, bird-like girl and that big man..."

He edged closer to be sure that she wouldn't be heard by Billy.

"I was a timid, scraggly little creature and afraid of most new people, but Carole was even smaller than me, and she was the new girl in town. So I wasn't afraid of her. Me and some of my friends we were glad to have a new playmate, but Carole was a loner. Even when you and she was together there was a whole lot of her that was somewhere else." She paused, nodding her head. "Even as a child, I wondered about her. Why was she so strange? With her father, she was so cold and automatic. I'd often think she didn't even like her father. She didn't like anybody, and maybe she liked her father least.

"One night, it was summertime, you could hear the peepers, the crickets, all the night bugs making a regular racket – one of those long, hot nights – windows were open, and there was a full moon. I had been walking back from my friend's house, by Mrs. Fleet's place, and made a shortcut through their property under the big trees. I heard some yelling, terrible yelling, crying-screaming like you'd have thought a girl was being raped or something. It was Carole. Then I peeked into one of the windows and there was Carole and there was Thomas.

"She was screaming things you can't repeat. And she was hitting him. And he was hardly doing anything! Then they were clutching at each other, and she'd picked up something in her hands, something heavy, a tool of some kind, and was trying to hit him. She just a little thing, and you know he is a great big man, and he was a lot younger then, but he had all he could do to hold her.

"I never forgot that night, of course. Mrs. Fleet and her brother never came out of their side of the house. And after that, for a good long time I hated her. And I felt sorry for him."

She sat still for long moments, gazing at the floor. Then she got up, walked over to the sink, filled a pot of water and poured it into one of the two mineral-encrusted pots on the stove, and then into two water glasses on the table, one for herself and one for Jim. She sat back down again, sighing as she did. She said nothing.

Jim said, "She must have been very sick."

If Euretha was anything she was loyal. And discreet. He doubted she'd ever discussed the old man with anyone. In the couple of weeks since he'd stayed with Doswell they'd come to know each other well. He was certain she was speaking as much to inform him as to confirm their unspoken bond, for which he was thankful. He sat, never taking his eyes off Euretha's face, bound to know more. A pan of peeled potatoes, boiling, sat alongside the pots of water on the wood stove at the far end of the room.

"Carole was a very sick girl. Yes. Very strange."

"Could he get help for her?"

She sighed again, drifting in thought. "She had the strangest eyes I've ever seen. Like they were filled with something she couldn't shake. And she hardly laughed. It didn't take long for folks to figure out she wasn't right. Those days folks would send people like Carole away to the lunatic asylum – the colored lunatic asylum – in the capital." She shook her head, grim.

Jim whispered, "Did he?"

"Of course not. He couldn't do that. He took care of her the best he could himself. But as she got older it got worse. It was a few years after they first came to Devon that he bought the place they're living in now. And soon after that she'd started running around. There were so many stories – half of them, I'm sure, untrue, but too many for them all to be lies. Then she left. For a long time he didn't hear from her. Luther and James Jr. were already in school and he was helping James with a loan from the bank and some other things when we were trying to get started – oh, he was like a father to us – but you could tell. Nothing he ever really said, but he was sick with worry about her."

"She just took off? Where?"

"We didn't know. But once he asked James about Philadelphia – he'd heard she was in Philadelphia and James had lived there not long before we were married. And then he went up there but couldn't find her. And when he finally got word later that she was in New York and where she was, he went there too, several times, trying to persuade her to come back, but she didn't until much later, much later after Billy was born."

Not knowing what else to say Jim said, "She finally came back?"

"Yes. And actually stayed for a while, a couple of months or so. And for a while we thought that maybe she'd stay for good and she might change. And I could see in those days the light in his eyes, that he was beginning to think that too. But then everything went bad again. I mean *bad.* Then she left with the boy. And after that

I thought, if this old man lives through this he'll survive anything."

"How did he finally come to stay?" Jim whispered. "I mean, like this?" He cast his eyes at the ceiling.

"When she left that first time he was about two years old." She spoke in a near-whisper. "But he was a real boy. He had energy enough for any woman. She'd gone to living alone for a while, but then, we heard later, with some people – not with very good people, at least that's what we heard. God knows a child can be a burden for a woman like that – maybe she saw the light…

"Anyway, she came back again about half a year later. She didn't stay long. But this time…" Euretha lowered her voice even further and gazed meaningfully once again at the ceiling, "she left him here."

Jim nodded. "Ah…"

"He was of course teaching every day at the college. A man alone. What could he do? How could he care for him? I had my family – six children already. Luther was a teenager. James Jr. was coming on. I stayed home all day anyway. I offered to take care of Billy while he was away during the day."

"He was lucky."

"Oh! He pays me! But even if he didn't, believe me…anyway, I love children. And that little boy is special. And I felt so sorry for him that she couldn't take care of him. I'm sure he was relieved that she'd left him here with us. I know Thomas feared more than ever for her, how reckless she was. Yet he never talked about those things with me at the time. Only later, after the news came – the news that she killed herself in some rooming house up in Philadelphia."

Euretha fell silent. Jim could say nothing. There was only the sound of the fire, the hiss of the water steaming on the wood stove.

After a minute or two she spoke again. "I'll never forget. To the day I die. I'll never forget those dark days. And after all that, he kept saying it was his fault. At the funeral that's all he said. One day when we were alone I said to him, 'Thomas, there's a lot I don't know but there are a few things I do, and I know it wasn't your fault.'

"'No, Retha,' he said, like the weight of the whole earth was weighing on his words, 'I'm not just talking. I'm not just saying it like any other man might say it. You don't know, but *I am to blame*.'"

PART 3

12

Old Friends Come Calling

In the stillness of night, the dark, very early morning hours, Thomas Doswell would hear, beyond the murmur of creaky walls and the faint, far pulse of pressurized water pipes, persistent voices from his long-ago past.

On this particular night there was no mistaking his memory. Even if in these many years some of that past had been forgotten, some of it was etched so sharply into his brain it was as clear as yesterday. And one such memory was of a single night and part of a day that had transpired twenty-five years before.

Carole Doswell was enrolled in the elementary school, the same that the university had run at its founding way back in the nineteenth century, and still ran as part of the mission of its School of Education. In the autumn of 1945 when Thomas still lived in the city, he'd been in the habit of picking Carole up from school and then, depending on whether he was through for the day at his office, he would either leave her at the university library under the watchful eye of the librarian, or, more often, spend the hour or two with Carole at play, or helping her with her homework. Then they would go out and eat somewhere in the East End as dusk began to fall, and from there go home to the small, whitewashed, run-down cottage which he rented, and was only blocks from the campus.

He'd been looking over his shoulder for two years now. In those days, when to be black was a handicap in all things pertaining to white people, in this matter it was a distinct advantage. Negroes in a Negro community were apt to be very tight-lipped when white men inquired about the whereabouts of a fellow Negro. And this, he had often thought later, had no doubt played some part in their having taken so long to catch up with him. Indeed, up until then, in occasional hopeful moments, he'd even thought that his former comrades might never catch up with him, or even – could he dare think so? – that they might give up on him altogether. After all, he'd broken with the Communist Party nearly two years before, and the Party had heard nothing from him for most of that time. Since they knew that it was highly unlikely that he'd go anywhere official with his tales, it might have seemed reasonable that they should simply forget him. But he'd never really believed this. For he knew that, for them, there was no forgetting.

And then recently there'd been signs and a message. The signs might not have been so ominous alone, for they were too tenuous to fully credit. The most significant: folks in the East End neighborhood told about two women – young women – being very interested in knowing *exactly* where he lived. They could easily be students, they could be secretaries or other employees connected to the school – and they could even be women with whom he'd had earlier liaisons and then joined against him! This last his laughing neighbor-acquaintances speculated. And yet they were more likely none of the above, certainly not the last. But then there was the message weeks before. He still had a few friends up north who were, if not in the Party, associated with some who were still in it, or within its orbit, and one of these friends recently passed on oblique bits of odd information which warned, like telltale cries from the forest canopy when the leopard is on the prowl, that his old comrades had caught his scent and would soon be in his vicinity.

He was fully aware he could be wrong. Obviously. He'd been wrong before. But on that day for some reason he'd felt a special uneasiness; something clicked that he couldn't pin down. He felt certain they were near, so he was decisive. Instead of coming home with Carole after dinner, as he would routinely do, he'd told his eleven-year-old daughter he had to work, and that he would leave her in the crowded Baxter library under Miss Jackson's watchful eye.

Alone, he'd gone back to the cottage with a .32 caliber pistol that he'd first purchased years before, and that he carried with him nearly all of the time, on the ready. The door hadn't been forced, everything seemed normal, there was not a sign anywhere of anything out of place, and his next-door neighbors reported nothing amiss. Still, he exercised caution. His neighbors were not the most sharp-eyed of people; often raucous and noisy, drinking seemed to be their main occupation. So he'd entered the house carefully, determined to follow through with his decision to examine it thoroughly before returning with Carole. It was just after slipping an apprehensive hand around the door frame inside his bedroom, and cautiously flipping the light switch while situated partially in the cottage's hallway, that there was a sudden scramble, and two men, one black, one white, fell on him, one of them swinging a blunt object which luckily only struck his shoulder and glanced off his back.

For months he'd been steeling himself for just such a moment! He'd twisted himself around instantly, striking desperately with his elbows first, then with his fists, then kicking violently to escape the hands that clutched at him; at the same instant, he heard from his daughter's room a man's voice yelling that "the girl" was "nowhere". In that moment rage welled up into an explosive fury, as the men screamed to their companion for help.

It was, of course, no more than seconds. Striking the white man a full blow in the face, he'd pulled himself back away from his assailants long enough to draw the gun from his holster, aim it and then shoot and hit one of the men. Near-simultaneously the third from the other room, another black man, appeared in his line of sight. Turning his gun on him, he was within milliseconds of pulling the trigger, but this individual, terror written on his face, suddenly dropped to his knees, pleading for his life. Gesturing frantically with both hands as if to ward off the bullet, he begged Doswell to let him help his "brother" who was lying on the floor, groaning and clutching at his leg. Of course the adrenalin had taken hold and he was feeling, amidst the fury and exhilaration, both a godlike generosity and the desire for a humiliating rout.

But it was not over. Threatening, in a convulsed fury, that he would kill them if he saw them again anywhere, the one leaning heavily on the other, they staggered out, leaving the white man who, yelling in a staccato Eastern European accent that they were "dirty, yellow cowards", jumped suddenly into action, striking Doswell's gun hand with the blunt object, causing him to drop the weapon, the force of the blow making it fly to the opposite side of the room.

There ensued a fierce second struggle. Crashing against the furniture – a small desk, chairs broken, lamp shattered – Doswell, a lot younger then, and desperate, just barely overcame his assailant. When it was over, this individual, whom he did not personally recognize but was sure was a Party goon, lay sprawled motionless across the floor.

The following day's evening edition of the *News-Herald* would report a foreign white man that had been mugged and found near a mailbox in one of the seedier sections of the East End. It was this incident that triggered Doswell and his daughter Carole's move in the night from the East End to Devon twenty-five years before.

It does not take a seer, or for that matter a physician, to see that an elderly man who is careless about drinking, suffers from insomnia, is careless about his weight, and lives a mostly sedentary existence, faces a greater risk from stroke or heart attack than most. A firm and loving wife might have persuaded Thomas, in this late autumn of his life, to be careful – or at least by her mere presence regulate his routines. But there was no such person, and Doswell had this not unwelcoming sense of death despite understandable anxieties over Billy. So burdened by the bone-weariness, there was an ever-renewed conscious determination that he should live for the sake of Billy, who had no blood relative other than himself. And there was something else too: a lifelong defiance which refused surrender, the pure will to endure.

Devon was a friendly place. He felt from these people in this little rural community, hardly more than a dusty crossroad in the Carolina Piedmont, much of the same kind of affection he'd felt from folks on the South Side of Chicago. And he knew the devotion of the Lewises. Yet he was alone. He was capable of talking the talk of Devon: appreciating a comic story about a neighbor, relating a tale or two inspired by the woods, the barnyard, or the fields; but he suffered an isolation few recluses know.

For despite many pleasant moments that would come with being among these unassuming neighbors of his, he could no more speak his mind among them than he could speak Attic Greek and expect to be understood. Jim had asked the old man, as others had on occasion, why had he chosen this exile? The younger man was satisfied with Doswell's assurance that he was fond of country living; and yet, while there was truth to this, it was hardly the whole truth, and while Mrs. Lewis knew more than anybody else, she barely knew anything.

It was more than his education, as immensely disproportionate as it was to their bare literacy, that set him apart from his neighbors in Devon. His life's experiences set him apart from everyone – even more from the people he knew in Colonus, and most of all, from those he knew at the university. Some of these humble people living on the edge in Devon, leading harassed lives of their own, might have understood something of what it was to be a fugitive. On the other hand, what could those at the school understand, amidst their middle-class self-complacency, their academic shop talk, about having to gather your possessions and run in the middle of the night from an enemy intent on annihilating you?

It would not have been unthinkable had the hunters been night riders hidden inside pointy hoods and behind white sheets, or had he been harried by racist local law enforcement officials. Such situations would have called for collective support for the victim, at least moral support. But what of this seemingly normal man in this seemingly normal time being pursued by an altogether different band of human hunters? Indeed, for some at the school, his tale of that one night, had he ever told it, would have been worse than unthinkable. Once the laughing died down from the melodramatic spy-story absurdity of such a tale, should these same individuals have begun to take him seriously, then rather than supporting him, a growing anger would have begun to flow over into their daily and familiar dealings with him. For to charge that the American Communist Party was an arm of the Soviet government, and that it was in the business of making off with and murdering people – this they would have viewed not only as absurd, but more, outrageous and contemptible.

Indeed, so thoroughly hemmed in was Doswell by the isolation of his living knowledge that on occasions he had fantasized – in a kind of bizarre reversal of paranoia – whether what he knew to be true actually *was* true! If what he'd lived he *actually* could have lived and not dreamed!

Tonight this ordinarily peaceful man thought not only of that furious battle, years before. He thought of his wife, long dead; he thought of Carole, in her childish innocence and trust, waiting for him that night in the library. In waves he thought of his parents, and of his early days at Harvard and in Moscow. Then he thought of Billy, and this young man sleeping soundly and alone in the room next to Billy's.

For years Doswell had stayed up through nights just like this, catching sleep when he could; and through those earlier years as sentinel he'd reinforced the habit of his insomnia. He'd stopped thinking of the future in the years since. But this thought had been with him throughout, even before he'd broken with the Party: the thought that *they* are fools. *All* of them. How can you be heard by those who refuse to listen, determined to repeat over and over again the same fatal errors? People who, willy-nilly, join forces with those others and seek to destroy anyone who disturbs their peaceful sleep?

After that long-ago night he'd gone on the offensive. He decided then that he would do what he could do. He would help those – anyone – who stood firm, convinced he could never win the bigger war but determined to fight it anyway; hoping at least to leave a legacy, some shard, some sign for the future amidst the refuse – and hopefully, perhaps, to purchase precious time for his own. But in all his pessimism about the future, he had not then guessed with a sufficient degree of pessimism the hopelessness of his struggle. He'd chosen to act as one who never admits defeat. But the bare fact was that his own had not survived, except for Billy. And as for the sign, the shard amidst the refuse, it seemed there was only refuse. And he'd thought about all of this incessantly following Carole's suicide, the despair redoubled in its burden by the troubles of these last few harrying years fighting Montbanc's new, very political regime at the university.

Over the last couple of months, however, there was something that lit up the darkness. And it couldn't be put any more succinctly than to say it had its source in those two young men. There was Vincent, vigorous, always on the move, restless, full of turmoil yet a pure flame; full of driving energy and seeking an alignment with him, even if in some misbegotten project of Montbanc's and his own. And then this boy upstairs, so melancholy and dangerously odd – at least to himself, talking of throwing himself off a mountain! For a while he didn't know what to think: white people have this strange way of talking to black people, telling them things they wouldn't dream of telling their own kind. Sometimes it's experimental, sometimes it's confessional. Sometimes merely crazy.

He thought of the passionate and earnest talk that Vincent so broadly ridiculed in the white boy, but which he had happily engaged him in from the beginning. For talk about matters which, for many others, would have been mere abstractions bandied about – intellectuals' playthings, ideas and words, solemnly frivolous – was not just a game with scores to be kept for Jim or himself, but a life-and-death quest after an elusive quarry.

With Jim's oblique remarks about life in New York and growing up in the Bronx, Doswell read between the lines. When he was a boy he thought all white folks led charmed lives. To be white was never to be caught out in the rain; and if you were, the raindrops miraculously changed their course to avoid striking you. Since then, he'd learned the rain struck.

Jim Allan reminded him of a different set of white boys. When he'd first arrived at Harvard fifty years before, he'd begun by noticing them riding in and out on the city's public conveyances. They were the same white faces mostly from older, slummier parts of the city where he and they both resided. They were from Eastern and Southern Europe, mostly, and they did not appear to him, this black boy who was fastidious about his appearance, who daily knotted a tie and ironed his pants, like they were very congenial. Some of them were among the least fashionable and most shabbily dressed of Harvard's students. But these individuals, comrades of the brown bag, waxed paper and baloney sandwiches, very oddly disconcerting initially because of their appearance as well as their rudeness, were, many of them, as fervent in their friendships as they were in their intellectual interests. They would also, in time, become his teachers, and he theirs.

They were different from Jim Allan, to be sure. Unlike Allan, they were immigrants, or first-generation children of immigrants. In those long-ago years they knew more about modern European history and literature than Allan certainly did. They also understood the literature of social protest better than he did then.

From a long, thin, ascetic Italian born in Sardinia, who would in time become a Jesuit priest, he'd heard the story of the southern Italian peasants' exploitation at the hands of big landowners, which Ignazio Silone would write about years later. From him he first learned about Antonio Gramsci, the leader of the Italian Communist Party who'd later be jailed by Mussolini, and who did not believe that the revolution should wage war against clergy, educators or others who were in daily contact with the masses. From him, he learned an alternative theory of the revolution: that it should win the masses over by staging a peaceful, gradualist, invisible revolt from the ground up.

Then from another, whose parents had come from a *shtetl* in Russian Poland, and who years later, as a distinguished scholar, would help him to get a summer job in Chicago, he became familiar with Isaac Babel and Gorky and Kafka, and the ideas and activities of the nineteenth-century Russian anarchists Bakunin, Kropotkin, and others.

He asked himself why Jim Allan reminded him of these, and a few other like-minded individuals, and the answer came back: because he had the same hungry, utterly serious need for truth that he'd seen in those young men. In talking with Jim he had the curious sensation of resuming a conversation that had begun half a century before. And it sometimes made him impatient that he had in the interim grown older and wiser, and his companion, deadly earnest as he was, had not.

One night Jim came back from an evening spent with Susan, Radhakathri and Chris Khalaf. On Radhakathri's invitation the four of them had gone to hear a talk given by Lillian Hellman, the famous playwright and author. Jim remembered

Radhakathri telling him Hellman was well known for her political commitments. She'd been on the blacklists in the early '50s. Her longtime lover, Dashiell Hammett, had gone to jail during that period, and she'd been uncooperative on being questioned before the House Committee on Un-American Activities, refusing to name names. She was also clearly something of a heroine among feminists.

The subject of her talk, *Scoundrel Times*, was the title of a book she was working on about the early McCarthyite period. But the presentation was more about President Nixon than Joseph McCarthy. Hatred for Nixon, and of course his Administration, was at its peak. Spiro Agnew had made his famous "nattering nabobs of negativism" speech, which only further infuriated people who'd never liked Nixon. Afterwards, for reasons having to do more with personal matters which had been evolving over time between Radhakathri and Chris than with political differences (Chris had always shown herself to be no more interested in politics than Susan), the two had a quarrel which centered on Hellman's argument that Nixon had started the McCarthyite witch hunts, causing the "half-drunk McCarthy" to "ape Nixon" in his earlier role as Congressional inquisitor. Hellman said it was he more than anyone who'd begun a "feeding frenzy" made up of politicians, the press, right-wing religious zealots, and assorted "kooks and crazies" that would lead to many going to jail, and thousands – like Hellman herself – to be legally harassed and persecuted over the next decade on vague charges of Communist conspiracy and disloyalty.

As they left the event and talked about it (Radhakathri having insisted on hearing the women's opinions), Susan made some vaguely favorable but essentially noncommittal comments intended to satisfy Radhakathri. But Chris surprised all, maintaining defiantly that she didn't like Hellman, that she sounded like a liar; that "those people would believe any lies she told". It wasn't clear what she thought were lies, or why she thought Hellman was lying. She could give no sustained reason for her opinion; untypically, however, she was adamant. Neither Jim nor Susan had ever known her to be a squabbler; she was not meek but she was old-fashioned in her belief that there are things about which men know best, and things about which women know best – and politics were hardly among the latter, especially with a man whose profession *was* politics! What's more, Radhakathri had had a hand in putting on the event as part of a joint committee of Political Science and History professors from both the Baxter and CSU faculties, and he was teaching a course on the subject. Chris' boldness was therefore profound.

Not surprisingly, Radhakathri was exuberantly vocal in his admiration of Hellman, and obviously expected nothing different from Chris, Jim and Susan. So the situation was a shocker for him. But even Jim and Susan, who'd seen it coming for weeks, were surprised at the way Chris had picked her fight.

"But my dear lady," Radhakathri said, shaken by this turn of events, "I certainly do value your opinions. This is why I asked you for them. But I do not understand. This is all a matter of record. No one disputes the facts."

"I don't care, Ramatha. I didn't like her. I'm sure the President of the United States would dispute her facts."

Jim told the story to Doswell in all its quirky detail, curious most of all for his opinion of Hellman's remarks. Of course he knew the general tenor of his mind on such things, and though he felt a strong bond of shared understanding on broad matters, he'd never been able to bring himself to go so far as the old man in many of the more practical details.

Doswell's response in this instance couldn't have been more concise. "The Political Science professor with the PhD gets an F. The receptionist with the associate degree from the junior college gets an A."

Jim laughed loud, a rare, belly-heaving laugh, for he liked Chris more than he did Radhakathri. And this spoke also to his long-held conviction that Chris had a whole lot more horse sense than her PhD-endowed Far Eastern boyfriend. Still, the disparity in the 'grades' was considerable, and he wasn't of the opinion himself that Radhakathri deserved an actual so-called F, or that Chris deserved a full A; and so he said after the laughter died down, "You mean there wasn't anything Hellman said that was true?"

Doswell chuckled. "Ask the young lady. She seems to understand, and can give both of you a lesson."

"Oh, come on!"

"Some truth is necessary, of course, when you are telling a big lie."

But amidst all the good humor the old man seemed to be debating with himself too. There followed a few seconds of thoughtful silence, followed by his rolling his bull-like bulk decisively up out of his couch. He stepped over to a corner of the room, and turned on an overhead lamp. His broad back was to Jim and the light fell over his large, balding ebony head as he rifled in a half-crouch through a pile of newspapers. After a couple of minutes of looking he pulled out a copy of *The State*, the Columbia, South Carolina newspaper. He opened and folded it, and then handed it to the young man, the obituary page face up.

Jim looked at him, puzzled. "What do you want me to do with this?" he asked, once again amused by this eccentric turn.

"I want you to read it, obviously." He pointed to one of the obituaries.

Jim thought it immensely strange, but he readily complied.

Heading the obituary was the picture of a dowdy, middle-aged white lady whose photograph, judging from the hairstyle and from the woman's age at death, had to have been taken some thirty-odd years before. The subject could have been Jim's grandmother, for the year given for her birth was 1882, the same as his much-loved maternal grandmother's, and he would always remember it for this reason. The subject was an eminently respectable local portrait painter who'd graduated from one of the nearby colleges, studied art in New York for a few years, and then returned several years later to lead a perfectly normal life in her hometown, dying there in the spring of 1969.

When Jim was finished he thought this had to be some kind of very strange joke, and he continued to look blankly at Doswell, smiling, and finally said, "Well, what's the punch line?"

He let what Jim had read sink in and then he said, "This little old lady was for many years a member of the Communist Party, and for several years she was in the Underground, engaged in wide-ranging clandestine activity, including espionage, for the Soviet Union. You would have been surprised to have found that in this obituary, wouldn't you? In fact you find what I'm telling you now incredible, maybe embarrassing, don't you?"

Jim's instant look was indeed incredulous, but it was wholly reflexive.

If a time had to be marked when they bridged the gap from the more general philosophic, literary and academic talk to personal and to political talk, it was that day more than any other. At least, Jim clearly remembered Doswell telling his stories after that: telling him not only about how he had come to join the Party, but about his recruitment into the Underground, his life in Moscow and in Erfurt, Germany in the early '30s, and his role in the textile strike which began in Passaic, New Jersey in 1926, and spread like wildfire throughout the East Coast textile region.

And it was also some time after that that Doswell spoke of secret matters he'd never spoken to anyone about before. In all of this there was the sense, then, but which would deepen in Jim in succeeding, more mature years, of an urgency – the urgent need to redeem the past, to bequeath this understanding won at so high a price, that what he'd learned should not be annihilated with his death.

13

Vincent Meets Gwen Randolph

Vincent's affair with Blissie Carter was losing its tang. There was the novelty of her being white, but novelties by their nature wear off. Then there was the fact that she was always pestering him about taking her to the Black Derby. He knew this was invested with symbolic racial meaning, a bid to becoming an honorary soul sister, but this too contributed to his growing boredom. And there was the annoying habit she had of preaching to him.

And then it happened: Gwen Randolph entered his life. Vincent first met Gwen at the Burwell estate. He'd gone down to Laurel Hill with Blissie, and following their usual habit, while Blissie was socializing in what was called the Great Hall, chitchatting with her usual coterie of conspirators, he wandered off on his own. Along the upper gallery of the hall, amidst the church-like interior vaulting and stone reliefs and sculptures, he'd suddenly spotted her, this gorgeous daughter of the Nile. Was she some wondrous hallucination amidst all the rich tapestry, portraiture and sculpture? Or one more treasure the Burwells had collected? No. She was flesh and blood. He was riven. And she was alone! But he was sure it couldn't be for long. Just then she moved into one of the big side rooms. After a few moments of frantic search he discovered her in a corner between the staircase landing and what they called the Blue Room. (Where, by coincidence, he'd first met his ivory-alabaster Blissie – quite a lucky place, that Blue Room!) There she was, studying some odd item of Renaissance art that he'd long thought belonged more appropriately in a museum somewhere.

"Manage to make off with that and you won't have to work another day in your life," he said teasingly by way of introducing himself. After giving him a quick, disapproving glance which read him in an instant, she raised her eyebrows ever so slightly, and went back to studying the picture. It wasn't an ideal situation. Blissie could join them at any moment, and put an end to the game right then and there. This required finesse. Vincent smiled handsomely, and said how pleased he was to see "a sister" for once at Laurel Hill. This time she turned to him ever so slowly, deadpan, a laughing glimmer in her eyes.

Her glance took on a conspiratorial look, and said something like: and what are *you* doing here? That was when he volunteered his name and began to tell her that he was with Baxter, that he'd come to Colonus from New York only recently, that he had few friends in the city, and that he wondered if she might be his friend.

The charm that he was quite capable of turning on in megawatts had broken through the initially icy exterior, and she came around to telling him a few things about herself: the fact that she lived with her mother and stepfather in one of the newer subdivisions outside Colonus; that she was studying psychology in the graduate school of the state university; that she liked playing tennis; and she told him her name. By the time her escort, a white professor of hers from the graduate school, appeared, prudence dictated he say his goodbyes (Blissie was, after all, in the vicinity). Later that night he telephoned Gwen from his hotel room. Those were the days when he was over in Chicago and to New York and out west, and it was all he could do to juggle his pressing concerns for his brother and his circuitous plans for the upcoming Alliance convention, not to mention his regular teaching duties. So it was another week before he called her again.

When he did on this occasion she was aloof, noncommittal, different from that first telephone call. He tried explaining what he could about his tight schedule, but he was shut out. He wondered if her coolness might be in response to something more than his failure to follow up sooner – that she might know about Blissie. And his suspicion about Blissie was confirmed when she stood him up on their first date at a noisy CSU student hangout where she'd agreed to meet him. It was obvious that something had happened. It was then, however, that his luck changed, for the long-awaited, long-anticipated Alliance convention came to town.

Months before Vincent had been assigned as a workshop leader, routine enough not to be affected by his changed situation within the Alliance. Every participating delegate and alternate delegate was assigned a workshop, meeting in assigned classrooms throughout the campus following the major addresses. The object was to discuss issues around themes the speakers raised. It so happened that in the first such meeting Vincent made a very surprising discovery. For when, following the welcoming address, he went to his assigned room for the workshop, there was Gwen's lovely, thoughtful – and startled – countenance. Thus providence took its cue from fantasy; that is, the incredible good luck of leading just that particular group with Gwen as a part of it, allowing him, altogether without guile, to radiate his many charming attributes as penetrative, analytical thinker, visionary and grand leader. He could capture Gwen's heart without trying – more significantly *because* he wasn't trying. For as Vincent thought about it later, whenever a woman like sweet Gwen, who is bright, her own person, and aware of men's wily ways, comes to understand a man is making a play for her, well, she can be very, very wary, especially where, as in this case, there are complicating factors. But this time he was just being his naturally beautiful self, like before the Fall, with no design on the fruit of the Tree of Knowledge of Good and Evil; yet the fruit was there, ready to be plucked.

*

So after that first session and then the several succeeding ones, Gwen and he began seeing each other. What's more, he knew Blissie knew this. And she had no objections! At that time she was active with visits of her own to Washington and New York with the political action initiatives of a reproductive rights organization that was engaged in "hardcore planning for the future". So she patted him on the cheek; then he kissed her passionately, feeling slightly deflected at her seeming indifference to his affair, and yet pleased at the prospect of having the best of both worlds.

The best of both worlds: but what about Gwen and *her* concerns about Blissie? When after those first workshop sessions they drifted off together for a Coke and a sandwich at a nearby diner, and she got around to asking about "the lady" he'd been seeing, he told her something very close to the truth. He said Blissie and he had been out together some, but it was "never anything very serious". This was true, of course; it wasn't very serious to him, but what did 'serious' mean for Gwen? And what might it have meant for Blissie? But to the extent that he gave this any real thought afterwards, he knew that Blissie and he were only a matter of time; that he was merely waiting for the right moment.

As for the meaning of this word 'serious' as applied to Gwen? He made accommodations for her that he never had with any other woman. She might say, "I have to be back early tonight, Vincent, Mom is expecting me for dinner", and he didn't instantly complain. Or, "No, I can't go out Saturday, my Aunt Lucy from Boston is visiting." She found it natural to ruin a great weekend night to be with her favorite aunt, and he didn't drop her then and there! And like so many attractive women she liked to dance; though he was never much for dancing and had never before accommodated his dates in this regard, he made clumsy contributions to this part of the package deal.

When they were together, though it wasn't always peaceful, it was never boring.

She talked a good political talk too; she instantly understood his purposes in the recent business of trying to bring Doswell into the convention. She'd never personally met the President but she quickly understood what he was like – "Oh, I know exactly the type!" she said. No, she wasn't surprised at his autocratic ways – "unfortunately there are too many like him!" And she shared his annoyance at the condescensions of white people.

He even thought enough of her to take her on a pilgrimage to meet Doswell. Afterwards she said, "I really do love him, Vincent – I can feel his intensity, the force of his personality, and his intelligence."

"I think you are more taken with him than you are with me."

"Oh, of course! I told you I love him! I might continue to go out with you so I can see him more."

"Ah, well, great! That's encouraging news!"

The trouble with exchanges like these was that Vincent feared Gwen wasn't entirely kidding.

Doswell liked her as well. She was, amidst the spritely warmth, the wrangling obstinacies and contentiousness, a very special woman.

But Blissie too was special, for Blissie was not only aware of Gwen, she was downright agreeable. How many women would have reacted that way? The same night he met Gwen, later in Blissie's bedroom, at an unlikely moment, Blissie whispered into his ear with a giggle, "Who, Vincent, was that black princess you paid so much attention to when you thought I wasn't looking?"

That night, she began pestering him about introducing her to "the goddess". This was entirely new: two women, one of whom was willing to share her man. It brought a great sense of relief – more, it was exciting. Was she hinting at a threesome? His supercharged, red-hot brain worked overtime. Were there other women besides Gwen that would fit her profile? But it also introduced doubts and confusions, making a simple matter complicated. Did he matter so little to Blissie? Or was this some labyrinthian woman's strategy that had nothing to do with his lascivious fantasies? All of this checked thoughts of breaking with Blissie. The perplexities gave rise to indecisiveness. There just seemed to be no point to it. And there was this, too: what if Blissie introduced herself to "the princess", throwing a monkey wrench into his affair with Gwen? He warned her that any "rational" approach to Gwen would sink everything for him. Furthermore, he stressed that he would view such a step as a very unfriendly act. This made her mad enough to trigger sermons.

"You want to love, Vincent, but I don't think you know how!" she told him late one night, in a voice pitched in high frequencies, as close to a quarrel as they ever came. "Love is spiritual, it's giving – you don't exclude, you include! You should want to share more and more, not to possess, to control."

Once again, his red-hot brain went overtime. Blissie and Gwen were both strong women, inclined at a moment's notice to straighten him out, but they were different too: Gwen's scoldings were meant for him alone, and he had to admit they sometimes hit the mark. Whereas Blissie's preaching was aimed obliquely, as much, he imagined, at his whole gender as at him.

"You know, Vincent, I need only one special person at a time," she said on another night, more subdued, in a preachy voice. "Maybe men are different in that way, I don't know." She grew more thoughtful, brushing her hair and looking at herself in her full-length mirror. "But I also think it's essential that you grow with the discovery of new personalities. Martin Buber says, *All real living is meeting.* I think that is *so* true."

There is another quote: *Hell hath no fury like a woman scorned.* But there was no fury. Though it could certainly be infuriating – and sometimes tantalizing.

In the meantime, when Vincent was with Gwen – and he was most of his free moments, both out of choice and Blissie's increased involvement with her own Washington-based politics – Blissie slipped from his mind.

One day Gwen and he were sitting in the Jolly Roger where they often met, and she was – what temerity! – playing a little game she called I'm Your Secretary: merrily pulling out memoranda and official communications he routinely stuffed into his briefcase after emptying his mailbox at school and then, later, with little more than a glimpse, emptied yet again into the first wastebasket he saw.

She was reading them aloud, teasingly poking him from across the table to get his attention, when suddenly something caught her eye. She paused significantly; after a moment his finely tuned ear caught a little trill of surprise as she murmured under her breath, "*This* is interesting!" She fell into silence, brows furrowed, intent on what she was reading.

After a while, his interest piqued, he said, "Damn it, what do you have there?"

She waved a sheaf of mimeographed sheets, two or three pages of blurry print on both sides, stapled together in the manner common to 'underground' student papers. The heading on the top sheet was in bold capital letters: THE LIBERATOR, with some crude scrollwork at each side. It was an article written, not surprisingly, by a Baxter student – and yet, also quite surprising. For while Baxter was no hotbed of student rebellion, this was an instance of that most common of student documents – a manifesto of insurgency. *LIFE* magazine, in those years an emblem of everything current in the nation's broad culture, only that month in a cover story, strewn with appropriate award-winning photography celebrating youth and dedicated to the new decade, had declared that being young was right. Everybody wanted to be young, and youth could now rightly claim superior moral qualities. This was a theme, of course, fully in step with the spirit of the Alliance, reflected in the pronouncements of Baxter's leaders; yet despite the swirl of enthusiasm and encomia to the superior wisdom of youth, actual student expressions of public dissent at Baxter amounted until now to nothing more than impotent grumblings. This exasperated Vincent. If there was ever a place where the exuberant idealism, the insurrectionary energy of youth was called for, Baxter was the place. But no, Baxter remained a bastion of peace and tranquility, and there was a ready explanation at its core: President Ronald Alfonse Montbanc. Ronny was celebrated everywhere as "one who could be trusted"; he was "a spearhead of reform"; he was "a man of the future".

The adulation was not always in words, either; words can often sound so trite. So there was Chuck Peter, Visiting Professor of Fine Art, in plaid work shirt and leather apron, who'd been working for weeks on a sculpture that promised to capture in welded scraps of junkyard steel, iron and abstract design the spirit of the Alliance movement, its heart and soul.

A regular chorus it was: these hen-squawks and mouse-squeaks which seemed to pre-empt any student dissent. But suddenly, from out of the gallery, from the standing-room-only section came this outrageous, this glorious *hoooooot!* This grand, protracted *hisssssssss!* Vincent thrilled to the spectacle of Ronald finally becoming the object of a well-aimed assault, launched by one of those selfsame exalted voices of reform!

Of course, it couldn't compare to what happened at CSU on the other side of town. Gwen reported that there, its president had been 'stoned' with marshmallows when on one occasion he'd allowed himself a timid peek from behind his office door. Ronald suffered no such airborne indignities. But yes, he was struck.

The article dared to say that the Alliance convention was a *PR extravaganza that might have been at least a partial success if there had been dissident voices!* (Was this a reference to Doswell's absence?) It also said that Baxter was at every turn, in its dorms, in its course offerings, everywhere, full of *bureaucratic red tape.* True, not earthshaking criticism, but tied to an attack on one of Montbanc's pet projects, his personally touted Baxter Plan of Education, as *a fraud and a gimmick*, it was an unheard of strike at this up-until-now acclaimed fount of universal wisdom.

So after breathing a giddy "whew", Gwen put the paper down, and eyeing Vincent with a mock scowl and barely concealed grin, said brightly, "You have anything to do with this?" And right she was in asking, for, while the piece had about it the tone of a collegiate effort, it was not badly written; it tickled the ribs and lifted the spirit. It was certainly not your typically club-footed Baxter writing project. What's more, it had some of the same sarcastically critical themes, and even a word or two Gwen recalled hearing from Vincent's own lips. (*Emperor Mountebank!*)

"Who's the author?" Vincent asked, his brightly smiling curiosity betraying itself to Gwen as having someone in mind.

She returned to the page. "It says, *Willi... Wade...* W-A-D-E."

He nodded, grinning, and as the seconds ticked past he started laughing, a rumble that started from deep down in his belly. For he was indeed familiar with the dark-skinned, slightly pock-faced student that came to mind with the name. He remembered him as part of a delegation of half a dozen students who'd come to him immediately after the convention. Willi seemed older than the rest of them by a few years. He wasn't the most voluble in his complaints about the administration and what they perceived as the failings of the recent Alliance convention. But later he told Vincent that he wanted to write articles outlining some criticisms he had of Baxter for the *News-Herald.* Vincent advised against this, but he also remembered not taking him too seriously either – a Baxter student writing something really effective? Publishable anywhere? He doubted it.

He said, "There's always a need for fireworks. Why don't you start an underground rag with some of your friends? Maybe it won't make you many friends, but it won't be viewed as a betrayal." He thought he'd never hear anything more about it; that it would never get off the ground.

Now as he gazed on that lovely vision sitting opposite him, into her bright, molasses-brown, large, laughing eyes, he confessed to his conversation with Willi Wade weeks before, and how wrong he was about his prospects as a writer.

"Well, are you planning to get started early running for political office?" she said teasingly, in what she perceived as a long-winded evasion.

"I didn't have anything to do with writing that article, but I wouldn't be unhappy if someone thought I did."

"You mean," she pressed, by way of picking up the paper and searching the article again, "that you didn't have *anything* to do with this business about... how did he phrase it?" She looked through the lines. "*Sometimes one feels that our dear U is less a modern American university and more an ancient Middle Eastern monarchy governed by a god-king or emperor whose word is divine writ.*"

Vincent laughed once again, a real, tummy-caving, chest-heaving laughter. Gwen had heard his description of the President on several occasions. It certainly sounded suspicious to her. It sounded suspicious to him! But he knew he'd never spoken such words to Willi Wade. And this was all the more satisfying, vindicating so thoroughly his own long-held view of the man.

14

We Will Achieve America in Our Lifetime

Weeks earlier at the convention, among those in the bleachers looking down among the row after row of fold-out chairs seating delegates from far and wide on the floor of Tenner Gymnasium, was an unexpected onlooker. Sitting unnoticed, Thomas Doswell would daily take in much of the day's events: listening not only to the often facile, importuning, even eloquent voices from the dais, but also voices from the past. It so reminded him of a similar gathering under similar auspices, with similar purposes, nearly fifty years before, that as he leaned an elbow to his knee, his palm to his chin, heaving a sigh, he could hear those other voices come to him on a long-ago, wind-driven, brutally cold Chicago night on the South Side.

"*...during the closing year of the first quarter of the twentieth century, we note with pride the worldwide stirring of the darker races...*"

General mayhem in that stuffy, smoke-filled high school auditorium.

They had brought together that gathering much as the Alliance convention had been called together: all the months in preparation, the grand hopes, the maneuvering behind the scenes, the backing and filling, political and personal quarrels over delegates that were to give voice to the soul of black America. Yes, then, too, they were to be a loosely confederated umbrella organization that would – at least on broad issues – be able to speak with one voice in the face of racist America. Planning sessions had begun a year before, and James Weldon Johnson of the NAACP, William Trotter, editor of the *Boston Guardian*, and Howard University Dean Kelly Miller had been instrumental in bringing that earlier assembly to fruition. Over the following months maneuvering took place over who and what organization representing portions of black America should have a place at the gathering.

At the opening sessions of the assembly, the founder of the African Blood Brotherhood reminded the many moderates attending that they should form "a united front on the interests of the race".

Dean Miller, one of those moderates, a man skeptical of the Communists' intentions, chaired the sessions made up of delegates from major organizations of the time: the NAACP, the National Negro Business League, the Urban League, the editors of major Afro-American newspapers, professors and teachers. Doswell, then as now, was an observer, not a delegate. Attached to no one, he was in his final year at Harvard. He had come alone in search of connections, possible contacts among men and women like himself, fired by the same revolutionary fervor that he felt. In his initial reaction he'd been sorely disappointed. On the school auditorium's walls were the patriotic and soberly stern likenesses of George Washington and Abraham Lincoln, and a large, unfurled American flag. Swirling about him were the cream – or the café au lait – of America's Negro bourgeoisie; the babble of businessmen, ministers, teachers, fraternity boys and sorority girls from Howard and Wilberforce, Morehouse, Spelman and elsewhere. In a few years he would come to view gatherings like these as little more than curious analogues for modern man to the rain dances primitive men once performed to magically bring on the life-giving waters; but then he still believed in magic.

He remembered even the smell, not unlike Baxter's Tenner Gymnasium, the accumulated odor of years of adolescent sweat-filled exercises and sporting events, only partially concealed by the vigorous use of strong, institutional cleaning solvents. And he remembered now the face, a surprising resemblance to the Black Muslims' Elijah Muhammed, with that slightly oriental cast to his eyes, which reminded him of a Buddhist monk when later he shaved his head. He remembered this not from that first night of the All Race Congress but out on South Side Chicago streets when Lovett Fort-Whiteman returned from his first journey to the Soviet Union decked out in a veritable rainbow, his silk *rabochka* that came to his knees.

"This is the way they deck themselves out in the land of the future!" he would say. "In the gay colors of the people, the colors of the rainbow, Russia's sturdy peasantry!"

Alone, he was like a later generation that discovered Africa and dressed African; he'd discovered working class Marxism in Russia and dressed Russian. Out on the streets of the South Side or on Lenox and Amsterdam Avenues in Harlem, he'd cut a fantastic figure in his peasant-style outfits, his high leather boots and fur hat. He appeared – as many of the comrades put it, some admiringly, a few scoffing – like a regular black Cossack cruising the streets of urban America.

Ten years Doswell's senior, Lovett Fort-Whiteman was a member of the Workers Party delegation – or was it African Blood Brotherhood? No matter. The Congress had invited Fort-Whiteman and the other laborites into this founding convention and they'd wasted little time in trying to move it in the direction of 'labor'.

"The problem of interracial cooperation has been discussed now from the standpoint of the YMCA and the church and every other point of view but that of labor! Although the Negro race is preeminently a labor group and its industrial welfare is bound up with the interracial cooperation of white workers, four days have gone by and labor has been ignored! We demand that the greatest of all issues before the Negro race be given attention!" Fort-Whiteman shouted, startling many in that till-then languid audience.

"You're out of order!" Dean Miller shouted back.

Otto Huiswood, a man so light-skinned he'd later be accused of being white by Marcus Garvey, rose confidently, demanding to be heard. Originally from Surinam, one of the members of the African Blood Brotherhood, he repeated his demand. The chairman tried vainly to shut him up but Huiswood couldn't be stopped: "I see that labor is an outcast here as it is outside."

The audience was applauding.

Again, Huiswood: "Dean Miller, you have been sabotaging this convention from the first day. You promised labor a hearing before the convention because it was the most important issue. We demand a hearing. Ninety-five per cent of the members of our race are workingmen!"

There was a burst of handclapping and an elderly clergyman cried out, "Ninety-five per cent? Better say ninety-eight."

Dean Miller was gaveling again and saying (his voice thinning with fatigue) that Huiswood was out of order, but others from the Brotherhood and the Workers Party were popping up now, demanding the right of labor to be heard.

Fort-Whiteman was among them, saying loudly that a labor discussion was urgent: "Negro girls are being hired in the garment industry not because the employer is favoring the race, but because they are unorganized and they can be easily exploited."

Miller, his face frozen, responding to audience sentiment and the hammer blows of the Party activists, finally agreed to turn the meeting over to a "labor discussion".

No one person in his life in those days would be instrumental in bringing him into the Party, but meeting Fort-Whiteman and Otto Huiswood and some of the others at that moment made it much easier. At a time when he was contemplating joining the Party, and not knowing a single person like himself who'd already done so, this bleak fact had given him reason for pause. Now at the All Race Congress, disheartened at first by what he'd viewed as the usually compromising stance of people with a stake in the racial status quo, he'd come upon these wild men, these – in the expression young people employed fifty years later – *in-your-face* African Party men, and he at once recognized in others his own inner passion.

It would not be long before he saw beyond the public personas of these Party men too. He would see in not a few of them burning personal ambitions, personal jealousies and rivalries, and yes, the Uncle Tom's anxiety to do the white man's bidding; and all of this he would put down to the reality of human foibles found everywhere. But on that day he found only the vitality, the comradeship, the affability of like-minded men pursuing a common and exalted cause, making all those other gray and boring time-servers around them seem even more irrelevant and inconsequential.

Huiswood was one he talked with that day. A senior leader of the movement, his Dutch-West Indian accent very much in evidence, still he had full command of his adopted tongue. A man of great vigor, and some stiffness, but in his presence you were aware of clear purpose.

And then there was Fort-Whiteman: an affable, vitally sociable man, he took an instantaneous interest in his younger cohort. It was he more than anyone that the young Doswell talked with after sessions, talked with about Harvard, about Baxter, about Fort-Whiteman's own career at Tuskegee. Or then again, the Texan shared with him the tale of his own politically short-circuited career as an actor, his dreams as a dramatist, his literary criticism for the *Crisis*, and his thoughts on certain contemporary playwrights and poets. When he returned a year later from an extended visit to the worker's paradise, they'd talk again. He'd report on how he and Huiswood, and others, had sat down and conferred with Zinoviev and Bukharin, two leading figures of the Russian revolution; how they'd exchanged ideas with those at the pinnacle of Soviet power, who'd known and personally struggled alongside Lenin. Yes, the greatest revolutionary experiment of all time! And they were a part of it!

Doswell was straightening up from sitting so long in this uncomfortable position in the bleachers of Baxter's Tenner Gymnasium. Kneading the shooting pain at the small of his back (sitting on these bare benches without back support always did this to him), he grimaced. There was absolutely no danger of Communists taking over here. He smiled grimly. He was listening now to President Ronald's keynote address, to the words coming from the distant dais, observing, not without some fatal humor, this small, coffee-colored man with the pencil-sharp moustache who at dramatic moments stabbed the air with his finger and rose on his toes, waiting again for the applause to die down. Not a man trained to the cloth, but who nonetheless spoke in the fiery mode of the preacher: by turns pleading, righteous – with indignation, lecturing, prodding, thundering.

"What must be done? What we face, you and I, is in reality the question of fundamentally altering American society… This is what must be done…

"In the past few years, indeed, we have witnessed, and during these last few days we have learned, of a developing resistance on the part of our political leadership to this emerging struggle. We have watched with growing alarm a steady retreat from the principles on which this nation was founded, and a steady march in the direction of repression and oppression…

"America the beautiful, in only a few short years, has become transformed into America the hysterical!"

Here and there on the floor, and up in the bleachers and beside him, there were piercing, impassioned cries: "Tell it to 'em, brother! Tell it to 'em!"

"Right now we face a most solemn moment in our nation's history. The wave of shootings, murder, the recent slaughter of black people by officers of the law, are but examples and symptoms of the deep sickness that afflicts American society.

"Throughout most of the decade of the '60s our nation has been torn and rocked by assassinations, riots, murder, police brutality, campus violence and unrest, calls for law and order..."

A woman, broader than he, wearing tight, pink stretch pants and bulky coat, pressed heavily to one side of him, mumbling something angrily as she sat.

"...and national guardsmen to meet protests and expressions of dissent with bayonets and bullets, and the rise of political leadership to positions of power, who speak and act in ways calculated to create deep divisions among the American people..."

His neighbor, jostling him, was up, cheering, pumping her fist violently. "Tell it! Tell it to 'em!" she cried repeatedly, seemingly louder than anyone.

"...and thus to render asunder the fabric of American society!"

Montbanc continued: "Clearly the nation is entering this eighth decade of our century, this looming two hundred-year anniversary of our nation's founding, in the throes of an internal revolt, clearly on the threshold of a revolution whose outcome no one can predict! The angry and the alienated young are outraged and will not be pacified by promises and slogans, or even stopped by imprisonment. If so, then you, the disinherited black, the disinherited young and black, even more so, outraged, fed up and determined to be free, will not be intimidated by threats of detention camps or stopped by guns and bullets, or fooled by the cosmetic window-dressing and powder-puffing activities of our government! No! This is why you – we, all of us – will be the vanguard! Yes! The vanguard to take up the challenge of this decade, born of this century, and with a new hope to usher in a glorious new and reborn twenty-first century!"

Roars of applause once again; this time everyone in the bleachers and down on the floor pumping fists, cheering wildly. "We will! We will! We will! We will!"

"For, if we as a newly begotten breed of black Americans will unite our voices, and our energies, and create a solidarity in our efforts, in our purpose, we can indeed, for a fact, fundamentally transform this land and redeem this society. But in order to do so we must have the courage to say to our country and to our countrymen, as Patrick Henry said in the late 1700s, but in words and actions appropriate to our time..."

Again thunderous cries: "We can! We can! We can! We will! We will!" The sound of feet, instantly dozens, then hundreds at once, stamping the gymnasium floor!

"Listen! Listen! We must ask our nation and tell them! Is law so dear and order so sweet that it must be purchased at the price of oppression and repression? God forbid! We know not what course other Americans may take, but as for us, we will achieve America in our lifetime! We will have freedom and justice for ourselves, and for our children and our children's children! Or… We…shall…have…death!"

The applause was electric; young and old thundering, standing up out of their seats everywhere. Doswell stood up to ease the pain in his back, and as a preliminary to leave. Beside him the woman was sobbing as she clutched at him; down on the floor, up in the bleachers they were standing and applauding and stamping their feet.

"We shall! We shall! We shall!"

Montbanc was trying to say something but his voice was drowned out; then he gave up and someone on stage rushed at him and embraced him; then another. On the floor and in the bleachers they were jostling and stamping and banging in a cadenced tattoo of wood and metal and striking fists; here, there, two, four, five, seven; in clusters of half a dozen or more, younger people were climbing on chairs and benches, and then each other, in a scramble of arms and clenched fists rising, outstretched, arms stiff in the black power salute.

But then suddenly, amidst the clamor, down below, he thought he saw a ghost, Patterson…could it be? An old man, but still recognizable; he strained to see for sure but only for several seconds; then the figure melted from sight as quickly as it appeared. If it was him; *if*– it had been more than twenty-five years…

Not long after the Alliance convention, following the appearance of the *Liberator*, following an afternoon spent with Blissie; then a late-night outing with Gwen, Vincent got a telephone call. It was Aunt Molina. At first it was impossible to make out what she was saying, but then in a hot flash he understood the hysterical words.

"Come!" she gasped. "Come home! Basil's been shot! He's been shot and he may be dying!"

15

Reconstructing Human Relations

When Vincent had last visited Brooklyn, the one thing he plainly asked Basil was "Who would want to harm you?" It was too obvious a question to go unasked even if he pretended he was only in New York for Alliance work.

But Basil, so brash in his contempt for normal human fears, would have none of even that little.

"I know Aunt Molina called you and wants you to straighten me out and save me, but believe me, she's overreacting – you should know Aunt Molina. The Party is working on these chicken-shit threats – I'm not the only one who got them, and I'm not the only one who wants to find out who's behind them. So just cool it."

"There's no cooling necessary," he'd lied then to his untypically surly brother. "I told you I'm here on Alliance business and I know you're big enough to take care of yourself. But hey, your brother can have an interest in you, can't he?" Which led Vincent over the next week to try and win Basil over to a different interest: the altogether reasonable prospect of assisting him in a task for which he had a genuine need – far away from New York.

Basil refused to talk about the threat on his life, but he didn't say he wouldn't go to Colonus. Over time, however, Vincent had no choice but to leave without him. Yet, over the several days he was in Brooklyn, as they grew comfortable again in matters relating to the Alliance, Basil did say this much: that the Black Panther Party had been infiltrated, and that there were police agents seeking their destruction.

Clearly this was not the first time Vincent had heard such charges. Many insisted on the government's campaign to exterminate militant organizations, that it used all means necessary: "dirty tricks", like assassinations blamed on rival groups or enemies within the Party, or direct assaults with SWAT teams on Panther and other militants' headquarters. No, there was nothing original in any of Basil's charges.

Even as he fearfully headed out to New York this second time, glancing through a couple of news magazines, the charges were confirmed. A glance yielded reports and commentary about recent shoot-outs between police and Black Panther members in Chicago, in Los Angeles and elsewhere, and the consensus opinion in those reports was that the Panthers had been targeted for destruction by the authorities. The Rev Dr. Ralph Abernathy was quoted in one news report as speaking of "genocide"; and "brutal and unwarranted slayings" was the way a civil rights organization associated with the United Auto Workers characterized the outcome of a recent shoot-out.

What's more, skeptical journalists pointed to anomalies in police accounts of Panther/police shoot-outs, and emphasized that from the beginning there had been disputes over who had begun the gunfights and why the police appeared to have used excessive violence. As Vincent folded the magazines shut, he sought to drive this whole ugly business out of his mind. But over the whir of the airplane's engines, gazing into the immensity of cloud-filled sky, his mind only quickened with racing thoughts of himself and Basil in moments of their childhood.

He remembered the policemen of their youth; cops who were into businesses of their own, that got payoffs from the local numbers men, and from legitimate businesses, too, with special needs. There was one he remembered from the street corner who was always extra-diligent with the kids on the block. He and his partner regularly accosted Vincent and his friends as they stood around harmlessly shooting the breeze, teenagers whiling away summertime nights.

"Hey, you bugaboos! Move on!" he'd call from the rolled-down window of his squad car. And then, stepping out of it with his partner, with brandished police-stick just barely, not quite touching – prodded, pressing as one might cattle through a head-chute. "Just how do you boys *see* each other in the nights anyways?" he'd taunt.

Resentments and furies welled up recalling such incidents of inconsequence as much as those of consequence. Vivid as if they'd happened the hour before – yes, and the stories of more than one joy-popping fool who was taken into the stationhouse and beaten senseless over some ridiculous, trumped-up charge.

So when it was clear Basil had no intention of returning with him, he'd thrown away all pretenses; he'd said the obvious: that if it was true the cops were behind the threat on his life, this made all the more reason to get out of the city.

But Basil would hear none of it. "You think I'm just gonna go scurrying off with tail between my legs, Chicken Little with big brother?"

What was strange was that it wasn't like his brother to talk so stupidly. He'd always been bold and he certainly could be defiant, but not just plain, stubbornly reckless. Nor had his brother elaborated on any of this; it was completely irrational and thus couldn't be argued with. But then recurrent and vividly conjured, long-suppressed memories of his own, insults which still brought a flush to his cheeks, demonstrated how much on the edge of irrationality Basil, he, or anyone sentient could go.

Yes, all of these thoughts converged and would have represented an impregnable wall of conviction, if it had not been for something else which kept resurfacing in Vincent's mind. On the night Jon Molumba appeared at the Alliance convention and gave his talk, a violent dissertation on a chapter in the revolutionary history of Haiti, Vincent met and talked for hours with the knob-headed, surprisingly articulate and coolly rational founder of the Mora. One of the things Molumba talked about from behind his wrap-around shades in the evening light was the Black Panther Party in his native California. He insisted that in the Santa Cruz Mountains near Oakland there were "killing fields" where members of the Party who'd fallen out with the Panther leadership were taken, bound and gagged, tortured and often killed. Of course, Vincent had realized that the fiercely nationalistic Molumba hated the Panthers. But now, as he thought about it, he couldn't simply dismiss the charges. Even if Molumba had blood on his hands himself and might indeed have made this up, on the other hand he'd also be just the kind of person who'd know if it was so, and would tell.

Vincent's stay in Brooklyn had to be indefinate. On his arrival he'd learned to his great relief that Basil was not only still alive, but his condition was stable. Still, Basil's doctors at Kings County Hospital stressed that it could still easily turn for the worse.

While he waited, Vincent lived in Basil's apartment, which had been made over from their father's former dental office. It still had the somewhat worn but functionally attractive carpet that had been laid out when Vincent was a child. Basil had brought into his transformed bachelor quarters furniture that he'd purchased, but most of it was odd pieces taken from around the house, which brought up memories from their childhood. Staying in Basil's apartment also triggered vivid thoughts about the life he'd lived before he was shot. The main room – dining and living room combined – had a small, oval, walnut-finished table that could be pulled out to seat as many as a dozen people. Vincent knew Basil often did, bringing in noisy gatherings of his friends to slump about on his mixed chairs, a sofa and a comfortable couch, playing cards or watching TV on a combination TV-radio-phonograph player. Could his assailant have been one of these 'friends'?

Waiting, Vincent wryly reminded himself, was particularly appropriate here since, after all, this was his father's former waiting room. But he didn't just wait; he spent most of his time reading current and future texts on his Great Books list, readying himself for the coming weeks, while also trying to catch up on those he'd let slide. So he read with care Plato's early dialogues, as well as the metaphysically and morally inverted Allegory of the Cave in the *Republic*, where the worst kind of ignorance isn't the absence of knowledge but false opinion embraced. He was determined that when he returned this time he would take on some of Doswell's seminars, and perhaps cover an extra lecture or two in the weekly assemblies. To this end, as well as keeping Doswell informed, he was a couple of times on the telephone with the old man.

He began his first call with profuse apologies. "I'm really sorry about having to be here like this, but Basil's life is still in danger. I'm not sure what I can do even if he does get better. They can always try again. You see what I mean?"

First a long silence over the end of the line. Then: "You stay as long as you need to. Jim has taken over most of your sections. I have one. We can hold down the fort here." Another several seconds of silence. "Maybe you should transfer your brother out of the Brooklyn hospital when he can be moved – no forwarding addresses. Move him to another borough. Or better yet, outside the city."

That was certainly an idea. Why hadn't he thought of it himself?

He visited Basil daily, and he was conscious now but still teetering, certainly too weak to be stressed by the kind of pressing questions Vincent wanted answered. There were tubes running out of virtually every orifice in his body; the doctors said he'd been hit three times. It was a miracle he was still alive.

In such circumstances as these, people typically try to keep their minds off the horrors. That's what Vincent did, not only by catching up with his reading but by writing and telephoning his lovely Gwen, keeping her posted on his brother's progress, and telling her about staying in the old house with the old memories, and the old haunts on the streets of Brooklyn.

One of Basil's friends – whether he was a Panther or not he wasn't sure – sought him out and said the "brothers" wanted him to "come by". He also started thinking of seeing the police. Aunt Molina and Miss McGirt, one of Aunt Molina's housemates, said they'd been to the house seeking a routine interview with him, but he kept putting that off.

Though there was the small kitchen in Basil's apartment (fitted into a recessed alcove slightly larger than an average closet), he took his meals upstairs with Aunt Molina and her longtime friends, Mrs. Violetta Hawkins and Miss DeWilda McGirt. This was something he did more to please Molina than himself, even though the meals were delicious, a pleasant change from his Colonus fare. The real reason was that Aunt Molina and Basil were his only family. She was obviously under a lot of stress and he worried about her; she could use all the support from him she could get.

But the old ladies could sometimes be personally trying. Mrs. Violetta Hawkins, a widow, was harmless enough, but not so her sister, DeWilda McGirt, a spinster. The sisters were long-established friends not only of his aunt but his mother, going back many years. And now a mutually beneficial arrangement had been struck among the old friends. When alive, his father had been in the habit of aiming irreverent jibes at the irksome "sisters tha Violent and de Wild", yet it was the tiny, prune-like DeWilda McGirt who was difficult up close. A retired schoolmarm, she acted like she was still in the classroom and Vincent was one of her pupils.

It was DeWilda who was largely responsible for his seeing the police. After being to the house on one occasion, the detectives who'd been assigned Basil's case had telephoned once again on another occasion, asking that he come to the station house for routine questioning. But Vincent had put it off even after he'd decided he'd have to go through with it for Basil's sake.

DeWilda, however, didn't let him procrastinate long.

"Vincent, did you call those police gentlemen yet, and make an appointment to see them?" she asked sternly one day.

He made no reply.

"Vincent, I *said* did you call those nice police gentlemen yet, and make an appointment to see them?"

"No. I've been busy, Miss McGirt, but you're right, I'll have to call them tomorrow," he said, hoping to end it there.

"What did you say? Speak up, Vincent, don't mumble."

"He said…he said," Violetta broke in, Vincent groaning within, "he said he's too busy."

DeWilda could always understand what Violetta or Molina said, but not what *he* said. "You're too busy?! Vincent, these are the police you are talking about. This is about your brother who was almost murdered—"

"Now, now," Molina had interrupted, "DeWilda, I think Vincent knows what this is about and he's old enough to know what to do."

"But he says he is too busy to *see* the police?"

Barely containing himself, he blurted out, "I *said* I would call them tomorrow!"

"Oh, call them tomorrow? You want *me* to call them tomorrow?"

"No. I said, I – *I* – will call them *tomorrow!*"

"Oh. You talk so *loud!* Why didn't you say that before?"

So one day, deciding that the lesser of two evils was seeing the police, he went down to the station house to visit with DeWilda's blessed boys in blue.

He'd expected them to be bad-tempered when he arrived at the station house, put out by the fact that he hadn't come by sooner. But these guys were tottering under an overload of cases, and the stress of disorganization; if they were put out by anything, it was that he'd come at all. They seemed equally surprised as sorry to see him. He could imagine them now, grumbling while they scrambled to find the right paperwork and file, psyching themselves up in preparation for the imminent appearance of this respectable black burgher, brother of the victim, an out-of-town college professor – some guy who'd be quick with complaints if they didn't have anything to show by way of progress in the case. When they explained defensively that they hadn't had any "citizen input", and that until they did, or got something from Basil, they'd have nothing to go on, Vincent decided to tell them a little about the situation as he viewed it. He mentioned his brother's condition, in fact making it sound nearly hopeless, and adding his fears for the continued threat. When he told them about moving him out of the city, they jumped at the idea, indicating they had no problem with that from the standpoint of possibly later questioning him.

"The further away the better. You got the right idea there." They suggested he stay away "a good long time".

Far from impressing him as schemers and conspirators behind the scenes, pulling the strings on agents who'd infiltrated the Party, they seemed amidst their chummy sports talk more like Peter Falk's Columbo twice over, but without Columbo's offhanded, probing questions. And in the months to come, neither would there be any signs of Columbo's forensic knowhow.

But there was one thing: as a matter of course they were sure Basil had been attacked by people from the Party itself. What the police thought and Jon Molumba thought were the same. So it became necessary to visit Panther headquarters in Brooklyn. He remembered Basil's friend, and within the hour got a return call and an invitation to visit Panther headquarters.

From the first there was something strange about the hastily arranged meeting: it was their place, a storefront in Bedford-Stuyvesant, seat of all their activities, a busy place, a community center, off a side street from Grand Avenue, but it was deserted that late morning. Even the adjacent stores were empty. Equally odd was that one among that little troop of three or four, a burly, not-too-bright-looking fellow in his early twenties with the characteristic diddy-bop walk of the 'hood', had to stand guard downstairs in the inside front entrance of the store as he and the others went to talk alone in the back end of the walk-up. The police were mentioned as the reason for all of this cloak-and-dagger, yet when Vincent walked past the area on previous occasions, and rode by in a gypsy cab the day before, the place was buzzing. Thus he wondered with a specific sense of the ominous why there were no other Party members around – yet, assuming the worst, why would they want to hurt him?

Over the store in the back they were completely by themselves, and everything was quiet, with virtually no sound from the street. The man who did most of the talking was tall, thin, goateed, and light-complexioned, probably in his late twenties. But the others were not completely speechless.

Jimmy Jones, their apparent leader, wasn't unpleasant. He was even gracious in a kind of rudimentary way, as one might expect given the circumstances. So first he made small talk about the recent Alliance convention and Vincent's part in it; mentioned favorably what he'd heard was "a great speech" by the college president. But all this talk had a certain hollow, perfunctory quality to it; that is, until he got down to business, a business that featured Basil only as a small part of a larger picture focusing on the problems the Party was having trying to build "a world community".

"Like you, we believe in a large alliance of poor people, hungry people, people with needs. It's especially hard on the poor with all this insanity and slaughter and suffering this man Nixon has forced on all of us."

Vincent cut it short. He asked him point-blank if he'd brought him there to talk world politics or whether he knew anything about Basil's assailants.

"That's what I'm trying to tell you, brother."

The other two or three of them, stationed around the room, added, "Uh-hmmmmmmmm."

"The pigs have got us under a siege. When we were still patrolling the police we were better able to keep police crime down. But police crime has gone up lately with Hoover's FBI and the local police using false warrants to break into headquarters, shooting up the brothers."

"Uh-hmmmmmmm..."

"You see we got a war on our hands, you understand, brother?"

Vincent nodded.

Here Jimmy took up an earlier theme of Basil's. "The police have been infiltrating our ranks. These are super-psychopaths. And they sometimes provoke younger, inexperienced brothers to turn on each other..."

"You're not telling me—"

"No. No. Listen. They try to incriminate the brothers. This is why we got to be super-vigilant. And I'm telling you we think we know who the agents are. Yeah. They're assassins, and they're informers too. These are some unscrupulous people. But we got to be careful, we got to investigate a little bit more."

One of the others, a slightly older, heavyset individual, wearing dark glasses and a black leather jacket, tunefully blended his baritone into the chorus. "They usually start showing these nervous tendencies when we pose some questions."

There was a snicker.

"And what are you going to do when you think you've found them?

They said nothing; only a faint smile was detectable on their faces, the kind of smile the cat smiles when it sniffs the mouse.

Then the guy who'd spoken of agents betraying nervous tendencies chuckled, and in a low, rumbling baritone that was chilling, he said, "We can't exactly turn their names over to the police, now, can we, brother?"

For a second Vincent was dumbfounded, running the impeccable logic of that through his mind double-time, and once again thinking of what Molumba had said about the killing fields in the Santa Cruz Mountains in Southern California.

"I don't want any more killings..." Vincent choked up momentarily and caught himself. "That is, whatever happens to my brother, I don't want any more shootings, no blood revenge, no matter what happens to him. There are too many people being shot and killed."

"We understand your concern," Jones replied.

"It's not concern. It's murder," Vincent said, regaining his composure. "I won't be a part of that, or have my brother made a part of it." Even as he spoke he felt a shock of humiliation in facing this Socratic thinker of the street who'd forced him to see something he'd been fighting tooth and nail *not* to see for so long.

"Of course not. Nobody's talking about murder. Don't you worry about that," Jones said, temporizing and seeking to blunt the effect of his comrade's words. He instantly began singing the Party's theme, his rap about the Party's benign purposes – its ultimate objectives: humanity, life, love, unity, reassuring Vincent with an updated, funky Robin Hood gab about giving to the poor and taking only from the rich...which he no doubt fully believed in.

Vincent said very little from that point on. And so the talk pretty much wound itself up.

Leaving, he made his way down the stairs and through the store, all his senses on the alert, noticing the political posters on the wall, cartoon pictures of uniformed pigs being garishly done in with knives and guns by Panther women and children. One he might have found funny: a sideways shot of a naked woman in advanced pregnancy holding her belly, a slogan in the recent presidential campaign below: *Nixon's the One.* But now he felt only a grim blankness and a churning within his soul.

The rest of that day he wandered the city alone, the conviction coming over him at first wordlessly; the uneasy feeling that he'd been talking to murderers.

After riding the subway a few stops, he got off and wandered around Prospect Park, ending up lingering in a half-trance on the footpaths of the small zoo on the park's Flatbush side. He began to think about Gwen back in Colonus, conscious of something he didn't remember feeling about a woman ever before, and that was an almost physically distressed sense of her absence – a yearning for her counsel, her humor, just simply her warm, womanly, knowing presence.

He watched now as he lit up a cigarette to steady his nerves; studied some preschool children playing beside their parents, remembering Basil and himself as children playing in this very same part of the park with his mother looking on. His mother so gentle and soft, and yet strong...ohhh, he missed her! She picked up after his father – not merely his cigar ashes, or his socks left carelessly about the house, but his broken relationships with people: he so foolhardy and vitriolic; she so utterly commonsensical and practical, and so insistent in her religion and her manners and courtesy. Then he thought of Gwen.

And he thought of his brother and himself, both of them as boys hearing their father tell about the whale-size fish he'd caught near his home in Trinidad, and the tales he'd spin about winning, and about not giving up, and not ever taking less than your fair share. He was sure he'd never been as close to any man as to his father – except Basil.

He had to sort out his thoughts. As he wandered over to the bears, the polar bears, the brown bears, the black bears, gazing into the expanse of their large outdoor enclosures, and at their man-made caves, the conviction came over him that not only had he been in the company of murderers, but that while his brother lay in a hospital bed with tubes running everywhere out of his body, the people who'd done this to him, these same people, had quite coolly invited him to a little chitchat over the world's problems... But then he rejected the thought. He didn't want to believe this. No. Not at all! And yet at each objection, instantly afterwards, like an underground seepage, a hidden spring, the thought stubbornly resurfaced again.

As he wandered and searched his mind, determined to think this through to get clear answers, he asked himself what rational reason would these comrades of Basil have for harming him? Maybe *he was* a police agent? No! Of course not! One of the few consistent convictions his brother had from adolescence, and which he shared with Vincent, was that the cops were the enemy. Anyone who knew Basil at all would know this. Vincent knew this. And yet did *they* know this? Having met them, he could easily imagine their collective paranoia falling like a gray cloud over Basil as it may have fallen over others – or maybe it was turf wars within the Party? As he thought about it, he thought how abrasive Basil could be. Maybe he'd gotten on someone's wrong side. Basil was never a diplomat; he routinely pissed people off. Even his friends, in fact especially his friends, were treated to his special brand of unpleasantness. Could he have said something to the thug with the sunglasses, or someone else, something half-serious and sarcastic, cutting at the pomposity or the stupidity, that would leave rifts, smarting psychic wounds which festered?

But why, why would they be quick to invite him to their lair if they'd ordered – or done! – the deed themselves? Why would they, when the natural thing was to lay low, to hug the sidelines, to stay a distance? When it would be the most natural, the easiest thing for them to do? Precisely. Precisely, the answer came quickly: precisely because it would be. He laughed abruptly: they don't merely want to avoid looking guilty, they want to portray themselves as innocents – as 'brothers' – and they half-believe it themselves!

Molumba had said something pretty much like that. And Vincent knew that on the street this was exactly, exactly the way hoodlums are: the impervious, in-your-face response to the victims of their crimes; that is the way, yes, the norm for criminals.

Beyond this there was a very logical reason why they would want to meet with him: to have some influence over the direction of his suspicions. Police crime is up. They are under siege. There is a war on. The police have planted assassins within the ranks. To the extent he believed such things, for him to cooperate with the police became impossible. To the extent *they* believed such things, what greater justification for murder?

Pulsing through and behind all these thoughts in Vincent's mind continued to be not only Jon Molumba's words about the Panthers, but his memory of what Doswell said barely two months before: that the revolution had a waste disposal system for ridding itself of its garbage, its refuse…

And now as he wandered the near-empty walkways of the park (it was a weekday), he remembered the words of Michael Fairlie, the celebrated white author who'd come to Laurel Hill the night he'd last spoken to Raskin. Fairlie cited a French philosopher: "The remoteness and inertia of past events transforms crimes into historical events seen as part of the natural progress of the future…" Spoken with the same breezy, knowing theorization about common sacrifices, founding humanity, the humanization of work, a redeemed future… "When one has the misfortune," he said, "or the luck to live in an epoch where the traditional ground of a nation or society crumbles and where man must reconstruct human relations, then the liberty of each man is a mortal threat to the others…"

Yes, when man himself must reconstruct human relations, then the liberty of each man – and maybe the life of each man – *is a mortal threat to the others!*

Standing there, rooted in that very spot, the words repeated themselves in Vincent's mind like a record, like they were free of any volition on his part. Taking in the not-unpleasant zoo smell, the sight of the spindly-legged pink flamingos, as he wandered from that spot once again, he fell aimlessly, with little thought at first, into prayer. He hadn't prayed in years. For an instant he thought to cancel the words, to check the absurd mumblings with the usual irony, but instead he redoubled the fervor. He prayed for his brother's recovery, and then (a believer might have thought a miracle) inside of days he learned in fact that his condition had taken a decisive turn for the better!

Things began to look up. The burden of the daily anxiety over his brother's survival lifted. The light of hope began to shine, and in his mind he turned now, still tentatively, but joyfully amidst the steady rumble of the great city, on the happy thought that he would be rejoining Gwen soon. So he telephoned her to share all the good news – but without any luck. Several tries and he was unable to reach her.

Interlude

In Devon, finding himself alone and with a rare free evening with Susan to look forward to, Jim settled, newspaper in hand, into one of Doswell's frayed but comfortable easy chairs.

A *News-Herald* editorial, addressing a growing problem, caught his bemused attention. It said that there was need for a *crackdown on drug abuse* in the schools. *Good old-fashioned discipline* was required to control the *scourge*. Among colleges and universities both locally and around the country, it insisted, and Jim smiled as he read, strict rules were required, with *the will to enforce them*. It wondered if such *grit* on the part of teachers and administrators would ever appear.

He looked up from the newspaper, hearing sudden, piercing cries from Billy and some of the Lewis boys playing cowboys and Indians. Then he returned his attention to the paper to search the amusement section, perusing movie schedules. Going blotto in a movie house with Susan was just the thing. Since Chris and Radhakathri's quarrel Susan and he spent all their time alone together, but there had been very little of it. Once again, Brown had taken off and left to Doswell and himself all the work of Great Books – and little time left for anything else.

It was cold early that February, the cold and the grayness of the days as dispiriting as anything New York could offer, but then suddenly a new current began to blow: warm, Caribbean almost, spring-like. In Devon Jim could smell the earth and see the rich, rusty-orange color of it in the bright morning light as Jim Lewis broke it into double furrows in preparation for spring planting. To take a break, he would wander, sometimes by the old log tobacco-curing barn, along whose walls still clung last summer's brush and brambles, the building now used for storing his furnishings.

Prevailing winds which blew across the Lewis farm, whose house and half-painted barn and dilapidated barn lots stood a few hundred yards to the west of Doswell's little place, carried the ammoniac odor of cow dung, mingled with the moist freshness of the upturned, plowed ground, near the Doswell and Lewis houses.

From his tractor seat, or passing in his pickup, Lewis would wave and gangly Billy, in his tattered overalls and visored baseball cap, sometimes called to him, trailing the smaller Lewis children, a sight as they kicked at dry cow pies and tumbled across the fields in search of adventure.

During the month or so Jim was with Doswell, passing many an evening talking into the late nights, Doswell hadn't been drinking as much. One night, standing on the porch, looking out over the dimly lit fields with Jim, Doswell had said something following one of those stories from earlier days: "We walk a thin line, Jim – we are tempted by illusion, and our nearest and dearest illusions are ourselves." But then he looked up, the chill air blowing through the crisp, crackling leaves; overhead in the darkness, glittering stars, mighty suns in their own orbits, mere pinpricks of light, and the old man said, "Remember this night, this sky, this eternity"; and then the peace of the night fell again.

Now he felt it. Without twitching a muscle, stillness itself, Jim watched for a sign of the deer, and sure enough, after a while, first one, then two, then three came very cautiously out from behind the cover of the wood by the stream, near the place of the fire-colored blossom which Doswell said appeared only in summertime. Jim remained as quiet as possible, not daring to move, careful not to make the slightest sound. And yes, it was like eternity, timeless; the moon casting a soft glow over the silent land, only the gentlest breath of wind in the trees, and those timid creatures by the edge of the moon shadow. Continuity is the eternity men know, he thought; and for a moment he knew, that *he*, the mystery of that *he*, the density of that *he* – suspended on the edge of that time, in the band of moonlight; and he looked again to the edge of the wood in the clearing where the deer had appeared minutes before, and now there remained only the moonlight and the shadows and the peace.

PART 4

16

Strike!

Passaic, New Jersey, 1926

It was late on a summer night in union headquarters in Passaic, New Jersey, the ceiling paddle-fan making a measured, rhythmic whooshing sound, the stir of the heavy air offering little relief from the oppressive summer heat. A man small in stature, black straight hair, of decided Semitic features, was speaking.

"I tell you, Thomas, I never heard of her. Colonel Johnson and the rest of the mill owners' flunkeys are behind this."

Albert Weisbord was nervous in his motions, but his voice was strong; he had the sound of a confident man of action speaking the truth.

"Still," Thomas said in a casual voice, "I thought you told me about her at least a month ago."

"No. Not about her. I never knew this woman…"

"You mean you never knew her…or her *true* soul? Or her name?" he asked matter-of-factly, without any humor.

Weisbord, pale, thin and bespectacled, was an unlikely ladies' man – but still a ladies' man, at least in the circle he ran in. The radicals among the chic along Park Avenue and the Upper East Side, back in the '20s, were not like the 'bloods' from the Black Panthers who became famous half a century later. If they were black they were made of tamer stuff, like Claude McCay, or Langston Hughes, or Abram Harris, writers of the Harlem Renaissance, men of artistic temperament. But if they were instigators, they were white, charismatic men like Big Bill Haywood, leader of the Wobblies, or, for that matter, Weisbord himself, the renowned leader of what was fast becoming the most celebrated trade union strike in America's history.

"Why don't you come with me one of these evenings? I tell you, they'll welcome you with open arms. Do it for the cause."

"For the cause?"

Heavy silence fell between the two men, alone in this barely furnished storefront union office facing Passaic's now quiet main commercial avenue. Thomas, a man inclined to severe restraints, knew he would find the chitchat amidst the gossip at these gatherings too much. He could not abide the breezy political and revolutionary talk any more than the steamier Freudian talk of Oedipus complexes, sexual repressions and whispered homoerotic liaisons. But still, it was over something other than these well-told tales that he felt some rising irritation.

"Do you think I go to see Eleanor Van Ormond to face those horse-sized teeth of hers, and all the chatter that comes out of that horse-sized mouth, with anything less than revolutionary zeal?"

Thomas knew the description wasn't without basis. He also knew Albert was involved with more attractive, if not more worthy, women than Van Ormond. Despite his denials, there was Rosalind Lapnore, who was bringing a lawsuit for breach of promise against the little Lothario, and trumpeting it in all the newspapers and tabloids. But Thomas decided not to pursue the matter. He studied Weisbord for a moment and thumbed through some papers on a desk.

"I told you last time we talked, Nancy Cunard is putting together a book entitled *The Negro Anthology*, made up of contributions from Negro poets and essayists, and she recently said she hopes to include as many Party people as she can. You could whip together an essay, or even a story, in no time flat that would put down the Party line for the workers – something, you know, that ties in with the strike. She'd love to publish it. She's got a special place in her heart for Negro causes. This is what I'm telling you about, Thomas: she's got power, influence, money – but she'd have to meet you."

It was true: the people you met at those little soirees could be tremendously useful. Nancy Cunard was a member of the English, aristocratic Cunard family, corporate owners of the Cunard shipping line, the *Queen Elizabeth* and the *Queen Mary* being two of their most famous ships. She would contribute to the cause of the Scottsboro Boys and continue to support the International Labor Defense, a legal defense arm of the Party. There was Elizabeth Gurley Flynn, an active Party member and firebrand speaker. There was Susan Brandeis, daughter of the Supreme Court Justice. There were others. There was Julius Hammer and his son Armand. Though both were already very wealthy, it would be several decades later that the latter would make a major name for himself as a roving (and unofficial) Cold War diplomat, philanthropist and billionaire founder and CEO of the Occidental Petroleum Corporation. And it would only be a few years before Thomas would come to know him intimately, along with other members of this powerful clan.

But Thomas certainly knew then the importance of such contacts. Only he knew equally well the importance of security. It wasn't the first time they'd been over this.

Weisbord wasn't through, but an uncharacteristic note of defensiveness had crept into his voice. "The movement has changed, Thomas. The old foreign language federations when Party members used to threaten to burn down America's cities, that's a thing of the past. Now we've not only learned to speak English, we've become progressives building the heavenly city. Just imagine, Thomas, where we would have been last winter if I hadn't made the contacts I made. The revolution needs people of power and influence within the establishment if it's to succeed."

"I don't need a lecture on the subject of alliances… And you know too much about alliances." Thomas glared, fixing Weisbord's eye.

"I know you don't…"

"What you don't understand," Thomas spoke with deliberateness, "is that the key to the change you're talking about lies in the control of information. Knowledge. We want them to know what *we* want them to know. Not what *they* can figure out with the help of our carelessness."

"They? Who's they? *They're* on our side." Weisbord had risen from his chair, nettled.

"You don't know who's at those parties – and then there are those affairs—"

"Thomas, you're obsessed with security. Like the committee!"

"Not obsessed, concerned…and that's why I'm here. Because you aren't. And because you can't take orders. And because of your breezy attitude and…" here Thomas paused, knowing that this was another sore point piled on other sore points, "your shoot-from-the-hip response to events."

"Shoot-from-the-hip?!" Weisbord suddenly jumped like he'd been touched by a live wire; the famous Weisbord temper pushed to the breaking point. He launched into a long list of complaints of his own: Thomas' disloyalty, the "ignoramuses" on the Textile Committee, his previous hopes that he'd be his ally, that he'd always thought better of Thomas and obviously overestimated him, and so on, and so on.

Had this exchange been witnessed by anyone, it might easily have been interpreted as a quarrel between a man answering Moses Walker's description to Vincent of Thomas Doswell, a leader of the largest textile strike in the nation's history – a hardline, confrontational individual – and another roughly equal, or even a subordinate. But this is not how the people of the time, nor the history books, viewed the man Albert Weisbord addressed as 'Thomas'. In fact the history books, as Jim Allan would come to know years afterwards, would take no notice of him at all. And those few people, other than Walker, who did in '25 and '26, if they gave him more than a moment's thought, imagined him to be a worker/bodyguard.

But Jim speculated that if Thomas Doswell as a young man was anything like the individual he knew forty years later, he would have been a brilliant leader. And no doubt the Party had something like this in mind, given that it already had an extensive resume to go on: in the first instance, while still an undergraduate at Harvard, having established a tenants' union on the South Side of Boston.

A sparrow does not fall to the ground without our heavenly Father's knowledge, Jesus said; and the Communist International, centered in its heavenly city in

Moscow, like God, had an interest in events as small as the sparrow – and even so small as a tenants' union. This was of consuming interest since the Party's inability to recruit and collectivize the sons and daughters of slaves had by then become a matter of grave concern. And Doswell's efforts in bringing his fellow tenants together on Dudley Street, in the heart of a neighborhood that was racially mixed, was thus a notable success. And yet, despite this success, and union experience later in Lawrence, Massachusetts, given the racial conditions of the day, naming Doswell as strike leader in Passaic would have been lunacy.

So there was Albert Weisbord, the face of the strike's leadership. He was a graduate of the Harvard University Law School. He'd shown himself to be a resourceful tactician, a charismatic leader, a man of manic energy. And not least of all, he was representative par excellence of the new kind of Communist leader. Though the son of an immigrant, he was a man removed from his immigrant roots, his Russian-Jewish father a generation ago having grown rich manufacturing accessories for men's coats. He moved in the best of circles; he had excellent contacts. But he also had glaring faults. He had a reputation for being impossible to get along with. In a movement which required discipline first, last and always, he was undisciplined, he was headstrong. And he was also a shameless womanizer.

Thus the Party's leadership struck a compromise: this brilliant Negro graduate of Harvard, more experienced in the day-to-day business of organizing, who'd himself been a worker in Massachusetts, would behind the scenes impose restraints, exercising influence, making decisions in conjunction with the publicly acknowledged leader of the strike. "Keeping Albert in line" was the way Weisbord himself often put it – sometimes half-humorously, sometimes not.

But how could the Party have hoped that Thomas Doswell would succeed in the task it had set for him? After all, Weisbord was "impossible to get along with". How could it expect to successfully pair him with this Bolshevik Napoleon/Don Juan? And after all, wouldn't Weisbord very naturally be expected to view him as an out-and-out spy sent from New York? As it would turn out, however, the two got along well. There were reasons. That Doswell was a man of careful, philosophic temperament, and that Weisbord no doubt respected his intellect, his self-possessed bearing – this must have played its part. That Thomas Doswell was indifferent to the power that Weisbord desired, and Weisbord knew this and knew also that Doswell, given his position, could be his most effective enemy, as he was his ally – this was crucial.

Smiling, Doswell summed it all up this way to Jim in Devon that early winter of 1970: "Someone in New York from the Textile Committee said something about us that got back to Weisbord, something like 'One is a calm, slow-going workhorse yoked to this very energetic, impulsive one – maybe together they can better pull the plow.'"

But perhaps the most compelling reasons they pulled the plow were two: that they'd known each other for several years, first as activist students, and then later as comrades in Lawrence; and the fact that, in a certain respect, they resembled each other as young men whose ambitious fathers had climbed from the depths and achieved a considerable degree of success in a hostile world.

Thomas Doswell knew that Colonel Johnson (the Botany mill's plant manager, company spokesman, and informal spokesman for the other mills in the region), or some other of Weisbord's many enemies, had encouraged this Lapnore woman to bring her recent lawsuit. This didn't change the fact that Albert, whom he knew only too well, had let himself be drawn into this ridiculous web of domestic folly.

He feared a repeat of what had happened in Lawrence. Thomas had been sent ahead and signed on as a worker in the mill there, his task being to document the brutal conditions of the workers by providing detailed descriptions and photographs. He had no trouble finding them: floors which were so slippery with accumulated grease from the wool, it was sometimes all he could do to put one foot in front of the other. He found toilet facilities that were little better than pigsties, and no places to sit and take a moment's rest, and lunch breaks that were virtually non-existent. The machinery, which was unguarded and dangerously crowded together, required constant and close observation lest the wool fibers suddenly snarl and create costly work stoppages. This led to accidents, some of them serious, and when it led to a work stoppage management was often quick to punish with peremptory dismissals.

All of this Thomas faithfully reported, including the tabulation of diseases that were all too common – tuberculosis and pneumonia and anthrax – secreting it to Albert through United Front agents for the press which they hoped could be convinced to write stories about the life and work conditions of textile workers. And then suddenly, there was Mary Nordquist! A part-time actress Albert had married in a whirlwind suddenly demanded a divorce. There followed a round of domestic squabbles, and the mountain of material that Thomas had been documenting began piling up in the United Front offices as Albert attended to the urgencies of his private life.

Doswell and Weisbord nearly broke over this. Their fight was carried all the way up to committee headquarters in New York. Since then, somewhat chastened, Albert had redeemed himself in one very important way: his successful contacts with the press were now yielding favorable results. Doswell told Jim that back then he would have worked with the devil if it would help to achieve the Party's transcendently urgent purposes.

"But it still had to have been infuriating, even for the calmest of workhorses, to work with a man who could be so fickle, so distracted by personal troubles," Jim observed.

"He wasn't fickle, and what happened in Lawrence never happened again. Although there were times – and the Lapnore situation was one – when I feared it might. I don't mean for you to think that he was incompetent or ineffective. Quite the contrary, that was the most infuriating part of it: he was a genius at organization, he was a man capable of working through night and day, and he could also put on the charm with the right kind of people. He was indispensable. There was no way we could have kept the strike going as we did had it not been for his strength as a leader."

Later Doswell told how, despite occasional squabbles, Weisbord and he had fought a successful battle against even cruder methods than gossip and cheap romance.

A month into the strike the Passaic Commissioner of Public Safety had ruled that mass picketing was illegal intimidation; so the police were ordered to disperse the picket lines.

Weisbord and Doswell secretly huddled in a nearby house. To sidestep the police order, and following a meeting with all the strikers, they had two thousand of them march quietly in pairs past the mill gates to their homes. The authorities and the mill owners went into a fury over this "sneaky, deceitful maneuver". The Commissioner of Public Safety within hours informed the press that no such subterfuge would work again. And then when it was attempted again, the line was stopped, the police closed the street, and the street leading up to the mill filled with striking workers.

"The order was given: 'Disperse that crowd!' Mounted police rode in – the chief of police himself was hurling tear gas bombs. Firemen arrived with water hoses to batter the crowd, sending people running like jack rabbits in all directions, policemen dashing after them with clubs, striking not only workers but onlookers as well."

"That was the way it was at Kelly Ingram. Police dogs were tearing at people's legs, the firemen were battering people with high-pressure fire hoses." Jim described the situation in Birmingham just before his return to New York in the summer of '64.

"Yes, and let no one say that violence rarely succeeds in its intended purposes. In Lawrence such tactics did succeed. But in Passaic and in Birmingham, ultimately they didn't."

"Is that how you got that?" Jim pointed. "Over your eye."

Doswell nodded after a moment. "Yes, yes..." He thought for a second, ignoring the scar. "It was all taking place a dozen miles from New York. The lessons we'd learned working with reporters in Boston, and through Weisbord's contacts in the city, allowed us to get the message out."

So reporters, photographers and feature writers, drawn like ants to sugar, converged on the strike scene in Passaic. And when they, too, became targets of the police, clubbed, kicked and beaten along with the strikers, this had the not-surprising effect of sharpening their focus in writing about what it was like to be clubbed, kicked and beaten. Furthermore, far from discouraging the newsmen, their numbers swelled, Doswell told Jim. Assisted by calls from strike headquarters informing them of impending new confrontations making for fresh stories, they appeared in ever greater numbers; only now they were covering events in armored vehicles and bulletproof limousines, and little airplanes with open cockpits that crisscrossed the sky. They had boxed the mill owners and the local authorities into a public relations debacle.

"It was heady stuff! But I wonder how the authorities could have been so stupid?" Jim interjected.

"They didn't see themselves. Or they saw themselves as righteous crusaders fighting mob anarchy. Their minds boxed them in. They could not have acted more contrary to their own interests if we had written a script for them."

"Like Sheriff Bull Connor and his deputies."

"Yes."

But not only the police had come into a permanent state of fury, Doswell said. The local courts had gone on a rampage, and it was all duly reported, not only in New York and New Jersey, but in newspapers and magazines across the country.

It had everything to do with a tactic employed from the start, which Thomas had come more and more to see as crucial, and that was to define the struggle, to project and define it for the world in their terms. And to be careful it stayed that way. It wasn't simply to remain on the high ground (non-violence); it was to do everything possible to use the press as an active ally. A method, he agreed with Jim, that Martin Luther King would employ decades later.

So were strikers' children getting enough milk? Thomas had thought to plant the question. Albert passed it on to one of the women journalists he knew from Nancy Cunard's parties, who worked for the gray but influential *New York Times.* And following the *Times*' lead, many other newspapers and news journals across America gave the milk story a prominent place in their reports. Then, naturally, for months following this compelling story, a campaign was waged, well reported in its many stages and headed up by Manhattan society matrons, to get sufficient supplies of milk to the hungry strikers' children.

But what about the strike children's opportunity to engage in wholesome play? News stories on the plight of children without adequate playground facilities generated discussions in city council chambers and in churches, among relief agencies and elsewhere. And then again, what about vacations for children? Or the opportunity "to breathe fresh air"? That became a feature of intense interest for the reading public, drawn to ever new, ever more engrossing tales of stark contrasts in good and evil, villainy and heroism – a heroism that the reading public itself could supply. In that summer of 1926 donations were taken up in churches, from civic organizations, from friendly unions, on New York City street corners. Strike children on their way to summer camps, or to sympathetic homes on Long Island, upstate New York, or in the hinterlands of New Jersey, invariably began their trips on parade routes through New York's midtown streets. The photo ops were endless.

And so it went. Studies were published showing that children growing up in New Jersey counties where the mills were located suffered the worst childhood mortality rates of the state. And now a new charge was leveled: they were unhealthy to the communities surrounding them.

Naturally there were outraged reactions from the mill owners and their defenders. Not enough milk? Sober assessments, they insisted, argued otherwise. The worst mortality rate among children? A counter-report was issued based on state-developed statistical studies. But the mill owners were always on the defensive. What are they *really* saying, people more generally asked – that strikers' children don't *need* milk? Or that people should be comforted by the thought that though children are dying, not so many are dying as previously thought?

And so the inevitable happened. A mirror held relentlessly in the face of the authorities led them – or at least some of those associated with them – to 'see themselves'. Wives and children were rising up against their husbands and fathers. The daughter of the police chief of Garfield was observed joining the picket line; the wife of the Commissioner of Public Safety in Passaic invited a delegation of strikers' wives and women strikers to tea.

"So you think with so much going for it, the strike was a tremendous success?" Doswell asked.

"Maybe not?"

Doswell nodded, a faint smile playing on his face. "Our United Front was intended as a transmission belt to convey the force of the Party to the people. This was originally Lenin's idea. But from the beginning, in the view of many, our method was very unorthodox. In fact there were those from one faction which had long and bitterly criticized the front for its left-wing deviationism. The front issued membership books and dues stamps. It acted like an independent labor union."

"Why was this so wrong?"

"Because the concept of the united front was to unite with mainline institutions and organizations. It was to work from within – boring from within." Doswell made a simultaneous motion with his hands. "It was to become part of some larger established entity which in time would be controlled by the Party."

"But if the front had been successful in 'transmitting its force to the community' – which is what you said it did – it *was* a big success."

"Yes, of course, but have you ever heard about the glass that is half-full? It is also half-empty. When it suited the critics within the Party, it was half-empty, when it suited them otherwise, it was half-full. It was a matter of maneuvering. Turf. Power and control trumping doctrine every time, but always in the name of doctrine, jockeying for advantage in a dialectical game that would advance one's personal interests. You see, they had not one but both – or one and a half – eyes on Moscow! All power came through the Comintern, and this one faction felt it had recently been filched out of a lot of power and was maneuvering to win it back from the other – the same one that had underwritten our efforts."

Doswell had been talking for hours that night, to the sound of the pelting, half-freezing rain against the windowpanes. It was well past midnight but the younger man hadn't lost any interest.

Aside from shelves and books lining the walls of Doswell's farmhouse study, a few chairs and the couch in which he sat erect like a monarch before an audience, Jim had taken notice of some pictures. He'd noticed them before. One was a turn-of-the-century formal wedding photograph. Within its faded frame it showed an eminently serious, stiffly-posed young bride of a lighter cast than her husband but equally as tall; and a stern, dark-skinned, equally stiff, balding man who could easily have been her father. The man's eyes seemed to take in different vistas: one resigned, perhaps dejected, the other blazing with an inner fire.

Jim, out of a deference, a sensitivity about secrets, had never asked his older companion anything about family. But studying this photograph he did ask about Doswell's father that night, and more exactly about how the elder Doswell responded to the knowledge that he had joined the Party.

He replied quite easily. "My father was a professor in the university seminary. He had great dreams for us. He believed that we had to make up for generations. Imagine if he'd known my first job after graduating from Harvard was to work as a laborer in a textile mill in Massachusetts?"

"He didn't know."

"Yes, that is certainly true!" He laughed. "I never told him that I joined the Party. I didn't want to needlessly upset my parents – and I didn't want to reveal anything in my letters that some third party might use against me. Yet, you have to understand, I was utterly convinced that I was on the same path he'd been – as they used to say, 'in lifting the race'. So I wanted him to know that part at least. I wrote my father a letter before I went to Lawrence that said for at least the near future I'd decided, not in a religious sense – though I didn't say in what sense – I'd decided to work as a kind of missionary among poor people both from the South who'd migrated north, and immigrant people in the North."

"He didn't ask for specifics?"

"I think he didn't really want to know more, frankly."

"It probably wasn't hard guessing at."

"Yes – I'd never talked about any of this but he spoke of white workers' hostility towards Negroes, that racial prejudice was just as real in the North, that my education, if I wasn't careful, could work dangerously against me in certain circles. And about all this he was right, of course.

"Then after I'd been in Passaic for a while I wrote my father another letter that was both insolent and that came ever closer to describing what I was doing. In a previous letter he'd ventured to say I was *irresponsible*. This was the closest we'd ever come to an open quarrel. I told him in that letter that I was hacking out a new path, except it wasn't only for my immediate family, or those nearest me, or myself, but for *all* the people. I reminded him of the story he told of his youth, when as a child of nine he'd been freed from slavery —"

"*Slavery?*"

"It wasn't that long ago, Jim. He was well into his forties when I was born. He told us about a northern officer in a neat blue uniform and a wispy moustache reading something from a paper near the end of the big war. And when the soldier was finished he told how everyone turned to the individual nearest him, wide-eyed: 'What did he say? What did he say?' And the soldier shouted, 'You're free! You're free! You can leave here and take whatever you have and go wherever you choose. You're free!'

"He said he would never forget that, and that we weren't to either. He repeated the story often: that those people who'd been suddenly freed were afraid, that they'd heard and finally understood the words of liberation, but beyond that they still had not yet understood, and in the days following they were much confused. He said some stayed on the land, making arrangements to attach themselves to the master and their past life, while others did what the Yankee officer said – they just wandered off with what they could carry on their backs and hold in their hands. Human streams moving towards whatever wind blew them their best hope. He said they were 'looking for a Moses to lead them to the Promised Land.'

"So I reminded him of that: of the people being afraid of freedom, of their drifting without direction. And I ended with a bit of rhetoric that came mostly from the stump, but which also mirrored his earlier sentiments and certainly my own: *We must chart our own future, we must seize the initiative and stop waiting for someone to lead us to the Promised Land.* Do you recognize in such words the arrogance of youth, Jim?"

"I guess you were puffed up with all the successes of the strike. You felt you were on top of the world and you were in command."

Doswell nodded. There was a long silence.

"Yes… I *was* puffed up. No question we were playing the authorities for fools. But in the end, you see, the situation in Passaic would make that kind of talk especially hollow."

Jim watched as he got to his feet and then, after a moment's pause, stepped over to a box containing firewood, slipping a log from the box into his wood-burning stove; carefully opening the flue to give the fire additional air. Then he returned to the couch, all of the time his brow furrowed as he slowly set himself down again.

"The workers were used by the Party. Their suffering was the Party's fuel, and it was spent lavishly in pursuit of its goals. This was all the worse because its goals could shift with the seasons – with the Party's internal struggles. So, in the end, the workers were defeated by the Party."

He turned his gaze away from Jim; he seemed in his mind to be deciding something. He looked upwards at the ceiling, expelling breath as he did.

"There was a Puerto Rican family I knew then. There was the husband and the wife and a grandmother, and half a dozen or so children, the oldest a teenager old enough to work at the mill. This child and the husband and the wife, all three worked at the same place. They were 'scabs'. People like that had to be cautious." He thought a moment. "Perhaps they weren't cautious enough. The younger children would sometimes come home bloodied, beaten up by gangs of children who'd be calling them 'scabs' and 'niggers'. Often that was too much for such people, they'd finally quit. Maybe you could criticize them for this, but these people were fierce – they stayed on. I never knew people that were fiercer.

"One day I started speaking to them in my school-book Spanish, which they just laughed at. 'Hey, you think you a Castilian black boy?' the father said. No one said 'black boy' in those days, but he knew that I was a part of the strike effort. Still, when they saw that I harbored no hostility towards them, they eventually tempered theirs.

"Some of the strikers who saw my friendship with this family warned me against them. 'These people, they don't listen to nobody!' they said. I told them we had no enemies among them, that they had to be educated, not hated. But then the strikers were right: I never succeeded in educating them.

"One day the father, the patriarch, a short, light-skinned, wiry man with a gold front tooth, said to me, 'But these Commies, Tommy, they don't have no interest in you or me! If there is a big crowd of people, then they are interested. They put on the show. But we are only one of thousands to them, grains of sand on the beach. And if one of these little grains of sand begins to talk back, eeeiiih! Then they get mad! Then they get frightened! Then they throw it away or they bury it!'

"The irony I felt at his speaking to me this way was great. The more I contemplated the fact that he thought me merely well-meaning, the more I savored the irony. And there was also this power that I felt, that I felt in being invisible to them – this too I savored. Of course I viewed them as hopelessly naive."

"Yet not so naive that they didn't know the strike was led by Communists."

"Exactly. They weren't naive. They were just as savvy as I was. More so, in a way. They were people who were desperate for a job and who considered the one the strikers were unhappy with desirable. They knew under normal conditions they'd be the last to be hired and the first to be fired. And I was trying to make them voluntarily wait for the strikers to go back to their jobs – make them understand and accept the notion that their immediate good had to be deferred to the greater and future good. You see? How could my efforts be squared with the goal of helping my brothers in the North when many of them were just like these people?"

"Were many of the strikers black?"

"Some of the strikers were Negroes, but surely the answer wasn't in counting heads and picking the number that happened to be greatest at the moment. It had to do with principle. Which was essentially to understand – and *believe* – in this mystical future where all the workers' interests would be reconciled."

"And never seen by them."

"They certainly couldn't see such a future. These people's plight nagged at me, hurrying me back to my work. And later there were times, unguarded moments, that I began to wonder: what would Marx say? That genuine justice is impossible in a capitalist society? To be sure he would say that, and we were preparing for the final end of capitalism...and so it was true, I thought: to fail to bring the revolution closer to fruition because one refuses to pay the cost in one's personal scruples? *This is immoral...* But what of these people?

"One day I saw Julio – that was the father's name – he was trying to get inside the mill through a back entrance and some strikers were blocking the way and cursing him out. I did nothing, I said nothing, I'd begun to think they were the enemy because they weren't joining the revolution – you see? They weren't willing to be led to the Promised Land...the *Promised* Land." He spoke with stone-faced resignation.

There was a lull in his talk. Jim broke the silence. "I guess...it was a strike, there was nothing you could do."

He said nothing for long moments. "Yes. I suppose so."

Doswell explained that the end of the Passaic strike was the end of a war that had as much to do with contending forces within the Party as it had with contending workers and mill owners. In New York, he told Jim, the Textile Committee would find itself under pressure from both sides inside the Party. The United Front was under fire from one faction – the Foster faction – for the "instigation of a parallel trade union", while the other, the Ruthenburg-Lovestone faction, following the recent Sixth Plenum in Moscow, seeing that its earlier policy was viewed from on high as a "deviation", quickly backpedaled, and sought to distance itself from both the strike and from the United Front as convincingly as it could.

The Party, embroiled in an internecine struggle that reached all the way up to Moscow, and no longer wanting anything to do with the strike, forced

Weisbord in the late summer to resign, turning it over to the American Federation of Textile Workers, which sought as quick a resolution to the strike as possible. So nearly a year after it had begun, the strikers went back to work with barely more in the way of concessions from the mill owners than they'd left with.

Despite the Party's immediate desire to put the strike behind it, and very bitter internal denunciations in its immediate aftermath (Weisbord was expelled from the Party by the end of the decade), in later years the strike won extravagant plaudits from the Party press as a legendary revolutionary event. So for Weisbord it meant the beginning of the end of his career with the Party; but for Doswell the opposite: it marked merely an initial phase in a much longer career in the Party, impelled by the Party's description of his work as "exemplary".

"So you came out a hero and Weisbord a villain – or the scapegoat."

"It would represent a big step up in my career (and a step down in my life). And yes, for Weisbord – in the long run, since everything that went wrong was blamed on him, and everything that went right other people who'd survived the factional fighting took credit for – it meant the end for him."

The story Doswell told Jim of Passaic in 1926 is what people usually imagine of the Party in the first half of the last century – the romance of the labor unions; the wild harangues and speeches; the clandestine meetings and smoke-filled meeting halls; the picketing and the street clashes. Jim's first impression on hearing it was to view it all as a great, largely spontaneous and collective splashing of bright and clashing colors on an empty canvas by dramatic and idealistic people – a kind of Jackson Pollock-style of derring-do, of artistic-politic on the world.

But now what Doswell would tell, in the many talks they had that winter, was that the canvas, despite its surface turmoil, was planned, devised, carefully executed; an engineer's mechanical drawing rather than an abstractionist's fancy. And to be sure, as in all human affairs, things don't always turn out as planned, though with the regime and the Party, he said, they always started out with every intention of exactitude.

17

From Passaic to the New Jerusalem

It was an early weekday evening. Vincent was still in Brooklyn. Jim was spending a lot more time on campus teaching nearly all of Vincent's classes, as well as his own, and hearing much about the war and Ho Chi Minh. `Uncle Ho' had died earlier in September and he was a hero and a legend with many at Baxter and CSU. Dinner was over, night had fallen, the dishes washed and put away. Billy, as sometimes happened, having gone to play with the Lewis children, ended up staying overnight. And Jim, though tired, more curious than ever, asked about the Party and the aftermath of the strike, and more about Weisbord and other major figures Doswell knew from that earlier time. The old man, in an expansive mood, went even beyond the scope of his very natural questions.

"I think they were more impressed with the way I handled Weisbord than in forming secret cells. But they needn't have been. For as difficult as Weisbord might be with subordinates, and as insubordinate as he often was with Party elders, he was a man with a humanitarian core." His Party comrade, he told Jim, could be grandly generous, and he had a human touch, making him widely popular among the ordinary strikers, especially the women.

During the strike, he said, he met Lovett Fort-Whiteman again, joining forces with him in hopes of bringing more blacks into the Party, a task it had put high on its list of priorities ever since Lenin had sent it a letter in 1921, expressing surprise that it had done so little work among them, and stressing that they should be recognized as a *strategically important element in Communist activity.* Fort-Whiteman had just returned from an extended stay in Moscow and was brimming with enthusiasm over what he'd seen and learned there. He eagerly shared Doswell's concern for black workers, but their efforts at recruitment were repaid with only a trickle of new members. And the Party's more aggressive efforts at absorbing Negro organizations through its 'united front' tactics were a disaster. Relations with Marcus Garvey's ultra-nationalistic United Negro Improvement Association (UNIA), whose militant membership made it an especially attractive target, in fact, ended in violent conflict.

"From the beginning I viewed my role in the Party as winning our people to the Party's banner, and when, after I'd left Passaic I was selected to go to Moscow to study at the Lenin School as Fort-Whiteman and a few others had before me, I took it as the beginning of a greater commitment to the race. But as it happened, this wasn't the plan."

"What did you study?" Jim asked, fatigued but still curious.

"Theoretical and practical subjects. The practical included techniques of revolutionary and guerrilla warfare: sabotage, uses of firearms and explosives, robbery, how to drive trains and blow them up, how to fight mounted policemen by sticking hairpins into their horses." He offered this list like items on a grocery list.

To Jim this crescendo of improbabilities was hilarious.

Doswell barely smiled. The practical lessons, he said drily, were more worthwhile than the theoretical. "Marxist dialectic is only profound on the surface – deep down it is superficial. The more I was called upon to study it seriously the more impatient I became."

He said he "bridled" under his teachers' "insufferable mysticisms… I'd left Christianity, I had no use for the God of my father. But at the same time I was not at war with Christians. And if Christianity was false, as far as I was concerned it had never done me any harm. Furthermore, its mysteries were acknowledged, they were reflections of human depths – the mysteries of the dialectics were carnival hucksters' tricks. They seemed to dare you: how many self-contradictions can we float before anyone starts speaking up and this whole absurd edifice comes crashing down? Certainly I didn't think any of this clearly. It was the last thing in the world I wanted to think, but getting anywhere near Marx's hocus-pocus with a critical mind brought you constantly to the edge of thinking it. So I ran from it, all the more ardently embracing the practical and political program."

And then there was the language. He explained that while Russian was not part of the curriculum, he'd made a special effort, working with one of his translators. On walks along the winding, cobblestoned, streets of old Moscow, talking to strangers as well as to Russian-speaking fellow students, he acquired a working knowledge of the language which would serve him in critical ways in future years.

Otherwise, most of those first several months in Moscow were spent doing nothing. He did not view himself as a student, even in an elite school that taught revolution. But before long, his previous preparation in the Party offered entree onto a new plateau of Party work. It also offered something not often done. When the subject of clandestine activities came up, manipulating unions and popular movements by "boring from within", the lecturer invited him to speak from his experience on the subject.

"It must have been an honor?"

"No. He was anxious to promote me as the American Negro Bolshevik."

There were a few others, he said, that were promoted in a similar way, among them a slightly older Vietnamese man who would later change his name to Ho Chi Minh.

That night, facing a long day, Jim, and later Doswell, retired early.

In subsequent days Jim became burdened following a telephone conversation he'd had with his mother. She'd called early one morning before long-distance rates went up, telling him that Chuck was buying a house north of the city in Rockland County and needed a loan to move on it right away.

"I think you know, Jimmy, how good it will be for them to get out of that apartment and in a home with a nice backyard for the children. He'll pay us back as soon as the estate is fully settled."

He wasn't really troubled by the request; he wanted to see his nephews out of that apartment too. Nor did he have reason to think Chuck wouldn't repay the loan. Chuck needed the money more than he did. But just weeks earlier, they'd quarreled about his not showing up for Christmas and Chuck said in a smug, offhanded way, "Mama didn't complain to me. Did she complain to you?"

He realized his brother was right. She *never* complained. She wore a sign that read *Walk on me* and Chuck had for years happily complied – as did his father. It infuriated Jim, but it saddened him even more.

His mother felt she had somehow to make up for the past. "He had it hardest with your dad," she often said. And it didn't occur to Jim to refuse the loan. Still, these painful thoughts filled his mind for several days.

But there was his Colonus life, which quickly crowded against his New York ruminations. There was Susan's sheer energy. Her tooth-jarring catcalls and her Bronx cheer at basketball games in CSU's Wilson Stadium; her bouncing, honey-blond ponytail, bold like a rooster's tail, held in place by bright flags of waving pink ribbon. She stirred his blood. Radhakathri was back in their lives, though, because he was back in Chris', glumly complaining about a mean-spirited America, addressing them as if they *weren't* Americans, and thus by the exemption condescending to offer supreme compliments. This, and life in Devon with Doswell, pushed dispiriting thoughts about his mother and brother out of his mind.

The next time he talked to the old man about his Moscow past Billy was in his pajamas, standing in the door to Doswell's study.

"Did you brush your teeth?" he asked Billy.

"Yes."

"You get all your homework done? I didn't look at it. Bring it here."

Jim could hardly suppress his mirth as he witnessed such exchanges.

"I did it all, Popeye."

He looked at him searchingly. "Come here then and give me a hug."

Billy furrowed his brow, sneaking a look at Jim, seeming to weigh this all very carefully; then he came running. Billy's hesitation wasn't borne of bashfulness in Jim's presence. Jim had become something of a household fixture by now.

"Popeye, you told me to check in the kitchen to see how much food we need for the week."

"We need any?"

"Lots." He ticked off the things they needed. "We need milk, and we need eggs and Frosted Flakes—"

"Give it to me later."

The games the old man played with Billy would break out at any time, allowing him to mix his roles as father, mother and grandpa into one, with sprightly results. He hugged Billy and then gave him a quick, very loud, emunctory-sounding smooch on his cheek that made the little boy scream. Which led instantly into a tussle, a "disgustingness" contest, each vying to plant the loudest, most revolting-sounding kiss on the other. When it seemed over, as Billy turned to leave, in a flash he pivoted and planted one lightning-like final strike to his grandfather's cheek, triumphantly laughing as he ran off.

Later that night, Doswell plunged deeper into his Moscow life than ever before.

"I came to believe that the control of information needed to be about more than simply keeping information secret. It needed to be about creating an alternative reality, providing a convincing narrative. Like winning the newspapers over to our side – in Passaic the way we saw the conflict with the manufacturers was the reality that the people who read the newspapers worked from. In that way they would be thinking about, talking about, acting in response to what we wanted them thinking about, talking about, responding to. As a practical matter, this meant only winning a few of the leading papers to our side, because the rest followed.

"The second thing I was convinced of then, and still am, was the importance of snob appeal to the revolution – that if you could make your politics appeal to those who viewed themselves as more discerning and superior, you could win over the most powerful, the wealthiest, to your banner."

"Snob appeal? Did you put it that way to your professors in Moscow?"

"Actually I did. I had a scathing opinion of what I called the 'aesthetes of revolution'."

"They didn't view you as a heretic and want to fling you out, as they did Weisbord?"

"No. It didn't touch on anything that was at the moment in real contention. It was all very theoretical. And it was in line with Lenin's concept of using the moral weaknesses of the bourgeoisie against themselves."

Doswell mentioned meeting some key people in Moscow at that time. One who would figure significantly in his future was J. Peters, a man who, using numerous pseudonyms, would for years head up the national underground – a shadowy figure.

Another to appear in his immediate future was an American of Russian or Ukrainian Jewish descent, Dr. Armand Hammer, the future billionaire. One of Weisbord's many tales in Passaic was that Hammer, a young physician and entrepreneur, along with his father, Julius, a physician as well, was the chief conduit for funds from Moscow which sustained the fledgling Party in the United States.

At a certain stage in their program of studies, when Doswell's fellow students' practical and theoretical work was supplemented by assignments to factories and agricultural collectives outside the capital, in his case his assignment was to the Hammers' palatial thirty-room mansion in the heart of Moscow. Thus began a relationship of long duration that would, amazingly, put him at the center of some of the regime's most sensitive and secret activities – a relationship which would also put his life at peril.

It was on the way, the first time, to this garish building on the fashionable Petrovsky Pereulok that Doswell told Jim he'd ruminated over other stories Weisbord had garnered from the gossip at Nancy Cunard's townhouse off Park Avenue. For one, he'd learned that Hammer's father Julius had served several years in Sing Sing for manslaughter, the result of a botched abortion. And the sequel: that the senior Dr. Hammer had not actually performed the abortion, that his son Armand had performed it in his father's clinic, Armand not yet having graduated from medical school.

Vying with these scandalous stories were a whole other set of thoughts impossible to quell: ever since the time of the All Race Congress he'd dedicated his life to the destruction of capitalism; he was now in the capital of the first government on earth dedicated to that end; he'd been assigned to a school whose purpose was to train in the overthrow of world capitalism; yet his contacts were admitting that the Hammers were no pretend capitalists. And now he'd been ordered to join the younger Hammer to become something of his partner in the service of their capitalist enterprise!

Doswell said he'd painfully pondered all of this as he came within sight of the Hammers' mansion, called the Brown House. They had said Armand was "shameless". *Shameless.* He repeated the word as he stood gazing meditatively, first at the gaudy, ample expanse of the mansion, and then at the squat, carrot-red Korsh Theatre across the street from the Brown House.

"He has been making excessive profits in his dealings with the regime," Sergei Strenskuloff, his tall, bass-voiced Lenin School advisor had said. He was in the habit of "deducting large sums for personal expenses, giving his friends and family discounts on items in his franchise agreements with the regime, siphoning off money". He simply couldn't be trusted! But Strenskuloff said he was immensely useful. And furthermore, he added, he was convinced Thomas could handle the task of being the Party's watchdog.

Doswell pointed out the obvious: he was no accountant. Strenskuloff replied they could teach him whatever he needed to know. They, Strenskuloff added, would tell him *when* he needed to know it. Doswell asked how if they didn't trust Hammer, they could choose to work with him. The usually poker-faced Russian laughed loudly – "that's where you come in!"

When they first met, he said, Hammer, who was about his own age, was profusely complimentary, praising his "compatriot" for what he'd heard about him: "They all say you are a fine young student – that you have the highest grades." Then he added something like this: "They have a proposition for me, Thomas – I'm sure you've been told about it. They want me to sell off the Romanoff treasure in the United States. There's quite a lot to sell, you know. The Crown Jewels should bring, oh, tens of millions, maybe a hundred million alone, and they had at least half a dozen palaces, and every one filled with precious objects. Of course I will get a commission for my services, like any sales agent."

This business of the Romanoff treasure was the way the regime was going to bail Dr. Hammer out of his financial fix, a matter which had been explained to Doswell at the Lenin School, and which Hammer alluded to, but with an understandably different viewpoint.

"Such money wasted in the past! No wonder the people had enough of them, those rulers who considered all Russia their treasure! We'll put it to good use now, helping to build a just and equal society here in the land of the future." He fell easily into reveries, a man already rich with memories; his gaze drifted to the lofty ceilings. "People in our country – our fellow citizens – don't appreciate the promise this new experiment holds out. I want to give it every opportunity."

The Hammers, Doswell explained to Jim, were at that moment in a difficult situation. Western businessmen whose investments they'd first helped to bring to the Soviets nearly ten years before, under Lenin's New Economic Policy, were now losing everything as their assets were being expropriated, their companies nationalized. And while the Hammers were the last in line to suffer these losses, they were the least able to sustain them, having put everything of the family fortune into Soviet deals and investments like pencil factories, a mining concession, an agency for importing Ford farm tractors, and an Estonian bank the Soviets had pressured him to buy, and which then went bankrupt.

"I heard you met Lenin when you first came," Doswell ventured.

Hammer drew a long, lazy puff of smoke from his cigar and then lingeringly blew it from his puckered lips. "Yes, that's right. They told you at the school? Well, you know the essence of it is, I'm just a businessman. And Lenin understood that I could help the regime with my contacts in the West. 'What we need,' he said, 'is American capital and technical aid to get our wheels turning once more.' That's when he offered me my first concession: an asbestos mine in Alapayevsk." Growing positively dreamy once again, he fixed on one of the trophy heads of wild buffalo high on the wall. "We lost a lot of our money in that venture. Our contract called for building houses for the workers, schools and a hospital and dispensary – it was all very costly."

Doswell had first agonized over why the regime would do business with a capitalist – a capitalist, worse, who'd given it a lot of reason to distrust him. Yet over time another question incessantly took its place, a question which Jim put into words.

"Why would this consummate businessman continue to do business with the regime if, after all, he *was* a businessman and he'd gained nothing but wrack and ruin from so doing?"

And Doswell, in the dim light of his Devon farmhouse, gave this much-considered question an answer, but only after long thought: "The notion that one defies reason when your choices run contrary to some simple calculus of profit and loss is a superstition. Even for a businessman. Guided by that superstition, ninety per cent of our choices would have to be irrational. No, even an international entrepreneur has to have something to live for..." He stopped mid-sentence, and then pursued a counter-thought. "Of course that doesn't mean you give up on staying at the top of the food chain. He became a billionaire in the West with his special contacts in the East. As for that mining concession..." The thought skipped a beat. "Alapayevsk was a bust – not because he spent lavishly on the workers. That was a lie. The workers were slaves."

So there they were: Doswell and Hammer – both about thirty – in the early stages of their careers. The two sat alone in this great, ornate room with ceilings seventeen or eighteen feet high, and lining the walls were rococo statuary and paintings and trophy heads of wild animals. From the beginning this was an operation that would be shrouded with the greatest secrecy. Within the family, only Dr. Hammer's father, Julius, and later a brother, would ultimately know the real nature of Thomas' position as partner in the Hammers' American enterprise. And at that moment most of this remained a mystery to Doswell, and unknown even to Hammer himself.

Throughout the long interview which followed that night, nearly half the century earlier, Doswell said he felt Hammer's calculated aggressiveness – controlling even in his facial expressions; unresponsive, condescending; constantly referring to him as a "fine student".

"I hope you keep up your good grades, that's important." Was he mocking him? Perhaps not consciously. His impression was that Hammer was so used to being in command that it was instinctive for him to make you feel a mere cipher in his presence, an underling, ready to serve. He admitted he felt this through the prism of his racial identity, but his mind told him – and experience would later confirm – that with virtually anybody who was a subordinate, Hammer could be similarly condescending, personally controlling and dismissive.

Of course it had been earlier explained to Doswell by the meticulous and martial Strenskuloff that he was *not* to be a subordinate, he was only to *appear* so. A cover, a charade for the outside world. Just as with Weisbord. He was to appear, in so far as there was any need to explain, as the Hammer family's loyal Negro retainer returned from across the ocean, brought to Russia to take over the domestic side of this huge and sprawling mansion. But here they were, alone, and Hammer's manner towards him was not in line with his status as the American Party's, and the Comintern's, representative, his partner in secret Party work, but as the factotum that was the cover.

As for the sale of this treasure of the Romanoffs', Hammer explained, it was to earn much-needed Western currency to pay for a quantum leap in industrial imports. It was to launch the first Five Year Plan – and it was now filling to overflow the warehouses of the Gorkham State Storehouse for Valuables.

"Thomas, there are those in the West who are spreading these wild stories about murder in the night, murderous labor camps, crazy, exaggerated stories you and I know, and they are already saying it was stolen from the people – can you imagine that? These same people, that the Romanoffs and their nobility ground into servitude, had *nothing! Stolen* from them?"

In fact, over time he told Jim he would come to know with complete clarity that it amounted to far more than the wealth of the czars. In the decade since the revolution, art objects, precious stones, jewelry, a vast array of valuables not only from the Romanoffs and the nobility, but from literally everywhere and virtually everyone – from monasteries, churches, synagogues, citizens of bourgeois background, prosperous peasants or kulaks, and not-so-prosperous peasants – any number of out-of-favor groups had been contributing vastly to this treasure in the Gorkham.

Selling these baubles of luxury over the next several years would not only bring a large infusion of Western currency to support the regime's grand industrial plans, it could also, if used rightly, bring a double reward: it could serve the regime by winning favorable opinion in the West.

"This is a wonderful cultural exchange," he said. "People in our country will have the opportunity to own valuable artwork – the glories of the imperial treasure – for ordinary Americans who can appreciate fine Old World workmanship."

The first and most obvious problem to be surmounted, then, was in making this treasure appear legitimate. Dr. Hammer was already trying out his first tentative steps in that direction with Thomas. It was a kind of practice session – a dry run.

Those many years later he told Jim, "It was spoken of as the Romanoff treasure. If there was room for thinking any part of it otherwise, it was what the 'filthy rich', those who'd 'stolen from the people' were now returning to them – albeit forcibly."

But what did Doswell think of it? Or, what did he know of the treasure's actual provenance? He at first deflected the question, but after an interval, staring into his own thoughts, he said, "The question to ask is, what did you *not want* to know? I suppose for many Germans thirty years ago, the answer would have been, 'I don't want to know where all those people are going in those trains.' It wouldn't have taken much to figure out. People traveling packed in cattle cars, that's not ordinary. But did they really not know? I'm sure, like us, many of them simply refused to think about it, because they did not want to know, turning their minds to more pleasant things, including what the regime promised for the future. On the other hand, they had a better excuse than I did in refusing to know, for the price of knowing and doing something would have been death. For us the price was to give up our dream."

And then he revealed something which Jim, at the time, found shocking in its unflinching self-revelation.

"I had this idea. I never put it into words, but it was there, unexpressed. It was that *they*, you understand, *they*," he let this sink in – "I mean, white people, had been at war on *us* for centuries, a war, you see, undeclared, all the worse for that, a war on all these generations, these countless innocents whose voices were never heard! And now the tables were turned – it was a war for the possession of the future, and if these people were killing their own – *if*, you see! – well then, so be it! That was surely not my concern."

"But they couldn't have had anything to do – even their ancestors – with—"

"Of course not. I'm not saying it was rational, not a shred of it! Some things like that are hidden in the depths because they can't admit the light of logic or reason. And I would never have admitted to it except that there was someone I knew that set me to realizing it. He said, and I forget how it came up, it was back in the States years later in Hammer's presence, he said, 'Those people sent to the camps for re-education, Thomas, believe me, they are the ones who in your South lynched people, they are the religious bigots, the Cossacks, the mob-exploiters who planned pogroms. I know. If they are getting it in the neck, that's just the medicine they need!'"

"When I heard him say this I found myself hot with shame. It took me a long time to fully appreciate why."

In fact, Doswell told Jim that back then with Hammer, he knew very little of the regime's plans. Virtually everything he related he first came to know as little more than hints. What he was told was either misleading or disappeared into a fog of speculation and conjecture. One of the things about which he was misled, both by his contacts at the Lenin School and by Hammer (Hammer himself had been misled), was that the sale of the treasure was for supporting the regime's ambitious industrial plans.

Now Doswell told Jim that worldwide revolution – espionage in all reaches of the American government, the nation's industry, and in far-flung other nations and governments – was the plan. And this would require a great deal of money.

No longer would one diamond necklace, gingerly lifted from the neck of an enemy of the people on the way to her execution, come near to providing for the Party's purposes. It would take the flow of hundreds of tons of priceless valuables to sustain the bold and worldwide effort the regime had in mind. And it would no longer be smuggled into the country. Times had changed. It would be imported, and sold through Hammer's Art Galleries.

The art objects of all kinds: paintings, icons, antiques, jewelry, precious and semi-precious stones, bric-a-brac – all ostensibly owned by Armand Hammer, while the regime's actual ownership was carefully concealed – would have to be overseen by someone outside the family. Yes, he, Hammer, was *Nashe*, "one of us", but the black American would be answerable directly to Moscow to see that the proceeds of the enterprise be directed to the proper channels.

Through all this, Jim's early '60s-sensitized thoughts of race flowed incessantly. Foremost: that the most brutally destructive ideological movement on the face of the earth, not only in its racial ethic but also in its practical life in America, was light years ahead of America's mainstream at treating members of the Negro race as equals. Hidden under America's collective nose, because it was oblivious in its frozen racial certainty, nothing provided a better cover for the regime's clandestine activities than Doswell's skin – a cover not only against American agents but ultimately Hammer as well. Only he could be at the hub, at the very center of things, directly involved with everything, and yet still be little suspected of engaging in sensitive and subversive activities.

Of course, once again, at that time Doswell did not yet know his eventual role in the regime's international schemes. In a fog about what his ultimate duties were to be, like a good soldier, he followed orders – not Hammer's but the regime's. He began familiarizing himself with the elementary tasks he would later have to perform in company with the Hammer family and its associates: the inner workings of the money-laundering, funny-money banking transactions and undercover arrangements; but also making specific preparations, not only logistical but political, for the Hammer family's eventual big move back to the United States.

18

A Sightseer in Erfurt, Germany

There were arrangements that had to be made prior to the Romanoff sale, which caused a delay in returning to America. For one, some of the proceeds from the sale would have to be forwarded to Moscow from time to time. But if the proceeds were Hammer's, why would he then be sending funds back to the Soviet Union? As a cover, Hammer would have to go into the cooperage trade for the distilling business, requiring shipments of oak from the Soviet Union for which he could then 'reimburse' its trading company, the Amtorg. There were other arrangements, and many more problems as well, not least of which was an unexpected legal one, not involving the treasure.

In England a raid had been conducted by the authorities on a London safe house that contained documents relating to the Hammers' long history of clandestine activities. Armand's Russian-born wife, Olga, underwent lengthy questioning at the American Embassy in Germany that was driven by information uncovered in that raid. As a result, his father, Julius, was instantly declared persona non grata in England, and in Germany worse: he was jailed and held on $100,000 bond until the Hammers paid debts owed to German firms that had sold them machine tools for a pencil manufacturing business they'd conducted in Russia years before. It was this last, Julius' incarceration in a German prison, which signaled Doswell's move from Moscow and return to the United States, but which included a several months stay over in Erfurt, a picturesque old city in the state of Saxony, in central Germany.

"I was to be a three-way messenger and go-between for Julius and Armand and the regime," he told Jim, repeating the story about how once before, Armand had been the cause of his father's imprisonment. Now Armand didn't dare to enter Germany for fear he'd be seized like his father, and he didn't dare return to the States for fear of what the US government knew about his activities. So he rented a house outside Paris and waited there with his wife and child, testing the waters before returning to America.

Julius' enforced absence in Sing Sing years earlier had not played well for the regime, Doswell told Jim. His being out of the loop once again brought hand-wringing all around. But this calamity was turned into an opportunity:

as go-between for father and son, he was provided access to inner secrets of the Hammers' business that the Hammers had previously successfully kept from the regime. Now they could be shared with the Comintern in Moscow.

"Of course I played the game so many of my race played for generations. I played dumb. Oh, I don't mean *dumb* dumb. But since accounting and finance were hardly my strong suit, I could easily give free vent to my feelings of inadequacy before the mysteries of business with Armand's close associates. I knew they would carry the impression of my inadequacy back to Armand. But the truth is I was probably the only student at the Lenin School who'd ever studied accounting while there."

Doswell's well-exhibited 'stupidity' in business was very crafty because although it had not opened the books for him while in Moscow, it lulled Armand into complacency. Armand had even taken to cracking sarcastic jokes about "Thomas' well-known business acumen" with his father and representatives of the regime in closed-door sessions, that caused much merriment among all present, and which Major Strenskuloff later shared with Doswell. Once in Erfurt, the Hammers' attitude well established, it became readily expedient that information among family members be transmitted through him, convinced that Doswell could never fathom what they were about.

At first, his task as go-between for all parties promised unremitting bleakness, but as the days stretched into weeks, though obliged to spend a good part of each day visiting with Julius in his prison cell, the remaining hours were his, and the city itself, a thousand-year-old time capsule, became endlessly fascinating for him.

"It was a strange time for me. In the past, serving the Party had sometimes meant simply waiting. I had done so in Passaic and New York after the AF of L expelled us. In Moscow, of course, I had waited. And now I was doing it again, but this time it seemed not just in another place, but in another age.

"I visited with Julius for seven or eight hours, spent to keep him from howling at the moon. Most days what business we strictly had to transact could be covered in fifteen minutes. But then there was the rest of the day outside the prison. And I had never been in a place so concentrated with history, with so much time on my hands and fully free to take it all in."

"It was your first experience as a tourist." Jim smiled.

"Yes, a sightseer... There was a great cathedral on a hill that you climbed a long stairway to reach, and on that same hill a smaller, beautiful, equally old church with magnificent stained glass, and intricately carved altars and statuary. I had never seen so many churches in one place. Yes, you might wonder that a Communist should have noticed or cared about churches. But of course we are human and we have our histories. I had virtually grown up in a church. My father had been a minister and teacher of ministers in a seminary. Unlike many Communists, not all, I did not hate Christianity – my memory of it was of a home that had nourished me. I thought of myself as going beyond it, but not against it. And I constantly asked myself: what would my father think of this, or that? In many ways I spoke more with him in those days than ever before, even though he'd been dead a couple of years. And yes, even to my Communist mind, and undoubtedly through him, I admired those many stunningly beautiful Gothic churches...all in one place...

Jim asked about the presence of Hitler at that time in pre-war Germany.

"In a short time Hitler would come to power. History wasn't just medieval history, it was also being played out all around us, as I was myself pummeling it forward."

Doswell wasn't doing any drinking that night. As he poured boiling water from a pot into two cups for instant coffee, passing one to Jim, he expanded on his impressions of those nearly forty years before.

"The political climate had been heating up for years. There had been a terrible inflationary cycle, and the Great Depression, much worse than in America, was on. The Social Democrats had a majority in the Reichstag but several nationalist parties, one of them the National Socialists, and the Communists as well, collaborated in an effort to destabilize the government.

"I was strictly forbidden to make contact with the local Communists. Though there were many of them, and they were not hidden, there was to be a firewall between me and the open Party in Germany as well as in the States. I was the Hammers' loyal servant, sent to comfort Julius. That was all. I assumed that persona throughout.

"So I looked on from a distance – literally, from my upper floor window in a rooming house which faced the city's main square – and I watched rallies which featured Communist and Nazi speakers on the same platforms, not vying with each other but taunting the police and taking turns assaulting the tottering power of the Weimar Republic."

"It was at least a fascinating place to wait..."

"Yes."

As he spoke Jim reflected on the irony that this was a man whose thoughts had been bottled up for years – a man who in his secret capacity had been at the center of transformative power, and was now living hidden in Colonus and this little Negro non-place, Devon.

"Moscow, on the other hand, that last year I was there, was nearly intolerable. Armand was hard at work, stuffing me into a long, narrow-necked bottle marked *hireling*. I think the isolation and the drudgery would have been completely intolerable if it had not been for the fact that Lovett Fort-Whiteman returned to Moscow.

"Whiteman came in like fresh air in a stuffy room – only it wasn't stuffy, it was airless, he wasn't merely a blast of fresh air, he was the paramedic who jerked me back from the brink of death. He told me he'd been assigned to the central office of the Comintern. He'd go outside Moscow on speaking tours to industrial and farming centers where he expounded passionately on lynchings, Jim Crow, the worldwide oppression of colored people by imperialist nations, that sort of thing. He told those workers and peasants how fortunate they were to be in the land of the future! But much of the time he was in the capital where he was something of a spark plug among the colored people living there.

"So when I could get away from the Brown House for a while and I wasn't having to meet with my contacts at the Lenin School, I would spend time with Lovett and these folks. We'd have these late-nighters with Russian women by our sides."

"No American women?"

"We were mostly from America. If a woman was there she was usually someone's wife. Talking about wives, Whiteman had a Russian wife, Russian-Jewish. They lived in a dank, dark room on Tverskaya Street. It was very near the city's Central Telegraph Office. I liked visiting him there, even though his wife showed great displeasure on seeing me."

"Why was that?"

"She knew that my appearance at her front door signaled that she'd be kept up late with our long talks. Imagine! She was stuck in the room with us! She should have thrown me out by the ear like a more assertive American wife would have, but she didn't." Doswell laughed suddenly, free laughter bubbling up out of a man reveling in saving moments from earlier years.

"There we were, with her in one corner of the room – glum, blank with fatigue – and Lovett and I at the other corner, me trying to steer him away from the Marxist dialectical talk which he liked spouting, and just wanting to talk about home. He had less knowledge of books than he thought he did, but as long as it wasn't fired by the dialectics, the conversation could get beyond slogans and labels tossed around like missiles, and something could be said. Noticing his long-suffering wife, I'd offer to go out and buy him a shot or two of vodka. But then instead he'd go and tell her to bring another bottle he had stashed away. I'd glance at her sheepishly, and he'd shout, 'Thomas, relax, man! Enjoy! Enjoy!' He was half-sloshed. 'You're in Russia now! Have some of the people's juice!'"

"Did you ever talk to him about Hammer and the Brown House?"

"No. Absolutely not. It would have been like the flood that breeches the dam. There would have been no stopping me once I started. Besides, security forbade it. I'm sure even Lovett didn't tell me half of what he was in the capital for."

"What made Hammer finally decide to return to the States?"

"I don't really know. But I had a theory that the regime had something to do with it. Maybe I was wrong. But someone I knew from the Lenin School that I met in Erfurt at that time gave me reason to think the Comintern gave him a green light – or maybe even gave him a little push."

"A push? You mean ordered him to?"

"Maybe not ordered him to. Maybe told him it was safe and the regime was getting impatient…"

Doswell cast his eyes downward in an attitude of meditation through the tent he formed with his clasped hands. Then turning his eyes to Jim again, and adjusting his bulk in his frayed, easy-back chair, he said, "This man I'm talking about, that I knew from Moscow? I met him in this little, dark tobacco shop I used to frequent. Dr. Julius was puffing away non-stop like a steamship in the Erfurt debtor's prison. I bought tobacco for him there. I liked to visit that place. The clerk was pleasant – he'd talk a carefully enunciated German, which was what I needed to hear with my uncertain knowledge of the language. I lingered as usual, putting my German to practice, and as I finished my business, I caught him out of the corner of my eye in the half-shadow. He was staring at me, a measured, almost wondering gaze. I instantly knew him. J. Peters. Short in stature. Dark hair. A head too big for his body.

"He approached me as he saw I recognized him, and started immediately to talk in English, and I remember his opening words almost exactly: 'I think you admire these churches in Erfurt very much, Thomas, do you not?' He smiled and chuckled.

"As his first appearance, so his opening words made an impression on me. For he was certainly letting me know that he'd been trailing me without my knowledge.

"We stepped outside the shop and we exchanged some words about Moscow, and he asked if I was anxious to return to America. I said I was. I said I dreamed regularly of a good ham-and-eggs breakfast. He laughed. 'Yes,' he said, 'Americans eat well. I, too, like their big meals.'

"Then he said, in the same off-the-cuff manner, 'The new President will soon be inaugurated. We expect not long after he gets into office there will be diplomatic recognition. About time too! Germany, France – so many countries already. Then it will be like a well struck. Oases in the desert!' He paused significantly, looking at me, a meaningful expression that read me as much as it spoke.

"We walked around the city, he leading the way, lingering especially long beside the churches which we gazed at like two tourists – I mainly listening and nodding, answering yes and no in response to his heavily accented but very adequate English. He got down to business then, explaining for the first time what the regime planned for me: that I was to be the 'bank' in America and the money was to come from the Romanoff treasure.

'The Hammers, of course, will not like it. We will not tell them until the time is ripe.' A big grin came across his face. 'Colossal opportunities in America!' He opened his arms wide. 'By the way,' he said, 'when does our capitalist prince plan to move back?'

"I was still digesting what he'd said, and then this question. I said I didn't know.

'You don't know, and you've been passing messages between him and his father for two months now?'

'He doesn't know himself,' I said. 'He's afraid to return to America. He thinks they'll arrest him and throw him in the slammer like his father.'

"He thought this quite funny. 'Ah, yes. Well. If we were religious men we might say that would be just punishment for his many sins against his father. But we are not religious men…' He paused and looked at me with a quizzical, bemused expression. 'At least I am not.'

"I said nothing. We walked in silence, absorbed in the sights.

"Then he said, 'The Americans are children. They won't do anything to Hammer. As long as they have their big breakfasts and their toys, they will be satisfied.'

"Seconds later, seeing a break in the heavy traffic, he cut across the street, saying as he rushed away, 'I'll contact you in New York. God be with you.'"

19

Inside the Haunted Wood

Jim watched Doswell as he helped Billy with his math. He led him through formidable thickets of gobbledygook called 'new math', which Billy was at pains to understand.

"A farmer exchanges a set, S, of strawberries for a set, M, of money. The cardinality of set M…"

"Popeye," Billy wailed, "Mrs. Clark says I'm ignorant 'cause I'm lost, 'cause I don't understand any of it!"

"Don't worry, Billy. Being lost isn't being ignorant, to be lost and to *think* you know the way, *that's* ignorance. We'll get it if we apply ourselves."

He had theories about what he was doing at the university that were not inconsistent with these words to his grandson.

And Jim had grown familiar with his theories: "What was the word you used the other day? Demolition? When we were talking about ignorance?"

"You mean at the office? About Plato?"

"Yeah. And I think you said, Freud's formulation."

"*The problem isn't with what you don't know; the problem is with what you know that isn't so.* But Plato had much more in mind than Freud."

"Yeah – so you have to demolish unsound, even dangerous structures of false opinion." Still, Jim had never seen anything resembling a wrecking ball in his dealings with Baxter's students, any more than with Billy.

Doswell greatly admired Greek thought, but not uncritically. "Plato thought construction materials were all of one kind: ideas. The Thomas Gradgrinds of Victorian England thought so too: only for them it was facts. Teachers make a fatal mistake when they find something partially true and ride it exclusively."

Billy and Baxter's young men and women, of course, were not Doswell's only pupils that year. Over the previous hour Doswell had given Jim a detailed account of the Byzantine intricacies of Soviet and Party apparatuses, agencies and political arrangements.

They'd returned earlier that evening from a banquet-like dinner at the Lewises' and Doswell had just finished a disquisition on some often misunderstood details regarding the open Party and the underground, about the Communist

International or Comintern; about 'legal' and 'illegal' work, 'legal' versus 'illegal' station chiefs, and how with diplomatic recognition a whole new chapter was being written in the regime's presence in America.

He explained that for many years J. Peters would slip in and out of the States, living within the country for long periods under half a dozen assumed names, heading up the CPUSA underground, organizing any number of espionage rings, and producing false passports, birth certificates and naturalization papers.

"So there was no withering away of illegal activities?"

"Of course not. Peters went right on with a very lucrative, actually pioneering business"

"I meant no withering away of an *illegal resident* or station chief. There continued unchanged agents working under the station chief – that is, *not* in the United States under a legal cover."

"Exactly."

"But why would they have two?"

"Two? Two categories? Why not? Why not half a dozen if they could?"

Doswell could see the glazed look. To Jim the old man seemed to be searching.

"What is the most popular sport in Russia?"

Jim suddenly drew himself up straight, looked up, knowing Doswell was preparing a parallel in the lesson for his slow student. "I guess I don't know. What is it?"

"Chess."

"Is chess a sport?"

"For my purposes it is. It requires cunning, employing multiple fronts, maneuvers anticipating remote moves, both offensive and defensive – you want to confuse and mislead your opponent in as many ways as possible. I guess you could say the other is weightlifting, and it involves a surge of brute and overwhelming strength."

"What you described is like some kind of wild, overgrown wood, or jungle."

"That's as good a picture as any. And like a thick wood it's very easy to lose your way, unless you know it from the inside."

"Or have a guide."

"Yes, one who'd been lost in it longer than anyone."

He said that all the divisions, the helter-skelter overlaps and apparent lack of logic, were intended to mislead and to create walls of separation among the agents, as well as keeping them, as much as possible, ignorant of the structure in general and each other's activities and identities.

"And outsiders?"

"Of course. Ten times over."

But they'd not entered far into the wood, or talked about the way into it.

"I went to Moscow assuming I would be continuing on the course I'd been on: labor agitation, winning the brothers to the revolution. It wasn't until I met

Peters in Erfurt that I began to understand where it was all leading…"

"Even when you were seeing Hammer in the Brown House you weren't thinking of espionage?"

"All we talked about was helping the regime to grow industrially. I think that's what he thought. The so-called Romanoff treasure was to be the means. Espionage was *never* talked about…" He caught himself mid-thought. Then he said, after a long pause, "No. I'm wrong. I forgot. Spying *had been* proposed.

"The Hammers used to give lavish parties. I was in the thick of them. There was my cover: the Hammers' loyal retainer. And they fully used my services. Brown House, you understand, was the closest thing to an American embassy before diplomatic recognition. Very important people came. Congressional delegations, foreign diplomats, famous personalities from the West, like Will Rogers, Jack Dempsey, John Dewey. The Hammers' house was the hottest social scene in Moscow. They asked me—"

"Hammer?"

"No, my contacts, they asked me to listen in on conversations and report back on any useful matters. I asked them: did they want me to blow my cover with cheap tricks?"

"Did you?"

"No."

"They never insisted?"

"I think they were testing my reaction as much as anything. And by that time there was the real task: to help prepare for the selling of the Romanoff treasure, then returning to the States."

"So you did after you saw Peters."

"Shortly afterwards."

"Oases in the desert?"

"Colossal opportunities. It wasn't just diplomatic recognition. That, of course, was critical. But it was the Depression. When I joined times were good – at least for most. That had changed. And with that, the harvest had grown immensely. I mean there were many more people sympathetic to the 'Soviet experiment', as it was called. Washington was awash with college types whose casualness and friendly competition with each other in joining the cause, as we say today, sometimes resembled more that of aspiring members of college fraternities than Soviet spy networks."

"There were *that many* spies?"

"There were many who said they wanted to help Russia. All kinds; bad times made for good times for the regime."

During those early February days when Jim and Doswell were twice holed up in Devon, and Susan in Colonus, during ice storms which covered everything under sheets of ice, Doswell told Jim about his return to New York. He told him about the 'roadshow' he went on with Hammer to open the Romanoff Treasure Sale, and about his arrangements with J. Peters and Strenskuloff, and then the 'banking' arrangements with the underground and the Comintern.

"Hammer opened an art gallery in the Waldorf-Astoria on Park Avenue, but first he wanted to sell all over America. He thought the provincials would be a lot less artistically critical and demanding. He planned on selling the bric-a-brac and poorer quality stuff first, out in the Midwest. I think it was in Chicago or Saint Louis, and it was at upscale department stores. There was a fifty-fifty arrangement with the proceeds from the sale, and he went from city to city for stays of several weeks. Like a circus, that's how he described it. And he was right about that...

"From what Julius said in Erfurt, and the regime studiously didn't say, for a while I thought that they were expecting me to go back to living with the Hammers again. But I decided I would quit the Party if it came to that. I was determined before I left Germany that on this I would not give an inch."

"The fact that you were coming back to the States, did that affect your willingness to quit the Party?"

"I didn't decide to quit the Party then. But I suppose it did affect my readiness to. Yes. Obviously I'd be a lot freer in my own country to take such a step. But I knew living with them was something I could never do again – that it would also be counterproductive. I argued this to Peters when I saw him in New York. At the time I was living on Lenox Avenue, just above 125th Street in a single room, little more than a flophouse, and I was anxious to get out. So I had a lot of things on my agenda. I wanted to find a place that would be roomy enough to provide a modicum of comfort, but with enough space and privacy to do the work they'd assigned me...and I was ready for a blow-up.

"I was on the road. I think I was in Chicago or on the West Coast when I got word that Peters was back and he wanted to see me. I'd given a lot of thought to what he'd told me in Germany, and what I'd need from the Party. I reminded him that I'd been handed an assignment that required two separate tasks, and one was to keep tabs on Hammer—"

"To spy on the spy," Jim said lightly, feeling by this time almost like a veteran himself of the spy wars.

"That's right, I needed an assistant, preferably from Russia, who could keep tabs on the details of the Hammers' transactions. Someone who knew accounting backwards and forward, and who could read and write Russian. Besides, I pointed out, I couldn't be in two places at once. 'Right now,' I said, 'Hammer's out on the road while I'm here talking to you.'"

"That got their attention?"

"It probably did. But actually, I wasn't too worried about Hammer being alone with his circus because I saw pretty quickly that the department stores he'd made arrangements with were very particular about accounting for everything, and the books he kept with them were difficult to hide from the Party. Also, I'd come to realize that the Party really expected him to cheat, and accepted his cheating as part of the price of doing business with him."

"So all the talk about stopping him from cheating them was...?"

"Naturally they would never say this outright. And this was only if he didn't get *too* greedy. They wanted to know other things. To gauge whether he'd be playing a double game. Spy on the spy, as you say. So I wasn't worried about a little cheating. But when he got back to New York, and some of the big, expensive items came along, major artworks, selling through his Waldorf-Astoria gallery, then I discovered he was way too greedy."

"How did he react when he learned about the bank, that all the money for it was to come from the sale of the Romanoff treasure, and you were going to oversee it?"

"He didn't. At least, not ever in my presence. His famous poker face never registered so much as a ripple of surprise or discontent. In my presence he even spoke favorably of the general idea, though I was told that in private he shared with Strenskuloff his concern that I was not up to the task of handling the tricky finances. I knew, of course, that this wouldn't be the end of it. That there would be intrigues.

"But in the meantime, I wanted a house to work from up in Harlem. It wasn't that far from where Hammer lived, midtown Fifth Avenue, and I knew I could more easily blend in and hide from prying eyes."

"Did you think the authorities, the FBI, were on your trail, or fear they might pick up your trail?"

"That crossed my mind. But more, frankly, Soviet government surveillance. I became convinced American counter-espionage was a joke. The American atmosphere in general was utterly lax. You could hold a Party meeting on the park benches right out in the middle of Broadway and the people would have gone right by, oblivious."

"Really?" Jim doubted this. "But how could you *know* that the FBI or other agencies were wholly in the dark?"

"I suppose if you put it that way, it is possible that they knew more than it seemed, that maybe there was surveillance I had no idea of. But I never had the slightest inkling or evidence of it. And that wasn't what I was most concerned about, even though I always used good spy craft. No, I wasn't worried so much about Soviet government surveillance either. It was Hammer and his associates. I knew that working with him would not be smooth – I wanted to guard against any possible eventualities with him. And I told Peters this – by the way, the first time, I met with Peters alone, the second time, no more than a couple of weeks later, Strenskuloff was with him."

"You mentioned Strenskuloff before when you were in Moscow. You said he was more a conventional kind of military guy?"

"Strenskuloff was a very different kind of man than Peters. He had this military bearing. He was tall, he was straight, and you could tell he was a little uncomfortable – he was uneasy in America. He was in the country illegally. And I think it was the first time he was in America. When we first met in New York, he mentioned the American secret police. I could tell Peters was suppressing his laughter. Peters was like a typical New Yorker. He too was an 'illegal' but he blended right in and was completely at home. He had a sense of humor too."

"A grim sense of humor."

"Yes, yes. Grim. That's true. And he had a memory. But even in Moscow, Strenskuloff was stiff. He felt the weight of his office. He was on a mission from the Comintern, and while Peters was, aside from the General Secretary, the most powerful man in the Party, it was Strenskuloff who called the tune."

"The General Secretary?"

"Earl Browder, General Secretary of the American Party. Peters was the head of the American underground.

"So we drove around the little park near Grant's Tomb and up and down Riverside Drive, pulling over now and then on side streets when we could (I was driving). It occurred to me then that this would be a very good way of conducting my banking transactions: in a car or limousine, moving around the city. The limousine, that was off the top of my head that night. A limousine service, yes, that would be the ideal cover, and my link to the Hammers and to whoever needed to make 'banking transactions'. I'd learned something from being around the Hammers. You could set up a business as a front, and you could be off and running if you had the connections and the funds and the knowhow. I had all three if I could win over Strenskuloff and Peters to my scheme. I'd learned from Hammer, too, that you could do that if you convinced the Party people that you could make it work for them. Capitalism in a socialist framework. So I made my pitch."

"Capitalism? But what about these so-called banking transactions you'd be making? Were you anything like a real bank?"

"Let me put it this way: Moscow wanted all of the national parties, as best they could, to support themselves. It wanted them to stop begging. This meant, obviously, the American Party first off, because it was judged to be so rich. The underground, for instance, was to generate income by providing what I mentioned before: phony immigration documents, citizenship papers, what have you. Peters had developed over the years a full-time industry with half a dozen researchers working out of the New York Public Library's genealogical division, looking up the names and dates of babies that were born and then died shortly afterwards, decades earlier. Then he used the names very creatively to get official American documentation for illegals traveling all over the world."

"This Peters character fascinates me. He sounds like a character from central casting. He seems like a regular entrepreneur of Communist espionage."

"Yes, a regular industry. And he also wanted to sell to the Comintern the documents and the secrets that his idealistic Americans were happy to purloin for free. But the Comintern drew the line at that. It didn't want to pay Peters. Anyway, the idea was that the underground was to 'borrow' from the bank if it needed money and then pay it back later. Same was true for the open Party. The American Party had always been subsidized by Moscow. Now that was changing. It wanted to erase the money link. It would be from New York that most new apparatuses would be funded with Romanoff treasure money. So an agent responsible for organizing a new network inside China, Japan, the Asian rim, Australia, Canada or Latin America would meet with me, requesting a 'loan' to cover start-up costs. These would be for legitimate-seeming businesses that would have reason to be in these countries. A news syndicate for instance, or a literary service – any kind of business that would justify heavy cable and human traffic to and fro would be a promising front within the target country.

"He'd give a general description of the activity, the type of front that would be employed, how many workers (both Party workers and legitimate workers if that was the case), material needs, whatever was necessary to determine if his request was reasonable. I might approve what he asked. Or not. We'd discuss it. I might even, though rarely, suggest more. When the decision was made (I 'approved the loan', so to speak), he would be instructed within a couple of days by code and through a mail-drop to pay a visit to the Trust Company of North America, a bank which an associate of Hammer's owned, who'd been laundering money for the Hammers and the regime for a decade already.

"Monies that came from Romanoff proceeds were deposited in this bank. Monies that came from several other Hammer businesses, including his cooperage business, his distilling and distribution businesses, and others, were deposited in this bank. The agent was instructed to go to the bank on a particular day and hour and there he would pick up the amount of the loan which was written up as a loan for the firm we had set up."

"But of course they weren't really loans. Or were they at all like loans?"

"They were virtually in every instance 'grants', if you will. Then on the books they'd be dealt with eventually in several ways. They could be written off as bad loans – of course they came from the treasure, so the bank really didn't lose money on them. Or monies that came from future proceeds of the treasure would be used in the name of the front to 'pay off' the loan."

"And no one ever paid any of this back."

"Actually that's not true. The American Party often did, though it was always in arrears. I think one network in Australia did make a payment, and everyone scratched their heads over that for years. Otherwise, national parties in other countries never paid back, but they did take some financial responsibility funding their own revolution with train and bank robberies."

Jim began to chuckle, thinking that Doswell had intended a witticism. But he didn't laugh.

"That was a common method of funding indigenous operations: criminal activities, which you know today have branched out into many other kinds of crimes. Many started like that – drug trafficking, for instance, especially profitable in Latin America with such a rich market to the north."

"Like some of these New Left operations? Like the Black Panthers or the Weathermen, which are no doubt engaged in similar operations now?"

"I don't know much about that. They're a lot about romantic revolutionism, playing at revolution, harking back to Bonnie and Clyde…"

"But it's as serious for the people who get killed."

"Absolutely."

"So did you get your assistant and your limousine? What did Peters say to your demand about living arrangements?"

"He agreed."

"Ahh, but did Hammer continue to try to 'stuff you into a long-necked bottle'?"

"No, but then again…" his thought trailed off. "Strenskuloff asked some critical questions that first night I made my pitch. And I wasn't sure of the direction he would go. But I could tell he could be guided by Peters' opinion, though he didn't want to be seen as anything but the man in charge. So if I could win Peters over without neglecting him, without alienating him—"

"He was no prima donna."

"Yes. He said we'd get back together. I knew he wanted to consult with the station chief in New York, and with Peters outside my hearing – but one thing I knew, they both liked the idea of the limousine service. Especially Peters. He told him, 'That is just the kind of business that a prosperous Negro living in Harlem would have – no offense, Thomas,' he said to me.

'No offense at all,' I said. 'That is exactly what I had in mind. Racist American authorities would never in a million years think to look into a Negro's business for such an operation.' I looked to Strenskuloff then, with the obvious question in mind.

"After a moment he said simply, 'Yes, yes, very interesting.'

"I didn't get a limousine. I got a fleet of limousines. In fact the most successful limousine service in Harlem…and I got my assistant."

Charlie, the underground name of this assistant, wasn't Russian. He was from one of the Muslim republics in Central Asia. An Uzbek. But he was an accounting whiz and he knew his Russian perfectly. And he efficiently handled all the details with the bank, the Trust Company of North America and its owner,

Schapiro. He also oversaw the books from Hammer's Art Gallery. And as time passed, he came to be in more routine contact with the Hammers than Doswell.

The Party also gave Doswell money for a modest house on West 144th Street. And nearby on Seventh Avenue he had a garage and an office which was also purchased by the Party, one of its many loans paid from Romanoff treasure funds. The limousine service was an ideal cover: it had no address, no identifiable physical location for the meetings, and it provided an easy connection with the Hammers and other Party figures.

"What were they like?"

"What? The agents?"

"No," Jim chuckled, "the limousines."

Doswell laughed. "They were typical of the time. Cadillac. Squarish. The kind you see in old movies. The one I used had a glass panel that separated the front driver and passenger seats from the rear passenger section. There was a partition; it could be slid open only from the front seats which I, sitting on the passenger side beside the chauffeur, controlled. The glass was also see-through from the front, and reflective facing to the front from the rear. As part of good spy craft, I did not look through the glass panel to see those who'd come with 'loan' proposals – in the majority of cases. During the last few months when I was breaking with the Party, I did. And as for the meetings themselves, they were always held after dark, and since the place of the meeting was my choice, I could arrange to shield myself from being seen when they entered or left the vehicle. Thus discussions could be carried out or transactions made without either party actually seeing the other."

"So both of you would know as little as possible about the other."

"That was the idea."

"No one ever suspected? The FBI never gave you any scares?" This was an improbability in Jim's mind. He had grown up on television and movies and popular stories which portrayed the FBI as a super-agency which knew all.

"The whole point of espionage is to keep everything very boring. Fictional spy stories are full of excitement because someone is always on the verge of catching someone. But if someone's on the 'verge' it's already too late. The operation is dead in the water – and the agents are lucky if they aren't dead too. So we took – or at least most of us – we took scrupulously careful measures. As I say, the underground insisted on them. I insisted on them. Making it all work meant taking no chances."

"What about your driver?"

"Hawpe was the only person that I hired for the limousine service that was with the Party."

"What about Charlie?"

"Charlie never appeared, at least I don't think he ever did, even at the office."

"But then your driver, Hawpe, he had to know you."

"But virtually nothing of what I was doing. Banking transactions never drifted into English – they were usually in German, sometimes French or Spanish."

"What if he guessed?"

"He was a Negro. He would prove himself utterly loyal to me, but even if he hadn't been, even if he'd known what it was all about, and he wanted to tell someone, who would listen to him? Who would believe him?"

"If he had a tape recording they'd believe him."

"Not even with a tape recording. They'd have had to listen to it first. I tell you, in those days you could have been wearing a sign that said *I am a spy*, and you would have been ignored. And then if you ever got anybody to listen, they'd have thrown *you* into the slammer. Anyway, Hawpe was utterly loyal."

But his description of his amazing global financial role from within one of the limousines of his limousine service – Uncle Big Bob's, the name intended to reinforce the jolly Negro patina – was not without a report of, so to speak, potholes, big ones, and they were in all cases created by the Hammers. This he told Jim one night when the power had gone off, Billy upstairs sleeping soundly, and the entire house lit only by the flickering light of two oil lamps.

"The day we arrived in America Hammer was complaining of losing money hand over fist. I'd barely stepped ashore in New York following months in Erfurt with his father, and Armand was accusing me of being responsible for bloated bills that were bankrupting him. There were warehouses in New York that had been storing the treasure piecemeal, in some cases for over a year. Some items were in the wrong warehouses. Inventory problems. All kinds of problems. I was in Erfurt and his brother Harry was in New York, but I was to blame for nearly all of them. I pointed out the strangeness of such a charge under the circumstances, and it became clear to me he was trying to maneuver me into responsibility for the 'pile-up' so he could exact some leverage with the Comintern."

"He was really strapped for cash?"

"I don't know if he really was at the time, but the bills were considerable. So then he'd 'borrow' large sums from the Romanoff treasure."

"He was only doing what Hammer did: cheating."

"No. *Large* sums which affected our ability to function. He'd try to do it on the sly by playing with the books. Charlie discovered this. Armand wasn't doing it by himself. His brother Harry worked with the books more closely than Armand. And so the game went in circles, in pursuit of the actual transaction or transactions that had been doctored to disguise the proceeds from different arrangements for different classes of artwork, with different New York galleries. When an irregularity would be demonstrated, there were phony smiles and laughter over the 'misunderstanding', along with reminders of his always-precarious financial situation with an unreasonably demanding regime. And then we'd go back to square one, and sure enough, eventually we'd start on another round when the time came for Hammer to cover his losses in some other venture with treasure money."

"But he was cheating, and you said the regime tolerated or expected cheating, so why?

"Up to a point, I said. Sometimes the funds weren't in the bank to cover the 'loans'. This Schapiro simply wouldn't tolerate. Which meant that there were occasions when agents would go down to lower Manhattan to draw on their 'loan' and it would be refused because funds were insufficient. This made for the unexpected – and the unexpected can mean disaster. For that is when you have serious missteps."

"And there was no one you could complain to, nothing Charlie could do?"

"Charlie was an easygoing kind of man. He was a short, round fellow whose great love in America was to learn the newest dances. He hated confrontations. So yes, I'd be drawn in. Of course the Hammers made it difficult in these situations for either of us to look at the books. Harry would make veiled threats which couldn't be discounted. There were stories of people from years before who, once they'd crossed them, had been killed or disappeared – nothing that could be proven, all just rumors. I looked on Harry as a sniveling coward and a bully, and I despised the man as much as his brother, but like all cowards in his position, and with the power and arrogance of his family, he could be dangerous."

"But his practices were a threat, as you say."

"I did take the matter up with Peters, but Peters in the end didn't want to be involved. The Hammers were too big. As for me, I knew that if the regime had to choose between us it would choose Hammer in a heartbeat. Still, I complained of his attempts at cheating the regime of large sums when that began to threaten our work. I even went to Moscow. For a while he became more circumspect. At least the loans stopped, though Charlie suspected the cheating continued on a smaller scale. But it was only a matter of time till he started borrowing against the treasure again, and there was nothing to cover loans. This time, though, he brought a complaint at the highest levels, in the Kremlin, that Charlie, or both Charlie and I, were embezzling funds. One of the oldest tricks in the Party's book of tricks: charge your enemy with exactly the crime you are committing, make the charge deafening, and make it stick with all the authentic details that you as the criminal know so well. Fortunately for us Strenskuloff was dispatched to New York to look into the matter."

"But Stalin was in power."

"Yes. Exactly. He was in power."

Outside they could hear breaking ice, the branches cracking and crashing out in the yard. Though the electricity had long gone off, the fire in the wood-burning stove made the room cozy – more than cozy, slightly over-warm for Jim.

"In fact I never went back again. And yes, they could have ordered me to return. But they didn't… I think it was pretty obvious. Strenskuloff eventually went back to Moscow and he must have reported that Charlie and I were innocent of the charges. Nothing further was said to us, but still, Hammer continued as before. He was too big. He had friends in the highest of places, going right to Stalin himself. As for Strenskuloff, I respected the man, I always thought of him as a basically decent individual – in fact, he would soon be swept away."

"He was killed?"

"He simply disappeared. At a certain point in time he simply ceased to be. It was the time called the Great Purge…"

"So Hammer just continued his merry way."

"What became clear was that I would have to handle the Hammers. The regime was taking the position, not so much by anything it said, but by its hands-off policy, that we had to work it out in New York…"

"Which meant nothing."

"Not exactly. One day something happened between Charlie and Harry. The account was depleted and I think Charlie pressed a mite too incautiously about some very large off-the-books sums he knew Armand had to be squirreling away. This time Harry began menacing Charlie in a very direct kind of way. Charlie then came to me and said he didn't want to go back to the Hammers. And of course he *was* very vulnerable in that situation. So I arranged a meeting with Harry and told him that he should pray that Charlie never has an accident, no, not so much as a scratch – this after Harry threatened Charlie by saying, 'accidents happen', that he thought Charlie could get badly hurt walking back to the subway at night. I said then that if he ever did get 'hurt', that I'd hold him personally responsible and kill him."

Only the occasional glass-like shattering sound of ice outside broke the otherwise blanketed quiet of the night which followed these words. After several moments, Jim ventured a question. "Do you think that you would have?"

"This was no game. When I said it I meant it. It is impossible to appreciate how desperate a situation it was unless you were in it. But of course I didn't." Doswell flashed a smile. "The mild-mannered cross between Mr. Chips and Uncle Remus that you have before you was in those days a different kind of…cat." His eyes lit up. But he finished his thought in a solemn tone: "I felt that if I did nothing, then that itself would be an invitation. Another futile effort would have been worse than nothing. It would have emboldened him."

"Did it work?"

"Charlie never had an 'accident'."

"He was never attacked."

"No. He never was. But in the meantime I did several things. I bought a gun, which I have to this day. For a while Charlie even came to live with me on 144th

Street. It was all I could do to convince him to go back to the Hammers."

"But he had no choice. He was an illegal and he was in America for one thing only, and that was to do that job."

"Exactly. And he did go back because he fully understood that. As I say, this was the time of Stalin's Purge. This was being in the frying pan, and if you jumped out you'd be jumping into the fire. But the fear he had, he couldn't control. I'm sure he was always extra-careful after Harry threatened him."

"If they were going to hurt anyone, it might have been more logical for them to go after you. They could have viewed it that way."

"Yes. I knew that. I purchased that gun. I was extra-careful. Hawpe, my driver, he was on the lookout too. And then I'd done something else a couple of years before – I'd purchased a house of my own. It was to be my own personal 'safe house'. You know that the Party had places few knew about – that woman in the obituary I showed you ran one, where agents could go, sight unseen, no questions asked, should things get hot and they were on the run. I bought this house with money from my parents' estate. My mother had recently died. I was left something. I took the money and the little I'd saved and purchased a place without telling anyone. It was the first piece of property that I'd ever owned. I guess you could say it was like a country home. It was in the city, but I could get away from it all. And when I went there I was very careful, I didn't want anyone to know. J. Peters taught me a very important lesson in Erfurt. I wasn't going to let anyone trail me as he did then. So I put my Lenin School training to a useful purpose."

"A kind of safe house from the Party."

"The building I purchased just north of Central Park in Spanish Harlem wasn't originally intended, though, as a safe house from the Party. I did have the Hammers in mind, but mostly when I purchased it, I just wanted a place of my own." And it was an ideal refuge. He told Jim a Spanish-speaking dentist rented the whole first floor of the building and used it only part of the week because he had another office in the city. Above the dental office there was a large apartment which he retained. The only other person in the building was there only some days. At night there was no one else in the building.

It suddenly came home to Jim that Doswell had been living through all of this, the strangest, most estranged life any man could ever have lived this side of full-blown schizophrenia. He said so.

"Yes, it was an insane life and the measure of its insanity was that this was the sanest part of it."

"I don't mean that I don't understand. I can imagine if you were looking to find some escape from the intense – I mean, it must have been intense – the crazy life of all that intrigue within the Party, you didn't want anyone to know about it."

"The Party wanted to rule every part of you and know everything about you. Wherever the Party rules it wants to fill everything up with itself. It wants full control. This is the reason why I took steps to keep this hidden, to keep an emergency security exit. Mostly I wanted to be free of anything or anyone who could break, yes, into my little corner of sanity and privacy. No one, not even Hawpe, could be trusted with this. The Party would have ways of finding things out from him if he knew."

"I would think that all of this in itself was a strong motive for quitting."

"The life of intrigue in itself, no, though it was exhausting, draining, insane – it came with the territory. If you believed in what you were doing you accepted it as a worthy sacrifice. But yes, once you started thinking seditious thoughts, then such a life begins to creep up on you, and one day you clearly understand that it is intolerable. And you must leave it."

There was one other thing which Doswell told Jim in the course of that night. It was an oblique remark made in the context of his saying that the Party wanted to control everything, but it was quite critical. He said that he'd begun in those years to write notes to himself; that this was in some way "a different kind of refuge".

"A diary?"

"No. That would have been viewed as nothing less than treason. In fact, if I'd been caught merely jotting down my thoughts from time to time as I did, that too would have merited serious reprimand. Literary efforts were off limits."

Jim looked puzzled.

"As I said, nothing is personal. They were most concerned, too, with what you might write that could eventually get in the hands of enemies, or be used by you if you later broke – and I can tell you, that wasn't based on paranoia."

"Yeah. Memory is served by written records. Did you use them in that way?"

"I recently found notes I'd written on a visit to the Detroit Museum of Fine Arts many years ago, when I was with Hammer's 'circus' there. Something I'd written in the museum on the back of a manila envelope. I'd kept it. I had this because I was going to use some of its ideas to write about Diego Rivera, the muralist, something on aesthetics. I long since discarded the idea. Lost the energy."

"What did you do with the rest of those notes then?"

"They were thrown away long ago."

In all of Jim and Doswell's talk at this time, Doswell never once thought to talk about his daughter, Carole, of whom he'd never spoken previously to Jim, nor certainly about any other matter pertaining to his life touching on Carole; and Jim was too discreet a man to have intruded in so private an area with even the most oblique of questions. And surely nothing of Carole's mother had been mentioned either. His secret house just off upper Fifth Avenue in Spanish Harlem he spoke of simply as a place he occasionally went where "sanity still reigned".

More than this meant stepping into a region of his past that he rarely visited even in his thoughts – the exception, of course, being a few desperate words to Euretha Lewis on the occasion of Carole's funeral.

But it is also true that it did not occur to him that this report of his house on East 112th Street would seem oddly empty to the younger man for the simple reason that for a while it had been just that – empty, that is, aside from his secret visits, his jottings and his notes. And this made perfect sense in an otherwise insane life, this place which offered a haven even before Zora Payton Doswell moved in.

20

Art Critic

Crowds of memories were overtaking Doswell in these final years, overtaking him as in a bad dream with an ever-growing, ever more ferocious crowd of ogres howling at his heels.

During the years he ran Uncle Big Bob's Limousine Service by day and was the Bank of the Comintern by night, the physical toll was great. Those who knew him saw him age rapidly. He grew fat. He lost much of his hair. He grew a double chin and pouches under his eyes. He broke out in sweats and winded easily. Drinking considerable quantities of coffee through the seemingly endless days, in the nights after his rounds were done he'd imbibe quick, bracing swigs of whiskey.

One might think that with the accumulated fatigue of these days, afterwards on the rides back with Hawpe at the wheel, sleep would come easily. But it didn't. Wound up physically and mentally by the wrangling, critical decision-making moments of long conferences and occasionally contentious applicants, with assistance from his good friend the whiskey flask, he'd often fall into a half-awake slumber as he gazed out over the city flying by, thinking in snatches of earlier, less eventful, more confident days.

Anything could come to mind at these times: his father, his days at Harvard, his early childhood in Colonus and his brother William; his mother, his sister Vanna; the years in Moscow or Passaic. As he gazed out on the buildings and the street lamps and the red and green reflected traffic lights slipping by along the rain-washed, nearly deserted streets of lower Manhattan, the far reaches of Brooklyn, and other parts of the city, sometimes he would think of the most trivial of incidents looming as large as if they'd happened hours before. Like when he'd first arrived in Cambridge and he'd learned he couldn't live in a dorm room. The dozen or so other Negro students, evenly divided between the sons of African chieftains and American athletes, having earlier found rooms among themselves – he, the odd man out… Such witless, foolish thoughts!

No, it didn't have to be. Nothing had to be, the words came in a whisper to his lips.

In those years he had sought out action, participation; he read voraciously the literature his activist student comrades talked most about. He joined in Boston politicking with 'Shag' Taylor; organized tenants' strikes, boycotts. Quarreled near-violently among old friends and newer acquaintances in the Yard over now seemingly pointless questions: is Bakunin right that only complete destruction is the answer? Is the proletariat so hopelessly corrupted by its priests that only a band of professional revolutionaries can save it?

And then in those earliest years, the nights restless and wakeful with personal demons he fought daily, he'd hear through the thin walls of his room on Dudley Street, between the strident screech of the El trains, the sudden sound of alcohol-sodden rages and beatings, shrieks and hysterical sobbing coming from some hapless neighbor's apartment, that would be magnified by the hallway acoustics of their garlic and urine-smelling tenement house. On those nights he'd begun serious reflection on what Marx was talking about when he spoke of alienation: alienation from self, from others, from nature, from one's labor and the products of one's labor.

In the South, he remembered, on some particularly lonely and cheerless evening, writing his father about his fellow Negroes who'd migrated north in search of jobs, *they are still close to the land, still part of something. But in the North they are on their own, the refuse, the useless flotsam, those alienated from their own uncreative labor, a people without even a memory of the land.*

His father wrote back, alarmed at the revolutionary ideas, *One has to exercise the proper precautions in a world only too anxious to punish the Negro.*

He wrote his father regularly, weekly – sometimes even more often. He would learn to mute his convictions and finesse the logic of his arguments, writing only enough to hint at his newfound ideas and his dream of changing the world. More often he wrote about his professors, especially one whose publications his father, a well-read man, admired. He especially appreciated hearing from him that Babbitt said he wished all his students had had the educational benefits he'd had. Oh! He knew his father would warm to *that!* He needed something good said about the severe training he'd subjected his children to.

But Irving Babbitt wasn't impressed by his political ideas, and this he did not report. "Yes, it is quite true, Mr. Doswell, that where there is no vision the people perish. But where there is a sham vision they perish even faster."

On his urging that Marx's vision of a world where the benefits of men's efforts would go to those most in need, where fraternity guided life, Babbitt cried, "Ah, yes! On the pain of death all men shall be required to love each other! Oh yes!"

During the years he was running his international 'banking service' on wheels, Doswell rarely picked up a newspaper. How could he find the time to bury his nose in a paper, occupying his mind with the daily flow and repetition of minutiae as others who lived normal lives did? But then there'd been a series of articles in the *New York Times* on the latest famine in the Soviet Union; and once he made the discovery, try as he might, he couldn't stop himself from buying every issue. The author, Walter Duranty, wrote his reports as though it was all essentially about two equally contending forces facing off: on the one side, the regime and its promising future; on the other, the unfortunate peasants, victims of their ignorant past – but he did so never really acknowledging that there was a famine!

RUSSIANS HUNGRY, BUT NOT STARVING.
DEATH FROM DISEASES DUE TO MALNUTRITION HIGH, YET THE SOVIET UNION IS ENTRENCHED. LARGER CITIES HAVE FOOD.

Special to the *New York Times*:

> *...the attempt to change the stock-raising nomads of the type and period of Abraham and Isaac into 1933 collective grain farmers has produced the most deplorable results...commissaries have made a mess of Soviet food production... But – to put it bluntly – you can't make an omelet without breaking eggs...*

He knew Duranty not only from the lavish parties he and other Western glitterati attended at Brown House, but from individual, more intimate visits alone with Hammer when they were discussing Hammer's writing of *The Quest of the Romanoff Treasure*; this book which was intended to quiet any suspicions in America about the origin of the treasure.

Now he feverishly read his old acquaintance's reports from Rostov-on-Don and Kharkov, from the North Caucasus:

> *...it is the touchstone – and by all accounts it has been not only that, but the Verdun-Gettysburg of the Bolshevik struggle with the peasants...*
> *There is no actual starvation or deaths from starvation, but there is widespread mortality from diseases due to malnutrition...*

What nice distinctions!

And yet, despite all the softening euphemisms and convoluted extenuations and false parallels, Duranty reported dire conditions, widespread death... Yes, he thought again of Professor Babbitt's dismay when he said that the key to the "properly human" lay in reordering the entire foundations of human life. "The entire foundations of human life, young man! Do you realize what that means?"

Now on these late-night treks, gazing out on deserted streets in the far boroughs of New York, he found himself in his wandering thoughts wondering why he'd been blind to so much in those years. Why, for instance, he hadn't listened more to those who'd said that the revolution had in its first years taken a wrong turn. Or even why, up close when he'd applauded Babbitt's attacks on "middle-class commercial culture", applauded his contempt for the confidence in materialist progress which he saw in Rotary and the Chamber of Commerce; why he hadn't seen this same blameworthy confidence in materialist progress which animated Communism?

The incident he remembered that clarified and focused so many long-held, seditious thoughts was in itself quite seemingly trivial, but large in its impact. It had been in the middle of the decade when Hammer was still occasionally going on his roadshows with the bric-a-brac of the Romanoff treasure, shortly after Charlie arrived from Moscow. To show the new man the lay of the land and something of America besides, he decided on taking Charlie to Detroit where the 'circus' had just opened. The Diego Rivera murals had also opened a couple of years earlier in the city's famous Institute of Fine Arts, and they had attracted much attention in the culture at large. They were of special interest to him because they'd generated bitter controversy among Marxist-Leninists, Rivera having been reviled as a Trotskyite apostate by American Party members who all towed the Stalinist line. So on one slow afternoon when he thought he could steal a few hours by himself, he'd left Charlie at the department store with the Hammers and gone off to see for himself the murals of the world-famous artist and Marxist revolutionist who'd attracted so much criticism from Party regulars.

Knowing full well the whipped-up passions of the Party faithful against Trotskyites, he still fully expected that Rivera would prove himself the great artist of the revolution, reanimating the faith of all believers with his proletarian inspiration. But his anticipated reaction, that of sweeping away all the backbiting pettiness of the Stalinists, went much, much further than that. Instead, in those hours he experienced a slipping away; as if a believing Christian, having viewed Giotto frescoes, or a Perugino painting of the Holy Family, discovered as a result that his faith had been shaken, not just in the norms and dogmas of his particular sect, but with Christianity as a whole.

What was so strange was that it was this that he remembered as the turning point. Whatever the reason for the precise moment, the fact was simply that in that quiet museum, church-like in the peace and seclusion, and the sustained concentration and opportunity for reflection, with nothing to distract him, he'd begun to see clearly something he would never succeed at shaking. For it was precisely because Rivera's work was inspired by Marxist ideas that in its inspiration it had demonstrated so fully what he could not evade seeing – his worship of the machine... And so clearly! He simply saw it. But was it not the people, he first argued with himself, the working class that Rivera more nearly worshipped? No! No! It was certain, it was the machine. Not the bourgeoisie. Not Mexico. The machine! Men, he reflected in a sudden rush of conviction, merely having importance only in so far as they are parts, mechanically regimented parts of a vast machine – the collective.

These were thoughts, he told Jim, he was certain had passed through his mind before but that had never been acknowledged. Yes, each figure, lacking the individuality of separate human beings — all of them in Rivera's mind ennobled, glorious proletarians, but in his art humanly debased, a part of the one great hypostatized absolute — the classless society.

He'd studied those figures for hours, remonstrating with himself, remembering Cafuoldi's words about the revolution, about the right kind of revolution being a culmination of the universally religious; trying to bring himself to deny, and unable to deny, to qualify, and having qualified, trying then to reconcile what he was undeniably seeing with the words of Rivera's harshest Party critics. Even this mere visit to an art museum to see Rivera's work would have been viewed by some of them, if only they knew, as an insurrection! To view a Trotskyite artist's work! But what if they knew the full burden of his thoughts?

He questioned himself: Rivera and the people? Or the Party and the people? Why, they no more care about the people than they care about the coal that comes out of the ground – the raw products of industry. The great, spinning dynamos generating energy for the assembly line. Oh yes! He remembered Passaic!

Marx is right, he thought, reality has been turned topsy-turvy, ideas have become reality, reality ideas. There before him lay the fixed vision of one vast ego which conceives the universe as material simply *there* – for the intelligence of men to manipulate.

He thought he must break. He must find a way to disentangle himself. But it was so complicated! And this was only art! And then – and this may sound absurd – he was so busy! He was exceedingly busy. Indeed, that very afternoon on return from his three-hour outing, he was instantly plunged into the shallowest, most quibblingly distracting of struggles with the Hammers over some matter he forgot within the week – only to be plunged again into some other equally quibbling affair. And then there were the people he saw daily in his office at the limousine service (not to speak of Charlie and Hawpe as well), whose working lives at the height of the Depression depended on him – they were altogether more real, more urgent, finally more important than anything else. More important, more real and urgent, certainly, than fugitive thoughts at a museum – or words found in a newspaper.

And then, as many can attest, however one's faith is shaken, often one goes about as always in the church that one has long worshipped in. Even at the altar, we are told, those under holy orders, some going through motions, empty rituals, find the unthought-of inertia one's surest crutch, the self-annulling doubts heaped against doubts a still-remote hope. This is how he persisted his final years in the Party, the doubts continuing to eat away at him even as he consciously put them out of his mind. Yet in off moments, in suddenly terrifying appearances, they came to haunt him, and then they could only be quelled by a whiskey flask – quelled, that is, until through a succession of accelerating events, the first of these the Hitler-Stalin non-aggression pact signed in Berlin on August 24th 1939, that fell one on top of the other, he turned irrevocably, violently against the Party.

PART 5

21

Vincent Returns

Nearly a month into Vincent's stay with Aunt Molina and the "Sisters tha Violent and de Wild", he finally got word that Basil was no longer in imminent danger. One doctor called it "miraculous"; he was a sensation among the hospital staff. Vincent could now pack up and go home. But he was hardly satisfied. Yes, he was incredibly relieved; he could certainly celebrate Basil's indestructibility with Aunt Molina, but there was still one unresolved problem. His brother's would-be killers were still at large. Miss DeWilda McGirt's gentlemen in blue were empty-handed, with insufficient evidence on a trail that was growing colder every day – though they knew who his attackers were, and Vincent did too.

It wasn't only the interview with Jimmy Jones at Panther headquarters two weeks earlier that convinced him that he did; there was something else now: a message he'd gotten from a woman he thought he recognized from the neighborhood. The message given in a crowded department store in midtown Manhattan, cloak-and-dagger style, was that Basil remained in danger – hardly a revelation, but an unwelcome confirmation. She refused to say how she knew and insisted she had no knowledge of who actually did the shooting, but she spoke with certainty when she said that the Party was "purging itself" of "police informers". When he pressed for more, not so much doubting her word (why would she go to so elaborate a ruse?), but seeking to strengthen his confidence that she was speaking from real knowledge and not just hysteria, she said this: that a member up in Harlem sometime the previous spring was taken to a city in Connecticut, questioned under torture about being a police informer, and executed. She insisted she knew no more and repeated her fear that if it leaked out that she'd told him, she herself would be targeted, reminding him nervously of the assurances he'd made over the phone when she first called to arrange the meeting. Then she walked off, disappearing among the shoppers. Vincent was left with a seething certainty but nothing he could concretely do, and up against the wire to return to Colonus.

Fortunately he'd since prevailed on a much-weakened and chastened Basil to transfer to Englewood Hospital in New Jersey, where Molina had a friend with whom she could live while he finished his hospital stay. Basil's assailants were still free, they hadn't answered for their crimes, and probably never would. But there was little chance they would trace him there. As for Molina, she seemed OK; and she insisted Vincent should "get going".

So after kissing and putting his arms lingeringly around the substantial armful that was his Aunt Molina, and gently hugging and thanking Mrs. Violetta Hawkins and Miss DeWilda McGirt for their help, he winged his way back to North Carolina on the first flight he could catch. The first item on his agenda was Gwen.

But here all was not sunny and bright. Over the previous week he'd been telephoning Gwen, and he'd not been able to reach her. Both her mother and stepfather on separate occasions answered his calls, and told him they would pass on the message, but she never returned his calls. He'd hoped to tell her that Basil had turned the corner, but he'd had to settle on telling Mrs. Malcomn. He was anxious to see her, not only because they'd been apart so long, but also because during the first couple of weeks, when daily he woke with the question, Is Basil alive today?, the thought crystalized: that he'd be a straight-out fool if he didn't break with Blissie and set himself right with Gwen.

On arrival in Colonus (a Saturday), Vincent called once again from the airport. Once again he got Gwen's mother, and once again she promised to pass on his message. Suppressing his anger, he asked if there was anything wrong. She denied there was. This time, through strangled words, he made his message very specific: that he would be in his hotel room most of the morning and Gwen should call the hotel. And if for some reason he wasn't in, she was to leave a message with the clerk. Otherwise he'd be in his office at Baxter, he explained, adding – feeling less and less as he spoke any hope she would – that it was *very* important she did. And she didn't. At one point shortly later he picked up the phone to call once again, then changed his mind, rising instantly from the edge of his bed to get over to the Malcomn house, knock on the door and insist on seeing her, or at least get a full explanation before leaving. But then, with his coat on as he stepped out into the hallway of the hotel, he stopped, thought long and hard, and changed his mind again. He feared his own temper! He would not add to indictable offenses if things were as his anxious conscience intimated.

So he went about his business in the morning as he'd told Mrs. Malcomn, and with his anxiety on high alert, telephoned Doswell, but got no answer. Then after a quick lunch near the hotel and a stop at the cleaners, he went to his office at Baxter and then, independent of Gwen, he got a jolt.

He learned about a campus-driven drug raid on student dorms which had taken place while he was away, among others the room of Willi Wade, who'd written the *Liberator* article. He'd been charged with possession and intent to distribute. The news was everywhere: in his mailbox, in back copies of *Baxter's*

Voice, on the lips of people encountered on the East End campus.

It was Saturday afternoon and he had the office and the building to himself, inhaling deep, desperate drafts of smoke from his cigarette, his thoughts ranging over a tangle of events through the many previous weeks. Then suddenly, independent of his conscious volition or the logic of his thoughts, in an instant he made a connection and the thought was pulsing inside his head like the flashing neon sign outside the hotel. He remembered he'd taken Blissie to the Black Derby on *two* occasions, once before he'd met Gwen and once afterwards, just before Molina called. That was it! Those women there…he was two-timing Gwen with a white girl! Fool! Fool! Naturally it got back to her. All it would take would be one; it was probably half a dozen of those women!

He sat there slumped at his desk, mute. The burden of his own stupid actions overwhelmed him as he gazed about his dismal, all-too-familiar office. He'd been sitting there for some time, and it occurred to him then that his office mate, Duro Ogunda, sometimes came in on weekend afternoons. Ogunda was always talking about registering students for his Swahili classes (Introductory, Intermediate, Advanced and Advanced Syntax, with only two students in Introduction, and one in Intermediate). He'd want to talk his usual bullshit! He decided in an instant to get back to his hotel room. At first thinking to call a cab to drive him back, but too weary to take the initiative to call, he put on his jacket, and quickly left.

Stepping out into the parking lot from Rogers Hall, the lot between Rogers and the east side of Harrison Hall (Baxter's rambling, gray-stoned science building), there was the sudden blast of sound from the cars and trucks on the busy avenue to the south of the campus as they roared past. As he walked from the parking lot to the sidewalk, weaving his way around the small, neglected weed-trees and brush on its edge, he spotted Jim Allan making for his car. Allan didn't seem to notice him, or perhaps he was pretending not to; Vincent walked back several steps, out from behind the trees, and called out.

Jim hadn't seen Vincent. His mind was too much on other things. Then he heard his name, looked up and saw Vincent coming in his direction.

Even when Vincent first saw him from more than a hundred feet away, he noticed that Jim seemed dejected. There was something in the way he carried himself, something especially sour and glum, which spelled defeat, but Vincent had no inclination to think, "Lemon Face". Instead he wasted no time as he came up to him.

"I want to tell you I appreciate your teaching my classes. The old man told me you taught nearly all of them. Thanks."

Jim said nothing for a moment. Then he said, "Don't mention it." His face was a blank.

They were standing beside Jim's little Volkswagen Bug. It was a damp, cool, overcast day, untypical for Colonus. To the side of them up the avenue there was a billboard, faded and torn at one edge, which Vincent for a long moment fixed his eyes on:

FACTORY OUTLET
WOMEN'S UNDERWEAR
LOWEST PRICES

"I couldn't help it, you know. It was a family problem. A serious one."

"I know, Mr. Doswell told me."

There was some hesitancy. "How is the old man? I arrived this morning and tried to call him. No one picked up the phone."

"I guess you could say under the circumstances, he's OK. You know what happened with this student, Willi Wade?"

"Yes. I learned about it just a little while ago."

"He was the boy who wrote the article – the most critical one – in that student paper."

"Yeah, I know him."

As Jim started to move towards his car, Vincent resumed his walk back to the hotel. Then Jim turned round as if reconsidering.

"So does the old man. Wade came to him beforehand, when he had the idea, and asked his advice. He told him not to. Told him it wasn't worth it; that what happened would happen. But then he did it anyway."

Vincent was facing Jim again, and dipped his head. "He said he knew the student? He told him not to?" But he seemed to be less asking questions than mulling over something.

Jim hesitated, considering a separate thought of his own. "There was an emergency faculty meeting that was called after it was learned who they were…"

"You mean the students?"

"Willi Wade and the others whose rooms were raided."

"There were how many besides Willi?"

"Just three others besides Wade, but they're only facing charges for possession."

"Did you learn anything at the meeting?"

Jim felt uncertain. He remembered it all too well. He remembered nearly everyone's reaction to his and Doswell's appearance at Ford Hall: the furtive and fixed stares, the buzz, parting like waves as they made their way through the lobby to the auditorium. In truth he still felt some lingering resentment at Vincent's many absences, even this last, even though it was unreasonable since after all his brother had been shot, and Doswell said he was close to death. Still he didn't feel right about Vincent. He had to get it off his chest.

"The two of us went to that emergency meeting. Doswell is convinced this whole thing was rigged. Even if Willi was selling drugs – and he doesn't believe it, but even if he was – he's convinced it's a vendetta. So we went to this meeting to see what answers we could get. When we got there everyone seemed surprised at our arrival, and real hostile. They stood back away from us like we were untouchables.

"Despite that, when the time came to ask questions Mr. Doswell wasn't shy. But Middleweek and Hyzak tried dodging every question, refusing to answer anything straight out. When he pressed them there were angry shouts for him to sit down."

"Who…?"

"Raskin and others. Middleweek, who was the chair, said that the meeting was getting out of order. But it seemed that was the signal for it to grow more disorderly. People were getting up and criticizing him, believe it or not, for his 'known indulgence' and 'recklessness' towards potheads and drug dealers, one person charging that it was only recently he'd been having parties where dealers had been plying their trade and getting high!"

"Middleweek didn't stop it?"

"Raskin got the floor and started talking about the convention and said that he was 'insufficiently distinguished' to be given a speaking role there…"

"Insufficiently distinguished?" Vincent frowned, incredulous.

"Yeah. Those were his exact words. He said a whole lot of other things about how the old man had tried to push his way into the convention – things I can't remember because they didn't make any sense. It didn't have anything to do with Willi and the raid. It was pure bullshit. You know him, you know what he is capable of. You're his old friend."

Vincent closed his eyes to this and said nothing.

Jim continued. "Oh yes! He was filled with righteous indignation! Shaking his finger in our direction, he was yelling something like, 'Have you no sense of shame? Young people who trusted you' – something like that – 'they were your victims.'"

"Did Doswell say anything?"

"What could he say to such garbage? He just ignored him. When he got up to speak again he didn't acknowledge anything Raskin said. He just pressed Middleweek and Hyzak about the search through the rooms: why they chose Willi's room, why they chose *his* dorm. Then Middleweek ended the meeting. He's up there on that stage, and suddenly pushes his chair back, gets up from his seat, says he's calling the meeting to a close, and walks off. And everyone follows him."

Vincent said nothing. He wasn't about to let loose. If it had been Doswell himself – or even a friend of Raskin's little troupe, any of his acquaintances at Baxter who'd told him what Allan just did – he would have. But it was precisely this same anger in Jim's presence which caused him to exert an effort at self-mastery. And in doing so he looked as he often did at such a time: like he was thinking and, most importantly, feeling nothing. And he said nothing.

Then he looked sidelong and said calmly, "I'm sorry I wasn't there. But frankly your description of these people doesn't surprise me. It sounds like they were acting out their usual parts. Listen, I'm going to get back to my room. I expect an important telephone call, and I'm going to try to get in touch with Mr. Doswell. You wouldn't have any idea where he would be?"

Jim seemed oddly thoughtful, as if this required careful scrutiny. He began reciting what he knew: "On Saturdays he and Billy go on their errands, grocery shopping. That could be where they are." Then he added, "It never occurred to you when you encouraged Willi Wade to start his so-called *underground* paper, and to write about the President, that he'd go after him with both claws?"

Vincent stopped in his tracks. For a long moment he stared at Jim. "You don't know what the hell you're talking about."

"That's what you always say."

"It's always true."

Jim began to laugh. "You know, Vincent, you stir up trouble, and then you run away. This time you had a good reason. But there were a whole lot of times you didn't."

Vincent started moving towards Jim.

Jim watched him. "Now what are you going to do? Beat me up?"

Vincent glared. He turned from Jim, and then turned again after a few steps. "Like I said, you don't know what you're talking about. What am I supposed to do? Willi, I'm sure, is over twenty-one. What is he, some kid I could just tell him to go running along? I didn't tell him to write the article. He already came to me with a plan, if you want to know, and I gave him some advice..."

"Not the right kind."

Vincent started to walk away.

"You of all people should have known Montbanc well enough to know he'd go after him."

"I've listened to enough of your shit. Don't bring this up again." Vincent continued walking away.

"I'll bring up whatever it occurs to me to bring up," Jim called back.

Vincent didn't turn around. He walked back through the trees and out onto the sidewalk.

Jim watched him as he disappeared, thinking bitterly as he did, there's a man with better things on his mind. And on a different track, a visual playback that kept repeating itself before his eyes since, pummeled by a part of the story he'd just told but which he'd withheld because it troubled him violently: after making it through that gauntlet into the auditorium, they'd sat in the same row a few seats to the side of their old friend, Mrs. Moxley – then she popped up out of her seat, like a jack out of its box, and flew as one might from some noxious, foul and fetid odor!

In response, Doswell turned to the front, voiceless and stiff, waiting for the meeting to begin. Jim remembered him holding, grasped tightly, his worn and stained fedora on his knee, noticing it trembling in his hands.

Back in his room Vincent once again telephoned Doswell. Once again there was no answer. Thoughts of Gwen contended with thoughts of this whole rotten Wade affair. He took some hotel letterhead and began scribbling down preliminary ideas for a letter he would write Gwen. Finding it impossible to shake Willi Wade and the inflamed sting of Jim Allan's impertinent words, he began to write out the reasons he was tied up with this mess, something as well that would tell her how important she was…

He'd try telephoning the old man again.

He dialed Devon. It rang for a while, then a tired voice picked up.

22

War Rages Round Us

Jim had an eventful several days. Late Friday he learned from Susan that she was pregnant. Not the way one wants to begin a marriage, but far from a tragedy either, he counseled himself; while the idea of a baby was daunting, he liked babies, he'd told Susan, grinning. He was determined to see the situation in a positive light. And when Susan finally came to believe him, her own anxieties (despite the many complications and her parents' anger with him on hearing the news) were considerably lessened.

So later the same weekend he'd telephoned his mother to tell her of this new situation, wondering how she'd take it, but before he could get it out she spilled some news of her own: that Chuck had recently been to the hospital with a ruptured appendix. His brother since was out of the hospital and fully on the road to recovery but Chuck and she had had a bitter quarrel afterwards, following, once again, something Clare had said – and in this case also done – at the height of the emergency.

While Chuck was in the hospital, Jim's mother was to stay over to help watch the kids, but Clare, no doubt under the stress of the moment and angry over something, had ordered her out of the house, and said she was "never again" to return. As he wondered what could have triggered such an eruption, he detected something in his mother's voice over the phone, unpleasantly familiar and alarming. It was the same hesitancy and jaw-clenched, mouth-filled slur she spoke with when the facial pain was upon her. It didn't instantly register, but after a minute or two, he asked, "Is the pain back?"

There were a few seconds of silence. "I have to be careful, Jimmy." The words spoken as if she were stepping on glass on the edge of a cliff. "If I stay calm, if I don't get excited, it may be short-lived. I may get through this."

It had flared up only twice since his father's death, the last time only a day or two of white-hot flashes.

He ended up not telling her about Susan, and dwelling gloomily instead on his mother's cursed affliction and the New York situation.

There was a lot going on at Baxter and in Colonus those days, much of it offering something to be gloomy about. There was the raid on the students' dorm, and

Jim's final move to his, and now Susan's soon-to-be, new apartment – a bane in Susan's eyes not only because of the neighborhood but because of the apartment's condition, especially its kitchen, whose walls and floor lay under layers of grease built up over the years by previous tenants' inattentions.

A few days prior to the encounter with Vincent, Jim had gone with Jim Lewis and Doswell in Lewis' pickup – rickety, rust-pocked, half broken down – carrying the big antique chest of drawers and mirror, and the antique oak desk which Jim had been kicking himself about getting ever since he'd moved the unwieldy monster from the auction barn where he'd first purchased it at a 'bargain' price. Could they get it up a narrow circular flight of stairs through doorways requiring twisting and turning this way and that? And Luther down with the flu? He feared they couldn't.

The three of them were packed into the cab with some odd tools and part of what looked like a carburetor and a piece of chain at their feet, and Jim Lewis, who Jim put down long before as a man of few and sober words, for some reason was now speaking non-stop; more in the twenty minutes they'd been driving to the new apartment than in all the weeks put together that he'd already known him. Perhaps, he thought, the floodgates had opened because Mrs. Lewis was absent.

Jim could just barely understand him. Lewis talked in a Southern Negro accent that was much of the time impenetrable. It little mattered, however, because as Lewis groped his way to Jim's place in a seedy, older part of the city, Jim's thoughts were painfully divided between the New York situation and the recent drug raid; the latter growing larger in his mind as they drove and he looked on Doswell's stone-faced expression even as he responded appropriately but minimally to Lewis' joke-festooned chatter.

Since the Monday following the weekend of the raid, in far-flung corners of the campus, everywhere people had met and talked, the buzz had been on little else, but not once, outside of the faculty meeting, did Doswell mention it again.

There was, Jim noticed, among a few of the white faculty that he heard, a caution, an anxiety about having a correctly postured opinion, especially when an editorial appeared in the *News-Herald*, long viewed as one of the state's most reactionary newspapers, which gave high praise to President Montbanc for his *courage in finally and at long last moving against drug dealers. News-Herald* editorials on previous occasions (during the recent Alliance convention, for instance, its scathing comments on rumored *mob-inciting by trouble-making speakers*) had been hailed ironically as a badge of honor for those who were targets of their rebukes. Now these same blithe-spirited critics fell into broadly temporizing meta-discussions, delving the underlying conflicting 'elements' and 'dynamics' that go into *difficult decisions for those with broad responsibilities.* Doswell, who would typically have had something penetrating to say about the many ironies in such a situation, on this occasion had nothing to say.

Even with the thickening blizzard of rumors, counter-rumors, self-justifications, analyses, editorials, radio and TV commentaries originating not only in Colonus, but in Raleigh, Columbia and elsewhere, none had kindled in him any response – that is, once again, except for his earlier probing of Deans Middleweek and Hyzak at the faculty meeting which was convened for the purpose of discussing the subject.

But Jim had also noticed the old man falling deeper and deeper into the lowest of depressions. Sitting beside Doswell in Lewis' truck, he knew, as he glanced sideways at him in a darkness lit up only by road lamps and the sudden glare and quickly receding light of passing vehicles, that it had overtaken his mind. For days now their long conversations about Doswell's life in the Party had come to an abrupt end.

On this night, following their victory over Jim's monster desk, out of step with the previous hours' mostly brooding silence, Doswell announced a sudden desire to "celebrate the occasion". At the house (Billy was staying over with the Lewises that evening), unlike his usual savoring and lingering habit, the old man was downing his beers like a sailor on shore leave. Then to Jim's chagrin, he pulled out a bottle of bourbon which he kept secreted in a kitchen cabinet, offered him a drink, and then tossed down one shot after another. For the first time, Jim noticed that the precision in his wide-ranging vocabulary grew blurry. His manner went from a forced, celebratory cheeriness to an undisguised bitterness. It was painful for Jim, whose veneration for Doswell was boundless, observing the old man for the first time – dare he even think it? – acting like a common drunk.

As he drank and came increasingly under the liquor's influence, he ranted on about murder being more often "legal in these days" than illegal. That there were those with the luxury of "keeping the stench at a distance" with more "imaginative ways to murder without breaking the law". For the first time he mentioned Willi, saying that Willi was his brother's name, a brother he'd last seen when they were both teenagers. He said, in a voice heavy with self-accusation, that he'd told Willi when he came to see him nothing good would come of attacking Montbanc, the university, the convention. But nothing he said could deter him. Willi couldn't imagine anything that would frighten him. What could Montbanc do, Willi had asked? Was he some kind of drug kingpin that would have hit men hunting him down?

"I sounded like an old woman telling him not to criticize them," he said bitterly of himself.

Doswell wasn't incoherent. The talk was understandable, that is, *what* he was saying. What was most alarming was the aggrieved, disconnected talk that followed: beyond the school, Montbanc, Willi, or even Vincent's brother, Basil.

He reminded Jim again of that past he'd spoken of so much, and then he spoke fleetingly – but for the first time – and alarmingly, of his wife, Zora, and his daughter, Carole, and that they were both gone – his voice coming shockingly close to breaking. He began raving about people who'd been long out to get him: active Communist cells in Columbia, in the South Carolina capital and in Raleigh – people that had connections in Colonus and were "in touch with people at the school". His wrath climbed, the words slurred, his thick hands joined in as he flayed the recent Peace Moratorium and the Student Mobilization Committee and Pham Van Dong, "writing love letters to each other" and "the fools, the millions of marching, useful idiots doing their bidding" and paying the price in "more corpses".

Jim, fearing his state of mind, stayed that night in his old room. He remembered earlier times when he'd overheard Doswell talking to himself, remembered Radhakathri at his hateful worst, his bantering and gossipy tales of the old man "speaking to his office walls", that he was full-blown crazy, and known to be so not only at Baxter but over in the East End neighborhood. And now Jim, of course, previously rejecting such remarks with contempt, feared he really was losing control.

But then after that dark night he noticed something. Doswell began to pull from the edge. Still fearing for him, Jim visited over the next few days as much as he could, even abandoning Susan, who was demanding and understandably clingy. It was extraordinary. The storm slowly subsided. As if on a silent search, like one out of a scene from a war movie rummaging through the rubble after the bombs have stopped falling, dawn began to break. One day the old man spoke for the first time of God. And he turned once again to the past, mostly the time which he described as days when he "was on the run", when he was out of touch with everyone – the Party, the government, everyone. And with this he recounted in an especially intimate way the days immediately following his open break with the Party.

"I'd found this church in the city. It had an upper and lower sanctuary, a basement church where the doors were never locked, and I could enter that place at any time of the day or night, lit only by a hundred flickering votive candles and by a few dim electric lights set in red lamps overhead. I was, of course, not a believer, I went there simply to be alone, to sort out my thoughts and my plans. And I was comforted by the seclusion, the dim light of the candles, and the lingering fragrance of incense –and the idea that no one would think to find me in such a place.

"I would sit there in the back, alone but for a few others that would come and go, mostly shuffling older women and occasionally an adolescent boy or girl, or a man, all of them kneeling most of the time and praying in silence, a few clutching rosaries with their heads bowed, others gazing absorbed at the front altar. I felt a profound peace in this place.

"For years I'd been trying to work things out. I thought that these people in the church, who believed what I could not believe, still had souls – even if I didn't. I began to think that in the world that denies souls – the noisy, frenetic world outside that church, which lives in the frantic pursuit of the latest ornaments and toys, crowded full of people seeking worldly adulation, power and pleasure and utility – there is only the individual, that naked naught of the ego. And in the Communist world which I'd abandoned, there too the same: nothing, despite the spurious, vaunted 'community' in its name."

He spoke of his childhood when his father, ordinarily very sparing of such pleasures, had once let his brother and sister and him visit the traveling circus which passed through Colonus in the summertime. "There was a day set aside for the colored people. I remembered for the first time seeing one of those horrible giant marionette clown figures they have in circuses, rocking in stilted mechanical motion in front of one of the exhibits, and how terrifying it was to me.

"Like that man-sized marionette, its hinged, painted smile intended to simulate life by the action of pulled strings and the rasping din of canned laughter, this, I thought, is the individual that is coming into being in both worlds – the kind of individual both are working to create. One largely unconscious, unacknowledged, incomplete, and the other, as it redoubles its demonic efforts...

"Occasionally, I would stay sitting in that church until late. There would be a benediction of the sacrament, the priest at the front facing the altar, solemnly raising and lowering and crossing from side to side the golden monstrance. (I had seen such a vessel in Hammer's warehoused collection – he was perplexed that it hadn't already been melted down.) The priest waved the incense, and the church only sparsely filled – a cold day outside, the people bundled in their heavy coats, the women with kerchiefs on their heads, and me sitting erect in the back, sometimes kneeling, mostly out of respect and so as not to appear out of place. These people, they sang Latin hymns that moved me deeply. Words I'd forgotten for years until a couple of days ago. The words and some of the melodies came to me! And the Latin came out of the mouths of ordinary working men and women and children like words and voices out of heaven!"

Doswell, in a loud whisper, chanted the bare line of melody and these Latin words: "*O salutaris Hostia, Quae caeli pandis ostium Bella premunt hostilia: Da robur, fer auxilium...* O Saving Victim, who opens the gate of heaven, war rages round us, give strength, bring help... You've heard that before, haven't you, Jim?"

Jim hunched forward tight-lipped, absorbed. He closed his eyes. He hadn't heard it since childhood but the old man's near perfect rendition brought it fully back. "I have. Many, many times at novenas. It continues like this," he said, a catch in his voice. He whispered the melody too, pleased with the accuracy of his own memory, and moved by the sound, though it was just barely audible until Doswell joined in his rumble.

"Uni trinoque Domino Sit sempiterna gloria, Qui vitam sine termino Nobis donet in patria. Amen."

Doswell smiled. "…and may He give us life in our home above. Yes. Well, we are a singing sensation, and it stirred my soul then as it does now. In fact I thought then, I have a soul. Men have souls. I thought – I think I felt it far more – I am alive as they are fully alive. And I was reminded of all of this a couple of days ago."

23

Going After the Drug Scourge

The grim, soft-spoken Willi Wade had grown up in the Temple Hill neighborhood of Paterson, New Jersey, with a record going back to grade school that included petty crime, numbers running as a teenager for local mobsters, and a drug bust that might have sent him to the penitentiary but for his youth and a sudden turn of good luck. Following this last incident, as part of an arrangement with the judge, he'd gone to Bridgeport, Connecticut to live with his mother's sister and her part-time preacher husband, and through him acquired a job as an apprentice machinist at a local gun manufacturing plant.

Vincent had learned this story recently from Doswell, and Willi himself had since filled in details, including his insisting that he'd stayed clean and saved a few thousand dollars for his first year's tuition and living expenses at Baxter. Since then (he was in his Junior year), he'd garnered nearly all As and was on a full scholarship at the school.

"It looks bad for me, doesn't it?"

Willi, out of jail on bail, and Vincent were sitting at a booth in the Jolly Roger, Doswell's gnomic friend, Mo Rogers, bustling about in and out of the kitchen and among the tables, helping the waitresses in this early evening busy hour.

"I'm not a lawyer. But we've spoken to another lawyer and Stein is encouraging. He thinks we've got a lot of leverage with the school. You should talk to him soon."

"In my application I wrote about my past. They knew about it when they raided my room because I told them in my application. But I swear I was no dealer here. I had stuff, but I wasn't any different than anyone else. Everybody trades it sometimes. But hard stuff, selling it? I know what that means. I know better than most because I was involved in that before. That life is long behind me."

"Professor Doswell believes you."

"I know he does." Willi hesitated, perhaps looking for the same affirmation from Vincent, but Vincent, while he was entirely behind Willi, wasn't confident enough about that one detail to say he was.

"President Montbanc, people like him, people like his friends over at the

Alliance, they want to work on you, and expect you to keep still – it's like they're telling you, 'Don't move' while they're twisting you and turning you and making you over, like I used to do with the lathe in the gun shops, and if you start fidgeting and resisting – that's what I did – that's when they do what they do. Or have one of their dogs do it."

Their strategy, worked out with Joe Stein, Willi's new lawyer replacing Johnny Beals, the pro bono ACLU lawyer who for about a week represented Willi, was not only to challenge the entire case against Willi on the basis of Willi's Fourth Amendment rights, but to initiate a civil suit charging the university with targeting him.

"It's certain," Vincent remembered Doswell saying, "that Montbanc didn't make this move to stem the tide of drugs. If he had he would have gone about it differently. He wouldn't have raided Smith Hall exclusively and put Willi's room first on his list."

No search warrants had been shown; and while, of course, university staff weren't the police, and the students' relation to the school was in loco parentis, the school had at least this specific obligation precisely because it was a parental surrogate: that Willi and the others not be targeted for felony crimes to satisfy some unrelated personal vendetta.

If a case could be made for just this being true, independent of the separate question of Willi's selling drugs, not only would this be basis alone for arguing the inadmissibility of the evidence, but as both Stein and Beals earlier maintained, those in the administration who were responsible for initiating such action could be subject to civil damages. Anything that would paint Baxter's faculty and administration as at least careless, or worse, criminally involved in the abuse of drugs, would support the case that the President had taken a sudden interest in the problem only as cover for punishing Willi.

Vincent better appreciated this angle than anyone. He knew firsthand Raskin's easy habits, certainly at Laurel Hill, and even at his Baxter digs beside the stage in Morris Hall. But not only had he never thought to pay any attention previously, he'd generally looked the other way. Now he realized it was possible Raskin even shared his stash with some of his more closely trusted drama students; at least he was certain he did with faculty friends.

At Laurel Hill he remembered the last time he was there with Blissie (they quarreled both before and afterwards), hard stuff was being used, with Raskin a leading player. He remembered the air, sweet and pungent, everyone lollygagging about, a dozen or so people absently sitting or sprawled within range of the grand, intricately carved granite fireplace in the library, taking in the flickering light of the fire. Goepels (everyone wryly called him Goebbels), the house's general factotum, who was more visible when Burwell was away, had retired for the night and someone was passing around some exotic weed of high quality.

Blissie, least susceptible to these drug-induced mental states, was musing aloud about learning to see herself in the "straitjacket" her "uptight" middle-class parents had "fitted" for her, which she'd finally learned to get loose of, when suddenly some guy broke out crying like a six-year-old girl who'd stubbed her toe. As he blubbered, his voice rose steadily to a near-shriek.

"They loved me! They never turned their love off. It was outside my middle-class home that I learned hatred and deceit! At school I learned that if you don't give them what they want they punish! With children, at play, I learned if you don't play their way, they *punish!*"

Suddenly there was Raskin, dramatically reciting in a high-pitched voice some lines from William Blake: "*Little lamb, who made thee? Dost thou know who made thee?*" He'd been in a sour state for weeks, and had come suddenly to life. His actor's voice growing especially resonant, reciting the words as if on stage with utter aplomb: "*Gave thee life and bid thee feed. By the stream and o'er the mead, Gave thee clothing of delight... Gave thee such a tender voice, Making allllllll the vales rejoice.*" Then Raskin started to bleat, and that solemn and richly sumptuous room broke into absolute, uncontrolled hilarity.

Gwen, long before, had told him, "They're creeps, Vincent! They're creeps!"

And on that night he was ashamed to say he didn't walk out right then and there – but it *was* the last time he went. That same guy Morris he saw one day at CSU, and he talked to him. Yes, he had a lot to say about Raskin's drug habits at Laurel Hill, and made it clear that "drugs and romances" weren't confined to Laurel Hill or Central University.

One day, shortly after Vincent saw Willi at the Jolly Roger, Vincent got a surprise telephone call from Raskin asking to see him.

Why, he wondered, would Raskin want to see him? No matter, he thought, he himself had a lot to tell Raskin.

He began without preliminaries the instant he stepped into his office. "I plan to testify to a lot of dope around here by you and a whole lot of folks. As for your friends, Willi is going to bring a lawsuit against the President and Deans Middleweek and Hyzak alleging that he was targeted. That's called violating someone's civil rights. And in case you don't know, Raskin, that's real, real naughty."

"You're going to tell them that you used dope around here too?"

"No, because I didn't. I might tell them that I used some pot at Laurel Hill – but a whole lot more about you over there."

"You know, Vincent", he'd come fully alive, "there isn't a thing you or that old Tom can do to me. If you try telling stories about me you'll find it's not easy to besmirch my name."

Vincent had begun laughing.

"If I'm not mistaken you have some obvious axes to grind. There are a whole lot of folks around here who see things different than you. Believe me on that! Didn't Dr. Montbanc fire you from that job you had with the Alliance? There were lots of people who heard you screaming and cursing and carrying on right there in his office not that long ago when he told you."

"That's what I'd expect from you, Raskin: Montbanc acts like a lunatic and you say I do."

"Vincent, you came in here threatening me, telling me all these nasty things, when all I wanted to do was to have a friendly conversation – in fact admit to you that I was wrong about something, seriously wrong. Yeah, wrong. You ought to be ashamed."

"I'm telling you these 'nasty things' because there's gonna be some sinking ships, and you can be on one of them or you can be off when they go down."

"Vincent, why don't you cut it out? You're not scaring me. But you know, you really ought to be ashamed of lining up with old Tom against me like this. If you knew—"

"He doesn't know you exist, Raskin."

"Doesn't know I exist?" For an instant there was a flicker of real anger in Raskin's eyes. "I think he knows."

"Well, let me tell you this: I'm not the only one who'll testify about all the dope around here: the buying, the selling and trading here and at Laurel Hill, and between you and some of your hotshot friends and students. When that day comes – and believe me, a lot more might come out – it'll get *real* ugly."

Raskin got up from out of his chair, stood behind it, and began fingering a pen from his desk. "Let me tell you about your lovely Mr. Tom Doswell."

"I'm not interested in any kind of lies you have to tell."

"No. I'm going to tell you that you were exactly right, that last time you came calling on me. You told me that you'd unearthed this old man in New York, dug him up in Brooklyn, didn't you say? And I'm admitting now I was wrong, wrong. I believe he really did tell the truth about Doswell. I learned recently that he *was* part of a progressive group, a radical textile union…"

Vincent started to actually listen to what Raskin was saying.

"This is why these conventions can be so profitable. You know, the networking. You get to meet these people you wouldn't otherwise get to know. This old guy, he comes over to me and tells me that old Tom was part of a progressive movement at one time. That he did some really wild stuff. 'Yeah, is that right?' I say. I want to know more. You can imagine I find it hard to believe. It turns out we've got some mutual acquaintances and he fills me in.

"He tells me that back in the '30s he starts informing, going to the government, spilling his guts about the people he knows in the Movement… Now just listen, just listen. Before you object and start crying about how I'm lying, you go check some major news reports like I did, which confirm the rest of what he tells me. He tells me that back in the early '50s, he volunteers to go to these congressional investigating committees: the House Committee on Un-American Activities – Senator Joe McCarthy and all those kinds of snakes. He doesn't just answer questions, you understand? No, he *volunteers*, says, 'Yessuh, boss, what else you want?' Kisses up to these white segregationist witch hunters and Joe McCarthy…"

Vincent started for the door, his back to Raskin.

"Just hear me out! You see, you *were* right. Tom had his days in the sun! Names names and places, ruins careers, even has a lot to say about one of your heroes and mine, Paul Robeson – yeah, Tom did know some *big name* folks in his day. Of course he probably made up most of what he told, but hey, a little inventiveness testifies to a rich imagination, my mother always used to say."

Vincent whirled round, facing Raskin again. "Who told you all this?"

Raskin chuckled. "It doesn't matter. You wouldn't have a clue who he was anyway. All that matters is that it's true. And there are public documents which prove it's true. Like I say, look it up. And by the way, something else that's true, though you won't find it in the back issues of the *New York Times*, I'm sure. He had a lover back in the '30s, a plump little fella that used to love to dance. They had a place all their own, a little private love-nest off Fifth Avenue in New York, bought it with money he swindled—"

Vincent raised his hand with just barely suppressed fury. "Alright, alright! I've heard enough of your slanders…"

"Keep that in mind when you start spreading shit about me!"

"None of this has a damn thing to do with Willi Wade and your selling drugs to students here."

"I never sold drugs over here, and you know that's ridiculous."

"I don't know any such thing! But I do know for certain, for certain, mind you, that you went to Laurel Hill and came back with all kinds of stuff and shared it like candy!" At that point Vincent opened and slammed shut Raskin's door before Raskin could say anything further. Then he stalked down the hall and out of the building.

But this last thing that Raskin said, this business about Doswell and a male lover, distressed Vincent to the extreme; for it also instantly and painfully struck a chord.

After he'd returned from New York and heard about the raid he'd spoken to Blissie about Willi having been targeted (a conversation which they had at her office between classes), and she'd asked matter-of-factly, or rather with a satirical matter-of-factness, "By the way, how are Jim and Doswell – those lovebirds?"

He'd drawn a complete blank. Doubting that he'd heard right, he'd murmured, "What did you say?"

She shrugged it off, and they returned to the business at hand: Willi's being targeted by Montbanc, and the university's drug scene. He forgot it nearly as fast as he heard it, thinking her words were part of some awkwardly phrased witticism. Now he realized its origin. And the malice of it, the sickness of the man who'd invented it, left him stunned. What's more, it was as stupid as it was evil.

He stopped and stood under the sheltering bare branches of one of Baxter's great oak trees, trees, no doubt, that were already of good size when the university was founded a hundred years before. But this other business… He didn't care about a love affair – if there was such a love affair – thirty years ago! But then this business about Doswell being a government informer, this *was* serious because – much worse – because it was possible! He could easily imagine such a thing. But no, he thought after a moment, whatever Doswell may have been at one time, and no matter how much he'd learned to hate progressive politics, he was no son-of-a-bitch-snitch, as Raskin would have it, running errands for the powerful. This couldn't be true…

Thankfully, when he arrived in his office Ogunda wasn't there. As he busied himself, he was seething. After trying to take care of a long backlog of student papers but not able to concentrate, he sorted through a pile-up of memos and directives that could no longer be put off, and then he called a cab to save the long walk back to his room at the Hotel Carolina.

As always when he'd been gone the whole day, he stopped for his mail at the front desk. And among the several pieces of mail which the desk clerk handed him was his grand hope: an envelope addressed to him in Gwen's sweetly familiar hand. The tingly rush of exhilaration which came over him was checked, however, by a discrete observation that was instantly followed by a sinking feeling not unlike stepping from the ledge of a building: the envelope was without a return address and it was postmarked *Boston, Mass.*

24

Family Problems

One late afternoon Doswell telephoned Jim from his office at the university to say he wanted to see him. This was not unusual. But on this occasion there was an odd formality in his voice which made Jim wonder what it was about. Willi Wade, of course, and as he made his way the short distance to Doswell's office, Jim grew irritable at the thought. Yes, he knew Willi Wade was being railroaded and he wished the best for him, but he had a very full plate. As far as he was concerned, this was Vincent's baby and he couldn't see anything that he could do. Still, he sensed an expectation from Doswell that he should do more, though he'd never said as much.

When he arrived, to his relief the old man was alone, but he was right: Doswell did want to talk about Willi and the case. They talked low, since at Baxter it was said the walls had ears. Doswell told Jim that Montbanc had recently been named to a Presidential Commission.

"Presidential...?"

"Richard Milhous Nixon, yes, a commission to 'look into the reasons and causes of student violence and campus unrest' around the country."

Jim shook his head in disbelief. After a few seconds he said, "How did this happen?"

A resigned smile played on Doswell's lips. "You ever hear the squeaky wheel gets the grease? Right after the convention there was an Alliance contingent Montbanc headed up which included a group of college presidents that went up to Washington and lobbied Congress, you know, about 'the growing agony of youth', 'the nation's problems'..." His voice trailed off.

Jim continued to shake his head glumly.

"This is good news."

Jim looked at him, his eyes questioning.

"He's got everything to lose. He's basking in the sunlight of a great reputation..."

"Yeah, even the *News-Herald* says he's a hero."

"That love affair won't last long. But you see, what happens if it comes out that he went after Willi as part of a vendetta? Right now, everybody thinks he's the best thing since...*chocolate* ice cream," Doswell chuckled.

Jim smiled too, and thought, he's certainly bounced back.

"Willi's lawyer, Joe Stein, said if we can gather some Baxter people's signatures on a well-crafted statement, that if it doesn't exactly *say* this is what he did, but that it surely *looks* like he did, that sort of thing, that would help him with a civil suit – that would win some leverage, not only with Montbanc (because you can be sure he's flying high with all this sweet attention he's been getting), but with the city's DA because he's going to have to contemplate charging those kids on contaminated evidence."

"You mean the dorms were wide open, and the rooms too?"

"All of that, and their Fourth Amendment rights."

Jim nodded, but the truth was his enthusiasm for all this Willi Wade business wasn't even lukewarm. Besides never having met Willi, thanks to the loan he'd earlier made to his brother, Chuck, his finances were shaky and he'd decided he couldn't afford to do anything to compromise himself with Baxter's administration.

Doswell had noticed Jim's sulky mood for days. He commented now in a way that he'd never before. "This situation with Susan. I know you must have your worries, but..." he spoke haltingly, "despite troubles with my daughter, I look back, and I realize the radiance of those days she was in my life – and, yes," he lit up, "what would I do without Billy?"

Jim smiled, surprised and, more, thankful that despite his reluctance to talk about Carole, and in fact that he never previously had, he had volunteered this to prop him up.

"I know what you mean. Believe me, this baby is welcomed by me." He hesitated. He found it hard to say directly what he really wanted to say. "As you know I just moved into this apartment. It looks like this is where Susan and I will have to stay...our first home...you saw the place. I had the money a few months ago to put a down payment on a house, a nice nest egg. But I lent the money to my brother so he could buy a house. Now we're stuck on Rigley Street." And stuck here at Baxter, he thought to say, but didn't. "That's not the worst thing in the world, but Susan's down in the dumps about everything. The neighborhood, the car, the apartment is pretty dirty. It's just not the way she wanted to start, nor did I..." He trailed off.

Doswell said nothing.

Jim hesitated. "My brother recently got out of the hospital. His appendix ruptured. He had to be rushed to the emergency room. There were complications..."

"I'm sorry to hear—"

"No, no. Actually he's OK. When he was there, in the hospital, my mother went up to his house in Rockland County – you know, north of the city. She's in the Bronx."

"I know the area well. We had quite a few regulars in Rockland County."

"Right." Jim nodded. "Uncle Big Bob's?" He talked on without waiting for an answer. "There were moments it actually looked bad."

"You could have gone up."

"I didn't even know about it. It happened so fast, and by the time I got word he was out of the woods. But my mother was up there a couple of days in the middle of it… I'm burdening you with all this crap."

"No, no, I wouldn't call it crap."

Seconds passed. "While she was there something broke out between my mother and my sister-in-law. They don't get along too well."

"Not uncommon."

"I know, I know. But Clare, my sister-in-law…my brother was still in the hospital and she tells my mother she's not welcome in the house. 'Get out,' she says. Tells her to leave. This, you understand…my brother's still in the hospital."

Doswell was acutely attentive, but he said nothing.

"Now, Clare is Clare. Even my mother says, 'She's his wife. He has to take her part.' My mother gets anxious easily. I guess she can be trying…and she's not well."

"Getting anxious when your son is in the hospital in an emergency like that, I'd say that's normal."

"Right. I think so too. And the fact is, my mother paid for the bulk of the down payment on the house. And it's not the damned money – if they showed an ounce of gratitude… He needed it at the time. I don't even doubt he'll pay it back. But you know, she made it possible for them to get the house…

"Now, the thing is, after my brother gets out of the hospital, as soon as he's well enough, he drives down to my mother's place and sticks up for Clare – as he always does. They have a quarrel and my brother goes into a tirade about how my mother is always doing – well, I don't know, something to set Clare off. I wasn't there…"

Doswell said nothing.

"I know you can't comment. This is all third-hand… I never talk about this. There's no point to it…"

"I wouldn't say that. Do you have any other siblings?"

"I have two sisters. They're a million miles away…in California. They have their own lives. They're smart. They don't get involved in any of this."

"Family problems," Doswell ventured. "When my brother was a teenager, one night he just up and left and was never heard from again."

Once more Jim was surprised. "What did they do? Why?"

"Why? My father was pretty demanding of both of us – all of us. Especially my brother and me. I didn't mind his Latin and Greek lessons – and all his other lessons – at least, not the way he did. My brother could sit at the piano for hours, though, and play ragtime, anything from memory. Beautifully. My father got impatient with all that – his 'lack of discipline', his 'mutinies'. Their quarrel simmered for years. One night, a big battle, and then he left."

"And they never found him?"

"They tried. In those days you didn't get much help from local authorities... anyway, they didn't."

There was a long silence.

"I didn't mean to...to burden you," Jim said.

"No, no. You didn't burden me. I just wish I could tell you something helpful. But like you say, I don't know enough. Who does? Even you, perhaps you don't know enough."

"I know my brother. I know him well... He has no love for the family, only contempt, maybe most of all for my mother."

As he said this Jim couldn't help noticing that Doswell's office was even messier than it had been when he'd first met him there in the summer. There were more boxes along the walls with student papers, books strewn about, along with an empty brown paper lunch bag. And there was his sweat-stained fedora which lay atop one of the boxes.

For a long minute silence reigned.

"But my brother had it very hard...with my father."

"Maybe you had a hard time too."

"No. Not like Chuck."

Doswell was silent. Finally he said, "One thing I know: you can't excuse someone from normal decency – and I don't necessarily say this applies to your brother, but I say if you do because of some past injustice, you say he's exempted, we won't hold you to the standards everyone else is held to, that's demeaning, destructive."

"I know."

Doswell hesitated, and the professor once again appeared. "Remember when Socrates was going to his death at the end of the *Apology?* He says to his friends that when he's gone, vex his children, punish them if they value the wrong things..."

"I know. That's his legacy. Not wealth. Not property. But true standards."

Again the silence reigned.

Doswell finally said, "So what are you going to do now?"

"I'm thinking my mother can't go on living in the city. She hates the place in the Bronx like I do. I'm thinking she should move away, closer to Susan and me. My brother and Clare...the family...they're killing her."

"Closer to you and Susan? Did she ask you that?"

"No, she wouldn't ask that... I mean after we get things sorted out." He smiled. "You know..."

"Ahh, I see," Doswell said.

There were no more classes for the day. It was growing dark. There was a knock on the door; a young man stepped in, noticed Jim and excused himself.

"I was seeing Dr. Trejo down the hall. I can talk to you some other time."

Jim started getting up to leave, thinking that he'd been here long enough.

"No, no." Doswell gestured to Jim. "What do you want?"

"You told me you'd read my paper and I should talk to you."

"That's right – we have class tomorrow? See me after class, you can do that, can't you?"

"Yep, I can." The boy stepped out of the room.

Jim was still standing.

"I was going to ask you to take this statement around and get some signatures, but you've got a full plate, I can see that. And we can get the job done without pestering you..."

"Are you sure about that?" he looked relieved.

"Definitely. You're not a very popular guy around here anyway. Being my friend, that sinks you." He laughed, big-eyed. "You're worthless!"

That ended their conference.

PART 6

25

Zora Payton Doswell, Wife and Mother

That year that Jim was privileged to know and to learn so much from Doswell, Doswell still didn't tell him everything. And he never would. During his final years working from an Uncle Big Bob's limousine by night, meeting with Comintern agents, there was one corner hidden on the edge of his life that he mentioned only once to Jim. This hidden corner was never revealed in their late-night conversations – and when he did reveal a part of it, facing the end of his life, in fragments, in pieces torn from the patchwork of his pressured memory, it was hardly a tale with a beginning and an end. But though Doswell would never tell it as he did so much else, Jim learned of it due to a series of providential circumstances. On one of those talks Jim recalled he'd mentioned that for some years prior to his break with the Party, he'd jotted notes to himself which he secreted in his 112th Street house. But he'd also said that later he disposed of them. And so he'd thought. However, to Jim's eternal gratitude, this was not so, and to Euretha Lewis is owed thanks for this different turn of events.

Fast-forwarding to sometime early in June of 1970, following Doswell's death, which no one anticipated, except perhaps himself, Euretha Lewis as executrix was faced with urgent tasks. In this instance it was Doswell's Will, which of course was of paramount interest to Billy. Euretha, failing to locate it where she'd always understood it to be, in the old man's bedroom bureau upper drawer, had gone hectically in search of the document. This led to a search of much of the house, through other bureau drawers, two closets, through nooks and crannies Euretha would never otherwise have looked, and eventually, it turned up. It turned up, however, with much else as well.

This was the first part of the story. She told it to Jim when she presented him with two cardboard boxes filled with miscellaneous papers that she remembered depositing some four or five years earlier, contrary to Doswell's instructions, at the bottom of an armoire which served as a closet for Billy's bedroom. And since Billy draped the few clothes he used over the backs of chairs, at the foot of his bed or halfway under it, it was rarely used except for storage. And thus forgotten.

"Maybe I shouldn't have done it," Euretha said, her voice subdued, saying that she was hardly proud of herself, but yet, Jim sensed, she wasn't really sorry.

"When Carole died Thomas was throwing out things," she explained. "In his frenzy he just started cleaning out. He started piling things in boxes and telling me, 'Get rid of this, get rid of that.' I did of course for much of it, but not all of it."

"I guess you could see that he was not himself, that he was acting in a way that he'd later regret."

"That's exactly right. I knew the state he was in, and I thought someday he might wish he hadn't thrown out all those things. That was the first and last time I ever ignored what he told me to do. I guess that's why I forgot about those boxes."

Now she said she'd peeked again and confirmed what she'd originally realized. There were letters both to and from his parents going back many years, and miscellaneous other papers, most of which no doubt *were* junk.

"Perhaps there are things in there not for Billy's eyes. I thought of going through them myself – and I have some. But he told me to get rid of them, and I know he talked to you a lot... Besides, I just don't feel right since it was me who hid them."

"It's obvious your intentions were what's best."

"Well," she added (and this was one of those things he knew endeared her so to Doswell, this rare wisdom and humility), there might be things there she "just wouldn't understand."

Jim laughed, embarrassed, both surprised and immensely pleased by Euretha's confidence and her intuition, and knowing no other way to respond, denying the compliment.

But Euretha, in her characteristically straightforward way, said, "No use pretending, if there was anyone he would have wanted to lay eyes on those things, and decide, it would have been you."

Naturally he was moved by this show of trust, and though he embraced the task with enthusiasm, he did so also with anxiety – an anxiety that, it turned out, was fully justified.

As he began this delicate foraging, he remembered in detail the short conversation they'd had: that his notes had been jotted down on whatever came to hand: on paper napkins, the backs of discarded envelopes, sheets of legal paper held together by rusted paper clips; the papers browned and faded with age, creased in odd places depending on the way they'd lain over the years. Some of what Jim found was in a small, careful hand on the backs of envelopes, some in larger but careless, barely legible fragments, and a few long, arduously drawn-out descriptions and reflections with startlingly clear references to his wife Zora.

The last, especially the earlier notes referring to *this lovely girl*, were often lyrically joyful expressions of this *wondrous discovery* of a *small-town girl in the heart of Harlem*. In them Doswell sounded like a lovesick adolescent! But then others elaborated on doubts and self-accusations with excruciating clarity – some with initially mystifying omissions.

Euretha was right. To understand much of what was in these often barely legible notes would have been a challenge, but not because Doswell was 'well educated' and she wasn't; but because of their disconnected – sometimes, it seemed, deliberately oblique – references, no doubt written by a man who feared that if they were discovered by prying eyes they would reveal too much.

But if Jim didn't instantly understand, he eventually did, amplifying them with the substance of their many conversations, and one especially revealing last conversation that was had not only with him but with Vincent as well.

So something scribbled on a sheet with unrelated fragments had this clear message: *She seems the perfect woman for me.* Another beside it, written at probably the same time, no doubt in the early '30s, referred to a *curiously spinsterish young woman* who had taken, he added, *the initiative in many ways*, adding in another place, *her earnestness, her willingness to try to do everything right.* But it was clear this efficiency of hers went beyond business, because it seemed Zora had early on taken a personal interest in him – though, he was careful to add, *in a shyly modest, maternal way.*

Of course, she wasn't unpleasing in her appearance either. There were photos of her, several taken at the time of her wedding to a younger, burly, but clearly recognizable, Thomas. Twenty-one, ten years his junior, she had a light brown complexion, clear skin, and an attractive figure which in the old photographs displayed curves in all of the right places. He wrote at the time that he felt in her presence *a sanity* which filled their moments together *with a wholeness and freshness* that he'd never previously known.

He described, then, what had to have been a time when Zora and he lived together, unmarried. It was the way of Movement Communists. But it was also clear that Zora was never a Party member, and for a long time apparently she was not even aware that he was. But then she became pregnant. Stalin had devastated the Soviet heartland; his Great Purge was swallowing victims by the thousands daily; in New York agents, both "legals" and "illegals" waited with dread for the call to return to the Motherland. Her happiness over the news of the baby was overshadowed by his unhappiness over this same news. This was one of those items which he dwelled on in some detail: *She has blossomed into a bourgeois, coffee-colored hausfrau, ready to raise a whole brood of little Zoras and Toms. Oh, for her easy blindness! Her obliviousness! She wants to add to the anarchy! She thinks all is wonderful with the world! She sees no further than the street corner and the sign reading UNCLE BIG BOB'S – HE TREATS YOU RIGHT, and my clowny face over the garage.*

Still, they kept the baby. He did not press his own preference on her, an abortion, a decision that the Party considered a matter of convenience, and that he considered a necessity, given the *hopeless world it would be brought into... Necessity, yes, but I am weak. She wants it so much. What can I do?*

Carole was born in 1935.

He wrote, in a painfully ironical aside, that his and Zora's relationship as live-together lovers had the underlying character of an employer-boss to employee-worker dynamic, admitting that while his life was *devoted to liberating the oppressed of the world*, in their secret intimacy *a domestic tyranny prevails*.

It was about this time that he began thinking of leaving the Party.

Why didn't he just walk out? Jim knew from their conversations that he cudgeled his brain daily for a way to do just that. If simply disappearing with Zora and Carole were possible, he would have. But there were the people at the limousine service, and Charlie and Hawpe. He was like a well-established plant whose roots are impossibly tangled and wound among others. To remove himself meant dislodging, destroying others. He said that he'd thought of leaving with the Party's blessing, asking and hoping to get permission to transfer to the open Party, and then as some others had, over a prudent period of time, slipping away. But he knew in his case this would never work. He was at the nerve center of the conspiracy's network of espionage; it was absurd to think that they would consider such a request. Uncle Big Bob's did legally belong to him, but he couldn't sell it without alerting the Party; there was a lien against it from the Trust Company of North America. He thought of making the case to J. Peters that he needed a partner, that the workload was killing him. The company would then be saved when he disappeared one fine day – the workers' jobs, at a time when breadlines formed round whole blocks in Harlem, would be secure. But this left too much to chance. The Party would certainly assign his partner, someone entirely new to deal with, and what new entanglements would be created? What's more, when he disappeared, the Party would not continue to use the limousine service as a front; there would be an explosion of recriminations, and those touched by him would come under instant suspicion of the gravest kind. What would happen to Hawpe and to Charlie, especially Charlie, an "illegal" in America at Stalin's sufferance?

Every plan he turned to had a dead end.

Now the notes made it clear: Zora had no understanding of what was taking place outside their life together, but he gave her no help. He acknowledged that his lack of confidence in her led to her meager understanding, and this fed in him a growing contempt and insane resentment at the isolation he often felt most acutely in her presence. It had never been in his character to use violence against a woman, or in the past, even to be harsh. But with Zora he admitted to himself that there were moments of great frustration – and then he would leave her for days on end.

When they were to be married, in the face of her astonishment, he was adamant that no one from Uncle Big Bob's appear as a guest; nor, he insisted, was anyone there to be told they were marrying. Here, after the difficult decision to keep their first and only child, there had come this second serious snag. And over this, he never budged.

These, no doubt, were days when his struggle with the Hammers had reached critical mass: the Hammers had accused Charlie and himself of embezzling funds; Charlie's life had been threatened; the Hammers' venality threatened the secrecy of the operation and its agents; while over everything hung the Purge. He explained to Zora that he didn't want office gossip – "Backbiting charges of office favorites." But to this wholly acquiescent, sweet girl who loved him, this appeared not only unreasonable but downright perverse. So for the first time she'd dared to openly rebel, and they quarreled.

Jim could imagine between the startling revelations in his notes, and from what Doswell told him on those many, many nights – and his final night – he could easily guess what they were like.

"But why, Thomas? Why wouldn't you want my friends, our friends, people who know us to be with us? To know?"

"I can't explain everything to you..."

"You've never explained anything to me, and I've never asked you to explain anything. But you can tell me this: is it because..." (the words no doubt freighted with anxiety and hurt) "because you are ashamed of me?" It was characteristic of her, her insecurity and innocence so great she could reveal her inner soul to this powerful man she thought might easily be contemptuous of her.

He'd approached her then, his face melting into a genuine warmth and radiant glow of love and affection, but an affection one shows more for a well-loved child than a grown-up woman lover.

She was suddenly confident again that he loved her and that he was *not* ashamed of her. And then he'd gone to great lengths to offer to pay everything to have her grandparents and anyone else she desired to come north (her widowed mother already residing in the city, along with younger brothers and sisters). He offered a wedding cake, bridesmaids, anything and everything – but no one from the limousine service. In the general good feeling and joy, she willfully overlooked his great, inexplicable strangeness. But then, neither did she ever get over it. Especially after he reinforced it by his insistence that she never go to the office, or have anything further to do with anyone there.

And then, having moved to the 112th Street apartment, he spread the story they'd broken up; that she was gone from his life, neither an employee nor the lover one of her friends had insisted she knew Zora had been. It was at that time when he learned that she'd whispered their secret to her best friend, contravening his *clearly communicated wishes*, that his harshness went beyond all earlier bounds. When she objected, in her fragile but newfound determination to rescue something of her rights as a separate person with wishes and desires of her own, he'd become furious, crushing her in a blistering verbal assault, telling her that she knew nothing, understood nothing, was an "empty-headed, silly, childish woman".

But why didn't he tell her *something* of his difficulty?

He did – a little. Overcome with sorrow, he insisted that these and other ugly things he'd said were not true. He explained that the business was not all that it seemed; he hinted at criminal types with whom he had from the beginning been associated. It made sense out of a lot of hitherto nagging quandaries and hurts, but it also frightened her; and she asked why he couldn't break with them, have nothing further to do with these criminals. And then later she wanted to know further details as their little girl Carole grew and wanted to wander at play in the park, or go out and play on the sidewalk without her mother.

In time he explained that the "criminals" were political in nature, that they were Communists. He said this to inform her, to reassure her, and it *did* reassure her. But because it didn't say everything, or rather it said virtually nothing of *why* he wanted to remain essentially hidden from so many people, why he'd insisted on no more children, why Carole was *not* to be left alone on the sidewalk, why Zora needed to always keep her in sight – it further frightened and confused her. She was left wondering and asking what was it that he so feared if they were only these scruffy, noisy, but essentially harmless political people from the Communist Party?

At that time, he often left her for days on end. But then when he would return, as the inner tensions and the outer pressures mounted, there was a widening alienation and incomprehensible resentment and bitterness. If she must share his life, let her share his *unsettled convictions!* If she must know – *but cannot, will not* – then leave her with some small knowledge of his *desolation!* And then this would require no provocations, as everything became impossibly worse in his other life.

In 1939 the Hitler-Stalin pact was signed. Within days of the pact, Nazi Germany invaded Poland from the West; two weeks later the Soviet Union invaded Poland from the East. As the opening events of the war played themselves out, the Party in America echoed the regime's line on all fronts of the war. It provided moral cover for the Soviet invasion by describing Poland as a criminal nation oppressing Ukrainians and Jews. It agitated against giving America's support, material or otherwise, to England, describing it now as a nation fighting merely for its "colonialist plunder".

Zora would come to him in those days with some hesitant domestic talk, something about new draperies and an article of clothing for Carole, the sharing of a happy observation about Carole; and he, with the burden of the world on his shoulders, this foolish woman presuming that he should concern himself with these petty matters, telling himself his sufferance could bear just so much, wrapped himself in silence, making no answer. Or he exploded in a fury of harsh words.

One incident he painstakingly described in a long, ramblingly convoluted several pages on Hammer Galleries letterhead. After one of those silences, in an agony of indecision following those recurring conflicts with the Hammers – then Schapiro's threats, then accusations and counter-accusations – she'd awakened in him some great wrath. It was compounded by a wholly innocuous comment as she returned in quiet distress to her work, chided by him on some miserable night near Christmas.

"I only *thought* you'd like to see what I did on Carole's new dress," she'd said – then returned to her smocking or embroidering on one of their little girl's outfits.

"What makes you think I've *ever* cared about all your fripperies?" he said, with rising bitterness. And when he saw the question in her face, pained but also like a child's face, confused, there was the thought, and the disgust in it: she doesn't know what 'frippery' means!

But it was clear it wasn't *always* this way. Sometimes on good days, and there were more of them during those first several months following the signing of the pact, he could be human – he could be meltingly, bountifully human with her, seeking to make up when he thought of it all, remembering guiltily his harshness. For a while his life at this time had grown more tranquil. Clandestine activities, especially those funding start-up operations in foreign lands, had come to a near-standstill. In the first instance, the war in Europe put a full stop to the Mississippi-like flow of treasure from the Soviet Union to Hammer's warehouses in New York. Funds for the bank dried up. For a while, which roughly coincided with the pact, following years of purge activity in the Soviet Union, the numbers of experienced legal and illegal residents and agents had been so diminished in Russia that there were an insufficient number of trained individuals to adequately replace them. And there was this: the FBI, under orders from the Justice Department, was taking aggressive action against espionage by a Communist party which was now de facto aligned with Nazi Germany. Deep in the underground, "under discipline", his usual strict orders to avoid all contact with the open Party, Doswell was to wait for messages from the *Rezidents*, and indeed occasionally did get orders and met with them – or their skeletal staffs – but outside of that he was to wait for better times.

But these were actually the best of times. Though the limousine service was as busy as ever, even busier, the traffic of undercover activities having come to a virtual standstill, the double life – at least in the busyness of his days – had nearly ceased. Life began to approximate normality. Thus he had the luxury of thinking more of those previously impossible thoughts about breaking again. And yet this period was short-lived. For it was also at this time that he made the searing discoveries that set him finally at war with the Party.

"In those days, as I say, I wasn't doing much. The regime had a skeletal staff in the States… One of the men they'd sent over, a younger man, was the most rabid Stalinist I had ever met. His admiration knew no bounds. And there was a hard anger in him, which he exhibited not against me but in his corrosively cynical attitude. His pet hatred was for Jews.

"One day I did something I never did in those days, except for a time with Charlie. I had this man over to the house on 144th Street. It may seem strange to invite such a person, but though I did not really want to, he so much desired a visit to my home, he asked so often, I knew that he had an immense hunger, a crying hunger for human contact, and for some reason he'd attached himself to me – I decided there was no harm in it.

"So we went to 144th Street, that's where I took him of course, and we began to talk late into that night under the influence of what Fort-Whiteman liked to call the 'people's juice'. I was surprised at how much he could drink. I'd been with some first class vodka drinkers before, Whiteman among them. But this guy was *world* class. He downed the vodka in glasses one after another, after another, and then he began to tell me his story, or at least a significant chapter in his story. He told me he was a Ukrainian, and that he'd been a teenager when the famine struck in '32 and '33.

'They were all Jews that came into my village. Komsomol from Kiev, directed by local Party Jews,' he said. He said they came into the villages like locusts and stripped them clean; ransacked, took all the food. Handfuls of grain, or pieces of old potato or turnip skins, waste used to feed the pigs (pigs long gone, as were the dogs and the cats, every animal that could be eaten), any pitiful scrap wrapped in old clothes and buried in holes or under furnishings. 'Everything, everywhere.'

"I said, to be sure he meant what he was saying, 'Only Jews?'

'Yes, Jewish murderers,' he said. 'There was the Jew who shouted into my mother's face that she must pay fair taxes!'

'Stalin had nothing to do with this?' I said.

"He turned on me – furious. 'Stalin knew nothing! This had nothing to do with socializing agriculture! He didn't order this! They did it without his knowing!'

"I said nothing further. What do you say to a man who's had such a vision? Who nearly died of starvation himself? Who's watched his family starving?"

"You don't argue with him." Jim had dipped his head and spoke little above a whisper.

"Yes – and I knew he was right in this regard: that this was not to socialize agriculture. This was extermination. Koestler, who'd traveled through there, described it years later. Whole regions sealed off. Scattered remnants from near the cities looking for handouts, rounded up and herded into arenas left to die. You don't do this, seeing children with stick-like limbs, babies with enormous, fetus-like, wobbling heads – no, you don't do this, you don't force this, except to kill them, to exterminate them!

"So you see, I hadn't known at all before what 'reordering the foundations of human life' meant. He howled at me, 'You'll see! They will get it! Hitler will give it to them! It is against the law to eat human flesh!'"

"So what Walter Duranty had written, even by admitting that there were deaths, was a clever cover-up."

When Doswell learned the full truth, not only the mind-numbing evil of the regime, and of the men of the regime and of Duranty, but *himself* in evading the real truth, putting out of mind everything that wasn't flat in his face, he'd fallen into a benumbed daze. For the very first time ever he didn't appear at the limousine service. He stayed away all day. But when he returned to Zora in the evening (having only had a little to drink, holding himself to strict limits), he was like one among the living dead. He sat in the big, overstuffed couch he'd bought when they were married and stared blankly into the space of their living room in the apartment over the dentist's office.

Zora had come to him late in the evening after Carole had been put to bed, sensing something terrible had befallen him, seeking to commiserate, to comfort, and once again to know something of his burden. In this department, this department of his life which occupied virtually the whole of it, the Party and the regime, never did he find Zora more of an interloper than when he needed her the most. And the burden he was now bearing was the isolating weight of the conviction of his own guilt, his guilt and cowardliness. Her commiserating efforts triggered an explosion, a fury directed really at himself, but at himself through her who was nearest and most intimate, and yet furthest in her impossible effort to be fully with him. This fool that adores *me!* How worthless she is, she who so blindly, so uncritically, so stupidly attaches herself to me! To *me!* And the part of him that sensed that she was his single, most precious link to life struck at her with an onslaught of destructive words aimed at her so very easily understood insecurities. To strike at her then was to strike at that link to life just as surely as a suicide puts a bullet into his brain.

What brought him out of a long, on-again-off-again depression in those late '30s, early 1940 days was his suddenly learning from Charlie that Hammer was assisting in the Nazi war effort.

"Hammer was buying huge quantities of used whiskey and beer barrels from major distilleries and shipping them to Mexico. Charlie saw the books. I was sure. The high prices he was paying for the barrels made it impossible he was reselling them to distilleries in Mexico. I knew the Mexican companies were fronts. I'd known them as fronts for years. The only explanation for what he was doing was that he was supplying the Germans with barrels for stockpiling fuel for their war ships in the western Atlantic."

This had shaken him out of his paralysis, had set him on his course to break without compromises, to make war on the Party.

But then something else happened – or rather, he learned something then – which became the occasion for the worst.

Most of this he told Jim one spring-like evening they sat on his Devon farmhouse porch after that day which led Jim to fear for his sanity. Jim had come for dinner, Billy had been put to bed, and they'd just finished listening to a new recording of Bach's *St. Matthew's Passion*, then an old 78 RPM recording of Paul Robeson singing rapturous, soulful renditions of Negro spirituals and slave songs made famous by the great baritone.

He told Jim he'd bumped into an acquaintance from the old Moscow days, who'd first recognized him. It had been in Harlem along Seventh Avenue near the limousine service, and the man, smiling broadly, introduced himself. He'd now grown careless about his many years of spy craft, grown largely indifferent to his fate as part of his general heartsickness; and motivated by this unexpected discovery of a link to his old friend Fort-Whiteman, inquired about him.

That Whiteman might have become a victim of the Purge had not escaped his thought in those days. But then Fort-Whiteman was an American, *and* he was a Negro, the former affording some protection against arbitrary abuse by foreign governments, and as a Negro he was a much-favored member of the proletariat. Though he hadn't heard from Whiteman in a long time, he was inclined to think he'd be shielded from serious trouble. The man, Van Holler by name, at first parried his questions, shifting instead to the reasons for his own long stay in Russia.

"You know I came down with the crew for the *Black and White* film production. We were invited by the Meschrabpom Film Studio. Whiteman was one of those who'd written the scenario. I didn't care about politics – it was a job, a great job when we first heard about it in the States. I still don't care about politics, never joined up with the Party."

"So you've been there all these years? Ever since '31?" he asked, Whiteman on his mind.

"I'm going back to the West Coast as soon as I've taken care of some business here. What about you? What have you been doing? You were working for some rich American family that lived in Moscow back then, I remember. Whatever happened to them?"

He told him that they were back in the States, and that he ran a limousine service.

Van Holler was astonished. "I never took you as a business type."

"Well, we do what we have to do, don't we?"

"That's for sure."

"But listen," he said, trying finally to get the information he wanted, "I used to hear a lot from Whiteman. I stopped hearing from him a few years ago. Do you know anything about him now?"

Van Holler grew silent. He seemed to be holding something back. Doswell felt a pulse of irritation at this, his coyness. He suggested a cup of coffee at a nearby diner. Together, mid-afternoon on a winter day, they entered this drab, otherwise nondescript eating establishment, sat down at a corner booth and ordered.

"I'd really like to know about Lovett. As you know, we were friends—"

"Everyone was friends with Lovett – that is, almost everyone."

Doswell waited for the follow-up. When still Van Holler only sipped at his coffee, he felt some real impatience. He would speak clearly: "I left not long after you arrived. So I know little of what happened when people were being arrested and sent away on all sorts of flimsy charges."

"That happened to a whole lot of people. Some good ones I knew."

"Stalin is a mass murderer, but he didn't do it all alone. Everyone knows this. Tell me what happened to Lovett, if you know anything!"

Van Holler nodded ever so slightly, averting his eyes, and glanced instantly to the empty space immediately beside them. Then he looked back, very deliberately, at Doswell, and he nodded, inching close. "Yes. That's what happened to Lovett... Only he didn't just disappear. I know he's dead. At least about as sure as anyone can be."

Doswell put down his coffee.

"We were favored there for a while, but they didn't always treat us so good later. And then we didn't always treat each other so good."

"What do you mean?"

"I mean some of our own people had a hand in doing him in, that's what I mean." A quiet anger had been creeping into the man's voice; now it broke out undisguised. "You know we often used to meet at the Foreign Club. There was a discussion there one day about Langston Hughes' *The Ways of White Folks*, and you know how Lovett used to like to talk like he was an expert about such things? Big shots would come to these meetings sometimes. This big shot from the American Party who was only in Moscow for a few weeks came to that meeting, he heard him and said that his criticism of the book was counter-revolutionary. I didn't know who he was. I'd never seen him before but one of the other people said he was a top leader in the Party. Anyway, he just said it out of the blue. Then he got up and left. Just as cool as a cucumber. It spooked all of us. We knew what it meant, saying that."

"Did Lovett say anything?"

"Lovett was speechless. It stunned him too. Then he started shouting. 'No, no. That's not counter-revolutionary. What did I say that was counter-revolutionary?' But he'd already gotten up and walked out. Everyone was deadly silent.

"It was like a man takes a rock or something, and just throws it and strikes an old alley cat – maims it, leaves it broken-bodied, dying. Then walks off. Cool as can be. And I swear I never saw Whiteman again after that."

"Then how do you know what happened to him?"

"You say he was your friend? He was my friend too. My wife's brother knew people, I asked around. I had to be very careful as it was. Someone said he saw him a couple of weeks later and he wasn't his old self. Then we stopped seeing him. But we heard he'd been sent into exile. It was much later, I mean several years later, that I met this Russian guy through my brother-in-law who said he'd known him in some camp up near the Arctic Circle. He said Whiteman had been assigned to his group of laborers and was severely beaten many times when he failed to meet the norm. He died of starvation or malnutrition, a broken man whose teeth had been knocked out."

Nearest them the booths and the tables were all empty. At a far table some patrons were sharing a joke. Van Holler turned nervously in their direction.

"Who was this so-called 'big shot' who fingered him?"

"I didn't know him. I never saw him again. Someone said he was a lawyer. That's all I was told."

A big shot in the Party of course meant the open Party. Doswell reviewed the names in angry seconds. There were a few possibilities for 'big shot', but 'lawyer' could mean only one. A man named Patterson, someone who could be seen on Harlem streets nearly every day. One of those open Party people who was something of a New York celebrity; a man who had occasional write-ups in the city newspapers, as often as not in association with his old and fashionable friend, Paul Robeson.

Van Holler added in a whisper, his eyes aglitter, that he had reason to believe he lived in Harlem.

Doswell glared at Van Holler. One of those loathsome climbers and manipulators, he could easily see Patterson ensconced in the Kremlin with Stalin's operatives, during one of his many self-important trips to Moscow. There'd been rumors that there were folks among the open Party Negro members who'd long had a grudge against Fort-Whiteman and wanted to get him "out of people's hair" in the States – yes, they'd gotten him out of the States and then out of this world.

But as quick as the thought came to him to find some way to avenge Whiteman's death, it occurred to Doswell that he wasn't any better than Patterson! He hadn't been personally responsible for the murder of an old acquaintance, but how much more responsible was he? How much more when furthering the goals of worldwide conspiracy, bringing Stalin's blessings to far reaches of the globe and numberless others who would die just as Lovett had?

That day he gave himself over to the booze, he told Jim. But his notes only summarily mentioned an encounter with *an acquaintance from the old days*, and *devastating news about a friend.* What they did tell was about the effects of the booze, drinking himself into a stupor, half-stumbling his way back late into the 112th Street house.

When he awoke the following day, stepping groggily out from his and Zora's bedroom, a fear weighed over him: his memory of the night before like a startlingly lifelike, self-revealing nightmare. As he frantically looked for her, he found a chair broken in the living room, other household furnishings scattered and damaged. Then he found Zora, Carole clinging to her, fearful and uncomprehending; Zora still trembly, the damning admission wrung from her lips – and he knew for certain that it was no nightmare.

He finished what he'd put down on paper in these words: *The criminal coward beat her, not the booze, not the misery – if you must kill yourself why not just yourself and be done?*

PART 7

26

Things Fall Apart

That spring, within Colonus and in cities around the globe, demonstrators were taking to the streets; in all corners of America students were coalescing into a nationwide strike to close down schools, colleges and universities. The National Council of Churches was issuing a call for repentance on a nationwide scale; the One Hundred and Third Convention of the Episcopal Diocese of Long Island was appealing to the US government to end the violence; a world renowned historian was reflecting aloud over his preference at being a Czech saved by the Russians than an Indochinese saved by the Americans.

In Colonus, voices along Baxter's and CSU's corridors murmured, "How could Nixon do it? He's found a way of destroying the last modicum of good will…"

Across the nation, and in Colonus and Baxter as well, more darkly anxious words were spoken: "They are planning to suspend elections and stage a military takeover of the government."

Then revulsion: Kent State, four students shot dead by National Guardsmen in Ohio…

Spring appears early in the Carolinas. Bright, mild days and birdsong are never wholly absent even through the short winter season. Then with spring, the radiance of the days and the balmy evenings, the cliché is that it is the season of romance. But in Vincent's case, that year of 1970, it seemed the season itself mocked him. He was the wilted leaf, stranded and to be collected from the previous autumn. For with Gwen's reply to his carefully composed letter, full of pleas for hopeful new beginnings, he received an answer more definitive than anything he'd worst imagined; not in bitter repudiation, but in the cool, calm tone of a woman who's made a carefully thought-out decision.

Her final words were:

> *Vincent, there is no hope for us in the future. Even if I was willing to try again, I'd never trust you and that's not the way to start out on anything permanent. I am not leaving my return address because I want to be certain you don't show*

up on my doorstep as you said yourself you would have, had it not been for your other concerns.

I am sure that with time I will fade from your memory.

Always your friend,

Gwen

She was inside his eyes, in everything he looked on, everywhere he went, the ghost of her ever-present. But at that time, unavoidably, much else pressed its way into his agitated mind. He heard, drearily and infuriatingly, more than he cared to about President Montbanc's preternatural gifts; yearned to hear bad news on some front for Ronald, but heard none. And he heard everything everyone heard about the state of the world, America and Colonus – including the nationally publicized Panther Trial in New Haven. This last, though, was felt personally and intimately, now that he knew what he'd been told by that secret friend of Basil's weeks earlier was every bit true.

Basil – a much chastened and wiser Basil – now living in a rented room across the river in New Jersey had recovered miraculously, but not without a lot of pain. And it was not over; he was still undergoing a hard regimen of physical therapy. He'd been shot three times! He'd never again be the healthy specimen he'd been before his ordeal. Yet he'd survived, and he and Vincent were thankful.

Basil and Vincent had since exchanged letters and even a couple of long-distance telephone calls discussing his "wondrous" survival, comparing it with ongoing news from the Panther Trial.

The strange and utterly incomprehensible thing for Vincent was that no one disputed the basic facts in this case which ended nearly the same for his brother: that in the spring of 1969 Alex Rackley had traveled with several comrades from Harlem to New Haven, where he was taken prisoner, incarcerated in the basement of a Party-controlled house in that city, questioned under torture about being a police informer, and then executed. The torture was recorded live on the Panthers' own tapes, with additional narration for the benefit of higher-ups in the Party! Yet everyone who was anyone – college presidents, church leaders, editorialists in leading newspapers and on America's TV screens – insisted that the Panthers were innocent. Police agents, it was said, had infiltrated Panther ranks; the comrades had been manipulated into turning on their own; the guilty were the police who'd "framed" the Panthers. Even if it were true, Vincent thought and now Basil acknowledged, what kind of human vermin would be so easily manipulated on so large a scale – and to do the things the tapes demonstrated they so obviously relished doing?

Vincent thankfully but also painfully pondered the differences between his brother and Alex Rackley. Obviously the one had survived, the other not. What seemed certain was that, unlike Basil, Rackley was singularly well suited for invisibility. For if there were friends or family in the life of this young man, there were no signs of them. Nor was anything said about him. It was as if he'd never existed. Or if he had, if his torture had ever happened, it happened eons before, or in some abstract present which reduced concrete facts to pure irrelevancy.

And only with Basil could Vincent talk freely about any of this. Among his colleagues he knew he'd be unable to contain himself when they spoke the invincibly oblivious words that would come from their lips. With Doswell he had once spoken of it when they'd met to talk strategy over Willi Wade, comparing the attempt to destroy Willi to Rackley's physical destruction; but there was now something which stood in Vincent's way which he suppressed both for itself and the perception that the urgencies of Willi's case took priority over everything.

The Willi Wade case had been occupying all the old man's thoughts. This "statement" critical of the administration had not had as wide a support as he would have liked. Vincent himself had gathered only five signatures.

But then suddenly, things were happening so fast. The winds were shifting in the opposite direction, and then came good news. What they'd long hoped for but never seriously expected, at least so soon: the judge summarily threw out the case against Willi. The reason: what Joe Stein had long stressed, that evidence gathered by university authorities was contaminated by staff and fellow students' ready access to Willi's room. The previously important statement became instantly moot; it hadn't even been delivered. Willi was free. And though he'd earlier been expelled from the university, Stein, waving the stick of civil action, was negotiating with the administration to remove that stigma from his record. The dust was settling on this battle over which Vincent and Doswell had fought so hard. Life was returning to relative normalcy.

Ordinarily, for years now, Doswell took his meals when away from home either at the university cafeteria or at Mo Rogers' Jolly Roger. But with Willi's case ending as it did, Jim's upcoming marriage, and the end of the academic year fast approaching, Doswell decided some kind of celebration was in order. A quiet place where conversation didn't have to be shouted across a table ruled out his friend Mo's diner.

One of those previously dyed-in-the-wool Jim Crow establishments which he ordinarily shunned, the Grand Hotel went back decades to the building boom early in the century. It had a reputation far and wide as one of the most refined establishments in the state, with authentic European and American antiques, eighteenth century American portrait paintings, walls covered in flocked, wine-red wallpaper, and grand crystal chandeliers that hung from its decoratively molded church-like ceilings. Not least important, with all of that, the ever-frugal Doswell knew its dining room to be reasonably priced.

Doswell, with a rare show of pleasure, raised his beer stein to Vincent. "And what do we drink to? Willi's release from the grip of the law? Or Jim's soon-to-be marriage?"

The absent Jim had begged off, citing the need to attend to preparations for his upcoming marriage. Susan, despite the urgent circumstances, was every day entering more into the spirit of the frantically gladful bride. Her parents having come around, she was planning a wedding celebration with many friends, out-of-town relations, flowers, professional photographer, a towering wedding cake, and there were a thousand reception details, all of which involved decisions, decisions and more decisions.

Vincent, feeling both slightly out of place in these surroundings, and pained by the reminder of Jim's grand fortunes in the love department, lifted his glass with a wan smile. "Both," he said.

Glancing upward at the Grand's vaulted ceiling and then around at its stiff portraits of antebellum gentry, Vincent wryly recalled an earlier adventure at another "old-time Colonus establishment". He told how he'd come close to getting the beating of his life in that place, and then Gwen's later upbraiding him for his foolhardiness.

They talked as well about Willi, and about the ever-resourceful Joe Stein's efforts at recovering Willi's legal expenses.

The main course came and they quietly ate. Vincent once again made some ironic talk about the dining room and the people in it, and launched into its well-liveried all-black service staff, the age of the hotel, its Jim Crow history, and its other near and presently outraged patrons.

"Look at that pair over there, they've been glaring at us for the last hour." He chuckled.

"My bet," Doswell said, "is that the Grand Hotel, what with all the motels springing up everywhere, will be demolished some time before the next decade. I wanted to see the inside of it before it's rubble."

"I'll bet they want all the business they can get from the likes of us now."

There was a long silence.

"You mentioned Gwen a moment ago. Since you came back from New York you haven't spoken about her at all. Is there something wrong between the two of you?"

"I guess you could say so. She's broken with me." Vincent fidgeted with his cigarette and drew a long draft of smoke, then exhaled. "It's unlikely I will ever see her again. She's moved north, somewhere around Boston. She won't give her address."

"She has a reason for this?"

Vincent straightened up, looked hard at the old man, and after a moment's hesitation said, "Yeah, a very good reason. I was two-timing her. By the way, she sends her greetings."

Doswell glanced at Vincent, but said nothing.

The main course was over. They had both turned down dessert and Vincent was lighting up another cigarette from his last, then pouring himself a long draft of beer from the tall brown bottle standing beside his still-cool glass.

"I guess I'm a man with regrets."

"You can't be a man and be without regrets," Doswell said.

Vincent had consumed quite a few beers. They decided on coffee before they left the Grand, and as they made for Doswell's car, after Doswell paid the check, Vincent said out of the blue, "Do you regret appearing before the McCarthy Committee, volunteering information? Were you pressured into it?"

As the words rolled from his lips, Doswell slowed the pace of his walk, then came to a dead stop – and a leaden-weighted pause. "Where did you learn to ask about that?"

"I read about it. Your name, even your picture, appeared a few times in the newspapers, as you know. In the *New York Times* for one."

"Ah. A twenty-year-old issue was delivered to your door this morning."

The truth is, few days had passed since Raskin first told Vincent about Doswell that he hadn't thought about those charges. But with all the busyness of those days, including, of course, Gwen weighing on his mind, amidst the bustle he'd sometimes forget it. But then, he couldn't completely. He was, for a while, simply going to ask him straight out, and then, when the Willi Wade affair ended, he changed his mind, deciding to find out what he could just in case there *was* nothing. Maybe I won't have to say anything; maybe it's more of Raskin's pure malice, he thought.

"No. Not this morning. I checked it out a few days ago. I wasn't going to mention it. I was going to bury it and forget it. Like you say, it was twenty years ago. But I had to ask you. I couldn't bury it. I can understand if you tell me you were pressured. I can imagine the government putting heavy pressures on people. And I can imagine a black man under still heavier pressures…" He suddenly broke off, thinking better of this whole foolish inquiry. "Forget it. Forget I asked. You don't owe me any explanations."

Doswell laughed grimly. "Forget you asked? That requires a degree of forgetfulness I haven't yet achieved in life. No doubt someone has gotten to you."

Vincent felt very unhappy about this. But yes, he certainly couldn't forget it. "When I spoke to Raskin about Willi weeks ago, he told me he met someone at the convention who knew you from years before."

Doswell nodded.

"He said that you'd known a lot of people in your time, important people in progressive circles. That you'd known Paul Robeson, even. He said that he was only one of the people you'd smeared. I didn't believe him. Raskin has lied many times before. So I looked it up in old newspapers. There was nothing about Robeson."

"What if there had been?"

"I can't say I would have admired you for that."

"The truth is, it's a lie about Robeson. And it's a lie about everything else. But not as you understand that..."

They stood a few feet apart on the sidewalk, facing each other, close to Doswell's parked car. It was a very pleasant night, typical for downtown Colonus at that hour, with hardly anyone on the streets.

"I didn't know him. And I never had much of an interest in him either personally or professionally. Nothing that ever left my lips at the hearings touched on him. But I can tell you this: he broke with the Communist Party as I did. Though it was different with him. It was common knowledge. He did it by going mad."

Vincent started to move off. "I shouldn't have brought it up. I really had no right to... It's not important. I don't know why I did."

"It *is* important. It's moral theology... Yes, I *did* inform. And I wasn't forced to. And it was not easy. But I don't regret it. I would do it again if I had to."

"You went to the Committee on Un-American Activities? To Joseph McCarthy? His ilk? And you say you'd do it again?"

"Did you *read* the articles? It was the Tydings Committee. McCarthy is one name. Is he the only name besides Robeson that you know? In fact they didn't welcome me because I was there to give testimony backing some of McCarthy's charges."

"To back him up? You're telling me that these people who destroyed reputations, who smeared hundreds with wild charges, Robeson included—"

"I guess that was my unspeakable crime: joining forces with America's arch-villains."

"You backed him up and approved of all that? And *still* approve of it?"

"You know nothing about any of it."

"I know a lot."

"That means you know *worse* than nothing."

Vincent started to move further away from the car. "I'm going to walk back. Goodnight!" He turned away, unwilling to say more – fearful of saying more.

Doswell followed him carefully with his eyes, the younger man quickly threading his way between parked cars and crossing the street.

PART 8

27

FBI Informer

One good thing about choosing the part of an informer: you have time to prepare. He might still be able to put into effect a plan he'd long nurtured to save his workers' jobs. He also surmised that with Stalin allied to Hitler, American authorities would now be keenly interested in the Party's activities. When he telephoned the FBI office in New Haven to say that he had critical information on its active assistance in the German war effort, the agents' response told him instantly that he was right. All of this and more Jim learned both from what Doswell told him in his Devon farmhouse, and from his furtively scribbled, salvaged notes months later.

Waiting nearly an hour, umbrella in hand, at a street corner in downtown New Haven for government agents who were late for their meeting with him, he never for an instant wavered. His hatred for the ideology he'd served all his adult life was unsparing; self-immolation was even welcomed, except, above everything, he wanted to strike a mortal blow. For that, survival was necessary, at least for the time being. And thus the hazards he faced were ever-present to his mind.

He remembered less than a year before admonishing a woman in the Foreign Agents Registration section of the Justice Department, who had access to FBI operations, and had been trying to recruit all her acquaintances. That none of them reported her to the American government (though obviously someone reported her recklessness to the Party) spoke to the risk he was taking. In going to the FBI (in New Haven, one small precaution), someone like Flora Wovschin – or someone like the many friends that had given her good reasons to trust them – could easily inform on him, or even unintentionally drop a fatal word that would have implications about a leak in Hammer's operations. But even as he thought these ordinarily daunting thoughts, they vanished and were replaced with something more urgent: the business of getting these strangers, these FBI agents he was meeting, to merely listen to him!

As it turned out, the two agents he met had arrived on time, but although as instructed he was carrying an umbrella and there was no one else in sight doing the same on that clear day, they'd waited, unsure that it was actually he who'd spoken to them over the phone.

"You figure its gonna rain?" Murphy, a red-haired, very Irish-looking man in his mid to late thirties, opened as planned; to which Doswell replied, in keeping with spy-story motifs, "I never take the weather for granted. I always carry an umbrella."

Clearly miffed, they told him to come along with them and then together they got into their car parked a few blocks away on a side street, ominously saying nothing as they went. After driving a couple of miles to an upscale residential neighborhood near Long Island Sound, they pulled over, parked the car, and began grilling him like he was a suspect – and he was: suspected of taking them on a fool's errand.

But by then he'd prepared himself for the questions they asked. They asked about the Hammer family. He said he'd long had an intimate relationship with them. He depicted himself as the family's previously loyal retainer, a faithful servant from years before in Moscow and Erfurt, who'd since, on arriving back in the States, owned and managed a limousine service in Harlem. He said he'd also been doing jobs for the Hammers in the States, especially for Armand. His story in all its particulars could easily be checked out. Clearly, however, it was a misrepresentation. But he'd calculated that telling the full truth would present an initial and likely fatal obstacle to his being believed. If he'd confessed his years as banker of the Comintern, and on the slim chance he overcame the Bureau's skepticism, he would be first in line for federal prosecution. Hammer, after all, had powerful friends in the very highest of places, not only in the Soviet government but in the American government. He feared such a fatally ironical twist. Once again, it would be so easy: the Party would not even have to exercise itself by direct action. It would be sufficient to pull an invisible string here, to nudge someone through someone there, to direct or to redirect attention on this or that activity through non-Party or even ill-informed anti-Party people, quickly suppressing his story by attacking him. All of this could be sidestepped. American authorities would be interested in ongoing Party activities as they related to the Germans, not to those past affairs. Therefore, in achieving his most urgent of purposes, to stop Hammer and the Party aiding the Nazis, he chose to depict himself in this onerously disloyal light.

Of course, no one likes a snitch. Thus his FBI contacts, when they ended their first meeting, said, "Well, we'll check out everything you've said, and believe me, we have ways of knowing. If you've been telling us fibs, we'll know, and you'll be a mighty sorry fellow if you have."

Their next meeting included an agent, Renner, based in the New York office, who opened with a sternly worded charge: that Doswell hadn't told Spencer and Murphy everything, that misleading government agents was a serious crime, and did he know that withholding information was misleading?

All three then stared at him, waiting for his reply.

Anxious though he was, he denied anything important was left out of his previous story. He guessed it was a bluff to test him.

The new agent, Renner, finally added, "You didn't tell us that Hammer made you a big loan to start you off in that limousine business of yours. How come he did that?"

"He didn't, he co-signed the note," Doswell said. He elaborated on this answer by stressing his long and faithful service in Moscow, running their house there, and later being in Erfurt with Julius and helping with the sale of the Romanoff treasure in St. Louis, Detroit and elsewhere. "I did a lot of work for them and wasn't properly reimbursed. I put myself out a great deal for them."

From that point on, in their year's long relationship, they never once challenged his veracity again. During that year he brought with him physical evidence to back up what he said: shipping inventories, records of transactions with distilleries, information on further leads the agents could check out for intelligence on the Hammer dealings. But during that year he'd grown increasingly restless. His immediate purpose in going to the government was to stop the Party's support of the Nazi war effort against Great Britain. He wanted to do as much harm to the conspiracy as possible. Now, during these days, he was growing increasingly suspicious of other ongoing activities. One of them involved America's sensitive relationship with Japan. But not being directly involved himself, and with no physical evidence, he could only speculate. As with his original suspicions about Hammer, however, they were not idle suspicions. They had a basis in a knowledge which only he possessed – but which would require telling the truth about his long-standing relationship with Hammer and his work with the 'bank'. Otherwise there was no hope of convincing anyone of their credibility. There was so much more he could do if he were not hobbled with this phony story about being a Hammer servant! He'd begun thinking that Murphy, Spencer and Renner might see the dangers if he could convince them to listen to him about his fuller past. But it was in the midst of these whirling thoughts, and the quiet decision to speak to Renner, that the course of history suddenly intervened.

In June of 1941, nearly two years after the non-aggression pact was signed, Hitler, sending his Panzer divisions on a front two hundred miles wide, racing headlong into the heart of the Soviet Union, ended the pact. Stalin was dragged kicking and screaming into war with Hitler, a war which many of his own people initially chose to fight *with* Hitler *against* Stalin – so brutalized by the Party's years of unspeakable tyranny – but then only turned against the Germans when it became clear that their incredibly stupid and evil race policies dictated that they murder and enslave the 'natural slaves' who'd first welcomed them as liberators. And the Soviet dictator, shining in the refracted glow of the stupefyingly heroic courage of his people – once he came back to his senses, following weeks of fear-induced paralysis at the thought that not only would the Germans quickly subdue his nation, but his own people would hang him from the nearest pole – thus cemented a wartime alliance with the capitalist exploiters.

From that moment on in the West near-total amnesia set in. Those twenty-two months when the regime was allied with Hitler would be forgotten. Which meant Stalin would gain a new lease on life; the Party and its revolutionary program would once again be honored among the best and the brightest in the West, sympathized with by millions more, and at the war's end rewarded with Eastern Europe.

At their last meeting in New Haven, Bill Renner was significantly absent. Doswell would see him again, however, a decade later, in another venue with a different set of inquisitors.

But in 1941 Agent Murphy announced, "I think you know, Thomas, recent events have forced certain changes."

"I know," he said resignedly.

"Yeah…one of them is that we've been reassigned. We won't be meeting anymore. As you know, the Bureau is just the investigating arm of Justice. And if Hammer was doing the Communist Party's bidding in aiding the Nazis, it's clear that's going to stop. There won't be anything to investigate."

"Who knows," Spencer added, "with Stalin no longer helping Hitler, maybe he'll start giving us some help. We'll surely be giving them help…"

They glanced at each other.

"I understand."

"Yeah," Spencer spoke up again, "we'll probably be handing them intelligence soon enough. They're on the right side now."

There was now nothing left for him to do but follow through with his well-laid plans of escape. On one meticulously prepared, sultry day in July of 1941, he deserted, thus openly declaring himself the Party's enemy.

28

Doswell Finds Powerful Allies

In the late summer of 1948, first Elizabeth Bentley, described in several dime store-style accounts as *the blond mystery lady*, then a few days later, Whittaker Chambers, a senior Editor at *Time* magazine, appeared before the House Committee on Un-American Activities, telling of their years of clandestine operations in the Soviet underground. Going beyond Doswell's own revelations to the FBI at the outset of the decade, they provided sensational accounts of Soviet agents in sensitive posts through much of the '30s and into the '40s.

Since those earlier war years when Doswell stopped talking to the FBI, once again there was a sea change in relations between the USA and the USSR. The Baltic states had been annexed and the whole of Eastern Europe was in the Soviet Union's grip. What's more, it threatened America and the world with an atomic bomb whose technical secrets it had acquired by successfully infiltrating America's supposedly super-secret Manhattan Project. Two years earlier, Doswell, as other Americans had, read in the newspapers about an obscure Russian cipher-clerk in Ottawa who'd defected along with his wife and child to the Canadian government, telling of an elaborate spy network in Canada and the United States. Unlike many others who'd read the story, however, Doswell never for a moment doubted the accuracy of Gouzenko's fantastic tale. What troubled him more, but did not surprise him either, was the incredulousness of many in places of responsibility. But now a score of American agents in high places that Gouzenko had brought to light were being named by these two embattled figures, and their earlier doubts were turning into active alarm.

Doswell watched from afar. He saw that many of those who'd championed the Soviet state in pre-war years, despite the treachery that the Hitler-Stalin non-aggression pact had demonstrated, couldn't believe the worst of her; and were disinclined to believe that fellow Americans, who were only slightly more committed than they to progressive change, could betray their country.

Doswell watched and listened. When he was deep in the underground, he had no time for anything but Party work and his Harlem limousine service; since then, in the enforced leisure of his academic post, he read everything he could. And he did nothing. And he said nothing.

He noticed that there were countervailing forces. In Europe a series of books documenting the existence of forced labor camps in the Soviet Union had been accumulating through the decade. All of them, from first-person autobiographical kinds like Victor Kravchenko's *I Chose Freedom*, to those made up of painfully long collections of concentration camp forms and affidavits documenting the identifiable existence of thousands of concentration camp inmates, were having an impact. To be sure, they were greeted by leading lights as slanders. In France the issue sometimes went into the courts for litigation, and her most famous philosopher, the novelist and playwright Jean-Paul Sartre, whose "existential analyses" of, among other concepts, "bad faith", fired the imaginations of post-war European and American intellectuals, insisted that these accounts were frauds; and he was later caught saying, to a small group of friends, that if true they should be ignored because the French proletariat would be "thrown into despair".

But Doswell was looking not only at Europe, or to the far ends of the earth, or to Washington, but at Colonus' own East End Negro community, which just then had a different set of troubles.

At the time of the hearings in the capitol, there had been a lynching. A black man, whom the *News-Herald* described as having intimidated a number of white men over a period of several months, had on one fatal night been attacked by about a dozen white men, beaten mercilessly and then strung up from the branch of a nearby tree. It was a lesson intended to warn other "lippity Negroes" about trying to frighten "decent citizens". Not surprisingly, the black community was in high alert over the prospect of this happening again. But it was also caught up in recrimination and counter-recrimination directed at the men who'd run from the scene and the man who'd been lynched.

Doswell, as a leading member of the community, had taken a role in counseling calm, of pleading for an end to its turning against itself. And along with President Robinson, he had visited the mayor's office to discuss the concerns of people from Colonus' East End, urging the vigorous pursuit of those involved in the lynching. So Doswell had much on his mind in those days, much to give him thought.

Ever since he'd broken with the Party, and then a couple of years after the Party's hired thugs had caught up with him, he was determined that he must inform and do so fully, holding nothing back as before. His crimes required atonement. He had intelligence no one else had. But no one knew better than he the nature of the forces that would be arrayed against him.

So he said nothing. He waited with only an ambivalent and self-accusatory hope for a summons from the FBI, and it didn't come. He watched impotently as Chambers contended with an army of lawyers and journalists and the ever-resourceful Alger Hiss, the most sensational of the secret agents he had named.

Hiss was one man, but one man whose friends included those in the highest reaches of government (Secretaries of State, Supreme Court Justices, and others). Chambers was being assailed from all sides: by much of the press as well as by a majority of those in higher rungs of society, including members of the psychiatric community who viewed him as a depraved character. And yet Chambers was not powerless; nor was he without powerful and influential friends – and he was white.

The importance of this last detail was joltingly communicated to him by the recent lynching of that forlorn individual in Colonus. He remembered Murphy and Spencer's first reaction to him. Chambers' whiteness was certainly never remarked on by anyone, friend or foe, because it bore exactly no weight at all. But if he had *not* been white? It wasn't literally a lynching that Doswell feared (though fearing physical danger to himself and to Carole was not unreasonable), but lynchings were not the only way to punish "a lippity Negro". Or to put it differently: there were other effective ways of lynching a man that didn't use a rope.

If Chambers was viewed as insane and depraved by many among the intellectual classes, given the extremity of his claims about his own and others' conspiratorial activities, what would many more among the general population think of him – indeed *do* to him, keeping in mind what they were already doing to Chambers? And indeed, Doswell's claims on their merits would be even more fantastic than his!

The burden of this problem, of course, had always weighed on his mind. But it was a fear redoubled by a changed set of circumstances that froze him. In coming forward and telling what he knew, there was Carole: Carole without her mother, Zora having died a sudden death some five years earlier; and Carole now a budding teenager, already showing signs of being seriously troubled.

Shortly after his encounter with the Party's thugs, Doswell had written a letter to the Party through J. Peters, warning it of his having written out a detailed account, naming Uncle Big Bob's, naming names, times and places of his clandestine operations; he explained that he'd left copies of the document with responsible individuals with instructions that it be opened should a successful attempt be made against him or Carole. But he was too circumspect to be sanguine about this stratagem, especially if the Party should have reason to believe that with changing circumstances he represented an urgent danger.

He was even less sanguine about it should the Party move using its friends in high places, and through legal means to strike at him through Carole. It was not hard to imagine. He'd heard about children taken from their parents by the state if a case could be made for the parents being unfit, mentally or morally. What sinister ends could the law be put to by evil men, or merely men who were foolish and frightened?

He was alone with Carole. He could not even see his way to sufficiently secure her safety while he went off to pursue a government agency which seemed thoroughly indifferent to, and would very likely spurn, any information he might offer – or might even turn it against him! And yet, despite the old concerns and his new ones, he finally did visit the local FBI office, telling the agents there his name with a request that they contact the Bureau's New Haven office, thinking that some way perhaps, if only indirectly, or by some remote chance, anonymously – known only to a few agents – he could offer some help.

This is the way things stood for two years. In the meantime he rededicated his life to his teaching, and ever more deliberately and self-consciously to his role as devoted parent. Then one resplendent weekend morning in the spring of 1950, he received a long-distance telephone call from an investigator who worked for Senator Joseph McCarthy, asking that he come to Washington to speak with the Senator and his aides.

Now the agony of decision had been thrust upon him. On the telephone, instantly perplexed, he thought only of the immense good work already done by Chambers and others, and the mountain of obstacles that would likely render any testimony from him worthless, paid for at the price of an ever-graver danger to Carole. How could he even consider such a proposal? And he didn't. His answer was that it was impossible to come to Washington. But this answer afterwards left him heavily burdened.

He turned through the facts he knew like the pages in a notebook. In the first case, despite the good work that was achieved by those others, he'd always known that what they'd uncovered constituted little more than skimming the surface. He knew not only much more, he knew the connections, the lifeblood that facilitated and sustained the purposes of the undercover system itself. And then there was not only the past but the future. For what had come to pass during those last two years was the fall of China, and he was certain that more than twenty years of Comintern work there, the result of funds channeled through the 'bank', his work in support of its agents, had achieved elsewhere a critical platform to the future which must not be ignored.

What's more, Senator McCarthy seemed to grasp, like no one else at so high a level of government, how little had been uncovered, and the urgent task of uncovering the rest of the sordid mess. But if only Senator McCarthy inspired greater confidence! Like the rest of the country, he'd learned of him only a few months earlier. Now he was suddenly forced to consider things he hadn't had to think about before, and that he had to decide about quickly. He wondered about this previously obscure Senator from Wisconsin who was making a name for himself on this issue of Communists in the State Department. The press reports were fearsome: not only in the immense political power ranged against him, but in their acid characterization of the man.

Reading *LIFE*, hardly a left-wing magazine (it had previously employed the admirable Whittaker Chambers), Doswell read under a half-page photograph of an imposingly stern and animated President Truman a fragment of the history of recent events:

> *JOE McCARTHY'S POLITICAL DYNAMITE*
> *CAN BLOW UP IN EITHER PARTY'S FACE*
>
> *Joe McCarthy's sensationalized case against the State Department was built on a rather casual foundation. Asked to give a Lincoln's Birthday speech on Communism, he had trotted out an assortment of shopworn stuff, much of it already investigated by the House Appropriations Committee. But as time went on and tips kept coming into his office, the Senator ran across much more important matters, or thought he did. Unfortunately, blundering Joe McCarthy was hardly the man to document and present them to a Senate subcommittee, and the headline-hunting approach was hardly the way to handle them anyway. His case against Judge Dorothy Kenyon of New York backfired when she entered a spirited and convincing defense. So did his attacks…*

Doswell read this ever so grimly. He knew nothing about Judge Dorothy Kenyon of New York, but he knew quite a lot about Judge Samuel Dickstein, a much bigger fish, presently of the New York State Supreme Court and formerly Chairman of the Immigration Committee in the US Congress. He was the man primarily responsible for drafting a resolution to form a new permanent investigating committee, back in the mid '30s when Nazism was the object of investigation, that had come so much in the news lately. It was called the House Un-American Activities Committee. And he'd been on the take from the Comintern all through this time as an agent of influence.

Doswell thought, with a mixture of bitterness and grim humor, of the *Rezidents*' Pavel Gutzeit first, and then Gaik Ovakimyan, and their tumultuous dealings with this same man over the years. Of course McCarthy knew *nothing* about Dickstein. So would he be helping Senator McCarthy by providing him with the lowdown on 'the Crook' (the moniker Gaik Ovakimyan employed for Congressman Dickstein), or would he simply be inviting him into another den of vipers from which he might never emerge alive? And even without such 'help', the hurricane blew week after week without letup. The verbal fury continued on the inside of pages even less inclined to restraint. Within hearing distance of coeds giggling amidst book stacks in Baxter's library, he read:

> *Secretary of State Acheson and President Truman talked publicly about the present attacks on the State Department, the Secretary extemporaneously at a meeting of the American Society of Newspaper Editors, the President in a broadcast speech before the Federal Bar Association.*

Acheson, after assuring his hearers that the State Department was never in better shape than now, lashed out at McCarthy and Company. First describing the orderly procedures in the Department for screening loyalty, he talked about "the wrong way" of doing this – meaning the one McCarthy is now employing:

"To smear everybody's reputation; to make charges on the basis that, if one is not right you try to find another one you hope will stick; to try to destroy the confidence of people in their Foreign Office and in their government in one of the most critical hours of this nation's history...is a madness, an insanity.

"It reminds me of a horrible episode in Camden, New Jersey, which happened not so long ago, when a madman came out on the street in the morning with his revolver. With no purpose and with no plan, as he walked down the street, he just shot people...

"As I leave this filthy business, and I hope never to speak of it again, I should like to leave in your minds the words of John Donne in his Meditations, in which he says, Any man's death diminishes me, because I am involved in Mankind; and therefore never send to know for whom the bell tolls; it tolls for me."

There were many more press accounts, equally damning.

Of course, the disinformation machine is operating at full throttle, Doswell thought, his mind ablaze. But how much can be ascribed to that? Is the man a blunderer? And if he is, should he give him more ammunition only to shoot himself? And yet...

McCarthy's speech in the early winter of 1950 that had ushered him onto the national stage had struck at a hornets' nest that had been building since the end of the World War. All that added to the confusion, and the contention was further uproar. Doswell suspected that that was his intention: to get attention. Was it wise? He doubted it. So was McCarthy a blunderer, or was he a man who'd blundered *once*, miscalculating in a situation which called for daring decision-making? Doswell, of all people, knew that these domestic political battles were not taking place in a vacuum. There was China. There was Stalin's power, now over nearly all of Asia: there were rumblings of war in the Straits of Formosa, in Southeast Asia, Indonesia and on the Korean peninsula. Many wondered, where next? And yet it seemed this Administration and so many of its supporters were stricken with a sclerosis of the spirit. And worse, what Doswell knew for certain: that a critical number of those who were a part of it were 'friends' of the Soviet Union. No doubt that's what McCarthy and others believed too.

But there were other things which made him wonder about McCarthy. There was this careless way the Senator had of talking about "card-carrying Communists". To speak this way, when the whole point of being a Communist *and* in government was to act covertly, was just downright silly. What's more, many who belonged to the open Party were, as he and other underground Party people used to say contemptuously, "display-window Communists": the literary and artistic types who liked the play-danger – plenty of mouth, yet were often clean as a whistle. Why give them a platform for their antics? Besides, fellow travelers who by definition were not Party members, how were they to be characterized? Under oath they could easily deny that they were Communists. When the Senator spoke of the urbane and prominent Professor Owen Lattimore of Johns Hopkins University as "the top Russian espionage agent in the United States", once again, no doubt, he'd sought the attention of the press. Yet, even if the substance of McCarthy's charges were true, he would not strictly have been an espionage agent, but something generally worse, an agent of influence – someone like Hammer or Duranty or Dickstein, not someone engaged in snatching documents.

Doswell, in short, was not happy with this cauldron of confusions. But he also recognized that war is confusing, that one's enemies are not obliging, one's comrades-in-arms not made to order.

Carole's mother, sometime after he'd defected a decade earlier, when he was still in a day-to-day struggle with the Party, had taken her own life. This is what he meant when he told Euretha Lewis years later that he was to blame for Carole's death. For he blamed himself first for his wife's suicide, and the shock that unbalanced Carole leading her eventually to follow her mother's example.

During those first days after his break, the three of them continued to live for a short while on 112th Street in Spanish Harlem. Ever since he'd begun his clandestine war against the Party, after that worst night that he never forgave himself, his abusive behavior towards Zora ended and his avenging angels were aimed at the Party. Still, there had been terrible frustrations and disappointments. The shock, for instance, when he learned that all his efforts with the FBI would be coming to nothing, had hit hard. In fact at this time his use of the bottle took a quantum leap. But it seems that throughout his life he always had this amazing capacity for bouncing back. It may have been due to his self-knowledge, and then self-corrective measures taken under the rigors of a stern self-discipline learned in childhood.

Still, it was a constant inner struggle which took its toll. Earlier when he did drink it was usually at home, to guard against observation. When he was at home, and the extreme drinking under control, there were his protracted and inscrutable silences, his presence in the house like a ticking bomb. Under such circumstances he would sometimes choose to get away from the house to lift the burden he was to his family – which was indeed a relief for Carole and Zora. But it was not an unalloyed relief.

When Zora had come to understand that he was taking dangerous steps, she had grown increasingly frenzied, even though he reassured her that he was doing what she'd long urged him to do. There was, as well, a long-converging and increasingly difficult situation that was evolving between Zora and him. Though he was hardly at his worst with her now, he was still not yet the man he would later become. His self-tormenting questions in those later years were answered by the retrospective conviction that if he had told her more, or helped her in some loving way to grasp his purpose, she might have avoided the downward spin that ended with the act which took her life. But he didn't. Was it his habit in the underground of never telling anyone more than what was absolutely necessary? Was it legitimate? Legitimate because in telling her that he was now informing, that this would be a danger to her? Or was it the long, faithless conviction that she would never understand, or just the sheer fatigue after round-the-clock, bone-wearying thinking and talking and doing on Party matters which were all a sham, that slammed the door on any further talk? All these reasons, and the fact that even from childhood he'd been inclined to keeping his own counsel, converged in determining his conduct in those days.

And there was something else. When he'd first met Zora she was a young woman of wholesome habits. Over the years, however, in some respects he had become a corrupting influence. In no behavior had he been more corrupting than in her later turning to the bottle herself. So at 112th Street, if he didn't already have enough problems, the problem of Zora drinking while she was alone and caring for Carole, and becoming a danger to both of them, became an additional burden.

Hence, after defecting, he'd decided on extreme measures. For he feared not only his own state of mind, he feared that the Party's hunters would soon learn about his personal safe house. He feared that, and Zora's own unhinged state in such extreme circumstances. He did not know what steps the Party would take against him, but that it would take steps, he was certain. He needed to remain hidden but he could not simply disappear because there were still unsettled matters. He also needed to know what steps to take in the face of Peters' and the *Rezidents*' altogether predictable efforts at neutralizing the effect of his defection.

Zora and Carole alone, however, could disappear. So he moved them to Washington. But why the capital of all places? Because Zora had an aunt living there. Washington was the only place where there were people whom he could trust. He had taken pains to keep the city of his birth, and even Zora and Carole's existence, hidden from the Party; but he was certain this knowledge would not remain hidden following his defection. It would be more likely to remain so if he 'lost' them in the large black ghetto of Washington, while he himself remained free to maneuver against the Party without worrying about them every minute. It was a decision fraught with perils, and which he would later regret. Now mid-century, in the year 1950, he thought of the time he had parted from them, and he pondered Carole's present state.

Since his return to Colonus at the end of the war, he'd told a few people who had reason to know something of his personal difficulties. President Robinson, his old friend from boyhood days, had given him the job at Baxter. He'd told

Robinson that he'd been a Party member. It was through Robinson that he'd found the place in Devon. Charlie Robinson, President Robinson's brother, living with his sister on the other side of the house, was a godsend, just as years later Euretha Lewis, the little girl who occasionally played with Carole, would turn out to be a godsend. When he was off teaching his classes at Baxter during the day, Charlie and his sister Bernice, a widow, watched over the child. It was Charlie who came to know more than anyone about his previous life. He'd been told, for instance (as had his brother), of the night he and Carole had had visitors. But only Charlie heard it in all its stark detail, the full violence of it, the real fear he continued to have for Carole. So Charlie, the retired policeman from the North, come prepared, as he'd told his brother and Doswell, for "friendly neighbors", had his gun at the ready.

But still, he could not leave Carole for days on end again. Not even with these good and faithful people. Since her mother's death he had not once seen the child smile or laugh, or show any signs of normal childhood pleasure. This other child, Euretha, said she sometimes saw her laugh when they played, but he himself could only remember genuine pleasure, pleasure and joy radiating from her face, years before when she was a little girl. That was when he would take her on the rowboats on the lake in Central Park, which was only a few blocks from where they lived.

Those were the relatively quiet days shortly after the Nazi-Soviet pact was announced, and he hadn't yet gone to the FBI about Hammer. 'Bank' traffic had slowed to a trickle. Even though he was running the limousine service, it seemed like he was on vacation. During those days he'd taken special notice of Carole, going on joyfully anticipated outings to the park. There was a rowboat slip located nearby. They'd rent out a boat, and he'd sit vigilantly at the stern, the great disproportion in their weights forcing the bow almost out of the water, while Carole, with great determination (all the while taking animated instructions from him), and with cries of childish glee, would try rowing it and avoid battering other boaters. What he would give to hear that thrilled little voice again! To see that determination, pride, and wide-radiating sense of triumph and pleasure in her face again! It was that laughing face which he wanted to remember. He hadn't seen much of it even before then, but that was because he was so rarely with Zora and Carole, and because he was always preoccupied – and because he'd been so terrible...

He would have to testify. But he knew he couldn't leave Carole. And he couldn't see how he could ever put this impossibly square peg in this one round hole. He would take one step at a time. When he came to that moment he hoped and prayed somehow there would be a way. So he telephoned the Senator's office and said he wanted to help, but explained that unavoidable problems in his family made it impossible to go to the capitol. McCarthy's aide promised to get back to him. Incredibly, inside of a few hours the aide called back and said that if he couldn't come to Washington, he would come down to Colonus and personally interview him.

When Dorwell spoke to Jim Allan weeks before the clash with Vincent at the Grand Hotel, he described his feelings about this young man who'd come all the way from Washington for this long-awaited interview. He admitted to a feeling of tremendous exhilaration that finally after all those years, and despite the color barrier, someone was seeking him out and willing to listen.

"He reminded me of another of McCarthy's aides with a more illustrious name: Robert Kennedy. Kennedy hadn't begun working for Joe McCarthy then, but the late Senator later reminded me of this individual. He was Irish, slim, slightly stooped. The Senator and he would have been about the same age at the time. Mid-twenties. Well-spoken, intense. Obviously intelligent. His name was Tom Gallagher.

"He told me straight out that they had my name through the FBI – which of course was obvious. He asked me if I was free to summarize what the substance of my discussions were, those years before. I told him. I added, however, that I had held back critical information then and told him why: that it seemed to me that the government was mainly interested in the Party's helping the Nazis, that it was the time of the pact, that most of all, I didn't think that they would believe me if I told them that I was more than Hammer's factotum. I told him that this was a front, my being simply his servant, that I had been in the Party's underground and engaged in clandestine operations for the Comintern, and had been for years.

"When I told him this last, his eyes grew large and he listened with an even more intense interest. This is a new generation, I thought. They see things differently.

"He asked me a question or two. Not to test me. I knew he believed me – or was certainly open to what I was telling him. Then I asked him a question: whether, if I now spoke fully, telling all, telling even of actions which constituted espionage, would I be the one the Justice Department would go after?"

"You trusted him enough at this stage?"

"It wasn't so much a matter of trusting or distrusting. You get to a time when you decide you've made the plunge, there's simply no holding back anymore. In fact, he told me something that was an instant relief. He said the statute of limitations had run out on espionage and on conspiracy. Then he asked me whether I would be willing to come and testify on some of these matters. Would I know of individuals who were engaged in clandestine operations who were *now* in the State Department?"

'Yes,' I said, 'and I'm pretty sure I can, but would I be believed?'

"He smiled. 'Those who want to believe you will believe you, those who don't won't.'

"Of course he was right – there was no predicting anything. He could give me no assurances.

'But I've been away from all of that for quite a while,' I said. 'I'd have to scour my memory. And I'd have to be brought up-to-date as to who is where in the government and elsewhere.'

"We talked for a while. Talked about a lot of things: Secretary Acheson's sanctimonious quotations from Scripture in defense of Alger Hiss, Laurence Duggan's suicide (or apparent suicide), former KGB agent General Krivitsky's apparent suicide and almost certain murder by Soviet agents in a small hotel in Washington, the great looming fact of China's fall the year before... We talked about the recent end of World War II, fought to liberate Europe and Asia, and now all those lives lost, the nation still facing war in half a dozen places along the Pacific rim, and along the Iron Curtain stretching across Europe.

"He was young but he was knowledgeable. He said he'd been lucky and had been in the recent war only at its very end. I told him about my unhappiness over this obsession with *numbers* of Communists in the State Department. I told him that if I were to guess, all the numbers which had been thrown around were modest in relation to the reality. But then all of this foolish talk allowed the issue to become sidetracked and trivialized.

'One well-placed agent can do more harm than a hundred agents stealing documents and passing on secrets,' I said.

"He agreed, and said Senator McCarthy had come to understand that he should avoid the trap that lay in talking numbers. But the public needed to be made aware of the enormity of the problem, and for that you needed to grab headlines. That this was simply in the nature of politics. 'People understand numbers and they vote,' he said.

"I told him I was very uncomfortable about naming names that would then be telegraphed to the world, that I could be mistaken in some instances. Public accusations often amounted to guilt in the public's eyes. It *was* all 'a very dirty business', as Acheson said.

"Then this serious young man suddenly burst into a very incongruous laughter. *Secretary Acheson* – he spat the name like it was an expletive. He quickly apologized for his outburst, stressing it wasn't really what I had said but in fact how very true it was, and how strenuously Senator McCarthy had said exactly the same thing.

'When the subcommittee which Senator Tydings now heads up was formed to examine the Senator's charges, the issue at its first executive meeting was whether the hearings were to be held in secret session or in public,' he explained. The majority insisted on public hearings. Senator McCarthy, who was not a part of the committee or the decision, stressed that some of the people could in the end, as he put it, 'get a clean bill of health'; so he was against public sessions. He raised precisely the points you just made."

Doswell said that Gallagher went into arcane details of cutthroat congressional politics, the wrangling between the majority and minority members of the committee, and the crucial role the press played in the back-and-forth as well. In the end, he said, it was just as the majority had demanded. They had maneuvered successfully for open hearings. They weren't interested in the cases themselves, they were only interested in embarrassing McCarthy by forcing him to make the charges in open session.

Doswell insisted to Jim that he found this hard to believe. For even at that very early date, less than six months after McCarthy's debut speech on this subject in Wheeling, West Virginia, his reputation as a man who carelessly smeared people troubled him.

"I must have shown some expression of disbelief, or surprise – or both.

"Gallagher grasped something of this because he said, 'I know it sounds insane. The thing is, Senator McCarthy has so enraged the Administration with his charges against the State Department, many in the Senate's majority who are in thick with the Administration, they're out to destroy him. And they've made it nearly impossible to investigate the Senator's charges of State Department malfeasance.'

'But how?'

'The President closed the FBI's files.'"

"This was sobering. I didn't press the previous matter. But I couldn't shake the thought that if they were *not* investigating the people in the State Department the Senator said were risks, then what was the point if it was simply an impossible task?

'Well, I didn't say it was wholly impossible. That's where you come in. The Senator's a fighter. And right now this is where the fight is. In the capitol and, of course, in newspapers across the country. In the end, it's the people. He's trying to speak to the people—'

'He's already lost the battle in the press.'

'If the American people see the truth, they'll back the Senator.'

'You said… I come in?'

'They've insisted on these public hearings so *they* can say McCarthy is making these wild charges, injuring everyone in sight, making him out to be a Goebbels – that's what Harold Ickes says, a Goebbels, and a traitor.'

'And I…?'

'They're figuring he can't make his charges stick without any way to back them up. That's where you come in.'

'You mean I make charges.'

'Well, you and Mr. Louis Budenz, Freda Utley, and maybe others. And then there is the public evidence outside the files, of course. But first you'd have to come to Washington and speak to the Senator and some of the rest of the staff.

We'd need a more detailed description of your activities in the Party. We'd need to know what you know. We'd have to know a lot more about you.'"

Tom Gallagher returned to Washington, leaving both his office and his home telephone numbers with Doswell, assuring him he could call if something new came to mind; and also promising to get back in touch soon. And after he left, Doswell reflected on the daunting picture he was left with. More daunting, yes, in certain respects than he'd expected, or at least hoped. More daunting, no doubt, than this young man Gallagher himself appreciated. And yet, as bad as all this was, *nothing* was worse than being alone. Now, as difficult, as insane as it was, as impossible as it seemed, he would be facing the impossible not as an isolated individual but along with others. That is, of course, unless in some way this smooth young man, or the Senator and his staff, couldn't be trusted. Or, then, if they came to more fully appreciate the liabilities he brought to the table and to discount the assets – *that* would be the traditional white way. And then Gallagher was only one man – an aide. It came back to this: what about McCarthy?

In days which followed, he wrestled with all of this, and of course, the problem of Carole. What to do about Carole if he went up to Washington?

29

Witness

When Doswell was going up to New Haven in a taxi to meet with the FBI he'd begun to see clearer than ever the shape of things to come. Late in the previous decade following the Nazi-Soviet non-aggression pact, he'd begun meeting with the New York 'legal' *Rezident*, Pavel Gutzeit, to discuss sundry matters, all financially related, and then when Gutzeit was called back to Moscow and shot, Gaik Ovakimyan took over.

Gutzeit, the dreamy-eyed *Rezident* who wrote poetry, and the slick Ovakimyan, a man who looked like a Mafia Don with a side business in used cars, were poles apart, not only in appearance but in personality. But both men had in oblique ways revealed in their meetings with Doswell, held over the highways and byways northeast and west and south of the city, the regime's plans for future activities.

Gutzeit, the dreamer, was the more creative. It was he who had come up with an aggressive project of recruiting agents of influence within the highest reaches of elected government. It was he who'd first recruited Congressman Samuel Dickstein, who ironically was the father of the House Un-American Activities Committee, the committee originally intended to snag recent immigrants friendly to the Nazis, but which roped in as well the regime's enemies: white Russians, Russian monarchists, Ukrainian nationalists, former Czarist officers and Trotskyites, all of whom came under the same broad umbrella of 'fascists'. This was one of the activities which he badly wanted to share with the FBI, and which he was about to do when Hitler broke his pact with Stalin, making Stalin America's ally.

The other which he learned about – or rather concluded, the result of many brooding deliberations, and then in full only long after the fact – was the more daring employment of Harry Dexter White, the Undersecretary of the Treasury, to promote a policy approach to Japan that would favor the regime. White had been serving it as a fellow traveler for at least a decade, and for a period of time after the pact there had been some concern he would no longer be willing to work for the regime. This anxiety turned out to be unfounded.

The international and policy situation that was relevant was Stalin's fear of Imperial Japan on the Soviet Union's eastern flank. This had never been a secret. Japan had been an obsession of the Soviets' for years. It was part of official

Bolshevik doctrine: the capitalist encirclement of the Soviet Union. Russian fear predated the regime, going back to the Russo-Japanese War of 1904–1905 that, under the czars, had ended with the nation's humiliation. It was also a constant and always very real danger; Russian and Japanese skirmishing had broken out numerous times along the Manchurian border through the '30s. This much had been clear: Doswell knew for years that espionage efforts conducted in Japan had been undertaken to find out Japan's intentions and then to steer it away from attacking the Soviet Union; just as it had been Stalin's purpose, on the Soviet Union's western flank, through his pact with Hitler, to keep peace with Germany.

The Soviet leadership never doubted Japan's ultimate desire to drive them out of the Far East, but they wanted to buy time, or even more hopefully to end the threat of Japanese power for good. They also fully appreciated Japan's growing fear of America as a power which threatened its control of the Pacific Rim. Thus Doswell had begun to see menacing signs, oblique hints from Ovakimyan, and something more: inferences he drew from agents he met in his limousine 'bank' who were making proposals for organizing or expanding networks in Japan; the nature of their specific proposals signs of their acting on a design to steer Japanese aggression towards the United States and thus away from the Soviet Union. But how this was to be done, and to what effect, he did not know.

He did know that within the White House itself, Laughlin Currie, Special Assistant to the President, was a "friend of the Soviet Union". He was not certain if Harry Hopkins, a personal advisor to the President, was also a 'friend', though if he wasn't a 'friend', Doswell thought, he was a friend. For at the very least, he was "in drive" under power of the "transmission belt", the term Lenin employed thirty years earlier when he spoke of the united or popular front's purpose in infiltrating and then influencing established bourgeois institutions. In the beginning it was trade unions. On the horizon, academic institutions and foundations, then departments of government, now Congress and the White House…

But what could they – or any of the many he knew about or suspected of influencing policy – do to steer Japan towards attacking the United States? Many things. But *what*, he'd racked his brain, *what specifically?*

He had noted the sudden appearance in the late winter of 1940 and early 1941 of Iskhak Akhmerov ('the furrier', so named because in his earlier long stay as an illegal *Rezident* in New York he had run a successful business in furs as a front). Akhmerov was the most astute intelligence operative he'd ever known. When the tall, suave, genial Akhmerov had been recalled earlier to Moscow at the time of the Purge, Doswell thought he had been shot like so many others. But he was wrong. Akhmerov returned at a time when most of the American agents were inactive. And he'd returned specifically to reactivate Harry Dexter White, with whom he'd had a very long and profitable relationship. The fear that White, being Jewish and a fellow traveler, might have broken over the pact was probably one of the reasons Akhmerov had been sent. Now they all learned that White had not broken over Stalin's pact with the devil, and that he'd recruited additional agents in the Treasury Department since they'd last been in touch. He was not only fully in drive, but able to put others to work as well.

Doswell also guessed, and deduced through things which Akhmerov himself said, in two conferences which they had at that time, that the Treasury Department was taking a hand in policy at State. Did this mean that Secretary Morgenthau was one of those White had recruited? He didn't know that. But he did know that there were important officials in the State Department who'd wanted a *modus vivendi* with Japan. These individuals wanted to gain time against the day when war became unavoidable. It was no secret that the United States was still woefully unprepared; it needed to build up its war production and these officials were pressing for a last-minute diplomatic effort that would put off conflict with Japan for as long as possible.

Doswell had learned that Laughlin Currie was telling everyone he could that the State Department was planning to sell China "down the river". And he later learned that White was furiously sending off memoranda to Morgenthau, who was then sending them up the command to the President and the Secretary of State. They urged communiqués to the Japanese in the harshest of language, making the most extreme and unrealistic demands: complete military withdrawal from China, Indo-China and Thailand; the leasing to the United States of up to half of Japan's naval vessels and airplanes; and the sale of half of its output of war material. The demands were diplomatically absurd, and a provocation. Morgenthau apparently did not always act on White's memos, and Secretary of State Hull did not always respond to the Treasury Secretary. But on November 26th 1941, the Secretary of State, in his ultimatum to the Japanese, used much of the harsh language in previous memos, making demands which Doswell later concluded Iskhak Akhmerov had suggested to White. Most of this he'd decided only years later on the basis of final pieces of the puzzle which he found in the most unlikely of places: Secretary of State Cordell Hull's *Memoirs*, wherein he spoke of his annoyance at Morgenthau's *persistent inclination to function as a second Secretary of State*, and the fact that he had allowed the Treasury Secretary to incorporate some of the harsh language and impossible demands which had originated in White's memoranda.

Even in 1950, of course, this was in many of its parts speculative. Whether, and to what extent, Harry White had made a real difference in American policy which resulted in an attack that might have taken place later, and if later, possibly not successfully, Doswell obviously couldn't say for certain. But that Harry White had *tried*, and had tried under Akhmerov's supervision, of this Doswell had come to be virtually certain. And more significantly, if it had been successful – or even if it hadn't been – what would such stratagems have boded for the future at critical junctures of policy? This is what concerned him – the future. He had ideas about this he'd often told Jim; and his speculations, not without evidence, included policy decisions involving China's recent fall.

He mentioned once again to Jim the notes he'd written to himself when he was still in the Party, and which he still had in those days immediately after he'd spoken to Tom Gallagher. And for a couple of years after his open break with the Party, he'd written not only detailed accounts of his previous activities but more reflective, evidence-laden analyses of what he suspected based on his knowledge of recent undercover activities. He did all of this not only to sharpen his weapon against the Party should it act against him, but in case he should ever have to talk to the FBI again. Now, he said, he was hoping "to re-anchor" his thoughts should he testify before the Committee.

But as he began, with the aid of his notes, to summon those long-suppressed memories, he realized how much of what he'd gathered and put down was simply outside the purview of the present inquiry. Given what Tom Gallagher told him, it was highly unlikely he could share any of the information about Samuel Dickstein or Harry Dexter White. In the latter instance, the mandate of the Committee's investigation was limited to the State Department. White and his cabal had been in Treasury. And what's more, Harry Dexter White had died two years before of a heart attack, days after he'd given testimony to the House Committee on Un-American Activities, categorically denying both Bentley's and Chambers' charges that he was a Soviet agent.

Judge Dickstein, whose brainchild was the since widely reviled committee, had never been part of the State Department. He was no longer a member of the House of Representatives, and granted his unhappiness with the waywardness of his committee, was no longer with the Federal Government.

But going over his notes and scouring his mind to try to recall the contexts of incidents and events, persons and places and conversations, many of which went back almost twenty years, much that had been forgotten began to take on a life again. As more and more came into focus, he realized that if Dickstein's and White's work was now out of date, or outside the purview of the Committee, there were other activities which did touch on matters that would be very relevant to its inquiries, a few of which included cases McCarthy named as security risks in the State Department.

One day, he told Jim, when he was cudgeling his brain over precisely these matters, Charlie Robinson appeared at his door and announced out of the blue, "You know, Thomas, me and Bernice, we talked it over, and we thought if it would be alright with you, since we haven't taken a vacation in a long time, how about if we go up to Washington together? Bernice and me, we can take care of Carole whenever you're doing whatever you got to do, and when you get back, why, we can all of us go out and paint the town red!"

Thus Doswell found the one square peg that miraculously fit the round hole which desperately needed filling if he was to go to Washington and testify.

Doswell waited in the back of the chamber of the Senate Office Building, listening to the testimony of the witness who was appearing before him. It was Earl Browder, the former Secretary General of the Party from 1932 to 1945. Iskhak Akhmerov had married Browder's niece some fifteen years earlier, shortly after he first arrived in America as a young Soviet intelligence officer and 'illegal'. Browder had known Doswell before he'd known Akhmerov; he'd given him an all-important recommendation which made possible his stay in Moscow at the Lenin Institute in the late '20s and early '30s. Thus he had been one of several mentors in Doswell's early days in the Party. The Senators on the Tydings Committee knew who he was; as the American Party's former Secretary General he was known in that role to most informed Americans.

Senator Hickenlooper of Iowa, one of two Republicans on the Committee (Senator Lodge of Massachusetts being the other), was questioning Browder about whether he knew this or that person previously or presently connected to the State Department to have been a member of the Communist Party. Browder was angrily refusing to answer.

"I want to declare to the Committee that I consider it outrageous that this hearing should be devoted to the development of new smear campaigns. I refuse to take part in such proceedings..."

Senator McMahon of Connecticut moved to intervene: "There are two names Senator Hickenlooper has presented to you. Miss Kenyon and Mr. Hanson were named openly and charged openly by Senator McCarthy. It occurs to me that whatever your answer may be, that to withhold an answer to Miss Kenyon and this other gentleman – that your withholding of an answer on them, if the answer is in the negative, is contributing to that smear. On the other hand, if the answer is in the positive, since those cases are before the Committee, I believe you should answer..."

Then Senator Tydings, the committee's chairman, was intervening as well: "Allow me to talk to the witness a moment. The chairman would like to bring this matter to your attention and in the interest of fairness and truth, and in pursuing the investigation which we are ordered to make, to ask you if you will not reconsider on those two names, and tell us whether or not you know or do not know they are members of the Communist Party."

Browder, somewhat mollified, replied, "I am quite willing to answer the question about those two persons, and I refused to answer before only because the question was obviously the beginning of a fishing expedition for new names to smear by association. I would say, without the slightest hesitation, that neither one of them ever, in my period of leadership in the Party organization, had any organized connection as members or friends."

"Thank you very much for cooperating," Senator Tydings said. And then Doswell heard him ask Browder a quick follow-up question: "To your knowledge, is Mr. John Carter Vincent or Mr. Service, is either one a member of the Communist Party? Those are the only names I shall present to you."

Browder's anger flared up again. "Yes – before it was two other names. Now, it is two, maybe one by one we will get into a list of thousands."

"I see your point of view. I am not arguing at the moment, but I do think you are defeating the purpose of this inquiry," he stressed this last, "in a way that you perhaps do not realize, if you allow this to be obscured, and if you felt that you could answer, in the cases of Mr. Vincent and Mr. Service, I would be very grateful to you."

Mr. Browder, once again made more agreeable, answered that to the best of his knowledge, they had never had any connection with the Party. He was thanked.

Then Doswell heard his name called. Ten years waiting, a flutter of butterflies in his stomach, he made his way to the front of the chamber. Flashbulbs flashing, klieg lights causing him to squint, hearing the buzz and hubbub as he approached the place where the little man with the pencil-sharp moustache was standing, he heard Mr. Morgan, the majority counsel, ask Browder to wait a moment, and to turn and to look at him as he approached the table.

"Mr. Browder, do you know this man?"

Browder appeared taken aback. "Do I know this man…? In what connection?"

"Do you know this man, Thomas Doswell, D-O-S-W-E-L-L, as a member or former member of the Communist Party? Before you leave, could you please help us in this one last regard?"

Browder seemed annoyed, but he approached slowly, bringing his face up close to Doswell's, scrutinizing it carefully. After several long seconds of this grim exploration, taking in ears and eyes and nose and forehead, Doswell feeling like he was being examined in prospect of being purchased, Browder said, "I can't say I've ever seen him before in my life. I certainly can't remember ever seeing him at any organizational meetings or gatherings."

"Thank you, sir, for your very helpful cooperation."

The chairman opened with some housekeeping details. "I see here, Mr. Doswell, that you are a graduate of Harvard University, Class of 1924. And you are a professor at Baxter College? Is that correct?"

"I am an assistant professor of Humanities at Baxter University."

"That is a very broad subject, is it not?"

"I teach Great Books. I have taught Spanish and French and Latin, and I occasionally teach courses in philosophy."

"Well, well, that *is* broad. You are a learned man, Professor Doswell… You were a member of the Communist Party from 1924 to 1943, you wrote in the statement you earlier turned over. And yet as you have just heard, Mr. Earl Browder, who was Secretary General of the Party for some thirteen years, and a longtime member before that, says he doesn't know you. Do you think he's just forgotten your name and face?"

"I don't know. I doubt it. But it's possible. It's been many years since we've seen each other and during most of the years I was in the Party I was in the underground."

As he said this last Senator Tydings made a blowing sound with his lips, and Doswell noticed him give the Senator to his right a significant look as he threw a weary arm over his chair.

"Mr. Browder doesn't recognize you," he said with rising irritation, "and when you first went to the FBI in 1940 to tell what you'd overheard listening to people talk about Party plans, did you tell the FBI then that you were a member of the Communist Party?"

"No. I did not."

"May I ask why?"

"I didn't share that information because I didn't think it necessary at the time."

"You didn't think it necessary at the time? I would have thought it was very important, considering especially that you were supposedly providing critical information about the Party."

"I was providing the FBI with information which it considered most urgent because it had to do with aid…"

"Excuse me. That is not the subject of this inquiry. If it is necessary to go into that, we may in executive session. It is not necessary that we smear anyone else's names here. I want simply to know why you didn't tell the FBI you were in the Communist Party then?"

"As I previously said, I didn't think it was necessary. What the FBI was interested in knowing didn't require that I divulge that information."

"You didn't say, 'I have information about a lot of other espionage in the government, in the State Department, and elsewhere' – you didn't say any of that?"

"I didn't believe I could interest anybody in any of that information at the time."

"But you do now? No. No. That's alright. You don't have to answer that. Just tell me this before you and I leave off: how much time, Mr. Doswell, have you spent with Senator McCarthy before you appeared here before us?"

"I spent about an hour with the Senator, and several hours with another of his aides on a few other occasions."

In that previous hour with McCarthy, Doswell told Jim years later, he'd said much that gratified the thickset but vigorous junior Senator from Wisconsin. He'd met with him in his office in the Senate Office building. McCarthy sitting leisurely sprawled behind his giant oak desk, Doswell gave the Senator names the Senator had never previously heard of; and he also provided facets of intelligence he'd never previously possessed. But Senator McCarthy, like a good poker player dealt an incredibly lucky hand, took it all in with little emotion, just as Hammer might have, sorting it out, calculating just what and how it could best be used in due time.

Senator McCarthy was also a very busy man and, small world, Bill Renner, whom he hadn't seen for years, now working for the Senator, questioned him low-key several times again in detail. What McCarthy wanted to know more specifically was: given Doswell's broad overview of the inner workings of the Party and the underground, could he remember ever having had any knowledge of agents in the State Department, more significantly in the *current* State Department – and most urgently, in the current State Department including or connected to Professor Owen Lattimore?

Senator McCarthy, who was present at the Tydings Committee hearing, broke in immediately following Doswell's answer to Senator Tydings' question about how much time he'd spent with the Senator. "Point of privilege, Mr. Chairman, if you please."

"You are not a member of this Committee, Senator McCarthy, but I will recognize you if you make it short."

"I do not have access to the State Department's loyalty files, nor do you, and I have been put in the extremely difficult position of having to develop and provide supporting evidence of the State Department's delinquencies on matters of security on my own. I am one Senator with very limited resources. I am submitting to the Committee information bearing upon bad security risks and disloyalty in the State Department. It seems to me you must understand the necessity of my finding witnesses with expert knowledge so that you can investigate my charges. After all, I am not in the position of knowing anything on my own. Therefore this impugning of the witnesses' credibility *before* they give evidence does not seem to me to be helpful to the purposes of this inquiry."

"I thank you, Senator McCarthy, for this enlightening disquisition on the subject of this Committee's responsibilities and the methods it is to employ in discharging them. Since I am presiding over this hearing, however, I will decide what is credible and what is *in*credible here on out. I have taken note of your words, and can we now move on?"

Senator Henry Cabot Lodge of the minority was next up.

Later, when testimony for that day was completed, Doswell was sitting in Senator McCarthy's chambers with McCarthy and his staff.

"Let me tell you – listen, you call me Joe from now on and I'll call you Tom – let me tell you, Tom, what Senator Tydings said to me the opening day of these hearings. He said, wagging his finger in my face, 'You are the man who occasioned this hearing and so far as I am concerned in this Committee, you are going to get one of the most complete investigations ever given in the history of this Republic.' That's what he said. So don't feel bad about his ragging you like that. It's because you're one of *my* witnesses that he does that. He doesn't like *me*."

They were sitting around in his spacious chambers with sandwiches, coffee and beverages. Besides the Senator, there was Tom Gallagher, Bill Renner, two or three other aides, and Jean Kerr. Kerr, who would in a few years become the Senator's bride, was in her early twenties, and strikingly attractive. She was also remarkably poised and well-spoken for so young a woman.

"Tom, just don't feel you have to tolerate any incivilities from them," she said. "You have a perfect right as a citizen to look them in the eye and to tell them what's on your mind."

"That's right!" the Senator chimed in, clearly smitten by the young woman who was young enough to be his daughter.

After a moment Bill Renner said, "Today was just the preliminaries."

"Tomorrow," the Senator added, "I hope we can go into the business on Lattimore."

30

Doswell's Oedipal Sin

Professor Owen Lattimore, Director of the Walter Hines Page School of International Relations at Johns Hopkins University, was one of Senator McCarthy's biggest fish. Though he'd never been a regular employee of the State Department, he had over the years gone on numerous official and semi-official missions and held numerous appointments, such as President Roosevelt's personal advisor on China, as well as chief of Pacific operations for the Office of War Information. He was also the editor of *Pacific Affairs*, a journal which had immense influence in the small but important world of Asian scholarship. An editor and prolific writer, he was responsible for books and articles which were treated with great intellectual authority by China hands at the Far Eastern desk at State.

Doswell told Jim, "Senator McCarthy, at that first and only meeting which we had alone together, said he believed that Lattimore was a conscious instrument – those were his words, 'conscious instrument' – of Soviet conspiracy."

This whole business of McCarthy made Jim feel very uncomfortable. He no less than Vincent recoiled at this characterization of McCarthy as a legitimate investigator of Communist spies. Making him out as anything other than America's storybook villain was to instantly render you a social outcast. Of course no one *said* this in so many words. Like any real taboo, the prohibition simply lay in never going unheeded.

So Jim, trusting Doswell immensely, and in awe of the terrible, lifelong price he'd paid for his knowledge, trusted him also to understand that he had to be certain.

"All those years you feared *no one* would believe you – and the Party believed no one would believe you, but McCarthy did so easily?"

"He did believe me. And quite readily. One might have said – and some did say – that he would believe anything and anyone if it served his purposes. And I was a case in point. I can say that, yes, he did take me quite seriously."

"But as you say, most believe, or would charge him – I mean, his name is a synonym for destroying people – they would charge him with believing anything if it served his purposes. Maybe it's hard to judge where you were, in your situation, but do you think he really wasn't reckless, that he wanted really to be as careful as Gallagher said?"

"This was politics that was an extension to war. Before the Tydings Committee McCarthy was more on trial than anyone was. And we were all of us up against a fortress with a very high wall. The lives of millions were at stake. They certainly were in China, they certainly were in Korea, and today they are in Southeast Asia. This was the most critical theatre in a World War that the enemy had begun decades earlier, only he'd never accommodated America with an open declaration. It was hardly a gentleman's game."

"And you knew that he was right? That Lattimore and maybe others had steered American policy in Asia to favor a Communist takeover?"

"I thought he was."

"But you didn't know him, you said. How could it be proven?"

"It was something difficult to *prove*, yes, Jim. But a great deal pointed to Lattimore. Much of it wasn't even direct action but ideas. Yes. But ideas that were used to persuade to one course over another. One policy decision rather than another. Those people you mention, of course they would say it was reckless. The charge was that Lattimore and some of his associates' work led over a period of time to a critical *tilting* of US policy away from the Nationalist Chinese and towards the Communists. This meant numerous policy decisions at critical junctures, few or none of which, taken alone, were demonstrably treasonous, but which overall had fatal consequences. It was the kind of charge that should have been investigated in executive – secret – sessions but *they* wanted public sessions, do you understand that? They *wanted* a media circus."

"Even Lattimore?"

"Of course. Lattimore was a hero in the press."

"But just the charges alone. Surely you couldn't *charge* him with bad ideas, even if they had fatal consequences."

"Well, yes and...yes. He was an advisor, therefore, if his ideas were consistently bad, his advice so recklessly bad that as a practical matter they tilted our policy to favor the Chinese Communists, then the State Department was remiss in failing to take note of that and not taking his advice any longer. At the least that, anyway. But yes, McCarthy *did* charge him with being a conscious instrument of Soviet policy at the outset. Perhaps that was a tactical mistake. I won't argue that. But it required a much more thorough investigation. What he was thinking was that it was like Harry White following Akhmerov's instructions when he went to Secretary Morgenthau. And it was my thinking as well: that there was a conscious line, and that he was in conformity with it."

"And did you have knowledge of the link?"

"Yes...But Jim, the standard of proof, or the demonstration that had to be made of such a link, was not, as in a criminal case, beyond a reasonable doubt. It simply had to be reasonable in the sense that any commonsense person with the facts before him would see the obvious connections. All of this is important to remember."

"But it *is* difficult to remember. And you know what people who criticize McCarthy say: that what this came down to was attacking a man for his ideas and the people he was associated with."

"That is what people say. But they are wrong. No doubt about it, for them it was scapegoating, a purely partisan and cynical attempt at finding a way to blame the Administration that had been in power – Jim, think about this – the *previous eighteen years, and at the time of China's fall.*" He stressed these words.

Jim blinked and shut his eyes momentarily, dipping his head and knitting his brows as he did.

"I myself returned from Erfurt in 1931. I began my work then: ten years of treasure and intense effort—"

"I guess that's true. They had been in power for all those years and China *did* fall under their watch."

"Exactly. But that's not how the press was looking at it. And it certainly wasn't how members of the Administration were looking at it. Hardly a day passed that someone from the Administration wasn't saying, and it was being loudly and approvingly reported, that McCarthy was a traitor, or he was doing Stalin's work for him, or he was another Goebbels. You throw that at a man day in and day out and eventually some of it sticks."

"But wasn't McCarthy doing the same?"

"No. He wasn't! He wasn't coming close to that – and if it was scapegoating, Jim, the goat was hardly a placid, defenseless creature. As targets go, the better image is that he was attacking an ever-rising oceanic flood. If he was reckless, he was reckless with himself, the target was inviting only to the suicidal."

Doswell's bull-like shoulders hunched, his head lowered, a dogged, angry edge entering into the sound of the words. "Of course it was dirty business. War is even dirtier. But whose responsibility was it? They – and I'm not alone talking about people inside the Party, but people outside the Party, from the Administration and elsewhere – from the beginning they'd wrapped themselves in the cloak of the First Amendment to conceal and to defend people who shamelessly abused it in support of an enemy power. And they could get away with that because they could play on people's ignorance and naiveté about Communism. They turned being a Communist into something merely eccentric. Unlike Nazism Communism wasn't supposed to be evil, it was merely about being a radical idealist, a progressive in a hurry."

But it wasn't just Lattimore's ideas that they had to go on, he stressed to Jim. And there were others who played important roles in the testimony: He told him that there was a one-time managing editor of the *Daily Worker*, Louis Budenz, who testified that Earl Browder, and others high in the Party hierarchy, had spoken numerous times of Professor Lattimore, both in matters of policy and intrigue as being a Party member.

As for his own knowledge, it was not limited to the Institute of Pacific Relations; he had *some* direct knowledge about Lattimore, and the journal, *Pacific Affairs*, which Lattimore headed up.

He remembered when he was still the 'banker' an agent made a request for a large sum for the Institute of Pacific Relations to sustain its "outstanding efforts in supporting the work of the comrades in China". He had in fact rejected the application back then, he said. He remembered that this had been one of those difficult applications. It was hardly routine, and he remembered it because the agent and he argued vigorously about the decision, which at that juncture, over much back-and-forth – and consultations with Gutzeit – he had sustained over the other's protests.

As for the Institute itself, he knew it back then to be a legitimate, old-line organization whose inactive board members were men of high repute in American business and professional life. And precisely that it was *not* officially a Communist front was a critical factor in his decision to refuse to fund it, because in the first instance it was well supported by those same conservative American interests – and more importantly, he'd wanted to keep it that way. He'd wanted to take no unnecessary risks at jeopardizing its impeccable credentials. One of the individuals involved was Frederic Vanderbilt Field. And Field – as his middle name indicated, a scion of the wealthy Vanderbilt family, and long a member of the open Party – had previously given large sums to the Party and its associated organizations.

"My thinking was, if it ever got out that the Comintern had funded the Institute it would be viewed as just another front." So paradoxically, not being another front made it a perfect place for a cadre of dedicated revolutionaries covertly peddling the Party line. This had been Lenin's fruitful idea of the 'united front' at the founding of the socialist state. And this had been exactly Doswell's thinking when he was himself a Communist Party member, working deep in the underground.

Now more than a decade later he was in the interesting position of undoing what he had previously played no small part in doing: concealing the effective revolutionary work of those within the Institute of Pacific Relations. Thus, he said, he intended to reveal what he'd previously gone to considerable lengths to hide: Field's generous philanthropy, which included, in time, over his oft-repeated objection, $7,000 for the Institute that could be corroborated by good researchers knowing what they were looking for. But would this be enough to nail Lattimore? Did it sufficiently demonstrate that Lattimore was one of the infiltrators, or just one of those unknowingly "driven by the regime"? In fact, it didn't really matter because the object of the inquiry was less his conscious purpose; it was, given the sensitivity of his post, whether he was under its influence and therefore a security risk.

But to make the case convincing to an American audience (and to vindicate McCarthy's charge), there was one other and quite different kind of arrow in Doswell's quiver. It was a piece of intelligence readily understandable by anyone.

Moreover, it hardly required textual analysis of Lattimore's writing which Freda Utley, another of the witnesses, a former Party member and friend of Lattimore's, had attempted to do to demonstrate that he followed a Moscow-dictated Party line. No, this was no textual analysis, postmodern or McCarthyite. And the evidence it offered was worth more than Field's $7,000.

"Alright," the Senator from Maryland was saying to Doswell on his second appearance before the Committee, "you know you could be the first person since this whole ugly business began that is charged with perjury for declaring himself a Communist when he never was one."

Tydings waited, the hearing room bursting into a gale of deafening laughter which the Senator had no intention of rebuking.

"Point of privilege, Mr. Chairman, may I be recognized?"

"The Senator from Wisconsin wishes to speak?"

"Mr. Chairman, as I have asked on previous occasions, I would like the privilege of questioning the witnesses. I would especially like the opportunity of examining this witness."

"Senator McCarthy, as I have already told you, if we allow you to cross-examine the witnesses, the witnesses will have a right to cross-examine you."

"And I have already said, Mr. Chairman, I am perfectly willing to be cross-examined by any of the witnesses – Mr. Lattimore, or any of the others."

"And we will take that up at the earliest possible moment. For now we will continue with the proceedings."

What followed was a short examination by Senator McMahon, whose time was cut short by the need to cast a crucial vote in another committee. And so there followed the patrician Senator Lodge of the minority.

Senator Lodge would later in the decade become something of a television personality when, under President Dwight Eisenhower, he served as Ambassador to the United Nations. There, often televised, he would, with dignity and precision of language, rebuke and refute verbal assaults both from the Soviet Union's Ambassador and its shoe-pounding Premier, as well as Third World representatives who most often sided with Communist powers rather than capitalist ones.

Senator Lodge, though not a friend of McCarthy's, was sympathetic to Doswell, and he led him through a series of questions which allowed him to expand on his knowledge of *Pacific Affairs* and its editor beyond the business of Frederick Vanderbilt Field's $7,000 gift to the Institute of Pacific Relations.

Now Doswell felt more comfortable in his role as witness. A fast learner, he had already become an old hand as he communicated the relevant information.

He told how in 1936 he had learned that Lattimore had put a request for a Chinese assistant through Comintern channels. He said that the man who had come to the United States to be Lattimore's assistant at the magazine was Chen

Han-shen, someone he knew as a highly experienced agent who'd first worked with another agent, Richard Sorge, a figure grown legendary after his publicized execution by the Japanese just before that nation's entry into the World War. For years Sorge had conducted successful espionage work for the Soviets under cover of being a German Nazi. Doswell said that after Chen arrived in the United States, he worked as a Chinese Communist operative, conducting espionage in New York while he served on Lattimore's special request as co-editor of *Pacific Affairs*.

"Mr. Doswell," the venerable Senator Green of Rhode Island opened, following this weighty revelation before Senator Lodge. The chamber was now quieter, more subdued than before. Green had previously been very critical of Doswell's testimony. "You have become quite the man since Senator McCarthy invited you here: the newsmen, the big lights, all of us waiting on your every word. You claim to know about all this international intrigue, these world famous spies – tell me, do you know what 'hearsay' means?"

Senator Lodge began rapping his pencil. "Mr. Chairman…"

"I will permit Senator Green to finish his line of questioning and then I will hear from the distinguished Senator from Massachusetts," Senator Tydings said, uncharacteristically short with his prominent colleague.

Once again Doswell felt his heart beat faster. "I think I do."

"Please tell us what you think it means."

"Testimony not based on personal knowledge, but told by another."

"Very good. Is there anything you know that you know from direct knowledge?"

"What I have told you is not hearsay. What I told, as I outlined it in my answer to Senator Lodge, is based on direct discussions with several high-level GRU and NKVD agents, and others, individuals whose names I have already given to you in previous testimony."

"So what you are telling me is that when you thought you heard something particularly interesting, you eavesdropped?"

"I didn't eavesdrop. I didn't—"

"I would like to remind you that you are under oath."

"I know I am under oath. I think if you ask me questions you need to let me answer them if you want an answer."

There was not a sound in the hearing room.

"Your conscience wouldn't have permitted you to eavesdrop?"

"The occasion never arose."

"Your conscience—"

Doswell broke in. "Conscience is an issue that arises when one contemplates doing something one ought not to. As I just said, the occasion for eavesdropping never arose. What I have told you here is based, as I told this Committee earlier, on discussions which I had with agents who were applying for Comintern funds to bankroll clandestine operations here and overseas. This is how I came to a knowledge of what I have told you. I was, so to speak, the 'banker' or the 'bank' of the Comintern."

"The bank!" Senator Green cried. He was now looking with great, wide-eyed merriment at the Senator from Maryland, who was smiling in return a look which seemed to say – didn't I tell you he was too much? But the hearing room, except for one or two audible chuckles, was soundless. He quickly added, "You seem to me to be a very smart man, Mr. Doswell, a very smart man. You are a graduate of Harvard, and I congratulate you on that. But Mr. Doswell, you certainly do not look like a banker to me."

He heard some less than robust laughter in a few quarters of the hearing room. "It is precisely the reason," he replied, "that you and several others here" – he glanced at all of the Senators as he said this, his eyes lingering for several extra seconds on Senator Tydings – "find it so hard to believe – that you find it so funny, even the idea of it – that I was effective in that role. The Party's thinking was that I would never be suspected. You have just proven what good thinking that was."

No one was laughing now.

When Senator Lodge was called on, a smile playing on his handsomely dignified face, he said he had nothing further at that point to add.

Owen Lattimore, professorial, "rumpled" as his wife affectionately described him, was up next.

"They are simply outrageous lies," he said confidently, his English accent strongly discernible, answering the plain, undramatic Senator Hickenlooper of Iowa, in response to some of Miss Freda Utley's and Budenz's charges.

"You also deny that Mr. Field ever gave $7,000 to the American Council of the Institute of Pacific Relations?"

"In the first instance, I don't keep a tab on who gives what to the Foundation. Although I do remember a large gift of ten times that amount from the Rockefeller Foundation. I hope you are not charging the Rockefellers with being Communists."

The hearing room broke into laughter.

"You deny," Senator Hickenlooper pressed, "that Frederic Vanderbilt Field is a Communist who has given support to the Communist Party and to Communist fronts in the past?"

"I don't know to whom he gives what. As far as I can tell he is a rather liberal young man."

"You deny that you had Communists on your staff at *Pacific Affairs?* Mr. Chi Chao-ting, for example?"

"I don't know that he is a Communist even now."

"Is there any doubt in your mind that he would be here as the proposed representative of Communist China to the UN if he is not a Communist?"

"It is possible, Senator. The Communist government in China appears to have taken over the services of a considerable number of non-Communists, especially where they were men of specialized training of various kinds."

"What about Mr. Chen Han-shen?"

"What about him?"

"I am referring to the testimony of Mr. Thomas Doswell, that he came to the United States on your request. That he was a highly trained and experienced spy, that he worked for you as co-editor at *Pacific Affairs*."

"This man is obviously working for the China Lobby. A very clever fellow, by the way. Cleverer than any of Senator McCarthy's previous witnesses..."

"Please just answer the question, Mr. Lattimore."

"I don't recall that even Mr. Doswell said that I asked that he come to the United States to work for me. I doubt very seriously that Mr. Chen Han-shen was a Communist or a spy. But then generally I was not then, nor am I now, in the habit of asking people if they are spies or Communists. I seriously doubt it but I can't say with certitude that he wasn't."

"Did he work as co-editor of *Pacific Affairs?*"

"I found him to be a very able man. Yes, he did work at *Pacific Affairs*."

"As co-editor?"

"I believe he did."

"You *believe?*"

"I think he did, yes."

On July 20th 1950, about three weeks after the North Korean invasion of South Korea, the Committee's majority issued its findings. It was a surprise to no one. The news report, widely read at the time, went as follows:

> *Last week the Senate foreign-relations subcommittee that has patiently listened to Joe McCarthy's charges that 205 or 57 or 81 "card-carrying Communists" are employed in the State Department released a stinging and conclusive report. Signed by Senators Millard Tydings (D, Md.), Theodore Francis Green (D, RI) and Brien McMahon (D, Conn.), the report states that McCarthy's accusations are "a fraud and a hoax perpetrated on the Senate of the United States and the American people. They represent perhaps the most nefarious campaign of half-truths and untruths in the history of this Republic."*

Besides finding that Senator McCarthy was a charlatan, the Tydings Committee also found that the State Department security division had been efficient and fully effective, and that those charged by Senator McCarthy as security risks were patriots.

But in fact, in the aftermath of its findings, Doswell stressed, nothing was really found to be conclusive, as the above commonly communicated reports of the finding said.

In the first instance, the minority had vigorously opposed the majority's conclusions, as well as its procedures. Senators Lodge and Hickenlooper raised numerous serious questions, not a few of which related to the examination of Professor Lattimore by the Committee.

Other Republican Senators and Democrats, as well, soon formed another Senate subcommittee in search of answers to questions raised by the minority. It was headed up by Democratic Senator McCarran. Its report, arrived at two years later, came up with an entirely different set of findings that had serious implications for, among others, Owen Lattimore. For besides being described in its findings as *a conscious and articulate instrument of the Soviet conspiracy*, he was later indicted by a grand jury for perjury in connection with several of the answers he'd given to the McCarran Committee.

Because the Tydings report was so clearly a whitewash, Doswell later told Jim, despite the mainstream press' support of its findings, McCarthy's supporters actually increased in numbers, and his popularity among many grew with an ever greater fervor. Senator Tydings, up for re-election in Maryland, where the campaign had been fought largely over the issue of Senator McCarthy and Communists in government, lost to McCarthy's hand-picked candidate by a greater margin than any Democrat had ever before lost.

Tydings wasn't the only one to feel the backlash that had come with the voters' general unhappiness with affairs in Washington. In California, Richard Nixon, who'd made his name as Alger Hiss' most diligent interrogator, swamped his opponent by 700,000 votes and became the state's new Senator. The tidal wave affected other states, coming close to sweeping a Republican majority into office.

But in those first days most of this news was still months away, except, that is, for the sudden flood of letters that came into Senator McCarthy's office supporting the Senator's efforts and damning Senator Tydings and his committee.

Though Doswell felt disappointment at the immediate outcome, with the more upbeat Senator's assurances that the people would be heard, he also felt relief. It's true that he'd known much more than he'd told, but then, he'd told all that he could. He had gone through the ordeal of testifying and he had more than survived. The pretty future bride of Senator McCarthy, Jean Kerr, said with wide-eyed, girlish merriment that he'd hit "several home runs". Clearly he wasn't being charged with perjury, as his Senate inquisitors threatened several times. The Party hadn't murdered him, and he felt a greater confidence it would not try in the future since, after all, it knew, at least he thought it did, how ineffectual his testimony had turned out to be. Indeed, he wondered at how much more credit he'd given to the effectiveness of the anti-Communist cause than he should have when he was a Communist. He thought of the needless anxiety he'd felt over Field's philanthropy, or even the proposal for Comintern assistance to the Institute of Pacific Relations; thinking of this he laughed at himself. But no, the fact remained, why should the Party come after him or Carole now; why should it bother? No one listened, anyway.

Of course, as he would tell Jim, his testimony would turn out to be not quite so futile as he'd thought, but still, in the lightness of the moment he agreed to do as Charlie Robinson had advised back in Devon, before they'd come to Washington: to paint the town red! Certainly no pun on Charlie's part intended.

So before he and his small entourage left the capital, Charlie Robinson, who'd happily learned that George Lewis, "the greatest clarinetist who'd ever lived", was playing in a nearby jazz club on U Street, persuaded his sister Bernice, Carole and Doswell to go and hear him play. Bernice, in her plastic-fruit and daisy-trimmed hat, and Doswell and Carole – who was curious enough to want to go "to hear the second greatest musician who'd ever lived", paraphrasing Charlie; second only to Lewis' former partner, the recently deceased trumpeter, Bunk Johnson – seemed happier than Doswell had seen her in a very, very long time.

Years later, in the stillness and quiet of a late night in Devon, Jim asked once again about the long-dead Senator that Doswell had come to know for a short period twenty years before.

"After the fiasco of the Tydings Committee report, and Tydings' defeat in Maryland, and the general elections which vindicated him with the voters, the people who hated McCarthy before hated him, impossibly, even more. They hated him with an intensity I had never in my life seen. He was compared to Hitler and Goebbels.

"Owen Lattimore wrote a book, *Ordeal by Slander*, and in it he coined the term *McCarthyism*. It encapsulated everything McCarthy's enemies had been saying about him, and brought under its umbrella everything that in their cornered fury they'd been saying about the anti-Communist cause and the people who'd fought it. It became one of the fatal wounds which eventually brought him down."

"Then what was he like? The McCarthy behind the 'ism'."

"I only knew him a short while, and I didn't know him that well. I guess you could say he was a patriot. I guess you could say he was driven. He was a Marine veteran. He was a boxer who'd paid for a large part of his college tuition by coaching his college's boxing team, he told me. He was a slugger. He was not a man whose strength was nuance. He came from rough beginnings. He could certainly be coarse, though most of the time I was with him Jean Kerr was around and he was a perfect gentleman. He was no dope. He was on top of everything when I knew him. He had a phenomenal memory. He was the kind of man who generated strong feelings. He and Senator Lodge (who was an entirely different kind of man, a Boston Brahmin) were barely on speaking terms, even though Lodge sided with him on the Committee. I liked him. He was utterly natural with me. Robert Kennedy said that he was someone who wanted very much to be liked, and this I found to be very true. He was loyal to a fault – a fault a public man cannot afford. That was one of the things that brought him down. He could be guileful, but he was way out of his league. He was also a man who had a problem with alcohol. A few years later, when the hate finally began to wear him down, he resorted to the booze without controlling it, without stop. Resorted to it, I think, suicidally. At least that's what Bill Renner said."

"Did he destroy people?"

"I don't think he destroyed anyone, or if anyone was destroyed whom he touched, it was more their own fault than it was his. But when he first entered the sacred grove at which his enemies worshipped, he touched off the campaign of his own destruction. Of course his name is itself an imprecation, it is virtually impossible to defend him because doing so instantly damages his defender, like defending Hitler – certainly in intellectual circles. In fact, my friend" – he suddenly gave Jim an acute, discerning look, not without a friendly twinkle – "you still find it difficult, I can read it in your face, that I thought well of this man, this man who is obviously, for you, the embodiment of all that is evil – you find it difficult, don't you?"

"No...perhaps...Well, I am trying to take it all in, just sorting it out, I imagine," Jim added thoughtfully. "Like you say, you'd been isolated for years. He was the first person, and a powerful person, who fought alongside you and believed you...Naturally you'd appreciate someone who'd done that."

"And our cause was right."

"Yes."

"You see, I've often thought, this was my sin – the sin of people like Budenz and Chambers and myself – that we were disloyal, not to our country, *that* could be forgiven, but to the people who'd turned against the country. Yes, *that* was the great sin! Never to be forgotten, never to be forgiven..."

That night when the talk ended it was nearly dawn. There had been a heavy, wind-driven rain that had come up suddenly, for short minutes coming down in sheets, striking noisily against the windowpanes. Fortunately it was a Friday and Jim had only a light schedule; still, he dragged himself through the balance of the day.

PART 9

31

The Tale of the Crow and the Hummingbird

The din and the clamor continued unabated through the week. There were calls for repentance on a national scale. In Colonus at Central State University students had gone beyond their earlier 'Marshmallow Riot', and were occupying buildings over the ongoing Cambodian incursion, and over a popular faculty member who'd failed to win tenure.

At Baxter, at a student-faculty assembly, President Montbanc warned of trying times ahead, cautioning patience and moderation: "You may have to learn to fight in the streets, you may have to learn to revolt, you may have to learn to shoot guns, you may ultimately be bathed in blood – but not this moment! The hour is not come!"

Curiously, this sermon fell on deaf ears because, outside of a handful, the body of Baxter's students all along had been, as some contemptuously called them, "hopelessly unengaged", but there fell a general quiet now even among the exceptions, as the workload of the impending close of the academic year descended.

In Jim's case there was in addition Susan, her pregnancy, and their upcoming marriage which absorbed him – Susan becoming increasingly agitated as both dates approached.

"We wouldn't have to be wearing our knuckles down to the bone scrubbing away like this, Jim, if you hadn't given away that money to your brother for a down payment on *his* house. We could have used it for a nice place in a nice neighborhood to move into ourselves – our *own* house!"

It's true Jim's apartment, especially its old-fashioned kitchen, was in a grimy, unredeemed state, and called for special attention.

Vincent, on the other hand, was burdened with a backlog of work accumulated during his long stay in Brooklyn – and burdened as well by morbid thoughts about his brother's still-enfeebled state, and the recent Alex Rackley case. He was also still occupied with Willi Wade, who didn't see the need for further wrangling to recover legal costs following his recent troubles with the university and the state of North Carolina – but there were bills to be paid!

All of them, of course, were swamped with student requests for conferences.

In the midst of the busyness, on one glorious Saturday in May, Jim decided to take a break by visiting the old man at the farm for an afternoon, bringing papers along to grade in the off minutes.

It was the first real break he'd had in quite a while. He drank in the day, the changing scenes along the way to Devon. First passing through a growing suburban sprawl on the main highway, past the Holiday Inn where, at the King's Table, he'd first met Susan through Radhakathri. Then down onto the gravel road he'd traveled numerous times before to Doswell's place, past the single-room log cabins, little more than ramshackle sheds poised on cinder and wood block footers, where bare-footed black folk no doubt lived much like their ancestors even as far back as slave times. He recalled stories Doswell told of his early life and his family. He thought of the tale he told of his father's slave past – amazing that they should be so near in time to events that had always seemed gripped in the dead hand of the far past. He slowed his vehicle, pulling his VW off the road, stopping on a slight rise a hundred or so feet from one of the cabins. He gazed at it with new eyes, and remembered what Doswell had said: how his father and grandmother, following emancipation, first lived in a log building that he himself, a small boy, had helped build.

"Laid up along a track of packed dirt," he said, "that turned muddy."

Jim gazed back along the road and saw children playing off in a field nearby.

"Along a road of packed dirt that turned muddy in the springtime and dusty in the summer heat..."

Jim started up his car again to go on his way. Ten more minutes and he pulled into Doswell's lane. As he drove up he saw him in overalls working his vegetable garden, striking nimbly with his hoe at weeds growing up between the rows; his grandson Billy beside him performing almost instantaneously and identically the same motions. In heavy overalls and a tattered, sweat-stained, visored cap, Doswell looked like the country Negroes beside the ramshackle shacks Jim had just passed.

He stopped then, leaned on the hoe and looked up with a grin as Jim stepped from his car.

"Ah, another worker, Billy," he said, and Billy instantly dropped his hoe, ran over to Jim and grabbed his hand.

"Alright, Popeye, let's take a break! We've been working for hours without any breaks!"

"A break, that sounds good to me," said Jim, smiling, looking down into Billy's beaming face.

"More like an hour," Doswell said. "He hasn't worked a lick, and he's already calling for a break." Laughing, he leaned his hoe against a wheelbarrow and urged Jim into the house.

As they entered the kitchen, Billy pulled a pitcher out of the refrigerator and began setting and pouring glasses of lemonade on the table.

"If you come here later in the summer you can help harvest some of these watermelons – you like cantaloupes? Billy, go get that container of cherries we're having for dessert tonight – let's start in on them *now*!"

Billy drew a bowl of glistening, fat red cherries from the refrigerator, grinning widely, grabbing a handful as he set it down on the kitchen table, Doswell and Jim laughing and following suit.

After they plucked at some of the fruit, spitting the small pits into their juice-stained hands, Billy suddenly jumped up, clutching another bunch of cherries and cried, "Let's all go down to the woods, Popeye!"

Billy ran ahead, down through the pasture and to the stream Doswell first showed Jim the previous fall, past where the clump of wild cherry trees used to stand, and where dead branches were scattered, waiting to be burned later in the fall.

As Jim and Doswell tramped along behind, they kicked at clumps of dry cow pies, talking as they went of many things: of the recent Willi Wade affair and Willi's joining the Army, of the academic year's imminent end, of the people who would or wouldn't be returning the following year. And of course, they talked of Jim's imminently changing marital status.

"You should bring Susan here more often. I'm sure she'd like to get away from the city."

"Oh, she gets away from the city all she cares to. She's moody now. Sometimes we get on each other's nerves...Chris Khalaf is no longer with Radhakathri. She learned he was already married in India, to a girl in her early teens. Chris comes over a lot, they hole up together for long, serious talks. Susan doesn't want me around then."

Doswell listened to this tale with conspicuous concern. "Radhakathri's leaving the city, right?"

"He's leaving the state, footloose and fancy-free – he found a position over in Arkansas."

They watched Billy disappear into the woods.

The two of them approached the stream where it took a turn at the edge of the wood and the still-open pasture, and Jim glimpsed the wild flowers, which reflected in the water, made it look flecked with fire. They plunged into the cool of the wood, stopping to watch Billy cast a stone into the foaming water of the stream. Silently they watched him step in, do a little dance, crying out how cold it was, and then perch on a rock. Suddenly a hummingbird, little larger than a moth, was darting away, flying in the boy's direction. Doswell called out to look, but the boy, thinking he was summoning him, came running. As he reached him Doswell took Billy's hand in his, drew him towards a big rock by the edge of the water and they sat down together, watching the white-crested water flowing swiftly through its channel. And he began asking him, "Did you see the tiny bird? The hummingbird, Billy?" He started one of his lessons.

"Oh, no, Popeye. You see one?"

"There was one just now, over here." He pointed upstream.

"I wish I'd seen it. I never see 'em."

"You've got to go real slow, and real quiet."

The boy shook his head thoughtfully. "Maybe I'll see it if I come back again later."

The old man nodded. "You come out here alone and see if you can find him. I know you will. But you've got to be real quiet. And you've *got to listen*."

The child was still. All his senses quickened at his grandfather's instruction. "Yeah, I'm going to come." The words were uttered like a pledge.

"You'll hear him hum. And if you're *real* quiet, maybe you'll even hear him talk" – the boy turned and beamed – "like a hummingbird, of course."

Jim noticed the boy's hand relax momentarily, and then tighten again, firmly clasping his grandfather's thumb.

"What does he say?"

"Once I heard him talk to an old crow who was sitting here, just about where we are now. The crow was laughing at him over the way he flies." Doswell gave the words a funny, imitation crow-like sound: 'You don't fly right, straight like a bird, like I do, and the robins and the buzzard, and any other self-respecting bird does. Why, you pretend to be a bird, but you're not really. You're just an *insect*!' He was very contemptuous. The hummingbird ignored him. He went on just as he was before. After a while, the crow started talking again. Yes, he had a raspy ugly voice. When he talked he sounded like sandpaper. 'Why all you can do is *buzz* around like, like a bee – buzz around,' he mocked. 'Now listen to me!' He was proud and boastful. 'The way a real bird sounds!' And he started to crow, and he made a lot of noise.

"After a while, the hummingbird, who'd been leisurely sipping the nectar from a hundred wild flowers and had his fill, turned to the crow. He didn't perch anywhere, you understand. He just backed up a little in flight and hung there, suspended in the air. He was still flying, but not going anywhere that the crow could notice. And he said, 'When you eat, you steal, and when you're not stealing you're living off dead things. I give as much life to the living flower as I take, and the flower rewards me with its sweet nectar. We have no quarrel, this flower and me – we need each other. You say there is only one way to fly: as you do. But if I did as you I couldn't live as I do, I would have to live as you – the flowers in the field would die and never return and I, I would be without the soul of joy, the sweetest drink in all of God's creation.'

"The crow was very angry at what the hummingbird said. He was particularly mad about that business of stealing and eating dead things, because it was true.

And he was a bully – he was used to picking on smaller birds, and even eating their eggs. So he made a quick move in the tiny bird's direction, thinking he'd frighten him off. But he didn't figure right. He hadn't bargained for what he got. He didn't know that the hummingbird, as small as he is, is also the toughest, the fiercest, meanest bird who ever lived when set upon. He lit into that crow, like he was all over him in a flash."

"That was the last of that crow?"

"I never saw him again."

There was a long pause, and Billy smiled thoughtfully with a far-off look on his face. Jim watched him, intently thinking, where have I heard that story before?

Then suddenly Billy beamed. "That was a good story, Popeye!" He slipped away and went to carefully overturning rocks in the stream in search of crawdads.

"Wasn't that a version of Swift's tale of the Spider and the Bee from the *Battle of the Books?*"

Doswell exploded with laughter. "You start them early, Jim," he said as his laughter subsided to a chuckle.

Jim and the old man fell into silence, each gazing at the stream and at Billy splashing around, getting himself thoroughly wet. They lingered there for part of an hour, and then they started back. It was on the way back that it happened. They hadn't said anything since they started walking towards the house. In fact Doswell had taken to walking ahead, Jim slowing down, looking to Billy, who was running to catch up. Then Jim turned to see Doswell approaching the house, and then turned again in Billy's direction, when he suddenly noticed Billy freeze, then terrified, yelling, "Popeye! Popeye!"

Jim turned again, and when he did he saw Doswell slumped to the ground, his body strangely twisted and rigid. He ran as quickly as he could. Within seconds Billy had caught up. They bent over him. His face was contorted. He couldn't speak. Billy kept crying, "Popeye! Popeye!"

32

Their Little Strength is Feebleness, Fast Bound in Darkness Like a Dream

Jim and the Lewises carried him into the house and laid him on the couch. As he lay there, limp and still, feeling the crushing pressure in his chest slowly subside, he gazed out a window to the wheat field Jim Lewis planted the previous fall.

In the kitchen Euretha Lewis was comforting Billy. Her husband waited outside like a sentry, scanning the distance of the gravel road for a sign of the rescue squad, listening for the sound of the siren. It seemed like hours, but it couldn't have been more than minutes before they arrived.

The days following were frantic. It was approaching exam week, the busiest time of the year. At the hospital, before Jim left, Doswell still experienced pain, but was able to speak. He managed to remind Jim to telephone Vincent. He also mentioned the name Ashbel Hawpe in Virginia, instructing Jim to call him.

Seconds after Jim's call, at his room in the Hotel Carolina, Vincent immediately began thinking the worst. Feeling a desperate flush rising to his face at the thought of the quarrel he'd started with the old man, and fearing he might die before he could talk to him again, for an instant he thought of rushing to the hospital, to catch a glimpse of him at least; maybe if the old man could see him, a confirmation, an assurance that he was with him, pulling for him…

But no, he reflected, his hands shaking as he lit a cigarette, trying to calm his nerves; Allan had said he was being closely monitored. He'd be in the way.

Allan gave him no reason to think that he should take a sudden turn for the worse, in fact he said he was already better; yet Vincent understood, from what he'd learned talking to doctors about Aunt Molina and others in Brooklyn, that following a heart attack one can easily have another and not survive. Maybe he should go out to the hospital after all, try and see him, try and find out as much as possible…

But first he called him back, the first time he'd ever telephoned Allan, who suggested waiting before going to the hospital. Their telephone conversation was cordial enough. They talked about the final days of classes, how they'd need to divide up Doswell's sections – and as for the finals, and Doswell's yearlong grade records and evaluations, wait and see what would happen. They agreed to that.

*

Over the next several days Doswell started to get steadily better. So much so that on Thursday morning they learned that the doctors had given permission for him to have visitors. As soon as Vincent got word, between classes at lunch, he rushed to the hospital, managed to speak a few words to the old man, and reminding him that he was on his lunch break under the pressure of time, promised to return in the evening.

And he did that evening, but to his chagrin he found Allan already there. He'd hoped to see Doswell alone, to have time to straighten things out from when they'd had that needless quarrel outside the Grand Hotel.

"I'll come back in a bit," he said, discomfited, especially as he saw Jim Allan turning to him with eyes and a slumped posture that suggested they were having an intimate conversation.

But as he started for the doorway, the old man called him back.

"No, don't go anywhere. I was telling Jim something I want to tell you, too."

It was this conversation he would never forget.

He returned and waited awkwardly.

"Pull up a chair. Sit down."

Jim got up, offered his chair to Vincent, went over and pulled another from the far end of the room, dragging it back near Vincent's.

A young, chocolate-brown nurse came in, brushed silently by them, checked several monitors at the head of the bed, then asked Doswell if he was comfortable. "Do you need anything, Mr. Doswell?" she added prettily.

He smiled and said he was fine.

"Then I'll leave you with your visitors," she said, making eye contact with neither of them.

For several seconds neither Jim nor Vincent said anything; then as Vincent cleared his throat, about to say something that would communicate as little as possible to Allan, but enough to the old man to let him know he regretted that night downtown two weeks earlier, Doswell spoke again. It was only slightly above a whisper, but his voice was strong; it didn't sound like that of a man with only hours to live.

"I was blessed this year. With the both of you. So I bless you in return," he said, smiling and gazing at Vincent.

Jim gently touched his shoulder.

Vincent's gaze, besides being drawn to Doswell, anxiously took in the maze of IV tubes and cords flimsily and ominously connecting him to monitoring equipment measuring vital signs.

"The doctors say I had a bad heart attack. That it was amazing that I pulled through...I'm living on borrowed time."

"You're as strong as a bull. You'll keep amazing them," Vincent said, wanting to believe it, struck by the strength of his voice and remembering Basil who'd survived three bullets.

Doswell nodded. "Yes, well, bulls die too."

They said nothing again for several seconds, the young men embarrassed by this word, 'die'. He started to speak again, but there was a longer pause as he seemed to be catching his breath, both Jim and Vincent waiting silently with only the background sounds, the public address system of a busy hospital sounding routinely.

"I've prayed for a clear mind. I wanted to tell about something more, something more important…I've confessed to God. Now I must ask forgiveness of men."

"You're tired," Jim said. "You need no forgiveness from us."

"No. I need to."

Both Jim and Vincent were aware of the other man asleep in the far bed, fortunately without visitors; the bed in between empty, aware of the drug smell, the clicking and ticking monitors.

Doswell first turned his eyes on Vincent. "Zora, Zora was the name of my wife. She never understood the allegiance that my faith in the Great New Order of the Future demanded. But I know she loved me…She, Jim, was one of the girls that would prop me up when I fell asleep at my desk at Uncle Big Bob's…" He smiled. "Once I fell asleep over the phone! Yes, on the phone with a client! She took the phone from my hand and finished the call, saying I'd been called away!" He chuckled. Then he coughed.

"The doctor said you're not to exert yourself. And you already told me that. This really can wait!"

"Don't stop me, Jim. No, I killed her…The battering of a human being over time takes a toll…"

Both Jim and Vincent were torn over what to do as he struggled under the strain of his emotions – stop him? How? Walk out and cause him even greater distress? Vincent got up halfway out of his chair and touched him. Jim held his hand.

He quickly added that Zora wasn't able to share the brooding, sullen, dark days of depression in the final years; that it was on her that he'd taken out his frustrations.

"When I thought I needed most the strength and the understanding of a woman who *could* understand, even as I did nothing to help her to understand, I deemed her a failure. She was not up to it. What burned inside I kept inside, and yet I resented her, her incomprehension, her inability to know…"

His eyes fell on Vincent. "*Listen*! I demanded the impossible of her! And I began to take everything out on her." He closed his eyes. "Yes, sometimes there was even a calculation in it." His voice rose to a near-frantic pitch as he glared up at the ceiling. "To confuse her, planting questions of doubt in her about herself, and about Carole, subverting her convictions, everything, our life together, to unsettle her as I was unsettled. To destroy her, and myself *through* her – *through her*!"

Jim pressed his hand. "Alright. Alright. We understand. That's enough." He was firm; his whispered voice rose. "That's enough!"

Outside in the corridor there was the occasional coming and going drone of voices passing. Vincent had been taking it in, much distressed. Mesmerized. After a moment he said, "You don't have to talk like this..."

"I robbed her of what made her so beautiful to me..."

He grew still. He said nothing for a minute. Jim stood up, hoping to end this, but he saw in his face a growing tension.

"In those days I was trying to work things out." His eyes fell on Jim. "Hammer was going nuts. I knew the Party wanted to lay hands on me in the worst way. It was dangerous. I stayed up through the night with a gun by my side. I couldn't have Carole or Zora around. All the while I little cared if I lived or died. That, too, is why I sent them away. Do you see? *I* was dangerous too...I couldn't trust myself.

"So I took them out of the city, and during the days sometimes, after I took them to Washington, to think clearly, I visited that church I told you about. I'd sit there for hours on end, thinking about everything. Thinking what I should do next. I rarely ever prayed, though it was a church, and where obviously people came to pray. That gave me a certain comfort, as if I couldn't pray then I could be near others who could. They'd come in, mostly older people, an occasional youngster, shuffling in, one or two, falling to their knees, losing themselves in God.

"There was a little Spanish lady who would come in often, at least once every day. I noticed her. A couple of times I spoke to her outside the church – she spoke poor English but a very good Spanish. She was very devout, and when she learned I wasn't Catholic, she was amazed. And then she explained everything: that she believed that God was inside that church, really, even physically there, on the altar. She told me she was coming there for her daughter who wasn't living the life she wanted her to.

"One day, about a block from the church we crossed paths, nodding as we passed. She stopped as if in thought, then called me back and asked if I was in trouble. I told her the truth. I said I was."

'Are the police after you?' she asked. 'No,' I said. 'Not the police. They aren't after me.'

'There is a man,' she said, 'a short man with black hair and a big head, who talks funny English, who asked about you.' And she said that he was waiting outside the church, with some men in a car waiting too. I knew she was talking about J. Peters.

"Peters remembered, Jim, you see? I feared that he'd found my house, too. I quickly left the area and the city that night and returned to Washington. When

I got to the apartment late…" He seemed now to be pushing himself against opposing currents, in a direction requiring an ever-mounting struggle. "This is the terrible thing, the price of my sins. When I arrived in Washington that night, Zora and Carole were nowhere to be found. They were supposed to be watched…

"I knocked at a neighbor's door, seized with the thought that the Party found them and had already taken them away. It was late at night. I pounded on the door. Someone finally came and told me. Zora had been drinking. Carole had come home from school and found Zora lying sprawled on the kitchen floor, an open bottle of lye on the floor beside her…"

An eternal-seeming several seconds followed. He barely whispered, "You see…You see!" The words stopped coming but his eyes were large. Then, "I live truly now."

After this he was like a man who'd come to the end of a grueling race. A minute or two later he said one or two other things besides, but they weren't important. He'd said what he'd needed to say, and he fell quickly into a tranquil state. Being glad of that, not wanting to disturb him, they slipped out when they thought they could without waking him. But it was those words, "I live truly now," that they remembered.

33

The Crowd is the Untruth

Vincent and Jim would be meeting in the dining hall. Together they hoped that by the end of the week they would have final grades ready to turn in. Jim, in Room 6 of Wirthlin Hall, pulled the old man's grade book from his desk. On the face of it was scrawled in his heavy hand, *THOMAS DOSWELL, GREAT BOOKS*. Below, three drawers were filled with student themes. The first two were papers already graded; the third, with twenty-five or so papers, he'd never gotten to. Bringing them together, with the last pile placed across the first, and with the grade book reverently placed on top, and then into a cardboard box that lay in the corner by the bookcase, Jim carefully lifted the box to his shoulder, slipped open the door and then closed it gently with his free hand, hearing it click locked as he did so.

He hoped that he wouldn't see anyone on the way back to his office. As he walked through the silent hallway, he noticed the odor of disinfectant. The janitorial staff had already begun cleaning up. Peeking in as he passed the seminar room Doswell used, he noticed the chairs neatly placed atop the single long table, the floor of the empty room having been waxed, and the free-standing blackboard washed and wiped clean.

Coming up the stairs at the opposite end of the hall at that moment were the giant Rev. Baker and Mrs. Baker.

"Ah, Mr. Allan!" Rev. Baker said, his head thrown back, Mrs. Baker standing there beside him with an expression of subdued grief. The Reverend's stentorian voice grew louder. "Wasn't it a shame? He was a fine man. It's been over twenty years that I've known him. We were hired the same year. A really fine man. He was a good friend...It happened late at night, I heard?"

"Yes...it was very early in the morning, they said, when it was still dark."

Mrs. Baker tilted her head, smiling sadly. Touching Jim's arm, she said, "He would have liked seeing the young people graduate. He always did."

"Well, you're busy," the Rev. Baker said, eyeing from his commanding height the contents of the box. "I know you have grades to get in. I know that!" He stepped back. "Now don't be a stranger! You know where we live. Just come on by anytime and we'll talk!"

They started moving away. Then he turned for an instant. "Oh, by the way. Have you seen the newspapers? I don't mean our Colonus paper. Have you seen the *New York Times* for today?"

Jim shook his head, anxious to be alone again.

"Well, be sure and get a copy and take a look at the second page. There's something in there, I promise you, that is *very* interesting!"

Vincent waited at a side table in the nearly empty dining hall for Jim to appear, thinking as he did how strangely things sometimes work out: that he couldn't think of anybody now at Baxter that he wanted to see other than – he smiled as he thought this – the Lemon Face. The kitchen staff had begun cleaning up following the noonday hour, a slow day since many of Baxter's students already had left for home, and many teachers that hadn't yet turned in grades were holed up somewhere hastily finishing up their grading.

He was no exception. In his hands was a paper that he'd begun reading when Sr. Mary passed by and said her goodbyes, saying that she'd be returning to Ohio within the week.

"Too bad about Mr. Doswell, I'd heard he wasn't well…The Sisters and I are having a Mass said for him. Is Mr. Allan doing alright? I know they were *very* close."

For an instant he felt a hot stab of anger, which instantly passed with the reflection that Sister Mary of course meant nothing more than exactly what was true, and hardly disgraceful.

"He's OK."

"Well, things will be very different next year. That's for sure. A lot of people won't be here. I won't be here, you won't be here, Blissie is leaving, Chuck and Rosie will be returning to Wisconsin. And Dr. Montbanc – isn't it wonderful? He'll be in New York. Well…we'll all have our work cut out for us, won't we? We did what we could. The task now is to get the message out…"

As he sat there, his blood rising a few degrees, taking in the clatter and clash of dishes, blending with the sound of the words still echoing through his mind, he tried once again to concentrate more calmly on the student paper written on the philosopher-theologian Søren Kierkegaard. The old man would have liked it:

> *The crowd is the untruth because it makes you iresponsible. Keerkigaard says that in joining the mob, one makes himself cowardly. One who is part of a mob that riots through the streets, destroying property and people, may escape blame for any responsability. But a mob isn't the only kind of crowd there is. You can be part of a crowd when all alone inside of your head you try to be like other people you think are cool. You don't stop to think why you really say this or think that…*

"He loved the orange juice..." Someone else wanting to talk about Doswell caused Vincent to turn, startled, and looking up he saw a dark brown, smiling face, a lanky kid with a huge 'fro, in an all-white dining-room smock. "Well, *you knew* that old man – he was really something special. I bet you and Mr. Allan are gonna miss him like we all will. Is Mr. Allan and you coming back to teach? I heard you were both good."

"No, I'm not coming back. Mr. Allan, yes, he will...Thanks..."

"Well, I loved that old cat. A whole lot of people are going to miss him."

"Yeah. I know. And thanks for saying I wasn't bad in the teaching department."

"Well, I didn't have either of you. That's just the rumor people tell."

"What's your name?"

"Alvin Foote." He began to giggle like he'd said something funny. "Yeah, well...see ya around!" He returned to his dining room duties, businesslike, clanging hoisted chairs up onto tables, seat side down.

Vincent's eyes scanned the row upon row of tables and upended chairs, still gazing anxiously and meditatively across the wide expanse of the now-empty dining hall; empty, that is, but for this boy hoisting the remaining chairs onto the last dining tables.

Epilogue

Effective Administrator for MUNY
Man in the News
Ronald Alfonse Montbanc

When early this spring turmoil erupted again at the Municipal University of New York over minority admissions policies, and then later Charles Wright stepped down after twelve years as president of MUNY the search began in earnest for someone who could effectively administer the now-sprawling, multifaceted and increasingly rebellious institution that MUNY has become. Those who have worked with him say Ronald Alfonse Montbanc, the man who yesterday was chosen for the vacant office of president, is uniquely well qualified and well suited for the post.

An effective administrator, a complex, erudite scholar, a visionary, Mr. Montbanc, less than four years ago, as a young man of thirty-four, inherited the office of president of Baxter University, a black institution located in Colonus, North Carolina, that had fallen into near-bankruptcy and general academic disrepute. In the short period since, he has not only brought Baxter out of its financial difficulties but made of it a leader among institutions of its kind for academic innovation and excellence.

"I believe that realism and idealism are two aspects of the same vision. Those who think that realists must be cynical and idealists must be feeble are both cynical and unrealistic. Bringing into being the change that is required to return America to its original vision is today nothing short of what is necessary for America's survival in a new and progressive world," Mr. Montbanc recently said in his characteristically forceful way.

And his realism has resulted in some very tough decisions. A few months ago, when it became clear to him that the abuse of drugs on the Baxter campus was getting completely out of hand, he gave the go-ahead for a search of student rooms notorious as drug centers on its campus. For his decision he received severe criticism from many. But as one of his original critics, Gerry Loewenstein of the psychology department at Baxter, put it recently, "He really showed in time that it was the only thing to do...In retrospect..."

Apparently this episode in Mr. Montbanc's career did not affect his overwhelming preference among the student members of the MUNY recruiting committee that met here yesterday with faculty members and narrowed the final choice to him.

"The drug scene isn't where it's at," Billie Williams, a pert, very pretty young sophomore on the recruiting committee said.

But Ronald Alfonse Montbanc has more to his credit than the Baxter Plan of Education and his formidable reputation as financial wizard of Colonus, as he's known to the banking institutions of this generally staid and conservative university town. He is known also as the founder and organizer of the National Alliance of Black People, a growing organization of very active, indeed restive, black Americans who look to bringing together a broad spectrum of people...

Earlier...he was named to the President's Commission of Inquiry into the Causes of Campus and Student Unrest. A forceful voice, he has argued that until America returns to its root convictions about human equality at home and a moral policy abroad "like a rudderless ship it will list dangerously, threatened by every storm, and surely will not survive far into a future frought..."

One student at MUNY, who is also a fledgling member of the National Alliance of Black People, recently said, "We knew then that he was one man we could trust." And even more than trust, what these young people so committed to change have come confidently to recognize is that "he is an inspiration to us all."

Dear Vincent,

I just finished reading that moving Man in the News piece in the New York Times. I never bothered to read it at the time, even though Baker told me about it too. I especially liked that comment by the student about trust. The man's life is obviously an inspiration for us all.

Yeah, after this year I'm moving on, even though Middleweek as interim President has so far avoided doing anything really harmful. I've already started looking.

Autumn has closed in I'm sure in the North, but I still go to Devon now and then to help Billy keep the weeds out of the old man's garden. It's also nice to see the Lewises and Billy. I brought my son, Peety, with me a few times and you should have seen the fuss Mrs. Lewis made over him! Billy, of course, lives with the Lewises.

The old man had an insurance policy and some money put away, and Billy got the farm of course. So he's inherited enough to keep him OK for a good long while, I should imagine. There were some heirlooms too. The most amazing were some mussel shells (for spoons, I was told) that the old man's grandmother brought with her out of slavery, and that Mrs. Lewis said his father found in a little tattered cloth handkerchief along with a few other odds and ends after she died, and left for him. Mrs. Lewis is going to keep them for Billy until he's old enough to appreciate them.

How is the Rotten Apple? I'm not going back there. That's one place I won't be looking for a job. Big cities are not for me, and New York is the ultimate big city.

Jim

P.S. How is your brother? I remember you were telling me that last day in Colonus that he was slowly getting better.

Dear Jim,

Basil is doing surprisingly well. He tells me himself the love department is fine. I'm not sure that is a blessing for the women of New York! But then maybe I'm just jealous because my own love life has been pretty anemic.

I'm still working in the mayor's office but things are going crazy here. The city is threatening secession! There's talk about moving it to statehood. I'm thinking of a mini-secession of my own. I mean, going back to the neighborhood and trying to do something worthwhile there…

Thank you for the tale of the mussel shell spoons his grandmother left his father. It's an amazing find – a family heirloom! Maybe it's not so amazing, or at least surprising. They are the kind of things he would have kept.

Here are a couple of tales for you. Remember that man Ashbel Hawpe, that came to the funeral from Virginia? That you telephoned? I took him out the night before he left and he said that when the old man broke he took pains to save the jobs of the people who worked at that limousine service he ran. He apparently owned it too, because Hawpe said he sold it right from under the noses of his handlers. By the time they learned he'd defected it was a done deal. They couldn't do anything about it without exposing the whole mess. He said he also secretly contacted him after his defection, and did the same with this other guy, Charlie, who was from Russia. He said he really risked his life doing these things, getting together with him, pressuring him to break. He could have just disappeared. He often thought later that he'd saved his life.

Well, there's my man for the news.

I know you say you hate the Rotten Apple but your mom lives here and that tells me you'll be coming back. When you do, make sure you call me. If you don't, I'll really be pissed. Besides, if you let me know, I'll buy you dinner. I know some good eating places in town.

Keep up the good fight.

Your friend,

Vincent

Acknowledgements

Journey to Colonus is intended to be true to life – the historic periods which it seeks to evoke and the lives of the individuals who lived through them. Numerous real-life figures appear in its pages, and to the extent possible in a novel I have cleaved to the historical record. Its major characters are fictional creations. Its protagonist was inspired in part by the story of Whittaker Chambers, who is mentioned in the novel's later pages. The novel's account of radical politics is based on personal experience, and reading begun in the '60s with Chambers' *Witness* and *Cold Friday*. Research continued over the years through the '90s with books published by scholars who had access to previously super-secret files belonging to the KGB and other governmental entities inside and outside the Soviet Union following its collapse.

Chapter 3: some of Blissie's words to Vincent in their initial interchange are taken from a Gloria Steinem essay, *Sisterhood*, which originally appeared in *Ms.* magazine in 1971. In the same chapter, demands made by the Republic of New Africa have their source in Theodore Draper's *American Communism and Soviet Russia*, Octagon Books, 1977, from the chapter entitled *The Negro Question*.

Chapter 8: *The Revolution Will Not Be Televised* was written by Gil Scott-Heron and is used by permission of the Bienstock Publishing Company.

Chapter 11: the phantasmagoric opening to this chapter is a report of commercial advertisements, billboards and graffiti actually seen in the Times Square area of New York City in the late '60s and early '70s.

Chapter 12: Doswell's thought that in first talking to Jim Allan he had the curious sensation of "resuming a conversation" rather than beginning one, is a thought which Whittaker Chambers shares with William F. Buckley, in a letter to him on page 55 of the Buckley collection of Chambers' letters to Buckley, *Odyssey of a Friend*, Putnam, 1969. The obituary Doswell shows Jim from *The State*, the Columbia, South Carolina newspaper, appears in *The Secret World of American Communism*, page 190, Annals of American Communism series, Yale University Press. This is one of the many books published since the fall of the Soviet Union which was earlier mentioned. The Yale Annals (others of which will be cited) publishes facsimiles and translations of documents from Soviet archives.

The Secret World is edited by Harvey Klehr, John Earl Haynes and Fridrikh Igorevich Firsov (1995).

Chapter 14's title, *We Will Achieve America In Our Lifetime*, and some similar words from Ronald Montbanc's speech, were suggested by Richard Rorty's *Achieving Our Country: Leftist Thought in Twentieth-Century America*, Harvard University Press, 1998. The words *What Must Be Done?* are the title of the famous pamphlet by V. I. Lenin. Much of President Montbanc's speech is taken from an unpublished speech given by a university president of the time. Most of the interchanges that are reported to have taken place at the Sanhedrin meeting of 1924 are excerpted and taken almost verbatim from *American Communism and Black Americans: A Documentary History*, Vol. 1, 1919–1929, Philip S. Foner and James S. Allen, Temple University Press, 1987. With the exception of Thomas Doswell, persons (described with creative latitude), as well as background description and facts about this meeting, have their source in this same text.

Chapter 15: reference to the *killing fields in the Santa Cruz Mountains in Southern California* comes from *Radical Son*, pages 386–387 by David Horowitz, Free Press, 1997. The Black Panthers were for a time the bitter enemies of WHO, a black nationalist organization headed up by Ron Karenga, the founder and creator of Kwanza, the well-known 'holiday' celebrating black African identity which takes place during the Christmas season. Some of the language employed by Black Panthers to Vincent in his conversation with them at Panther headquarters in Brooklyn is taken from a *Newsweek* interview with Panther members on the occasion of the Alex Rackley murder, which made the national news in the spring of 1970. The French philosopher that Michael Fairlie quotes in Vincent's memory is Maurice Merleau-Ponty, and comes from *Humanism and Terror*, trans. John O'Neill, Beacon Press, 1969, page 2; and from Merleau-Ponty's preface to *Humanism and Terror*, page XVII.

Chapter 16: much of the information on textiles and the Passaic textile strike of 1926 comes from *American Communism and Soviet Russia*, cited earlier. The detailed contemporary descriptions of the strike, the textile industry itself and Albert Weisbord (with creative latitude) come from an unpublished Ph.D. dissertation, *The Passaic Textile Strike of 1926* by Morton Siegel, Columbia University, 1953. It also comes from references to events and personalities from contemporary news reports in the *New York Times*. The description of 'radical chic' in the '20s comes from *Blacks and Reds* by Earl Ofari Hutchinson, Michigan State University Press, 1995. Doswell's description of inner Party politics comes mainly from Draper and from Chambers.

Chapter 17: the description of the Lenin School and its curriculum comes from page 22 and 187, *Operation Solo* by John Barron, Regnery, 1996. Doswell's words, "Marxist dialectic is only profound on the surface, deep down it is superficial," are Robert Conquest's, I believe, from *The Great Terror*. But perhaps it is from one of his other books, because an examination of this text fails to find the words. Information about J. Peters comes from many sources. Here it is in substance from Whittaker Chambers' *Witness*. Information about Armand Hammer comes mostly from *Dossier: The Secret History of Armand Hammer* by Edward Jay Epstein, Random House, 1996.

This book offered a goldmine of information on Hammer, on the Hammer family, and virtually everything associated with the Hammer family and its clandestine activities over the years with the Soviet Union, except of course Doswell's fictional association with the Hammers. I used this readable and crucially informative biography very freely. For instance, the description of the interior of the Brown House comes from and is quoted by Epstein in *Dossier*, and originally comes from Eugene Lyons, *Assignment in Utopia*, Transaction Publishers, 1991, originally published in 1937 by Harcourt Brace & Company.

Many of Hammer's words to Doswell are also taken almost verbatim from Hammer's words in *The Quest of the Romanoff Treasure* by Armand Hammer, The Paisley Press, 1936.

I allowed myself the least possible latitude with the character of Armand Hammer. In succeeding chapters, many of his words to Doswell, interwoven with the description of Hammer's situation vis-à-vis his relation to the Soviet authorities, comes in places (allowing for Doswell's fictional interaction) almost verbatim from his own words in *The Quest of the Romanoff Treasure*, cited above, that are sometimes also cited by Epstein in *Dossier*.

Now Doswell told Allan that worldwide revolution, espionage in all reaches of the American government and the nation's industry, as well as in far-flung other nations and governments, was the plan. The pages in the novel which support this statement, reflecting Doswell's knowledge, have their source in the previously mentioned books and numerous post-Soviet books that were mentioned earlier, specifically, the Yale series. The books that I used from the Yale series in addition to the *Secret World* are: *The Soviet World of American Communism* by Harvey Klehr, John Earl Haynes and Kyrill M. Anderson, 1998; *Venona: Decoding Soviet Espionage in America* by John Earl Haynes and Harvey Klehr, 1999; *The Unknown Lenin: From the Secret Archive* edited by Richard Pipes, 1996. In addition, *The Venona Secrets: Exposing Soviet Espionage and America's Traitors* by Herbert Romerstein and Eric Breindel, Regnery, 2000; *The Haunted Wood: Soviet Espionage in America – The Stalin Era* by Allen Weinstein and Alexander Vassiliev, Random House, 1999; *Special Tasks: The Memoirs of an Unwanted Witness – A Soviet Spymaster* by Pavel and Anatoli Sudoplatov with Jerrold and Leona P. Schecter, Back Bay Books, Little, Brown and Company, 1994 and 1995; *The Black Book of Communism* by Stephane Courtois, Nicolas Werth, Jean-Louis Panne, Andrzej Paczkowski, Karel Bartosek and Jean-Louis Margolin; trans. by Jonathan Murphy and Mark Kramer, Harvard University Press, 1999.

The subject of two of the above books – the Venona documents – was Soviet cable traffic that was intercepted and some of it decrypted by American agents beginning in the 1940s and revealed only after the fall of the Soviet Union. The information from all these sources is woven into the narrative in such a way that it is difficult to identify one bit of information as distinct from another in origin In many cases there are several sources. All of these books are quite readable, especially Epstein's *Dossier* and Barron's *Operation Solo.*

Chapter 18: the Hammer family's troubles in England and Germany come slightly altered and simplified from Epstein's *Dossier.* The political climate in Germany is described in *Dossier* and in *Stasi: The Untold Story of the East German Secret Police* by John O. Koehler, Westview Press, 1999.

Whiteman lived with his Russian-Jewish wife in a dank, dark room... The words describing Whiteman's life in Moscow come from *Black Man in Red Russia: A Memoir* by Homer Smith, page 78, Johnson Publishing Company, 1964. Most of the information about Lovett Fort-Whiteman comes from this book and from Robert Robinson's *Black on Red: My Forty-four Years Inside the Soviet Union* with Jonathan Slevin, Acropolis Books, 1988, and from the *Soviet World of American Communism*, already cited. Additional details, especially Whiteman's description found in earlier pages and here, are found in *Black Bolshevik: Autobiography of an Afro-American Communist* by Harry Haywood, Liberator Press, 1978, *Communists in Harlem During the Depression* by Mark Naison, Grove Press, 1983, and from Draper's *American Communism* and Foner and Allen's *American Communism and Black Americans*, already cited. Peters' sanguine account of future espionage work in the United States is recounted by Chambers in *Witness.*

Chapter 19: this chapter's title and the striking image given by Heda Gumperz, a Soviet agent, of competing 'college fraternities' to describe Soviet spy networks comes from *The Haunted Wood* by Weinstein and Vassiliev, already cited, page 5. Information regarding the intricacies of Soviet undercover work and the Party comes from *The Haunted Wood*, and from the two previously cited books on Venona, and the several books based primarily on the Soviet archives, and from Chambers' *Witness.* Doswell's words, "American counter-espionage was a joke", is a theme sounded time and again by numerous sources, none more strikingly than by Nadia Ulanovskaya, who with her husband, Alexander Ulanovski ('Elaine' and 'Ulrich'), worked closely with Whittaker Chambers as espionage agents in the early '30s. Many years later, after she had emigrated to Israel in the '70s, she told an interviewer, "If you wore a sign saying *I am a spy*, you might still not get arrested in America when we were there." The quotation comes from *Perjury: The Hiss-Chambers Case* by Allen Weinstein, Random House, page 108, originally published 1978, from the revised edition, 1997. Another book providing additional background information on this and other matters is *Whittaker Chambers* by Sam Tanenhaus, Random House, 1997. Stalin's name for the foreign Communist parties in the Comintern, and the description of Peters' 'industry', are details recounted by Chambers in *Witness.* The story of Hammer's 'roadshow' and the Trust Company of North America, and its owner Schapiro, its money-laundering operations for Armand Hammer, as well as Hammer's financial situation on returning to the States, follows Epstein's description in *Dossier.* The arrangement with Doswell is, of course, made up.

Chapter 20: Doswell's racial situation at Harvard is based on *The Half Opened Door: Discrimination and Admissions at Harvard, Yale, and Princeton, 1900–1970,* pages 83–84 and elsewhere, by Marcia Graham Synnott, Greenwood Press, 1979. Chambers gives an account of his freshman year at Columbia in *Cold Friday* on pages 124–127, which in some respects paralleled Doswell's at Harvard. Irving Babbitt's imagined conversation with Doswell is based on several sources. Most of it, the man's personal character, comes from F. Manchester and O. Shepard, *Irving Babbitt, Man and Teacher*, Greenwood Press, 1969, originally published in 1941; also from Babbitt's own *Rousseau and Romanticism*, Houghton Mifflin Company, 1919, and from *The New Laokoon.*

Russians Hungry, But Not Starving, comes from *The New York Times*, March 31, 1933.

Chapter 22: The Latin hymn, text by Thomas Aquinas, O Salutaris Hostia, and translation come from *Latin Hymns* compiled by Fr. Adrian Fortescue, Roman Catholic Books, pages 80 - 81, originally published in 1913.

Chapter 25: the description of the Ukrainian Famine that is given Doswell through the eyes of the 'younger man' comes from *The Famine The Times Couldn't Find* by Marco Carynnyk, *Commentary* Vol. 76, #5, Nov. 1983, pages 32–40; *Famine in the Soviet Ukraine 1932–1933: A Memorial Exhibition*, Widener Library, Harvard University, prepared by Oksana Procyk, Leonid Heretz, James E. Mace, Harvard University Press, 1986; *Execution by Hunger: The Hidden Holocaust* by Miron Dolot, W. W. Norton and Company, 1985. Some time in the '80s, as well, there appeared on PBS television an excellent documentary on the famine, with an appearance by its British producer, hosted on William F. Buckley's *Firing Line.* Blaming it on the Jews was a tactic employed by the Party and reported as such in *Execution by Hunger*, already cited, pages 82–84.

Hammer's probable attempt at assisting the Nazis during the Nazi-Soviet pact is reported in Epstein's *Dossier*, pages 147–148.

Van Holler's description of Fort-Whiteman's involvement in Meschrabpon Film Studio appears on pages 23–25 in *Black Man in Red Russia*, by Smith, previously cited. Fort-Whiteman's end, including William L. Patterson's likely part in it, is given on pages 218–226 of the *Soviet World of American Communism*, previously cited. The description of "beatings" and how he died are verbatim from the same source, and from *Black on Red*, by Robinson, previously cited, page 361. Patterson's connection to Paul Robeson, and Robeson's "defense" of the Soviet

Union over many long years, is described by Martin Bauml Duberman in his favorably written *Paul Robeson: A Biography*, Ballantine Books, 1989.

Chapter 27: the story of the woman Doswell had to admonish in the Justice Department who had access to FBI operations refers actually to both Flora Wovschin, who did the energetic recruiting, but while in the State Department, and Judith Coplon who had the job in the Justice Department, and who was later caught red-handed (no pun intended) handing over Justice Department counterintelligence files to a KGB officer. Wovschin's story is told in *Venona* by Haynes and Klehr on page 200, and Coplon's story is told on pages 158–161. Haynes and Klehr make the point that the Coplon story was far from isolated. Though easily convicted – twice – because the evidence was overwhelming, *admissibility under the complex standards of US criminal justice* was impossible to uphold under appeal. In general, those facing charges of espionage were either prominent people or had the backing of highly prominent people, and they could buy some of *the finest legal talent in the country.*

The notion that only with the Hitler-Stalin pact, Stalin's alliance with Hitler, did American authorities take a serious interest in Communist espionage, finds support in much of the source material but it is specifically found in *Venona* by Haynes and Klehr, on page 151. And the fact that when the pact was dissolved, the US government once again lost interest in Communist espionage, is referred to on pages 158–159 in the same book. Stalin's reaction to his learning of Hitler's attack on the Soviet Union, the reaction, on the other hand, of many of the Soviet people, and the events which followed, are treated at length by Nikolai Tolstoy in *Stalin's Secret War*, Jonathan Cape, London, 1981, pages 224–261.

Chapter 28: *Joe McCarthy's Political Dynamite, Life*, April 10th 1950, page 802. The Joseph McCarthy saga, opening with his speech in Wheeling, West Virginia, in February of 1950, is told here based primarily on two books: *McCarthy and His Enemies: The Record and Its Meaning* by William F. Buckley, Jr. and L. Brent Bozell, Henry Regnery Company, 1954, and the recently published *Joseph McCarthy* by Arthur Herman, The Free Press, 2000. Tom Gallagher's words to Doswell in Doswell's home are taken substantially from *McCarthy and His Enemies*, page 157 and pages 41–74.

The story of Western intellectuals' refusal to believe firsthand testimony of those who had escaped the Soviet Union, even those who had escaped concentration camps, is told in *The Great Terror: A Reassessment* by Robert Conquest, Oxford University Press, New York, 1990, pages 464–476; Jean-Paul Sartre's part in this episode, page 472.

Chapter 29: the story about Congressman Samuel Dickstein, with its many associated players and parts, is taken from *The Haunted Wood*, Weinstein and Vasiliev, previously cited, pages 140–150, and from contemporary sources, including *Samuel Dickstein, Chairman of the Immigration Committee* in *The*

New Republic, October 18th 1933. The story involving Assistant Secretary of the Treasury Harry Dexter White and his attempts to influence American foreign policy is found in *The Venona Secrets*, Romerstein and Breindel, previously cited, pages 34–44. Doswell's self-questions are answered, at least in regard to White and his additional efforts at influencing American foreign policy, in *Venona* by Haynes and Klehr, pages 138–145. The exchange which takes place between General Secretary Earl Browder and Senators Hickenlooper, McMahon and Tydings, are in the record and quoted almost verbatim from *McCarthy and His Enemies*, pages 182–184.

The exchange between Thomas Doswell, Earl Browder and members of the Committee, while radically altered to accommodate the fictional character and story of Thomas Doswell, is not wholly made up. It is based on actual incidents, and sometimes the words of minor historic figures, and in a different venue. Browder's insultingly dramatic denial of Doswell's identity is taken from Hiss' initial confrontation with Chambers at HUAC investigations two years earlier. Senator McCarthy's words, "I do not have access to the State Department's loyalty files..." at the Tydings Committeee, and Senator Tydings' words to Senator McCarthy, quoted by McCarthy in this novel, "You are the man..." are verbatim, or almost verbatim, taken from the record and found in *McCarthy and His Enemies*, pages 66–67.

Chapter 30: Senator Green's tone and words to Doswell about being "quite the man", and his asking Doswell for a definition of 'hearsay', are those of Lloyd Paul Stryker, defense counsel to Alger Hiss, put to Whittaker Chambers, and Chambers' reply, in the first Hiss perjury trial. His question regarding conscience and Doswell's reply was put to and answered by Julian Wadleigh at the same trial. These exchanges can be found in *A Generation on Trial*, by Alistair Cooke, published by Alfred A. Knopf, 1950, pages 131 and 172–173. The exchange between Senator Hickenlooper and Professor Lattimore is derived in substance, and portions almost verbatim, from *McCarthy and His Enemies*, page 158. The news on the Tydings Committee majority report comes from *The New Republic*, a contemporary issue, cited in *McCarthy and His Enemies*, page 167. Buckley and Bozell wrote, *Senator Lodge had written that persons named as having been connected to Professor Lattimore had not been called to testify*. The fraud involved in the Tydings Committee's procedures and final report, reflected in Senator Lodge's questions and objections, and their suppression, went far beyond what the novel describes. An appreciation of it can be found in pages 167–172, *McCarthy and His Enemies.*

The information about George Lewis, *the greatest clarinetist who'd ever lived...*was gleaned from *They Had A Right To Sing The Blues* by Tom Bethell, *National Review,* July 8th 1991.

Chapter 31: President Montbanc's words, "You may have to learn to fight in the streets…" are the words of a distinguished academician of the time.

Chapter 32: the title of the chapter comes from lines in *Prometheus Bound* by Aeschylus.

About the Author

Franklin Debrot was born in Willemstadt, Curacao, Netherlands West Indies, in 1941. His family emigrated to the United States two years later, settling in New York City. Mr. Debrot grew up in Brooklyn where his father, a dentist, was active in the West Indian community.

In the early and mid 1960s he studied at Fairfield University in Connecticut and later at the University of Toronto, Canada. He first started teaching philosophy in 1966 at Shaw University, a traditional African-American institution in North Carolina. Since 1978 he has been teaching at James Madison University.

He was a contributing editor of *The Southern Partisan* from 1987 to 1992, and published stories and essays there, and in *The Hillsdale Review*, *New Oxford Review*, *Perspective*, and other journals over the years. One of his articles appeared in the anthology, *Continuity in Crisis: The University at Bay*.

Presently he is working on two other novels, *The Love Experts* and *Grandpa's Gift*, as well as a philosophy text, *Love of Wisdom: The Self-Examined Life*. To keep up to date with Franklin Debrot's most recent publications visit www.DebrotNovels.com.

He has two grown children and lives with his wife in Virginia.

CPSIA information can be obtained
at www.ICGtesting.com
Printed in the USA
FSOW01n0438180217
30810FS

9 781781 325032